ABOUT THE AUTHOR

Marion Leigh was born in Birmingham, England. After receiving her M.A. in Modern Languages from the University of Oxford, she worked for a year as a volunteer in Indonesia before moving to Canada where she enjoyed a successful career as a financial and legal translator.

Marion divides her time between Europe and North America. She loves boating and living close to the water.

This is her second novel featuring RCMP Marine Unit Sergeant Petra Minx. The first book in the series, *The Politician's Daughter*, was published in 2011. An excerpt is reproduced at the end of this book.

DEAD MAN'S LEGACY

MARION LEIGH

Matador
9 Priory Business Park
Kibworth Beauchamp
Leicestershire LE8 0RX, UK
Tel: (+44) 116 279 2299
Email: books@troubador.co.uk
Web: www.troubador.co.uk/matador

ISBN 978 1784623 487

British Library Cataloguing in Publication Data
A catalogue record for this book is available from the British Library.

Printed and bound in the UK by TJ International, Padstow, Cornwall
Typeset in 11pt Aldine by Troubador Publishing Ltd, Leicester, UK

Matador is an imprint of Troubador Publishing Ltd

To my parents for giving me life, love and education

CHAPTER

1

Cliff Graceby had never actually seen a dead body. Only in the movies or the tortured dreams of a disturbed night. So he didn't know if the man next to him was alive or not.

In the silence that followed the crashing and rending of the impact, he heard a faint tick from the engine and a hissing noise from the radiator. There was no sound from the two people in the back of the car.

Cliff licked his dry lips and tasted panic in the back of his throat. The smell of his mother's perfume, the new one he had given her today for her birthday, hung in the air. Elizabeth Taylor's White Diamonds. Jokingly, he had called her Diamond Lil as she opened the package.

Beneath the air bag, his right forearm throbbed with excruciating pain. He felt blood, sticky and warm, flow over his hand onto the front of his shirt. He couldn't move to reach out and touch the figure beside him.

A moan from behind echoed his own. Then a small pleading voice: 'Help me, Joe.'

Another voice, metallic, emanating from the system: 'The ambulance is on its way.'

And a third, full of anger. 'What the fuck have you done?' Asking the same question he was asking himself.

'Shut up. I need to think.' Secrets came out after death.

★ ★ ★ ★

The taxi in which RCMP Marine Unit Sergeant Petra Minx was sleeping screeched to a halt at the foot of a grandiose flight of marble steps. To broadcast his arrival, the driver gave an extra-long blast of the horn. Petra's head jerked backwards and her eyes flew open. For a moment she was unsure where she was. Then she remembered: *Neptunis*, the fabled Bahamian resort. Disney World, Gaudí and Heath Robinson rolled into one. A joint venture between Joe LePinto and a South American media mogul whose name she couldn't remember. Home to LePinto's widow, the legendary Betty Graceby, Canadian singer and ex-Vegas dancer ... Exhaustion after a long night on the plane, trapped between Tweedledum and Tweedledee, a screaming baby in front, and a whining toddler behind.

Petra caught sight of herself in the rearview mirror and grimaced. Bags under her eyes and a stain on her shirt. A.K. should be shot for insisting that she take the next available flight to the Bahamas – an overnight charter special. Surely another few hours in London would have made no difference, and the day flight would have been less of a nightmare. But Sergeants in the Royal Canadian Mounted Police didn't question orders, and A.K.'s had been clear: she was to go immediately to Nassau. So instead of returning to Canada at the end of her previous assignment, here she was.

The passenger door of the taxi was pulled open and a wave of humid fragrant air collided with the semi-cooled dust and perspiration inside the car. A brown face topped with a shock of black hair peeped in. 'Welcome to *Neptunis*, Miss. This way please.'

The bellboy's bright eyes and cheeky grin lightened Petra's mood and she found herself responding with a smile. In his blue suit with brass buttons he would not have been out of place at the Ritz or the Savoy in London. He seized her leopard-print bag on wheels and bounded up the steps. At the top stood an immense statue of Neptune on his throne, holding his trident and surrounded by mermaids.

The bellboy led Petra into a cavernous reception hall. Tanks full of multi-hued tropical fish lined the walls on both sides. He nodded his head in approval when he noticed her interest in the fish. 'That's nothing, Miss. Wait till you see our aquarium and the shark cages, and the mermaid caves down by the pool.'

Looking around the hall, Petra could hardly believe her luck. For years *Neptunis* had been on her bucket list of places to visit when she had time, but she never dreamed A.K. would send her there to meet Betty Graceby. He had come up trumps, even if he had put her through a night of misery.

Acting on A.K.'s instructions, Petra had gone straight from Oxford to London to meet RCMP Liaison Officer Tom Gilmore who had briefed her on the unexpected assignment. Petra smiled to herself as she remembered their conversation.

'Why the rush to get me to Nassau?' she had asked. 'Do you have any idea?'

'All I know is that Betty Graceby has filed a number of complaints against her grandson, Kendall, accusing him of harassment and violence. A few days ago, the police and the medics were called to her apartment. My understanding is that there are serious concerns for her welfare. Your job is to get to know the Graceby family, assess the situation, and report back as quickly as you can.'

'And how am I supposed to do that?'

'A.K. has laid the groundwork. You're the daughter of a friend on your first visit to the Bahamas. Betty's expecting you, but you'll need to come up with a storyline if you want to get really close to her and her family.'

'Another of A.K.'s special investigations! He must think I can work miracles.'

'What you want is something simple and believable, like I told you before you went off to the Med,' Tom added.

'You don't have to remind me. The trick is to stay as close to the truth as possible. There's far less risk of being caught out and a much better chance of the cover being effective.'

Ticking off points on her fingers, Petra had a sudden vision of her father.

'My father loved Betty Graceby,' she said. 'Once, when I was working on a school project with my sister, Mira, he called us to come and watch the news on TV. There was Betty, arriving at the opening of Joe LePinto's latest restaurant and nightclub in Las Vegas. He was so excited. "You girls, take note," he shouted. "She's a legend. You could do worse than be like Betty Graceby." My mother kept pulling his leg about it. Mira and I were mortified to see him acting like a teenage groupie. Now I cherish the memory. Hardly a day goes by that I don't miss his presence and his advice.'

Tom ran a hand through his salt and pepper hair and grinned. 'That's just the ticket, Miss Minx!'

Petra gave him a puzzled look.

'Your father – he could cook, couldn't he?'

'Yes. He loved to cook Polish specialties at the weekend, to give my mother a break.' She thought fast. 'So he could have worked for LePinto ...'

'And now you can offer your condolences to Betty and let her know that your father died recently.'

'Actually it was not long after her husband, Joe, was killed.'

'You don't have to go into detail. You want to create empathy through sympathy and ...'

'OK, OK, Mr. Gilmore. I get the point. Why do you guys all treat me like a rookie?'

'It must be your porcelain complexion and those blue-green eyes. I come over all protective!'

At Heathrow Airport Tom had handed her a large manila envelope. 'Some light reading for the sleepless night ahead,' he had joked with prescience. 'From your alma pater.'

Tears had sparked at the back of her eyes as he gave her a quick hug and pushed her towards the boarding gate.

She opened the envelope on the plane, after using her elbows to clear her space. Whoever had put the material together had done a decent enough job. There was a good summary of Betty Graceby's career and a striking photo of her in her prime. This was followed by some background information on her deceased husband, Joe LePinto, including a description of his dealings with the media mogul who had co-founded *Neptunis*, and some pictures of the resort. Where the package fell short, Petra felt, was in its lack of detail on Betty's relationship with her son, Clifford, and, more importantly, with her grandson, Kendall, against whom she had filed the complaints.

According to Tom, Betty had become something of a recluse since Joe's death two and a half years ago. She had survived the car crash that had killed Joe but ended up in intensive care with a broken hip and a fractured leg. Although she had recovered from her physical injuries, she had never given another show.

Death was hard to deal with under any circumstances, Petra mused, but especially when it snatched away a loved one. Twice she had faced that situation in her own short life: first when her teenage love, Romeo, was killed in a motorcycle accident, then when her father dropped dead at the age of sixty. As she had told Tom, it was strange that the embolism that felled him had occurred shortly after the accident that had killed Joe LePinto and injured Betty Graceby.

A shrill voice brought Petra back to the present.

'Excuse me, can I help you? Are you waiting to check in?' From across the desk, the receptionist was peering at her through owlish black glasses.

Petra glanced round at an invisible queue. 'Of course I am. The name's Minx, Petra Minx.'

The young woman typed a few words on her keyboard and studied the screen in front of her. She entered a command, paused, then clicked her tongue. 'I'm sorry. Your room's not ready. The occupant hasn't checked out yet. You'll have to wait.'

The energy Petra had directed at her thoughts drained away. 'Can't you give me another room?'

The receptionist shook her head. 'I'm sorry, the standard doubles are all full. Changeover day is usually Saturday, and today's Friday.'

'Really? Since we didn't cross the international dateline, I …' Petra broke off when she saw the bemused look on the girl's face. 'Never mind. What about a different type of room?'

'I'm sorry, there's nothing. As I said, you'll have to wait. Why don't you go to the pool bar and enjoy a cocktail – on the house, naturally? Sam will show you the way and fetch you when your room's ready.'

'Coffee might be somewhat more acceptable at this time of day,' Petra said, unable to keep the acidity out of her voice. The sun had hardly risen, let alone moved over the yardarm.

'As you please, Miss …'

'Minx, Petra Minx.'

'Ah yes, Miss Minx. I'm sorry …'

As much to escape the constant apologies as to keep a hold on her anger, Petra turned to Sam who was dancing at her side. 'This is a waste of time, Sam.'

'Let's go then, Miss, let's go.' He grabbed her bag and waved her on.

Petra doubled her pace as she followed Sam through the rear doors of the reception hall onto an open terrace that overlooked the resort. In the distance, the turquoise waters of the Bahamian sea shimmered in the sun. A blue golf cart decorated with gold tridents was parked at the side of the terrace. Sam threw Petra's bag into the cart and swung onto the driver's seat. She climbed in beside him.

Tropical gardens tiered downwards to a vast semi-circular swimming pool that was built around an artificial cliff. As they drew closer Petra spotted the pool bar, half hidden under a waterfall in the centre of the cliff and linked to terra firma by a narrow suspension bridge. It was an unusual place to be sent to wait – and a long way from Reception. A coffee, though, would help her organize her thoughts and work out how to approach Betty Graceby. On the other hand, she might wait there all day for her room.

Before she could voice her misgivings to Sam, a dull boom like distant gunfire sent flocks of coloured finches chittering into the air. From somewhere beyond the sundeck, a plume of smoke drifted skywards like a slow-motion Indian signal. The early morning sun-worshippers lying by the pool remained where they were, showing few signs of arousal.

Sam could hardly contain his excitement. 'It's down at the marina, Miss. Let's go see!'

As he spoke, a second, much louder explosion echoed through the resort. This time, there was panic. Sam urged the golf cart on with little regard for its welfare. Ignoring the display of topless sunbathers now agog with excitement, he roared round the end of the building that shielded the marina from view and continued along the dock at a furious pace. He jammed on the brake and punched his fist in the air. 'Wow! Look at that!'

A black cloud hung like a pall over the marina. The source of the cloud appeared to be a top-of-the-line sportfishing boat that had been heading for the exit to the sea. Behind the vessel's damaged mid-section, two of her four rods still stood tall in their holders. Petra watched in awe as the boat's tuna tower teetered like its leaning namesake in Pisa before folding into the water. With a gush of hot air, flames rushed upwards. Another explosion rocked the hull and debris flew in all directions.

A man wearing a cap that said "Harbourmaster" was shouting into his portable VHF, urging the police to dispatch the fireboat. Nearby, a young dockhand was yelling for help to man the marina's workboat. Petra leapt out of the golf cart and raced towards the water. In the course of her career in the Marine Unit, she had seen how rapidly a burning boat could turn its neighbours into funeral pyres. Fortunately, the sportfish had been almost out of the marina so there was little danger of the fire spreading to other vessels. She prayed that the crew had had time to abandon ship.

As she ran to the edge of the dock, Petra thought she saw two figures in the water, one waving its arms, the other floating like a bag of sodden rags. She kicked off her shoes, took a deep breath and dived in. Swimming strongly, she covered the distance to the first person before the marina's workboat could reach the crippled vessel. She caught hold of a bobbing life ring embossed with the name *Geyser* and pushed it into the hands of a dark-haired young man. Then she turned her attention to the second, less able, casualty of the explosion.

Treading water, Petra grabbed a handful of clothing and rolled the victim over. The face was that of an elderly woman, lined and grey. As Petra lifted her up, she opened her eyes. They were a clear lavender blue. There was only one person who had eyes like that.

'You're safe now,' Petra said. 'Just relax and keep your back towards me. You'll be fine. I won't let you go under.' She clasped an arm over the woman's chest and began to tow her to safety.

Maintaining a steady rhythm, Petra soon reached the dock where the first emergency workers were waiting to relieve her of her burden. For a minute or two, she lay floating on her back. Then she climbed out with the help of Sam, whose anxiety kept him jumping.

'Miss Petra! Are you OK? You're a good swimmer!'

'I'm fine, Sam. Just tired.' Petra took the towel he thrust into her hands and dried off her hair before draping it round her shoulders. She gestured to where a team of paramedics surrounded the woman she had rescued. 'Is that who I think it is?'

'Yes'm! That's Miss Graceby, and that's Mr. Ken's boat.' Sam pointed to the blackened hull of the sportfish. 'I saw him this morning, early, getting ready for a cruise.'

'So the guy in the water was Ken Graceby?'

'Yes'm! He was taking his grandmother out.'

'He must have a good relationship with her then.'

'Yes'm!'

Petra nodded thoughtfully.

She looked up to see a portly man bearing down on them. He was wearing a pinstripe suit, a yellow tie and a pink shirt that was too tight and the wrong colour for his auburn hair. 'Don't you have anything to do, boy?' he shouted.

'Yessir, Mr. Reed, Sir. I'll fetch the golf cart.' Sam scuttled away in the direction of the abandoned cart containing Petra's bag.

The man stuck out a sweaty hand. 'Dick Reed, Resort Manager. You must be Petra Minx. Miss Graceby mentioned you were coming. Sorry I wasn't around when you arrived. A fine show. Lucky you were here.'

Petra took an immediate dislike to Dick Reed. He was a pompous ass. Wryly she wondered if he was referring to the smoke and fire as a "fine show", then concluded it was his way of expressing admiration for her actions. Words continued to drip from his mouth. He didn't seem to have noticed that so far she had said nothing.

'I'm sure Miss Graceby will want to thank you once she has recovered. She asked me to put you in the Mermaid Suite. Of course, it's usually reserved for our royal visitors and our wealthiest patrons.'

Reed's condescending tone set Petra's teeth on edge, and she bit back a testy reply. If he'd been there when she arrived or had organized things properly, she wouldn't have had to waste her energy doing battle with the receptionist. She noted his pudgy fingers and the pink face only a shade lighter than his shirt. Definitely the wrong man for the job. And useless in a crisis.

The sound of rotors caught Petra's attention. A helicopter bearing the resort's name and trident logo was flying in from over the sea. It hovered above the building that faced the marina and landed on the roof. Petra turned to Dick Reed to ask him who was expected.

'Not now, not now! Just stand clear.' He waved her away and began to waddle towards the building as fast as his short legs would allow.

A few minutes later, the glass elevator on the side of the building began its descent. The man who emerged was tall, slim, perfectly groomed and casually elegant in a cream tropical suit worn with a black open-necked shirt. "Debonair" was the adjective that leapt into Petra's mind. Only his silver hair suggested that he might be older than he appeared. Petra immediately christened him "Black-shirt". The guys in her unit often assigned simple nicknames to unknowns. It helped them to sort the wheat from the chaff in difficult situations and to remember details later.

Dick Reed stuck out his hand in greeting and opened his mouth to speak. Black-shirt brushed him aside like an unwelcome fly and strode to where Betty Graceby lay on a stretcher wrapped in blankets. He began to talk to her. When she struggled to sit up, he placed a restraining hand on her shoulder. Petra was too far away to hear what he was saying. Unsure of his role, Dick Reed was hovering a few paces behind Black-shirt. No one was taking any notice of her at all. She moved closer.

'I don't want to go! There's nothing wrong with me,' she heard Betty say.

'You've had a terrible shock, Mother. You must!'

'I won't. They'll fuss and mess me about.'

Black-shirt began to wheedle. 'Please, Mother. Just for observation. I would hate anything to happen to you.'

'Well, it nearly did, didn't it? Anyway, what are you doing here, Cliff?'

There was a momentary pause before he answered. 'I don't know. Call it a premonition or a whim, if you like.'

'You must have better things to do than fly around on a whim.' Betty's eyelids fluttered. 'All right then, tell them to take me to Lyford if you insist – but no siren.'

'Fine. I'll follow you in my car.' Black-shirt exchanged a few quiet words with the paramedics, who lifted the stretcher and carried it to the ambulance.

As the ambulance pulled away, the fireboat drew near the dock. Kendall Graceby was standing on deck, a furious expression on his face. He had stripped off his wet shirt and was naked to the waist. As soon as the boat was close enough, he jumped onto the dock.

Clifford Graceby marched across to meet him. 'God almighty, Ken! What the hell have you been doing?'

'What do you mean? Leave me alone!'

'You could have killed Mother with your antics.'

'You think I arranged this?'

'It sure looks that way!'

'Fuck off!'

'Don't tell me to fuck off!' Cliff lowered his voice. 'Look, let's not shout. There are too many ears around.'

Petra watched the interaction between the two men. Apart from their colouring, father and son were remarkably similar in height and build. Clifford Graceby had the well-toned physique of a much younger man. Ken, as everyone seemed to call him, was no stranger to the gym either, but his skin was darker than his father's and his features coarser with a faint African cast.

The Gracebys were now talking quietly. Dick Reed temporarily gave up trying to make his mark and homed in on Petra. 'My goodness! You're still here! And dripping wet! We must get you settled in your suite.' He snapped his fingers at Sam. 'Bring that golf cart over here, boy! Take Miss Minx to the Mermaid Suite and make sure she has everything she wants. Do you hear me? Get going!'

Petra smiled at Sam. 'Right now, I'll take that coffee I was promised – followed by a brandy, a hot shower and a comfortable bed. That will be more than enough.'

CHAPTER

2

The mermaids were too much. Petra had expected them, but not in such numbers and such a variety of media. Painted, gilded, carved and sculpted … on canvas, in metal, glass, wood and porcelain … girls with fish tails and flowing golden locks adorned every inch of the luxurious apartment.

Above the door to the master bedroom, mermen joined the maids, their scaled nether regions closely entwined. The theme continued in the tapestries that hung on the walls, giving the bedroom the feel of a medieval château without the nymphs and the satyrs. Petra could only blink at the antics of the half-fish in their watery world and guess at the quantity of gold thread used in their creation.

What Petra didn't realize until she sat down on the edge of the super-kingsize bed was that it was a waterbed. Experimentally, she rocked back and forth. A wave threatened to swamp her. She would have to learn to control her movements. The mattress was warm to the touch but in her post-crisis fatigue it felt comforting, and water was after all her element. She threw a baleful look at the mermaids and their mates, lay down carefully on her back and closed her eyes.

An insistent ring dragged her out of a deep dreamless sleep. After sending Tom a quick text, she had forgotten to turn her phone off. She rolled onto her right side and threw out an arm. The bed swayed alarmingly. A good job she never got seasick. She searched the night table with one hand and sank back onto the soft pillows when she found the noisemaker. Only one person could be calling: her boss, A.K. She put the phone to her ear.

'So you're there!'

'Yes, Sir.'

'Have you spoken to Miss Graceby?'

'No, and I probably won't today.'

'Why not?'

'She's been taken to hospital after an explosion on her grandson's boat.'

'Is she badly hurt?'

'No. I pulled her out of the water.'

There was a brief pause.

'Are you OK?'

'Fine. Tired. I could have done with a bit more sleep.'

No reaction from A.K.

'Any idea what caused the explosion?'

'Not yet. I'll see if I can get a look at the boat this afternoon.'

'Find out what you can. I've arranged for Miss Graceby's file to be handed over to you tomorrow. 10 a.m. at the Canadian Consulate. I'll call you afterwards.'

A.K. rang off without wasting time on a goodbye or giving Petra the opportunity to ask questions, like why was he so interested in the affairs of a retired Canadian singer who spent most of her time outside the country? And why the urgency? She knew from experience that A.K. would never impart what he considered "superfluous details" – probably to protect his staff. As a result, some pieces of the puzzle were always missing.

Another question niggled at the back of Petra's mind: why had Betty Graceby gone out that morning on her grandson's boat if she had contacted the authorities less than a week ago to complain about him? It didn't make sense. What ruse or argument could Ken have used to convince her? Judging by his behaviour and bad language on the dock, he had difficulty controlling his emotions and temper. His father seemed like a much smoother operator – except for his initial outburst, which was no doubt the result of stress. Cliff had had little trouble persuading Betty to go to hospital for observation. Perhaps he had been the one to suggest the outing with Ken, to bring the two of them closer. For the moment it was a mystery, but she could use the time until Betty returned to find out as much as possible about both men.

Half an hour later after a long hot shower, Petra felt rejuvenated. Clad in a bathrobe embroidered with mermaids, she took a banana from the platter in the sitting room and walked out onto the balcony. Surveying the boats in the marina below, she made a rapid estimate of the capital tied up there: sportfishing boats like Ken's, each worth a number of million dollars; immaculate motor yachts in the same price range and more; racing sailboats, say half a million each; day cruisers and runabouts ... The total was significant, and the vessels' names as varied as their make and size. Those she was able to read from the balcony revealed a great deal about their owners: *Nice'n easy*, *Lazy Days*, *Tranquillity*, *Hotrod*, *Surfchaser*, *My Reward*, *PhilAnn III*.

Ken's boat *Geyser* had certainly lived up to her name, exploding like a head of steam from an over-pressurized boiler. During the few hours Petra had been asleep, the boatyard staff had worked quickly to haul her out. Now she hung forlornly in the straps of the larger of the yard's two marine lifts.

Petra scanned the marina again, looking for Betty's classic motor yacht. As far as she could tell, *Gloriana* wasn't there. She would put on her bikini and a cover-up, walk around to make sure then take a look at *Geyser*. But first, she wanted to find Sam and ask him about the Gracebys – he seemed to know everything that went on in the resort.

Sam was loading suitcases into the luggage compartment of a large bus filled with red-faced tourists. She watched him for a few minutes as he concentrated on his task. He was older and stronger than she had thought at first. Hefting the last bag in, he closed the compartment and banged on the side of the bus. The driver acknowledged his 'All clear!' and the bus jolted away with a belch of diesel fumes.

Sam beamed at his visitor. 'What are you doing here, Miss? You should be resting.'

'I was until something disturbed me. Can we talk for a few minutes?'

'Sure. Come with me to the marina. I have a package to take to the harbourmaster.'

Riding in the golf cart with Sam, Petra couldn't help anticipating another explosion. It was the same feeling she had whenever she looked up into the sky at a plane in the days following an air crash. Each one had the potential to break into pieces before her eyes. Her mother would have said she was tempting fate even to think about it.

'You said you saw Ken Graceby this morning, Sam.'

'Yes'm! Mr. Reed gave me three boxes to deliver to Mr. Ken's boat.'

'What was Mr. Ken doing when you delivered them?'

'The usual – checking things, I don't know what exactly. I put the boxes on the side deck and left.'

'Do you know what was in them?'

'Drinks, or supplies maybe. Mr. Ken told me yesterday that he had some trouble when he took the boat out on a fishing charter, but everything was fixed.'

'Have you any idea what the trouble was?'

Sam giggled. 'Whatever it was, it was worse than he thought!'

'Sam! That's a mean thing to say. Don't you like Ken Graceby?'

'I don't like the way he treats people sometimes.'

'How does he treat them?' Petra asked. 'Does he treat you badly? And what about his grandmother? Is he nasty to her sometimes?'

The barrage of questions confused Sam. 'I don't know, I can't tell you anything.'

Petra realized she had been pushing too hard too soon. She tried a different approach. 'You have a busy job, looking after the luggage as well as making deliveries to the boats.'

'Yes'm, but I don't mind.'

'I expect Ken Graceby often takes people out fishing.'

'Yes'm. He does lots of charters. He loves the water.'

'What about you? Do you like the water?'

'Me? I like boats but I can't swim, so I stay on land. Once I went with Mr. Ken when nobody else could.'

'Does he take his grandmother out much?'

Sam hesitated. 'He spends the summer on her yacht, *Gloriana*, but he isn't captain any more.'

'Oh?'

Sam lowered his voice. 'She replaced him. He was entertaining friends on her boat, you know. James Freedy is captain now. Before, he was just one of the crew …'

Now that Sam was on a tack he was comfortable with, it was like a broad reach on a summer's day. Petra could sit back and enjoy the flow of information. And she had dozens of questions to ask him.

'Yo' man, Samson, you' a real gossip! You watch what you say now.'

The reprimand came from a man who stepped out of the Marina Office as the golf cart cruised to a stop. Petra recognized him as the harbourmaster. His bulk took up the whole doorway, and his sailor's striped T-shirt and cut-off pants made him appear even wider than he was in reality. The grizzled hair suggested a man of middle age, though the skin on his face was as smooth as Sam's was weathered.

'Thanks for the ride, Samson,' Petra said. 'Let me take that package.' She gave Sam a conspiratorial wink and handed the box to the harbourmaster. 'I'd like to walk round the marina for a while if that's OK.'

The harbourmaster crossed his arms over his copious belly and scrutinized Petra.

'You' de girl who rescued Miss Graceby dis morning,' he said in a lilting Caribbean accent. He scratched the top of his head. 'Dat was a good t'ing you did. She'n swim too good.'

'That's surprising for someone who enjoys boating as much as she does.'

'She say she growd up in a li'l ol' mining town in Ontario and don't have no chance to learn. But it no stop her goin' places on dat beautiful boat o' hers.'

'Where is her boat? I don't see it in the marina.'

'Should be here dis week. Hurricanes 'bout over and de big boats is comin' back. Cap'n Freedy know what's right. He'd never let no boat of his get in trouble.' The harbourmaster looked pointedly at Petra, who gave a solemn nod. If he was deliberately trying to confuse her by not speaking standard English, he was succeeding. He stood watching her reaction.

She was wondering how to respond when the radio inside the Marina Office began to squawk. He turned away to answer it. With a wave, she walked along the dock towards the boatyard.

It was a shock to see the extent of the damage to Ken's Viking. The explosion had blown a large hole in the rear section of the salon. The side windows were shattered, the fishing tower and rigging had collapsed. Everything was black or bent.

Petra ducked to examine the underside of the hull. To her surprise, it was intact. The force of the blast must have gone upwards, and the vessel's heavy sole had been enough to save the engine room from destruction. Betty and Ken had been exceedingly lucky. She had witnessed many boat fires where the ending had not been so happy.

In one incident, a man and his mother had been driving from the upper helm on the flybridge of his powerboat when a fire started below. They had issued a Mayday call and jumped overboard. By the time the fireboat reached them, the boat had sunk and the woman had drowned. As with most fires, the cause had been difficult to establish. In the end, it was attributed to faulty wiring and the inquest had returned a verdict of accidental death.

Standing in sombre contemplation, Petra failed to hear the approaching footsteps.

'I suppose you've come to gloat.' It was Ken Graceby, his voice surly.

'Why would I gloat? I don't take pleasure in other people's misfortune. It's a tragedy, although it could have been worse.'

'It could have been a helluva lot better too.'

'What do you mean?'

'It's obvious, isn't it? Even to someone like you.'

Petra shot him a threatening look.

'Well now I won't get a new boat,' he said, shuffling his feet. 'The insurance company will pay to have *Geyser* fixed, but if she'd been a complete write-off, they'd have given me the cash.'

And a million or two was not to be sneezed at, Petra thought. Plus, if Betty's complaints against her grandson had any substance, he might have wanted her to die in the explosion.

As if he could read her thoughts, Ken jabbed a finger in her face. 'Now I know who you are! You're the broad who saved my grandmother!'

'You too, buddy, in case you've forgotten!'

'I'd have been fine without any help from you or anyone else.'

'Possibly,' she admitted, 'but in times of crisis those distinctions are hard to make. The worthless get rescued along with the worthy.'

Ken's eyes narrowed. 'Who are you anyway? You're Canadian, eh? Are you on vacation?'

'Ten out of ten for recognizing my accent, boyo.'

'My grandmother's Canadian and my father's half-Canuck, so I should; we spend a lot of time up there in the summer.'

'Ah, yes! On your grandmother's boat, *Gloriana*.'

'How do you know about that?'

'My family's from Sudbury, Ontario. In summer we get together at my uncle's cottage in Killarney,' Petra said, adapting the truth to fit her cover story. 'I've seen *Gloriana* there. She's a Trumpy if I'm not mistaken.'

'Wrong! A classic Burger, 1969.' Ken's lips curled into a supercilious smile.

Petra laughed to herself. Her ruse had worked. He was the type who needed to feel superior. 'Of course! They can look quite similar.'

'Not if you know about motor yachts.'

'As you obviously do.'

'I know that boat inside out.'

'You used to captain her, didn't you?' Petra asked, remembering what Sam had said.

Ken feigned indifference. 'What's it to you? Anyway, you didn't answer my question. Are you here on vacation?'

'I am,' she said, looking him in the eye. 'I've always

wanted to visit *Neptunis* and I needed a break. When I told my mother I was coming here, she asked me to let Miss Graceby know that my father died recently. As a young man, he worked for your grandfather, Joe LePinto. Joe took a liking to him and they became friends.'

Petra's words had an astounding effect on Ken. He turned on her like a pit bull. 'Joe LePinto was never my grandfather, he was a mean old bastard. He hated my father and he hated me.'

Petra had expected bad blood between Ken and his grandmother, but this was an added dimension. 'I'm sorry, I had no idea.'

'Fucking right you don't!' he said. 'I've got a party booked to go fishing tomorrow, and no boat to take them out on.' He paused. 'And what do you think my chances are of being able to beg, borrow, steal or charter another vessel in time, eh Canuck?'

'Not good I would think, if you call people names,' she retorted.

Petra left Ken supervising the moving of his boat from the marine lift onto blocks and stands. The encounter had made her realize how important it was to properly establish her cover and act like a tourist. She spent the next hour wandering round, exploring the resort and marvelling at the architect's ingenuity. His creations reminded her of Gaudí's fantastic constructions in Barcelona where form and function existed in counterpoise.

One of the apartment buildings represented a coral reef. Colourful protuberances sprouted from the walls:

anemones, corals, fish, even the head of a conger eel. Another was built like the side of a Spanish galleon. It was a kingdom where kitsch reigned supreme, yet the overall effect was impressive.

In one corner of the resort, she discovered a lost city of gigantic carved blocks of stone – broken statues, columns and arches – artistically arranged around a marble piazza. At the outdoor café, she ordered a fish burger without fries and sat down at a mosaic-topped table bearing the head of Neptune. When her plate came, it was loaded with fries: the willpower test again.

After consuming the fish and a handful of fries, Petra followed a winding pathway marked with tridents to the aquarium. The dim interior was full of treasures, from tiny yellow seahorses to vast diamond-shaped rays. When she entered the shark tunnel, though, it unsettled her. She wished she had a harpoon in her hand for protection as a tiger shark dogged her footsteps and a hammerhead swam above her.

When she emerged from the deep, the afternoon was drawing to a close. She made her way to the semi-circular pool near the bar. It was a time of day she looked forward to. Most guests had gone to their rooms to shower and change for the evening, leaving the pool for serious swimmers.

Petra took a towel from the lifeguard's kiosk, placed it on a sunbed with her cover-up, kicked off her flip-flops and dived into the pool. The water was pleasantly warm and slightly salty. She lay floating on her back as she had done that morning after rescuing Betty. Then she flipped onto her stomach and began a strong rhythmic crawl to the far side of the pool.

One of the lasting benefits of her previous assignment aboard megayacht *Titania* in the Mediterranean was a blue and gold bikini that showed off her figure to advantage. She had worn it only once before for a recreational swim. On other occasions, she had found herself in deep water, literally and figuratively, in far less suitable attire … like the afternoon when Don León had taken her in his Lamborghini to visit his magnificent villa on the Costa del Sol …

A faint pink suffused Petra's cheeks as she rolled onto her back and swam lazily, using just her feet for propulsion. It seemed such a long time ago yet it was hardly more than three weeks since she had fooled around in the pool with him … She visualized his massive head with its curly mane of hair, his muscled chest and legs, the amber eyes, the roaring laugh. The rapport between them had been intense – a sensual connection that still tugged at her insides. Several times she had wished she could succumb to his advances, but his moral code was not hers; she had fought against those feelings and triumphed over them in the end.

Petra kicked harder and brought her arms into play to increase her speed. Why, when she was attracted to a man, did she favour the older ones? It was a rhetorical question. She didn't need a psychiatrist to tell her that the answer lay in the tragic accident that had stolen Romeo from her before they could unite in matrimony. Ten years on, the wound was still raw.

CHAPTER

3

Cliff Graceby was on his second drink of the day. Despite the shock of finding his mother being attended to by paramedics, he had managed to stay off the liquor until the sun had begun its descent to the western horizon. He exchanged quips with the barmaid, a buxom blonde in a shimmering sheath that resembled fish scales, then turned away, tired of her lack of imagination. A sledge hammer was more vibrant.

Cliff contemplated the golden brown liquid in his glass. It was too early for people-watching and too late for rating the bathing beauties. He shifted his weight to ease the pressure on the back of his legs. Whatever the designer's intent, the barstool was beginning to feel like a lump of coral. He swivelled to face the pool.

A slender arm broke the surface of the water, arced backwards and disappeared. As it did so, its twin rose and dipped, followed by the first in perpetual motion. The swimmer covered the distance to the end of the pool in record time, executed a tight turn worthy of an Olympic contender and continued to the bridge in the middle.

Cliff watched as two hands reached up and grabbed the lower edge of the bridge. It swayed as the swimmer – a girl with long black hair – drew herself out of the water. She held the position for a few seconds before lowering herself back into the pool. She repeated the manoeuvre several times, apparently for exercise, before launching into a robust breaststroke.

The barmaid tapped Cliff on the shoulder and he almost fell off his stool. 'How about it then? I get off at eleven.'

'Some other time, darling, I have plans for tonight.'

'Is that so?' Désirée followed his gaze as Petra emerged from the pool and shook off the excess water like an excited puppy.

'You'd better be quick or she'll slip through your net! I'll be here when you want me.'

'Désirée, you're one in a million.'

'I know my limitations.'

Cliff downed the rest of his scotch, slid off the stool and walked with as much nonchalance as he could muster to the pool deck.

'You have goose bumps right along the top of your bikini bottom,' he murmured, coming up behind Petra. He kept his voice light, sweet as honey, as he drew his finger across the small of her back.

Petra whirled round, clutching her towel. 'What the hell do you think …' She stopped in consternation when she realized she was facing Betty's son.

Cliff's eyebrows lifted as he recognized the young woman the resort manager had pointed out as his mother's rescuer. Her face was pink with exertion and anger at his impertinence. His gaze dropped to her chest. The gold edging on her blue bikini top formed a deep V between her breasts, mirroring the heart-shaped line of her chin.

'Forgive me, I should know better. That's not at all the proper way to behave towards a lady.' He held out his hand. 'I'm Cliff Graceby, a black-hearted rogue.'

The words were said with such mock seriousness that Petra laughed aloud.

'Petra Minx. Accepted.'

'Would you also accept an invitation to dinner tonight? I know a fabulous place.'

Petra's instinctive reaction was to decline his offer. To accept might be construed as forwardness. Yet it would be an opportunity to get to know him and assess his relationship with his mother and his son. Betty was still in hospital, Ken she had already met … There was nothing on the agenda until ten o'clock tomorrow morning.

'I may be a rogue, but I'm not an ogre,' he urged. 'And it would be a small way of thanking you for rescuing my mother this morning.'

'All right then.'

'Don't sound so enthusiastic! Meet me in the lobby at eight and wear your dancing shoes.'

Back in her suite, Petra riffled through the clothes she had unpacked earlier that day. They were hardly suitable for a vacation on a subtropical island. Fortunately, she had kept a few of the items provided for her to wear on board *Titania*. She unearthed a gold silk shirt, some midnight blue Lycra leggings and a pair of gold high-heeled sandals. When she tried them on, the effect was tasteful and faintly sexy. She pulled back her hair, revealing clean high cheekbones, and pinned it into a neat chignon. She was ready well before eight and decided to arrive early to capitalize on the element of surprise.

The lobby was crowded with incoming tourists. From their fair colouring and guttural language, Petra guessed they were Scandinavians. Sheltering behind a noisy family group, she saw that Cliff was already there, seated in an armchair opposite his son, Ken. Intent on their discussions, they were unaware of her arrival, and she had ample time to observe them both. Although the din in the lobby made it difficult to hear, she could lip-read some of their conversation.

'I don't understand you, Ken,' she saw Cliff say. 'You're heading for big trouble if you're not careful. What went wrong this morning?'

'Nothing went wrong, fuck it!' came the irate reply. 'I tell you these guys are serious and they'll pay top dollar. We should at least look at what they want to do.'

'They're serious all right. The risks are enormous, boy. Don't underestimate them.'

'Look, if you're not interested, I'll do it myself.'

Cliff sighed. His son sounded like a petulant child who hadn't learned to curb his appetites and emotions. 'Listen to me, Ken. At the very least, what happened this morning was a warning. At that level, you play for keeps. I'm not rushing into anything, and don't you go making anybody any promises.'

Petra moved closer as a man with an impressive beer belly obstructed her view. She strained her ears but was unable to catch Ken's reply. Whatever he and Cliff were talking about sounded a great deal fishier than deep-sea charters.

At that moment she heard Sam's excited voice rising above the hum of the crowd. 'Miss Petra, Miss Petra!'

'We'll discuss this some other time,' Cliff said. 'I have to go.' He stood up and looked around.

Ken's expression turned thunderous as his eyes fell on Petra. 'What's she doing here?'

'We have a date,' Cliff said smoothly.

Ignoring Ken, Petra stepped towards Cliff and raised her hand in salute as though she had just spotted him. 'There you are! It's so crowded in here. I hope I'm not late.'

'No, no, right on time, as I would expect.' He appraised her from head to toe. 'Beautiful! You'll turn more than a few heads tonight.'

'Miss Petra!'

Sam was pushing his way through the masses. She could no longer pretend she hadn't heard him. 'Hi, Samson! You're working late tonight! Don't you ever go home?'

'That's OK. My home is here.'

He paused and Petra thought she detected a flash of sadness in his eyes before he continued.

'There was a message for you at reception. It's been there since this morning. I wanted you to have it,' he said, handing her a small white envelope edged in silver.

Cliff glimpsed the ornate lettering and immediately recognized the handwriting. 'It's from my mother.'

'I'll read it later,' Petra said hastily, seeing the questioning look on his face. She placed it in her beaded purse and slid her arm through his. 'I'm looking forward to this evening and I must warn you, I'm ravenous!'

'Good! I don't like girls who pick at their food. Let's go.'

Petra eased into the gleaming red Viper SRT-10 and waited as Cliff closed her door and walked round the long hood to the other side of the low-slung car. As the engine roared to life, she wondered what kind of driver he would be. Would she feel the same fear as she had on the first day of her previous assignment – the day Monica had raced Don León's Lamborghini along the Grande Corniche to Monte Carlo? Or would she enjoy the experience as she had when Don León himself had taken the wheel of the Murciélago a few days later, the chemistry between them helping her to overcome her phobia? Logic told her she probably didn't need to worry: she was on a small island with limited highways.

The Viper was sleek, powerful and fast off the mark, the fanged head a fitting logo. Once they were out of town and past the airport, the road narrowed. It was winding but not hair-raising like the South of France, and Cliff maintained a steady speed that gave her confidence. Petra noticed his hands on the wheel: long strong fingers, manicured nails. A man who took care of himself.

She threw a covert glance at Cliff's profile. His nose and chin were well defined, the proportions classic. His face was clean-shaven and tanned, his silver hair carefully styled. The black linen suit and green silk shirt he was wearing set off his tan and suggested a touch of the Irish. He would be an easy person to like if you took the smoothness at face value.

Because of her profession – and perhaps her early experiences with love and death – she tended to distrust until she was completely sure of her footing.

Petra remained silent, waiting for Cliff to speak, knowing there would be questions. Under his suave exterior, Cliff was shrewd and nobody's fool. It would be better not to volunteer information, just respond. She knew from interviewing suspects that the nervous ones divulged far more than was necessary in the first few minutes of a conversation. She also knew how difficult restraint could be in situations where there was a primordial connection between the parties.

Cliff looked sideways at his passenger. 'You're quiet. Are you all right?'

'I'm fine.'

'The place we're going isn't far, just a few miles along the coast. It's an easy drive. Are you familiar with the Viper?'

'Not really.'

Then, instead of asking another question, he threw her off balance by saying: 'Tell me about yourself.'

'What do you want to know?'

'Whatever you want to tell me.'

Petra lobbed the ball back into his court. 'What do you want me to tell you?'

'What do you think I should know?'

She returned the play, trying to force him into submission. 'What about you? I'd like to know about you!'

In the end, Cliff won the rally with a masterstroke. 'I asked first,' he declared, in a tone that brooked no argument.

'OK, I'm beat. You're a tough opponent!'

She spent the rest of the drive telling Cliff the same story she had told Ken. Unlike Ken, he did not react badly when she mentioned his mother's husband, Joe LePinto. He insisted, however, that he had no recollection of Petra's father ever working for Joe.

'I was living in Vegas at that time – not with my mother and stepfather, but I knew most of their friends. People were always at the house. I don't remember anyone called Ludo.'

To Petra's relief, they turned right onto a track leading towards the sea before Cliff could pursue the matter. As they negotiated the corner, she caught sight of a large illuminated sign.

'The Coco Caverna Club – is that where we're going?'

'That's it! One of the top places in the Bahamas: members and special invitation only. I'm sure you'll enjoy it.'

Halfway through a sumptuous seafood platter accompanied by a crisp Pouilly-Fuissé, Petra had no complaints – at least as far as the meal was concerned. She put her wineglass down and looked across the table at her host. The silver St. Christopher he wore round his neck glistened in the candlelight and she caught a whiff of lightly spiced cologne as he leaned towards her. Hugo Boss, or perhaps Armani.

Since their arrival at the Club, Cliff had kept the conversation on topics of general interest. At first, she had been happy to sip a Bahama Mama on the terrace and talk about holiday destinations. But once they were seated at their table on the edge of a vast cave, the Caverna of the Club's name, she tried to focus the discussion. Not allowing himself to be led, Cliff launched into a detailed history of the island and the caves. Petra refused to let him get away with it any longer.

'You've obviously spent lots of time on the island, yet I get the impression it isn't your home. Do you still live in Las Vegas?' she asked. He could hardly refuse to answer a direct question.

'Where else would a rogue like me live? I'm a dyed-in-the-wool Vegan – not to be confused with a vegan, since I eat everything under the sun!' He laughed at Petra's wry grimace. 'I can see you don't appreciate my little joke.'

'Your stepfather, Joe LePinto, made his fortune in the hotel and restaurant industry in Las Vegas, didn't he? Have you been running his businesses since his death?'

A flush suffused Cliff's cheeks. 'Why would you think that? I have my own hotel. It's one of the best boutique establishments in the city. We win awards all the time. You should come and visit.'

Cliff's colour had returned to normal, but she had definitely touched a nerve. She dug a little deeper.

'So who looks after his interests?'

'My mother,' he said tersely.

'Of course. How is she? Did you go to the hospital this afternoon?'

'Yes, she's fine.'

'I am glad. That means she should be home soon and I'll be able to meet her.'

'I'm not sure about that. My mother's a virtual recluse nowadays. She hardly ever goes out and doesn't like people, especially new ones.'

'But she went out on Ken's boat this morning.'

Cliff shrugged. 'Family's different.'

'Have you any idea what caused the explosion?'

'An engine problem, who knows? It could have been anything.'

Not quite true, Petra thought. Diesel tanks did not explode easily and if they had, the damage would have been much greater. If she had to hazard a guess, she would say that somebody had sent explosives aboard in the boxes Sam had delivered.

Running through the possibilities in her head, she didn't notice the hostess who had come to clear the table until the girl squealed as Cliff caressed her buttocks under the turquoise and gold mini-skirt.

'You should know the rules by now, Sir! You can look but not touch.' The Rubenesque mulatto batted her eyelashes at him before flouncing off to the kitchen.

'I'm sorry, I shouldn't have done that,' Cliff said. 'I miss female company since my wife died.'

'Your wife?' There had been nothing about a wife in the material Tom had given her to read on the plane. Petra kicked herself for her stupidity. Ken had to have a mother.

'Yes. She died of cancer three years ago. That's when my hair turned white.'

He sounded so forlorn that Petra gave him a look full of sympathy and murmured her condolences.

'Do you want to talk about it?'

'I'd rather not dwell on it. Let's have another drink.' He called the nearest hostess and ordered another bottle of wine, then sat staring at the lone couple smooching on the dance floor in the centre of the cave. He seemed locked in with his memories and Petra finished her food in silence.

The vocalist who had entertained them during dinner left the stage with his back-up trio. Oblivious to their surroundings, the couple carried on dancing. Not until the steel band struck up and the tempo changed did they cede the floor to scattered applause and a few loud catcalls. Petra began to tap her foot to the beat.

Cliff rubbed his hand across his face. 'I can see you like the music. Shall we dance?'

'Yes, it'll do you good.' She glanced at her watch. 'Just don't forget I flew in from London this morning. I'll turn into a pumpkin at midnight.'

'That's when the fun starts.'

He was right. By the witching hour, the Club was packed with assorted glitterati, fathers and daughters – just like Cliff and herself – sons and mothers, well-heeled locals, and tourists with special passes. Cliff had an innate sense of rhythm and soon Petra was dancing her jetlag away. Any unresolved issues from their earlier conversation dissipated in the throb of the drums.

When the limbo dancers arrived, the hostess who had batted her eyelashes at Cliff pushed him to the forefront. He had already taken off his jacket to dance; now he stripped off his green shirt and gave it to Petra to hold. His muscles rippled as he bent his knees and leaned backwards to inch his torso under the pole. The watchers applauded as he made it with clearance to spare.

'Incredible!' Petra said, handing him his shirt.

'Lots of practice,' he replied. 'And they don't hold the pole quite so low for me.'

'Still very impressive!'

The noise level mounted as the goombay drums beat out their message to the assembled crowd. The hostesses in their black coconut brassieres and sequined skirts hurried back and forth, bringing a constant supply of drinks to the thirsty dancers.

As Petra bopped away from Cliff, he grasped her shoulders and spun her round to face him. She sashayed forward, closing the gap between them. In the canyon between her breasts hung a black and silver cross. He brushed it with his fingertip.

'Nice talisman! It hides like the pearl in an oyster, waiting to be discovered.'

'Ah, but discovery is a long, slow, frustrating process,' she said, pushing his finger away with a bewitching smile.

It was two o'clock in the morning when they left the Club. Petra sank exhausted into the Viper and snoozed most of the way back to the resort. She was conscious at one point of Cliff's hand on her thigh, but decided it was a light friendly touch and did nothing to remove it.

Cliff parked the car at the bottom of the marble steps and helped his sleepy passenger onto her feet. 'I don't think you can walk back to your suite. Sit on this bench. I'll get a golf cart.'

Petra had no energy left to protest. While she had been on the dance floor, everything had been fine. Now she felt as weak as a malnourished child. She sat dozing on the

bench until Cliff returned and lifted her into the cart. The
gardens were silent and deserted as they whirred by, the
pool bar closed and in darkness. A handful of lights shone
in some of the buildings, though none in Petra's block.

'Give me your key card, I'll take you up,' Cliff offered.

'There's no need.' Petra drew herself upright. If she let
Cliff accompany her, there was a good chance she would
end up having to fend him off, and that she didn't want.
'Really, I'll be fine. The elevator goes straight to my suite.
Thank you for a wonderful evening.' She gave him a peck
on the cheek, pulling away as he caught at her hands. 'See
you tomorrow sometime.'

The private elevator took only a few seconds to reach
her suite. She stepped out and stripped off her sandals. The
relief to her feet was immense. Enjoying the feel of the cold
marble, she crossed to the sitting room door, which was ajar.
First stop the bathroom, then a glass of water on the balcony
to wind down. In the end, she decided to forgo the water as
tiredness overwhelmed her.

She gave her teeth a cursory brush, switched off the
bathroom light and made her way to bed. As she walked, a
phosphorescent strip illuminated her path, giving her the
feeling of being deep under the sea. The feeling intensified
when she sat on the side of the bed and the water moved
beneath her. She peeled off her gold silk shirt, now damp
with perspiration, and deposited it on the bedside chair near
which she had dropped her sandals. Her bra joined the heap.

With reverence, Petra touched the crucifix that hung
round her neck and sent up a silent prayer for Betty
Graceby's well-being. Betty's son, Cliff, was an intriguing

mixture of charm and bravado and disconcertingly well turned out. Ken Graceby was the opposite – a diamond in the rough. The intensity of his hatred towards Joe LePinto had come as a complete surprise. Her eyes began to close and she pushed all thoughts away. Now was not the time to attempt in-depth analysis.

Almost too weary to undress further, Petra nevertheless stood up and rolled down her Lycra leggings, removing her thong at the same time. As she bent over to move one of her sandals that could be a trip hazard if she got up during the night, she felt her skin prickle. At the Police Academy, they had been taught never to ignore the signals sent by mankind's deeply buried primordial instincts. She snatched up the sandal and reached for the bedside light switch.

'Nice, very nice!'

The lazy male voice came from immediately behind her. Before she could move, two hands grasped her breasts and jerked her backwards. Petra gasped with shock. She could feel her attacker's arousal through his jeans as he rubbed himself against her. She struggled to break free, but her efforts were futile against his superior strength. In the male-female equation tonnage always ruled – unless you could find the weak spot.

What was it Tom Gilmore had taught her in London about using down and dirty tactics? *Don't panic; don't waste your energy fighting randomly. Think. Focus. Find some unexpected method of attack.* His words reverberated in her head.

Deliberately, Petra sank back onto her aggressor's hardness, making herself soft and accommodating. When she heard him moan, she tightened her abdominal muscles and thrust her pelvis backwards with as much force as she could. The unexpectedness of the move startled him into relaxing his hold on her breasts. She twisted out of his grasp. Before she could put some distance between them, he grabbed her arm and pulled her back.

'You bastard!' she shouted. 'How did you get in here?'

With a muttered curse, he seized her left wrist, the one that held the sandal. His grip was like a vice, crushing her bones. She was forced to drop the sandal.

'You're a wild one!' he grunted. 'The way you were dancing with my father, I didn't expect any resistance at all.'

His left hand dug into her shoulder and she could smell the rum on his breath.

'What were you doing with him, anyway? Gold-digging? He's twice your age. You need a young stud like me!'

Still struggling, Petra tried to knee Betty's grandson in the groin. He kept out of range, dancing lightly on his feet like a well-trained boxer. Each of the muscles in his naked torso was carefully sculpted through hard sessions at the gym. She waited for an opportunity to hurt him.

Suddenly, he pushed her backwards onto the soft sponginess of the bed. 'Huh! I'm wasting my time. You're not worth bothering with! I came to ask if you'd be interested in a gangbang. Now I know the answer.' He enunciated carefully to avoid slurring his words. Then, swaying slightly, he turned and left the room.

Petra sat up and rubbed her wrist, listening to Ken's footsteps as he made his way through the sitting room and into the hall. She didn't think he would come back, but he was so unpredictable that she wanted to be sure. Still listening, she pulled her gold silk shirt from the pile on the chair and shrugged it on.

When she heard the outer door click shut, she let out a breath and kicked the sandal Ken had forced her to drop across the room. He had taken her completely by surprise. She should have guessed that lust was his Achilles' heel. And though she had tried to put Tom's advice into practice, she had hardly given a stellar performance. Fortunately, a little feeble opposition had taken the wind out of Ken's sails. Another time she might not be so lucky.

CHAPTER

4

'You're late!' Jayne Birch puffed out her meagre chest and tapped her fingers on the massive desk behind which she sat. It wasn't difficult to imagine her as the headmistress of an upper-class girls' school chiding one of her charges.

Petra took a deep breath. After her face-off with Ken, she had lain awake trying to figure out how he got into her suite and the real motive for his attack. Apart from the basic sexual aspect, it seemed to be linked to his relationship with his father. Had he felt slighted, seeing her go off to dinner with Cliff who was old enough to be her father? Had watching her dance with Cliff aroused feelings of jealousy and a desire to get his own back? Did Ken have old scores to settle with his father? Or was he taking revenge on her for saving his grandmother and his boat? There were far more questions than answers. Finally she had slept and overslept. Although the taxi driver had done his best, motivated by the promise of a generous tip, she had arrived at the Canadian Consulate half an hour after the appointed time.

'Unforeseen complications, I'm afraid. It happens in my profession.'

Jayne Birch frowned and gave Petra a sceptical look through the top half of her bifocals.

'Attacked in my own quarters,' Petra murmured.

'What did you say?'

'Nothing. I apologize. As you know, I only arrived yesterday and there was an explosion at the marina.'

'Yes, we heard about that.' Jayne Birch pulled a beige file folder towards her and opened it. 'In the normal course of events, I wouldn't be able to pass on this information, but I have been instructed to do so. I understand you're RCMP.' She paused, waiting for an answer to her implied question.

'Correct. However, I'd appreciate your keeping that in confidence. I'm here in an unofficial capacity. My late father was a friend of Joe LePinto's,' Petra said, sticking closely to her cover story. 'Do you know the Gracebys?'

'Everyone knows the Gracebys. Clifford is a staunch supporter of our local museum and his son, Kendall – such a nice young man – has made generous donations to our bird sanctuary.'

With Betty's money, no doubt. Jayne Birch had spoken with complete sincerity yet Petra couldn't imagine either of them as a philanthropist, and Ken was hardly a nice young man. 'I believe Betty Graceby has made several complaints against her grandson,' she said. 'What can you tell me about them?'

'It's all in the file.'

'Yes, but I'd like to understand how the Consulate came to be involved.'

Miss Birch pursed her lips. 'This is highly irregular.'

'It would help me to have your perspective on the issue,' Petra insisted.

'I wasn't here when the first incident occurred last November, about a year ago. Miss Graceby called the police, claiming that Kendall's girlfriend had gone into her bedroom and stolen some jewellery. When she confronted the girl, Kendall became aggressive and verbally abusive. The girl swore she was innocent and the subsequent enquiry produced no evidence to support Miss Graceby's allegation.'

'So an enquiry was conducted?'

'Yes, by the police.'

Petra leaned forward. 'What about the second incident? Were you here then?'

'I was. That was in February this year. Miss Graceby called the police again and accused Kendall of pressuring her for money and stealing from her wallet. The police promised to investigate but let it drop. Then, at the end of April, Miss Graceby's houseboy, a Puerto Rican by the name of Luis Morales, made a third call to the police. He reported that Kendall had been threatening his grandmother and refused to leave the premises.'

'Did the police respond?'

'No. They declined to intervene, so she contacted us. There wasn't much we could do, even though she is a Canadian citizen. She was not in immediate danger and family politics are not part of our mandate. In fact, Clifford advised us that his mother suffers from Alzheimer's disease, which might explain her delusions.'

Miss Birch seemed eager to dismiss Betty's complaints as delusions, which they could be, Petra thought, but the

Graceby boys' support for her pet projects might have coloured her thinking.

'Three incidents in six months,' Petra said. 'Then nothing until last week. How do you explain that?'

'There were no problems during the summer because Miss Graceby was away on her yacht. She flew back here three weeks ago, leaving *Gloriana* in Bermuda for maintenance.' Miss Birch checked a note in the file before continuing. 'Again, it was her houseboy who telephoned the police to report that her grandson had forced his way into the apartment and was raising hell. Miss Graceby was so distressed that the doctor had to be called.'

'Yet she was on Ken's boat yesterday morning when it exploded,' Petra mused. 'Something doesn't compute.' She needed to talk to Betty and find out what was going on. 'I appreciate your time, Miss Birch. May I take the file?'

A reluctant nod was the answer. 'Please return it when you've finished with it.'

'Certainly. Is there anything else I should know?'

'Not that I am aware of.'

'Well, if you think of something, please contact me at the resort. I'll be there for a few more days at least.' Petra stood up to take her leave then stopped as a way of playing tourist and placating Miss Birch occurred to her. 'Does anyone run tours to the bird sanctuary? I'd like to see it.'

Miss Birch softened immediately. 'I'm a volunteer there. I could take you myself on Monday afternoon, say four o'clock. Would that suit you?'

'Perfect! I'll look forward to it.'

When Petra got back to her suite, the light on the telephone was blinking. There was a message from Betty Graceby. She was home from hospital and wondered whether Petra would join her in her suite for lunch at one o'clock. Petra picked up the phone and dialled quickly. It was already close to noon.

After speaking to Betty's houseboy, Luis, who assured her there was no problem at all, Petra remembered the envelope Sam had given her the evening before. It was a note from Betty, as Cliff had been quick to recognize. The handwriting was old-fashioned and elegant. "*Dear Miss Minx,*" she had written. "*My apologies for not being able to greet you on your arrival. Make yourself comfortable and please do not worry. I will telephone you later. I look forward to meeting you. Sincerely, Betty Graceby.*"

Petra read the note again. It contained nothing unusual apart from the suggestion that Petra might worry, which could be just an elderly lady's way of being polite. She put the card back in the envelope and added it to the beige file folder.

For the next three quarters of an hour, Petra immersed herself in the file Miss Birch had so grudgingly handed over. The first incident had occurred almost exactly a year ago. It was the only one involving anyone other than Betty and her grandson. Some of the details were sketchy, and it appeared that the police had arrived too late to be of much use. How strange that Betty had called them rather than Resort Security. Security would have responded much more quickly and been able to hold the girl until the police got there.

The police had identified the girl as Bianca Casales and her job was listed as hostess at the Coco Caverna Club. Petra ground her teeth. What a wasted opportunity! Ken had been drinking at the Club the previous evening and Friday nights were busy, so it was quite likely that Bianca had been working there. Had she known what she knew now, she would have tried to find Bianca and ask her a few questions.

Petra put down the file. On each of the last three occasions when Betty or her houseboy, Luis, had complained to the authorities about Ken's behaviour, there was no evidence to support their claims. It was their word against his. Yet based on what she had seen of Ken so far, she would be inclined to side with Betty.

A few minutes before one o'clock, Petra went down to the lobby to meet Luis. The picture she had formed from talking to him on the phone and reading the file proved close to the truth: he was dark, stocky, pleasant-faced, well-trained and tough. With a smile, he led her to the glass elevator that served the Siren Suite. It was built on the marina side of the building and gave Petra a bird's eye view of the boats as it whisked them to the upper penthouse level.

'I must admit I'm a bit nervous,' she said.

Luis laughed. 'Don't worry. Miss Graceby is a darling. Everyone loves her. She's wonderful to work for.'

The elevator coasted to a stop. Petra stepped out into an enormous roof garden surrounded by a colonnade of Corinthian columns. Immediately she thought of the temples she had seen in Rome. The centre courtyard was inlaid with mosaics; in the middle stood an elaborate fountain. Betty was seated under a canopy near the fountain, waiting to greet her.

As Petra approached, she extended a slim white hand. 'Petra, my dear! How good of you to come! Forgive me if I don't get up. My hip's giving me trouble, no doubt because of yesterday's immersion treatment.'

Petra took an instant liking to the handsome silver-haired woman in front of her, who exuded warmth and confidence. 'I'm so pleased to meet you. Thank you for inviting me.'

'Thank *you* for coming to my rescue. I'm not a strong swimmer, and the shock might have been the end of me. Come and sit here beside me. What do you think of my garden?'

'It's amazing.' Petra scanned the tiered marble steps that framed the courtyard and the ceramic pots overflowing with tropical plants. The flowers were a riot of colour against the cool cream of the marble. The fountain in the centre seemed to be comprised of long-legged birds with female torsos and heads. The same curious motif was repeated in the floor mosaics.

'My husband, Joe, built this for us. He loved being on the water, as I do, and we have a beautiful balcony overlooking the marina, but he said we needed a private retreat where we could look inwards and concentrate on each other.' Betty gave a coy smile. 'I was so much in the limelight in those days, and he was so busy with his restaurants and nightclubs – and well known too. It was hard to go anywhere without being recognized.'

'I'm sure you still have a large following. My father was a great admirer of yours. He used to boast that you gave him your autograph while he was working in Las Vegas for Joe. As teenagers, my sister and I used to tease him about it.'

'Then I must have met him! What was his name?'

'Ludo, Ludo Minx.'

'I can't say that I remember him. How old is he?'

'He would have been sixty-two this year. I'm sorry to have to tell you he died recently.'

'How sad, my dear! You have my sympathy,' Betty said. 'Joe passed away two and a half years ago, and I still miss him as though it were yesterday. He was so full of life and fun, despite his age and the extent of his businesses. It should never have happened.'

'It was an accident?'

'Yes. A terrible thing. Cliff was taking us out to dinner for my birthday. Actually, I should say for *our* birthdays because we were born on the same day, ten years apart. But Cliff never really hit it off with Joe, even after all the time we were together.'

Betty made a dismissive motion with her hand as Petra leaned forward to interject. 'I don't want to talk about it now. I'm forgetting my manners! Let's have a drink. Luis makes a mean banana daiquiri.'

Luis's daiquiri was not so much mean as lethal. Petra felt herself unwinding to the point of becoming light-headed.

It appeared to have no effect on Betty. 'Have you noticed the fountain, my dear?' she asked.

Petra nodded. 'It was one of the first things that caught my eye. But I don't understand the significance of the birds.' In fact, she thought them rather weird.

'If you look carefully, you'll see that they have my face. Joe loved to watch me dance – something I find difficult now with this leg and hip – but he always told me I had legs like a bird. It was my singing, he said, that lured him.'

'So they're sirens, and that's why your suite is called the Siren Suite.'

'You've guessed it! When I sang, he said, no one could resist me, my voice was so sweet yet so powerful, like the sound of the waves and the pull of the ocean.' Betty closed her exquisite eyes and gave a deep sigh.

'Do you give any concerts nowadays?'

'My agent keeps asking me to perform for the high rollers in Atlantic City or Vegas or here. To be honest, I don't feel ready. It's not the same without Joe by my side. Those were golden days.'

'It sounds as though you had a wonderful relationship.'

'We did. Let's go in, my dear. I'll show you the rest of the suite after lunch. Give me your hand, just to steady me.'

Petra saw the pain in Betty's face as she stood up. But Betty kept her smile and walked unaided across the terrace, limping very slightly. Of course, Betty's business was show business, and the show must go on. She would never allow herself to display signs of weakness or give in to her injuries.

Inside the suite, Petra noticed that the siren motif reappeared in the wall hangings lining the corridors. It featured too in an elaborate carved frieze that ran the length of the dining room where Luis had set a regal table for their lunch.

After the meal, they went to sit in the library. Betty continued to reminisce. She was particularly proud of her gallery of pin-ups, as she called them, from her heyday, thirty years earlier. 'I was as much of a beauty at forty as I had been at thirty – you can see by the pictures. I never lost my figure as so many of the girls did by the time they were in their mid-forties. Joe liked that. Let me show you some photos of him.'

Betty paused in front of a shelf of gold-tooled albums bound in different colours, each marked with a year. Petra's heart sank. It would take until nightfall to go through them all.

'1978, that's the first one,' Betty said. 'The year we met. Joe swept me off my feet like a tornado. We married almost immediately.' She pulled the blue leather album off the shelf and opened it. 'There he is. You can see why I fell for him, can't you?'

Petra examined the photo: a man of medium height with a full head of wavy dark hair, Hispanic features and a ready smile. He looked like a nice guy. In later pictures, his hair had turned grey, though his bearing was still upright and his tailored suit and tie impeccable.

'You did say he was born in the United States, didn't you?' she asked.

'Yes. His parents were Puerto Rican immigrants. I never knew them. He grew up in Miami then moved to South America for a while. That's where he met his first wife, Sofía. They divorced in 1968.'

Betty picked up a dark green album. 'There are a few pictures of her and their daughter Elena in here. I was never the jealous type, and they'd been divorced for a decade by the time I met Joe, so I kept the photographs for his sake.' She turned a few pages and pointed to a black and white print of an attractive woman and a young girl. 'There you are! That's Sofía with Elena …'

Immersed in the photographs, neither Betty nor Petra heard the door open and Cliff enter the room.

'Mother! You're not going over ancient history again, are you? You should be resting, and I'm sure Petra is bored,' he exclaimed.

'I'm quite all right, Cliff, and this "ancient history" as you call it is part of our family's pedigree.'

A sour look flashed across Cliff's face.

'And I'm not bored at all. It's fascinating,' Petra added, smiling innocently. Cliff's emotions were not far below the surface. How would he react if he knew about Ken's incursion into her suite?

Cliff arched an eyebrow and addressed his mother. 'I came to ask if you'd seen Ken. We were supposed to meet for lunch. There are a few matters I need to discuss with him, and I'd like you to sign some cheques before I go.'

'You're leaving? I thought you'd at least stay to welcome *Gloriana* back. And what do you need my signature for now? You and Ken always seem to be after money. If it's not one of you pestering me, it's the other.'

'The cheques are for parts and supplies we ordered for your boat, Mother,' Cliff said, drawing a deep breath. 'And I have to go. A foreign delegation's coming to the hotel to see how we do things in Vegas. I'll fly back in a few days' time. When is *Gloriana* due?'

'She should be here on Tuesday. I asked Ken to fly up and join James, but he said he had an important appointment and couldn't leave until tomorrow. I never know whether to believe him or not. That will be too late anyway.'

'Don't worry. James will manage with the crew he's hired locally. The weather's fine and he's a good captain.'

Petra listened to the exchange between mother and son and observed their body language. Cliff was adept at deflecting criticism and seemed able to manipulate and appease Betty at the same time. Her querulousness disappeared as he made the right reassuring noises. But there was no warmth or body contact between them. Rather a physical and an emotional gap.

Cliff turned to Petra. 'I'm sorry I have to leave just as we were beginning to get to know each other.'

'So am I. Can I buy you dinner before you go? I'd love to go back to the Club. The food was fantastic – and the music,' she said, thinking of Bianca Casales.

'I know a dozen other places where *I* would like to take *you*,' he replied, 'but I can't stay.'

'No problem,' Petra said to hide her disappointment.

'I'll take a rain check though. Before you even notice my absence, I'll be back. Then, I promise, I'll show you all my favourite places.'

Petra realized Cliff had mistaken her interest in the Club for interest in himself. 'I'll be waiting,' she murmured, to flatter his ego.

'I don't know what you two are cooking up,' Betty interjected. She looked at her watch. 'Goodness, you were right, Cliff! It's past time for my siesta and you have something for me to sign. You'd better explain to me what it is.'

Petra took that as her cue to leave. 'I'll say goodbye to both of you and thank you, Betty, for a wonderful lunch and afternoon. Perhaps you'd show me the rest of your photographs some other time.' She would never continue in Cliff's presence, that was for sure.

'I'd be delighted, my dear. The physiotherapist is coming tomorrow to work on my hip and leg, so it won't be before Monday. How about coffee here at eleven and stay for lunch if you like?'

'That would be divine.'

The glass elevator carried Petra swiftly to ground level. She had pulled away from Cliff's embrace, but not before he had planted a light kiss on each of her cheeks – just enough to make her wonder what it might be like …

Lost in her thoughts, she stepped out of the elevator and walked right into a man who was waiting in the lobby. She stared at him in disbelief.

'Martin! What on earth are you doing here?'

'Good God! Petra! I could ask you the same question. I didn't expect to run into you. Isn't that the elevator to Betty Graceby's suite?'

'What if it is? What do you want with her?'

'There was a wire service story yesterday about the Gracebys and an explosion on a boat. I've come to get an angle and some pictures. A little of the rich and famous goes a long way towards improving my income. What are you up to?'

'Just having a vacation.'

'You really expect me to believe that?'

'It was worth a try. Look, Martin, can we talk later?'

Martin's presence was a problem. Petra hadn't seen him for over two years, but he knew her well. He could blow her cover in a heartbeat if he said the wrong thing to the wrong people. She needed to put her thoughts in order and decide how much to tell him. As a journalist, he would not give up until he had his story. On the other hand, he might be useful.

'Let me take you to dinner tonight. I'll see if I can worm some secrets out of you. I have a pass for the Coco Caverna Club,' he said.

Petra opened her eyes wide. 'You do? Awesome!'

CHAPTER

5

GRBY 2 was parked directly in front of the hotel, as it had been on Friday evening. Ken Graceby, sleek in white jeans and a black shirt, ran down the steps, past the guests lining up for a taxi, and round to the driver's side of the red Dodge Viper. He let himself into the car, slid into the seat and revved the engine, grinning as the heads began to turn. It never failed to make an impact, and with his father gone he could pretend it was his car.

Through the rearview mirror, he spotted a leggy blonde of about his own age standing a short distance away: touting her assets in killer heels, skinny jeans and a super-low-cut top that showed off her D-cups perfectly. She was not in the taxi line and appeared to be waiting for somebody. The resigned look on her face convinced Ken to try his luck. He revved the Viper again and put it into reverse. This time she reacted to the sound. He lowered the window on the passenger side and leaned across to speak to her.

'How about coming with me instead?'

'Whichever way you mean it, it sounds wicked.'

He laughed as she opened the door and slipped into the seat.

'OK, muscle man! Show me what you can do!' She crossed her ankles and folded her hands in her lap.

'First I'll show you what this snake can do.' Ken pulled away and drove at normal speed to the end of the driveway. He turned onto the deserted boulevard and braked hard. Then he took a folded U.S. one hundred dollar bill out of his shirt pocket and threw it onto the floor in front of the blonde. 'That's yours – if you can pick it up after I get moving and before I shift into second!'

'You're on! Take her away!'

Ken put the Viper into gear and accelerated along the road. Zero to sixty miles an hour in 3.4 seconds. The G-force was huge. Of course she couldn't do it. In skilled hands, the sports car was a dynamite plaything, like a girl with guts and spirit.

The blonde laughed and spiked the bill with her killer heel. 'If you want what I think you want, this is just the deposit.'

'Let's see if you know what you're doing, then we'll talk.'

When they arrived at the Coco Caverna Club an hour later, Ken congratulated himself on his choice. He preferred women who knew when to keep quiet and breathe through their noses and when to crackle and spit.

It was Saturday night and the Club was humming. Ken tossed his car keys to the valet and draped a proprietary arm round the blonde as he escorted her through the palm-lined entrance. Her diamante-studded top sparkled with a million tiny stars in the reflected light from the cavern ceiling. He elbowed a pathway through a group of dancers and grabbed two Piña coladas off a passing tray.

'Here you go; this'll wash your mouth out. I'm Ken. Cheers!'

'Cheers! I'm incognito.'

For a split second, he thought that might be her name. Then his forehead creased into a frown. Idiot! Well, two could play at cat and mouse.

He raised the glass to his lips. Before he could drain it, a coffee-coloured hand reached out and grabbed it. 'That belongs to somebody else, buster. And that's not yours either, darling,' Bianca Casales said as she relieved the blonde of her drink. 'I'd be careful if I were you – both of you.'

From their table on the edge of the dance floor, Petra and Martin observed the scene.

'What a chancer!' Martin spluttered. 'He's got some gall.'

'He thinks he's the cat's whiskers.'

'Does he have a reason for that?'

'No, just a famous grandmother.'

'Aha! Do you know him?'

'We've met briefly a couple of times,' Petra conceded.

'And the girl?'

'Unknown. Incognito.'

'I sense there's something you're not telling me,' Martin pursued.

Petra refused to be pushed. 'There's a lot I'm not telling you at the moment. I can't, Martin. Just accept that. And please keep quiet about my background.'

'So the party line is that you're on vacation?'

'Yes.'

Martin was the last person Petra had expected to meet in the Bahamas. It was over two years since she had told him, shortly after her father died, that she enjoyed his company and his friendship, but didn't want their relationship to go beyond that. He had made no secret of his disappointment. After trying to persuade her to change her mind, he had accepted a position as foreign correspondent in the Tokyo bureau of one of the major wire services. He had sent her a postcard a month or so after he left; then she had heard nothing. After a while, she forgot to wonder how he was getting on.

'Are you still living in Tokyo?' she asked him.

'No. I've been in Toronto since September.'

'What made you come back?'

He shrugged. 'Hard to say. The job was challenging at first, and I met my objective of learning basic Japanese; then I decided to branch out on my own. Officially, I'm an investigative journalist. I go wherever I need to go to find a story.'

'Sounds fun.'

'It is. You should try it yourself.'

'Me?'

'Yes, you. Become a private investigator.'

'I suppose I could think about it.' Petra paused, as if she were considering the possibilities. Then: 'How come you're interested in Betty Graceby?'

'I'm not, my public is.'

'Surely a good journalist is interested in the same things as his public?'

'Petra, you'll tie me in knots as you always did.

Naturally I'm interested, because I'm keen to uncover facts that no one else is aware of, but sometimes I investigate subjects that don't hold any intrinsic interest for me. It's all part of the job. Betty Graceby still has a huge following in Canada. She's one of only a handful of Canadians who've made it really big in the United States. And her recent life has been marred by tragedy. That's why I'm here.'

He paused and looked searchingly at Petra. 'You're very aggressive where Betty Graceby is concerned. What's your connection with her?'

'I saved her from drowning.'

'You're not serious?' His eyes lit up like a child's in Toys Plus at Christmas time.

Petra nodded and, for a moment, felt sorry for Martin. She had always been able to twist him round her little finger. He was the good, solid, riding-school plodder rather than the thoroughbred racehorse she would have liked him to be. That's why the spark had been lacking. She hoped he could turn his dogged persistence into a viable career as a freelancer.

'It was sheer luck that I arrived just before the explosion,' she explained. 'I went to look at the marina while my room was being cleaned. When I saw two people in the water, I jumped in. I had no idea who they were. Had I known, I wouldn't have bothered to rescue Ken Graceby.' She pointed across the room to where he stood with the blonde on his arm and a scowl on his face. 'He's a jerk.'

Martin studied Petra through his glasses but made no comment.

'Betty's a sweetheart,' she continued, 'feisty and tough.'

'Just your sort of woman.'

'I suppose she is. I feel very drawn to her, even though I don't know her well. She's so upbeat, nothing seems to get her down. Someone told me she was a virtual recluse, yet everything I've seen and heard so far points to exactly the opposite.'

'She might not be active in show business like she used to be, but according to reports I've read, she's involved in a lot of charities,' Martin remarked.

'And she covers huge distances every summer on her boat, taking it to Canada and back.' Petra leaned across the table, glad to have someone with whom she could share her impressions of Betty. 'She talks about the past a great deal, which is understandable given her age and recent loss. She was extremely close to her late husband, Joe LePinto, and devastated by his death. He was a man of many talents and a very successful businessman. The suite he designed for her here is eye-popping.'

'You say you don't know her well, but clearly you've spent time with her.'

Martin was fishing for information. *When you tell lies*, the Police Academy instructor had declared, *be consistent*. Petra remembered the raw recruits' swift intake of breath and some of the sanctimonious comments that had been bandied about before he brought them up short with his next words: *Your life may depend on it*. Since that time, she had come to understand the value of his advice and no longer worried about her place in heaven.

Petra kept her story congruent with those she had told the Gracebys. Martin might suspect it was cover, but she knew she could trust him.

'When I told my mother I was coming here on vacation, she asked me to let Betty Graceby know that my father had died. Apparently he knew Joe LePinto in Las Vegas way back.'

'What a coincidence!' Martin said with a touch of irony. 'So is the fact that I've been interested in LePinto for some time. He's a fascinating character. Before I read about the explosion and decided to fly down here, I was researching the United States' foreign policy with regard to Cuba. It's an issue for Canadians, as you know. Business travellers have been denied entry into the States after spending time in Cuba.'

'What's that got to do with Joe LePinto?' Petra asked.

'About ten years ago, there was a scandal involving a major real estate corporation that had been using Hispanic workers. There was a terrible accident at one of its development sites in Florida. A portion of the building they were working on collapsed and more than a dozen people were killed. During the investigation, it was found that half of them were Cuban refugees with no papers. One of the directors of the company was Joe LePinto. He was suspected of having ties to Cuba, though an extensive background check turned up no evidence. There was more talk about him five years ago when a similar incident occurred.'

'I still don't see the connection, except that he was born in Florida. His parents were from Puerto Rico.'

'How do you know that?'

'Betty told me when we were looking through her photo albums.'

'Are you sure it's true?'

Petra's initial instinct was to jump to the defence of her friend. Then she recognized the validity of Martin's question. The image of the instructor flashed up again on her internal monitor. *Never take anything at face value. Don't trust the information somebody gives you just because you like the person.* 'You're right, Martin. I'm letting my feelings cloud my judgement.'

She looked up as a shadow fell across the table.

'Well, well! What have we here? You didn't lose any time! My father only left this afternoon and you've found yourself a new man already.'

'Hey, watch your mouth.' Martin scraped his chair back and stood up. 'That's no way to talk to a lady!'

Ken Graceby took in Martin's tousled sandy hair, horn-rimmed glasses and pinkish cheeks. 'Another Canuck, eh? Birds of a feather! Be careful with him in the sun.' He turned to the blonde, who was standing just behind him. 'He looks about as soft as they come, wouldn't you say, darling?'

Martin's cheeks turned a darker shade of pink and he balled his fists.

Petra reached across the table towards him. 'Don't, Martin. He's not worth it. I told you he's a jerk.'

'Been talking about me, have you?'

'The way you behave, I'm sure you're used to that.' The sardonic grin on Ken's face made her want to wipe it off with a boxing glove.

The blonde took a step forward and glared at Petra. She dug her French-manicured nails into the underside of Ken's wrist and tossed her head. 'This isn't my scene, lover boy. I'm leaving.'

'No you don't!' Ken grasped her arm as she tried to pull away. 'We've some business to finish.'

Despite her show of independence, she allowed him to lead her back into the throng of people on the dance floor.

Martin raised a hand to attract the attention of a nearby hostess. 'I need another drink. Petra, what would you like? Have you tried gin and coconut water?'

'No thanks. I'll have a Rum Runner. I'm sorry he behaved like that, Martin.'

'Don't worry, I can stand up for myself, but what about you?'

Petra thought about Ken's incursion into her suite the night before. Martin would be furious if he knew, and concerned. She decided not to mention it. 'I have a few tricks up my sleeve if ever he attempts anything.' Her eyes wandered in the direction Ken had taken with the blonde. She scanned the crowd of dancers to see if they were still there.

A hostess arrived with their drinks. 'Thank you, Bianca,' Martin said, reading the girl's nametag as she set the glasses down on the table. 'What does the C stand for?'

'Casales, Sir.' Bianca threw him a look from under her false eyelashes.

'And very nice too!'

Bianca Casales. For once, Petra forgave Martin his annoying habit of asking waitresses their names. During the early part of the evening, she had been on the lookout for the girl Betty had accused of stealing her jewellery. Then the confrontation with Ken had driven all thought of trying to find her out of Petra's mind.

She turned to face Martin and the waitress. Instantly she recognized her as the girl who had been on the receiving end of Cliff's caresses. 'Haven't you served me before? Last night, when I was here with Cliff Graceby?'

Bianca Casales glanced at Petra. 'I might have. I see so many people, I don't remember them all.'

But I'm sure you haven't forgotten Cliff fondling your buttocks, Petra thought, or the flirtatious look you gave him. The skirts worn by the waitresses – or hostesses as Cliff had told her the Club liked to call them – were designed more to reveal than conceal, and Bianca had plenty to reveal. In her case, the African-Spanish mix had produced a robust woman of fine proportions. Martin, like the majority of men on hand, was clearly appreciative of the T and A on display.

'I remember you though,' Petra insisted, 'and you must know the Graceby boys.'

'Yeah, well, who doesn't? They're regulars here. Why do you want to know anyway?' Bianca placed her hands on her ample hips.

'No particular reason. I thought I saw you talking to Ken Graceby and a blonde earlier. It looked as though you were putting them in their places.'

'She's trash!' Bianca spat out the words like an old-timer expelling a mouthful of tobacco juice. 'He's just a playboy, all mixed up, doesn't know what he wants.'

'That must upset his father and his grandmother,' Petra remarked.

'They've only themselves to blame if you ask me, especially her. After what she did to me, I hope she rots in hell!'

Bianca's vehemence was so unexpected that Petra found herself at a complete loss for words. Realizing there was a problem, Martin leaned forward and stroked the front of Bianca's skirt.

'She can't have done anything that bad to a great girl like you!'

'Don't you start! First she fired me then she tried to get me into more trouble when all I was trying to do was help her stupid grandson.' Bianca turned away quickly, but not before Petra had seen the dampness in her eyes. 'I shouldn't be talking to you. I need this job.'

'What was all that about?' Martin asked, as Bianca disappeared from view.

'I'm not sure. Thanks for bailing me out. I really didn't know what to say. Look, will you excuse me for a minute?'

Petra got up and threaded her way through the dancers, keeping an eye out for Ken and his partner as she headed for the ladies' room.

Her hunch had been correct. A heavy sniff and the sound of nose blowing came from the furthest stall. Petra tapped on the door. 'Bianca? Can I talk to you? My name's Petra. I know how you feel.'

'You can't possibly know that!'

'I know you used to date Ken Graceby. You were in love with him, weren't you? In fact, I'm guessing you still are.'

'What is it to you anyway?'

'I know what it's like to feel so strongly about someone that you would do anything for that person, even something you know is wrong.' She was trolling, praying that Bianca would take the bait.

'But you don't know what it's like coming from nothing and fighting to survive, then one day being offered a chance at a new life.'

'It must have been a dream come true!'

'It was.'

'So what happened?' Petra asked.

'Why should I tell you?'

'Because you'll feel better and I might be able to help. Open the door and we can talk.'

Petra listened without interrupting as Bianca talked about her teenage years in the Dominican Republic, in the slums of Santo Domingo. It was a story that played itself out over and over again in the ghetto areas of cities around the globe.

Forced into prostitution at the age of fifteen, Bianca had managed to keep on the right side of her pimp and secrete a bit at a time from her earnings. The tiny amounts grew until she had amassed what seemed like a small fortune. Wisely, she trusted no one and hid the money in several different locations.

One day, her pimp failed to appear to collect the night's take. Nor did he show next day. Bianca knew it was time to disappear. She had planned every detail of every step yet the thought of carrying out her plan made her quake. It meant leaving behind the life she knew, however sordid or difficult; it meant handing over her hard-won cash in exchange for a muttered promise; it meant trusting a shadow to keep his word when the last person she had trusted had deserted her more than ten years before.

'It took everything I had!' Bianca cried. 'But I made it! And I met Joe LePinto and he saved me. He gave me a job and everything was all right ...' Tears the size of tropical raindrops began to fall on Bianca's chest. She wiped a hand across her eyes, smearing her make-up.

Petra leaned forward. 'Look, I don't know if there's anything I can do, but if I can, I will. I'd better be going. Someone's coming.'

Bianca nodded and closed the door to the stall.

Petra hurried back to Martin, her emotions in turmoil. When she saw his white face, she realized how long she had been gone.

'Jesus, Petra! Where've you been? I was so worried about you. Ken Graceby left just after you did. I didn't know whether to follow you or not.'

'Sorry, Martin. I was comforting a distraught woman.' Petra slumped in her chair. Her response sounded weak even to her own ears.

'Oh? Who was that?'

'I can't tell you right now, I'm exhausted. How long are you staying in Nassau?'

'My flight's on Tuesday, early afternoon.'

'Good. Then I've plenty of time to fill you in. Please will you take me home to bed?'

CHAPTER

6

Petra lay luxuriating in the warmth and softness of the whale-sized waterbed that dominated the master bedroom of the Mermaid Suite. There was no reason to hurry. She could lie in bed for another hour and still have plenty of time to go for a walk or a swim before her rendezvous with Martin at one o'clock. With the shutter closed, the room was quiet and conducive to sleep.

Ten minutes into her dreams, the damn phone roused her. She had kept it switched off for most of the previous day but put it on again after dinner.

'Where were you yesterday?' asked the familiar gravelly voice of her boss.

'In meetings.'

'Hmm. Any problems at the Consulate?'

'No, Sir. I've got the file.'

'What about Betty Graceby?'

'She's fine. I had a good session with her yesterday.'

'So what's going on?'

'I don't know yet. I can't see her today, she's having physiotherapy. I'll see her tomorrow.'

'You need time then?'

'Yes. I'd like to be here when Betty's boat, *Gloriana*, arrives. When do you want me back?' Petra held her breath as she waited for A.K.'s response.

'No rush. You call it.'

The phone went dead. Petra took it away from her ear and stared at it in surprise. She had expected to be recalled to duty in Canada within a few days. A.K. was not usually so munificent. He liked everything to be resolved instantly.

His call had driven out her desire to linger in bed. Pulling on the resort's bathrobe and slippers with their mer-motif, Petra padded through to the sitting room. Housekeeping had done its job and the fruit platter had been replenished. She picked up the banana that lay on top and walked out onto the balcony.

It was a perfect day. Overhead the sky was the sort of blue usually found only in re-touched advertising material. The lightest of breezes ruffled the fringes of the palms and cooled Petra's cheeks. She studied the marina. In the far corner, in the boatyard, she could make out Ken's boat, a blackened carcass sitting low on the stands. There was still no sign of Betty's motor yacht.

As she turned to go inside, a gangly figure caught her eye. Martin, his hair lifting in the freshening breeze, was walking along the dock towards the harbourmaster's office. A camera hung round his neck and a couple of expensive lenses crisscrossed his chest, bandolier-style. He was making no secret of his profession today.

Poor Martin. Two years in Japan had done nothing to cool his ardour. Petra knew he had been overjoyed last night when she'd invited him to accompany her to her suite. She felt guilty about raising his expectations, but with Ken Graceby on the loose she had wanted reassurance. After giving Martin a quick tour – mostly to check that no one was lurking in a dark corner – she had asked him to leave. He had stood at the door expressing amazement at the lurid scenes of mermaids and mermen in unimaginable poses until she suggested meeting him for lunch. It had been the only way to get rid of him.

Now she leaned over the balcony railing and shouted down to him. It would be useful if he could take some close-up pictures of the damage to *Geyser* for her to analyze later, when she had access to her unit's database and research capabilities. He continued walking and she realized he must be too far away to hear her. That, or he was ignoring her.

He remained oblivious to her presence until she gave a piercing wolf-whistle that caused him to look up. She pointed to Ken's boat and made the shape of a camera with her hands. Using her index finger, she pushed down on an imaginary shutter then pointed to herself. After repeating the pantomime several times, she succeeded in getting her message across. Martin gave her a big smile and a thumbs-up before striding off in the direction she had indicated.

Once Petra was certain he was on the right track, she gave herself up to her thoughts. Since the moment Tom Gilmore had handed her the package from A.K. to read on the plane, she had been wondering why there was such interest in an ageing Canadian singer. Certainly, Betty could be considered an icon of Canadian culture and a magnet for Canadian national pride, but her fan base was dwindling and she had lived outside Canada for over thirty years.

Many young people wouldn't know who Betty Graceby was. Yet the Canadian authorities seemed inordinately interested in her welfare. Why? That was the huge unanswered question. She would ask Martin during lunch. He might have some ideas. In the meantime, there was still no need to hurry. She could sit on the balcony and reread the file Miss Birch had given her.

With the breeze playing on her face, Petra concentrated on the account of the first incident, the one involving Bianca Casales. In her statement to the police, Betty asserted that she had found Bianca in her bedroom helping herself to a pearl necklace and earrings Betty had worn the night before and placed on a glass tray on top of her chest-of-drawers. Bianca was adamant that she had gone through the wrong door into Betty's bedroom on her way back from the bathroom. She had been admiring, not stealing, the items in question. But if that were true, why had Bianca told Petra last night that she had been trying to help Ken? And what had she meant when she said Betty had fired her? There was nothing in the file to indicate that Betty had been her employer. According to Bianca herself, it was Joe, not Betty, who had given her a job.

An hour of reading and reflection turned up no new information. Petra put on her bikini and a loose shirt and took the elevator to the lobby. The entrance door had been propped open and a golf cart overflowing with boxes of groceries, tropical fruit, strange vegetables and a crate containing live crayfish stood outside. Luis was busy unloading the cart and stacking the boxes next to the elevator to Betty's suite.

'Luis! That's enough food for a party!'

Luis smiled broadly. 'Some of it's for tomorrow. Miss Betty wants me to make you one of her favourite dishes. I hope you like spices.'

'The spicier the better. The food yesterday was delicious. I didn't realize you were the chef. Have you been with Miss Graceby long?' Luis's age was difficult to estimate. His skin was clear and unlined, yet his expanding waistline indicated a man in his forties.

'Close on twenty years, I guess.'

'No! You don't look old enough!' Petra's deliberately flattering response brought another smile to Luis's face.

'Oh but I am! I started with Mr. Joe in Las Vegas when I was in my teens. He tried to help any of us immigrants who came from the island.'

'You mean Puerto Rico?'

'Of course. When he saw I had a flair for cooking, he sent me to train at his Culinary Institute and Hotel School in Florida.'

'I don't know anything about that. Tell me more.'

'It's a private foundation that takes students from across America. A new six-month course starts every month. Ten percent of the places on each course are reserved for Puerto Ricans.'

'Does that include Nuyoricans?'

'I'm afraid so,' Luis replied. 'Mr. Joe didn't discriminate against our New York brethren. He said we were all from the same stock and deserved a break.'

Petra made a mental note to find out more about Joe LePinto's foundation. His concern for his fellow 'Ricans undoubtedly benefited his hotel and restaurant businesses, but he might have been a genuine philanthropist too. Cliff and Ken's charitable endeavours could be a nod to the old man and his benevolence. On the other hand, she had already witnessed Ken's hostile reaction to any reference to LePinto. She helped Luis load the last cartons into the elevator and walked out into the sunshine, pondering on the real reasons behind the Gracebys' apparent desire to do good.

She had agreed to meet Martin for lunch at the open-air restaurant next to the pool. Mindful of Ken's sarcastic warning about her friend's ability to withstand the sun, Petra found them a place in the shade. From there, they could watch and comment undisturbed on the vagaries of the human race.

One of the things that still endeared her to Martin was his caustic sense of humour. He was realistic about himself and knew people had a tendency to underestimate him because of his sandy hair, flushed cheeks and boyish looks. He confided that he was learning to turn this to great advantage in his new profession.

'No one really takes me seriously. When I present my *Jetalong Magazine* business card, they scarcely give it a glance. I'm too puny to do much damage.'

'So that's how you got us into the Coco Caverna Club! I was wondering.'

'Yes. The manager was delighted when I phoned to say the magazine had asked me to do a review, but I'm sure you noticed his face when I introduced myself. He wrote me off straightaway. I fade right into the background. In some ways, it's a fantastic attribute to have. You could do it too.'

'What are you saying, that I fade right into the background and no one takes me seriously?' Petra demanded.

'Not at all. You have presence, but you don't look like a cop.'

'Shush, Martin. Enough. Remember what I said.'

Secretly Petra was flattered by Martin's comment. And she admired the resilience that enabled him to make the best of his shortcomings. A lesser man might have lost his confidence. 'Did you manage to get some close-ups of *Geyser* in the boatyard?' she asked.

'No problem at all! The harbourmaster was quite excited when I told him I was writing a piece for *Power & Motoryacht*. I took a great picture of him in front of the stuffed marlin on the wall of his office. He's a teddy bear!'

Petra turned her eyes heavenwards. Where did these guys come from? Still, Martin had connections and might be able to help her get to the bottom of what was going on.

'There's something I don't understand,' she said. 'Why are the Canadian authorities taking such a keen interest in Betty Graceby? Her grandson's been harassing her for over a year and nobody did anything about it; now all of a sudden it's as though they don't want anything to happen to her.'

Martin thought for a few moments. 'It can only be one thing: money. Betty's a wealthy woman, as you know, but since Joe died her fortune has quadrupled. Apart from a few staff bequests and an endowment to ensure the future of his foundation, he left everything to her. And I did hear rumours in Northern Ontario recently about a major benefactor.'

'That would explain their desire to keep Betty safe and healthy!' Petra exclaimed. 'Or should I say alive and well, just like the mercenary streak in all of us?'

'When I get back, I'll do some research and see what I can find out.'

'I'm sure you're right, Martin. Betty doesn't need all Joe's millions and would likely want to do something to benefit people in her home region, just as he's done for Puerto Ricans.'

'As I said, follow the money! That's the key, I'll bet you anything.'

CHAPTER

7

Bianca Casales was perplexed and wary. It was well over an hour since they had left the marina at *Neptunis* in the Cheoy Lee sportfishing boat Ken had chartered to meet his obligations. The captain he had been forced to hire along with the boat showed no sign of slowing down. In the past when she had helped Ken with his charters, they would run for perhaps thirty or forty minutes before finding a suitable spot. Most guests wanted less running time and more fishing time. Today's pair were definitely unusual.

Ever since the two men had come aboard that morning Bianca had had an uncomfortable feeling about them. They were dressed like twins in batik shirts and khaki chinos yet their demeanour was very different. The taller of the two was clearly the leader. He was older, probably about fifty, more talkative, more demanding and, to Bianca's way of thinking, quite obnoxious. He boarded the yacht first and walked straight past her, ignoring her polite 'Welcome aboard, Sir.' His sidekick was silent, creepy and, she judged, exceedingly dangerous.

They appeared to have no interest in the boat and even less in the state-of-the-art equipment and unrivalled opportunities for deep-sea fishing. For the time being, they were sitting in the air-conditioned salon with the blinds drawn, watching a movie about a bank robbery on the giant plasma screen.

Ken had instructed her to make sure they had everything they wanted. Bianca was under no illusion as to what that might mean. She didn't want to spend time with either of them, but if she were forced to, she would choose the taller one.

To make matters worse, Ken had brought along the blonde who had been with him at the Coco Caverna Club the night before. Evidently, he had offered the girl a handsome wage to come and entertain his guests without explaining that she would also be required to help Bianca prepare and serve food.

On the galley counter were two tins of *mousse de foie gras* waiting to be opened. After listening to the blonde gripe and watching her struggle with the can opener, Bianca had sent her below. If the girl had any skills, they weren't in the culinary department. She wouldn't have made it through the first week at Joe LePinto's Hotel School.

The coffee machine pinged. Bianca poured the steaming liquid into a vacuum jug, added a plate of cookies to the tray and carried it carefully up to the salon. Through the door, she heard a burst of gunfire then the men exchanging a few words in accented Spanish. When she made her appearance, they fell silent and carried on watching the movie as if she didn't exist. She deposited the tray and left them to it.

The Cheoy Lee was racing along, her bow well out of the water. With great care, Bianca climbed the ladder to the flybridge to let Ken and the captain know that there was coffee if they wanted it. She glanced at the chartplotter that showed their course.

'This is a long run,' she said. 'How far are we going, Ken?'

'It's none of your business. You'll see when we get there.'

Bianca planted her hands on her hips. 'And when will that be?' she wanted to ask, but quickly decided against it. Snubs she could handle. She gave a mental shrug and returned to the galley.

A little over an hour later, they reached their destination – a coral cay Bianca didn't recognize. They dropped anchor a few hundred metres off a white crescent beach. There were no signs of habitation and no other boats in the vicinity. The breeze was just enough to alleviate the heat of the sun and ripple the surface of the clear blue water. The Cheoy Lee swung lightly on her anchor chain as Bianca announced that lunch was ready to be served on the aft deck.

The blonde appeared in a shiny white swimsuit with a plunge neckline and an inviting black zip from cleavage to pubis. The second man, the one Bianca considered dangerous, sat up in his chair. Bianca was conscious of a small current of jealousy as she compared her own fuller figure to the blonde's svelte tanned body. She wished she had been sensible and put on a one-piece swimsuit instead of the red bikini that did nothing to hide her well-padded stomach and hips. In the candlelight at the Coco Caverna Club, she could flaunt her voluptuousness among regulars like the Gracebys and take pleasure in their flirtatious comments. Now, in the company of these sleazy men and the willowy blonde, Bianca felt ill at ease and unsure of herself.

Ken was drinking steadily. He drained his glass and snapped at the blonde who was whispering to the second man. Bianca watched her take the bottle of white wine from the ice bucket and begin to fill Ken's glass. The girl didn't stop in the normal way when the glass was half to two-thirds full but carried on pouring.

'Stop! Stop!' he shouted. 'Have you no idea how to do anything? You never fill glasses that full.' He turned to Bianca. 'Can't you do anything to train this idiot?'

The blonde gave Ken a tight-lipped smile that did not reach her pale blue eyes. She gripped the bottle hard, pretended to sway on her feet as the boat pulled on its anchor chain, and poured the remaining contents into his lap. Before he could grab her, she moved away muttering profuse apologies. Bianca stifled a laugh and hurried forward with a napkin, but Ken was already pushing past her.

When he returned to the deck in fresh clothing, Bianca was serving coffee and liqueurs. The blonde did not reappear. Either she was licking her wounds or Ken had exercised unusual restraint – perhaps because he had business to discuss with his guests and didn't want to alienate them.

'You seem to be having trouble,' the taller man said as soon as Ken sat down.

'The girl was upset because I scolded her, that's all. There's no problem. Forget it. Let's talk about your requirements.'

'This isn't the boat you showed us before. We heard you had an accident,' the taller man continued.

'It was nothing. Just a small fire on my boat yesterday. She's in the yard for minor repairs. That's why we're using *Magnum* instead of *Geyser*.'

The taller man spoke again. 'You should have let us know ahead of time. We don't like surprises. How long would this trip take on your boat?'

'About half an hour less with *Geyser*'s 2000+ Man engines. Two and a half hours, I'd say, in normal sea conditions. This boat tops out around thirty-five knots. *Geyser* can deliver forty.'

'What about at night? Could you do it at night?' asked the same man. His companion maintained his watchful silence.

'Easy!' Ken declared.

'What if we wanted you to do regular trips?'

'That could be arranged, depending on the value you place on them and the merchandise to be transported.'

'It wouldn't necessarily be the same every time.'

'Then we'd have to work out a deal based on the risk factor.'

Bianca paused halfway through the salon on her way back to the galley. She could still hear what was being said on the aft deck and liked it less and less. Ken was getting involved in something that sounded shady, even by his standards. As his girlfriend, she had tried to straighten him out and show him that money wasn't everything. He had told her repeatedly that when he had enough to buy whatever he wanted without a second thought, he would think about retiring. This didn't sound like retirement. She listened hard as the man who always did the talking spoke again.

'Providing everything is to our satisfaction, you will receive adequate compensation.'

'I'm sure everything will be fine.'

'Let's hope so.'

Troubled, Bianca tidied up the galley and went to find the captain who had been fishing from the foredeck. He had reeled in his line and was looking up at the sky. High above, a few herringbone clouds were forming. For the time being, they were thin wisps, as filmy as gauze, but the wind they heralded could blow the sea up quickly and make the return voyage slower and much less comfortable. Together, they left the bow and made their way along the port side of the boat to the aft deck where Ken and his charter guests were talking in hushed tones. Bianca hung back, letting the captain take the lead.

Ken looked up with a frown on his face as the captain approached. 'What is it, Raf?'

'I'd like to get underway. The wind's coming up and we've a long run ahead of us.'

'OK, let's get going. We can continue our discussions inside, Gentlemen.'

The taller man rapped his fingers on the table. 'There's nothing more to discuss at this point. If we're interested, we'll talk again. Now we'd like to relax.'

'The girls will make sure you have everything you need,' Ken said.

'Good. Send the mulatto to my stateroom and the blonde to my colleague's.'

Bianca made the sign of the cross and sent up a small prayer of thanks.

The more Petra considered what Martin had said, the more convinced she became that he had hit the nail on the head. Everyone was after money, and the super-wealthy were expected to dig deep into their pockets to sponsor all kinds of projects.

After lunch, they went into town. On the way, she told him about Miss Birch and her admiration for the Graceby "boys".

'Their support of local institutions buys them a great deal of goodwill, but I have a feeling there's more to it than that. I'm sure Cliff and Ken skim off as much as they can from anything they persuade Betty to contribute.'

Martin nodded. 'Not unusual. Charities are wonderful fronts for shysters. If the public knew what a small proportion of the money donated gets where it's supposed to go … When I'm successful enough not to have to rely on commissioning editors, I'll do an exposé.'

'I'd still like to go to the museum and see what Cliff's contributions have made possible.'

The museum was housed in a restored colonial building painted a conch shell pink. A sizeable area was devoted to Bahamian history and culture. As she read about Calico Jack and the female pirates who had terrorized the area in the eighteenth century, Petra remembered how compellingly Cliff had spoken about the islands during their dinner at the Coco Caverna Club. The extent of his knowledge suggested that he had spent some time studying the subject, yet she had the impression he had been a tearaway in his youth. Nothing she could pin down, just a feeling that he was too suave by half.

The Gracebys continued to occupy Petra's thoughts as she followed Martin to the straw market where he belatedly bought a sun hat. After pushing their way through the throngs of cruise ship passengers exploring the shops, they had an iced coffee at the Green Parrot and took a taxi back to the resort.

As the taxi drew up at the foot of the steps below the colossal statue of Neptune, Sam scurried down to greet them. He pulled open the door and gave Petra his usual cheeky grin.

'Sam!' Petra exclaimed. 'I missed you. I haven't seen you all day. What's up?'

'Lots of guests in and out, Miss Petra, and Mr. Ken needed supplies for his charter. He went out this morning with Captain Rafael on *Magnum*. They're on their way back now.' Abruptly he stopped and looked distrustfully at Martin and his cameras.

Petra caught the look and realized that Sam hadn't yet met her friend. Immediately, she pulled Martin over to introduce him.

'Martin, this is Sam, my driver, guide, advisor and absolute best buddy at *Neptunis*.' Sam's eyes lit up as she spoke. 'Sam, meet Martin, my friend from home.'

'I'm honoured to meet you, Sam. I know you'll look after Petra when I leave.'

'You can count on me, Mr. Martin. Miss Petra is a real lady.'

'Not always, Sam,' Petra laughed. 'What are you doing now?'

'Going to the marina to help Mr. Ken unload. He's due in any minute. Why don't you come and watch?'

Sam brought the golf cart to a halt very close to the spot where Petra had plunged into the water to rescue the victims of the explosion just two days earlier. It already seemed a long time ago yet, in the curious way time compresses, Petra felt she had been at *Neptunis* only a few hours.

Beyond the breakwater, a powerful sportfishing boat was bearing down on the harbour entrance. Petra estimated she was doing over thirty knots. She showed no signs of slowing until the last possible moment when the captain throttled back and turned the yacht neatly between the red and green entrance markers in a cloud of spray.

Martin had already unslung his camera and telephoto lens and begun taking pictures. The sun was sinking to the horizon as he turned his attention to the spreading tendrils of pink and orange. He wandered along the dock with his light meter, eager to capture what promised to be a glorious sunset.

Sam jumped up and down in delight as the sleek white vessel approached the dock. As soon as the boat pulled in, Ken vaulted off. He grabbed the stern line off the side of the boat, cleated it, then ran forward to deal with the rest of the lines. Once they were all secure, he signalled to the captain on the bridge and the engines faded into silence.

Petra took her hat off to the two of them. Docking a boat was a complicated manoeuvre that required perfect coordination between captain and crew. She had judged it best to stay out of the way while Ken was working. Now she stepped forward to congratulate him.

'Nice docking!' she said.

'What the fuck are you doing here, and what do you know about docking?'

'I've spent a lot of time on the water at my uncle's

cottage,' she replied, remembering her cover story. 'Sam said you'd gone out on your charter. How was the fishing?'

'Fine!'

Petra noticed how he glared at Sam and was sorry she had mentioned his name. Then she saw Bianca step out of the salon onto *Magnum*'s aft deck, followed by two men and a blonde. Petra recognized the blonde as Ken's date from the night before at the Coco Caverna Club. She waved to Bianca, but Bianca gave no indication that she had seen Petra or knew her.

'Can't you mind your own business?' Ken shouted at Petra. As she turned away, he caught sight of Martin with his camera, filming as he walked back towards the Cheoy Lee. 'Now we've got the fucking paparazzi!'

He rushed at Martin and tried to wrench the camera from his grasp. Martin held on doggedly and they struggled, perilously close to the water's edge. For a few long seconds, Petra was sure Martin would fall into the water with his expensive equipment. Then she saw him duck sideways and reach to his left. In a move his old school rugby coach would have been proud of, he rolled to the ground, away from Ken and the edge of the dock.

'Mr. Martin, give me your camera! I'll look after it for you!' Sam's voice cut through the melee as he scampered towards Martin. He took the camera from him, leapt into the golf cart and sped away from the marina.

'I'll get you, you little bastard!' Ken screamed, shaking his fist after him.

'We'd best get out of here,' Petra muttered, seizing Martin's arm. 'The man is not happy.'

CHAPTER

8

At ten minutes to eleven the following day, Petra was standing in the lobby of her building waiting for Luis to escort her to the Siren Suite. It was Monday morning. Her appointment with Betty wasn't until eleven, but she didn't want to be late. The elevator door opened and Luis appeared, a frown on his forehead. His brow cleared as soon as he saw Petra.

'Good morning, Miss, you're nice and early! Please go up. I have an errand to run for Miss Graceby.'

'Can I do anything?'

'No, no. Miss Graceby's expecting you. Her grandson's there but he won't be long.' Luis activated the elevator with his key card and sent Petra soaring upwards.

The glass cage seemed to take forever to reach the penthouse level. Petra drummed her fingers on the rail, scanning the marina. There was no sign of Betty's yacht *Gloriana*, and *Magnum*, the Cheoy Lee Ken had been using the previous afternoon, was no longer at the dock.

After the skirmish with Ken, she and Martin had settled for a quiet dinner at the resort. Sam had reappeared with Martin's camera and lens and an extra twinkle in his eye. 'That was some move. You must have been a good rugby player.' From the look on Martin's face, he didn't appreciate the "has been" element of Sam's compliment.

Petra wondered anxiously what Ken was talking to Betty about. She stepped out of the elevator into the foyer of the Siren Suite and was about to call out to announce her arrival when she heard their raised voices from behind the sitting room door.

'I'm not senile! I saw you come into the marina yesterday afternoon, you and that trash, Bianca Casales, and some other whore! And you can't tell me those were fishermen you took out on the Cheoy Lee,' Betty shouted.

'They were business people.'

'My eye! You were all drunk.'

'That's not true! It wasn't what you think.'

'I think,' Betty said deliberately, 'that it's the same as last time and the time before that, and exactly why I had to replace you as captain of *Gloriana*. You're a disgrace to the family.' She paused before continuing her tirade. 'You should remember which side your bread's buttered on. If you're not careful, you won't get a cent from me!'

'So that's it, is it? Following your old man's example, eh? He left everything to you. It doesn't matter what happens to Dad and me, you don't care.'

'Don't talk to me like that, young man! Leave now and don't come back until I invite you.'

Petra stood motionless in the foyer. What would Ken do? She could imagine the anger working in his face. If he refused to leave, it could get nasty very quickly. This time they might come to blows. The seconds ticked by. She waited, poised to intervene. But there was no showdown.

Instead, Ken stormed out of the apartment and lurched past Petra to the elevator without even a glance in her direction.

After he had gone, there was silence. Petra decided to give Betty a few minutes to compose herself. While she waited, she examined the marble frieze that ran round the foyer. Now that she knew what the female figures with birds' legs represented, the siren theme was evident. It was a little too grotesque for her taste.

Somewhere in the apartment a clock struck eleven, clear and bell-like. Then Petra heard a muffled sob. Immediately, she crossed the foyer and entered the sitting room. Betty was sitting on the elegant Biedermeier sofa by the fireplace, her head bowed, a hand over her eyes. She looked up when the door opened and wiped away a tear.

Petra couldn't hide her dismay. Betty's skin was as grey as on the day she had pulled her out of the water and in her face was a frightening degree of despair.

'I'm sure you overheard some of that,' Betty whispered, dabbing at her eyes.

'I'm sorry, I couldn't help it. Are you all right? Did he hurt you?'

'No, no, it was nothing like that. I get so angry with him and I know I shouldn't. He has talent, intelligence, good looks – just like his father – yet he won't use them. Instead he carouses and keeps company with the most awful women, and men for that matter.'

Petra placed a comforting hand on Betty's shoulder. 'It's not your fault.'

'Sometimes I think it is. You know the old adage: "Like father, like son"? Well, Ken's behaviour is just like his father's was twenty-five years ago. I blame myself for that.' She sighed heavily before continuing. 'I had Cliff when I was barely twenty. I was in the early stages of my career, singing in nightclubs, doing road shows. Life was tough. I pretended that having a baby made no difference. I carted him around with me or left him with anybody who'd help. There was no continuity. It wasn't the right environment for a child. Children need structure and stability. I never gave Cliff either.'

'Children are also extremely resilient.'

'Maybe, but I always felt out of my depth as a mother. I never knew how to handle Cliff, so a lot of the time I didn't. I let him run free. By the time I met Joe, Cliff was a motorcycle gang member and had been in trouble with the police several times. I protected him and bailed him out, but I couldn't make up for what I had deprived him of. So, you see, I blame myself.'

'You mustn't! There are so many factors that come into play. I'd say Cliff has turned out fine. He's had a good life and wanted for nothing.'

'That's one of the reasons I married Joe. Not the main one,' Betty added hastily, 'because I fell in love with him the moment I saw him. But I was forty and worried about maintaining my career. There were always younger girls pushing themselves forward, willing to do whatever was necessary to make it on the stage. Joe represented peace and security.'

Betty looked at Petra and gave a wan smile. 'You caught me at a bad moment, my dear. This isn't at all what I had planned for today. Let's go up to the terrace and get some air.'

In the space of a few minutes, Betty had shaken off her sadness and regained her poise. Petra was full of admiration. Revealing one's insecurities or explaining complex motivations was never easy, although sometimes it helped if the confidant was not a person you knew well. It was as Petra had suspected: Cliff had been a tearaway in his youth, and once again she wondered what lay beneath his glossy exterior.

Up on the roof, the sun was strong. Sitting under the yellow and white striped canopy, Petra listened as Betty regaled her with stories about her early concerts. Talking about those years was the best therapy there was. Betty was proud of her successes and matter-of-fact about the rare occasions on which the audience had failed to respond as expected.

On one particular evening, she had been invited to sing in front of a prestigious audience at a fund-raising function in Washington, D.C. She was unusually nervous and her agent's exhortation to "break a leg" did nothing to calm the butterflies in her stomach. The audience was older, difficult, and heavy on politicos, lawyers and socialites.

'During my third number, I decided to strut my stuff to liven up the crowd. I waved my arms about, twirled the microphone, tripped over the cord and wound up sprawled on the floor in front of the band – which played right on. I was lucky to get away with a twisted ankle and a bruised ego. You should have seen their faces, my dear! Those stuffed shirts didn't know what to do. For them, it would have been the end of the world. For me, it provided a good laugh and dispelled my nerves.'

Petra shook her head. Betty was a case. It was hard to

believe she was in her seventies. They chatted comfortably until Luis came to tell them that lunch was ready.

After a spicy jambalaya full of shrimp and chicken followed by a homemade mango and coconut ice-cream cake, Petra felt relaxed and replete. Instead of asking Betty about her relationship with Ken as she had intended to do, she found herself talking about the motorcycle accident that had killed Romeo.

'I know what you went through,' Betty said, 'because I howled and screamed when Joe was taken from me, and we had over thirty years together. You were in the throes of young love, a love that had yet to mature. As I was, when I fell pregnant with Cliff.' She hesitated then said: 'Let me show you some more photos before you leave.'

Ten minutes later, they were ensconced at a mahogany table in the library and Betty was leafing through one of the gold-tooled albums. 'I have only one picture of Cliff's father. There! It's not very good, I'm afraid.'

The faded print showed a dashing young man with thick, dark, curly hair and an aquiline nose. In drainpipe trousers, black leather jacket and sunglasses, he could have been any teenage rock-and-roll idol from the late fifties.

'Was he a singer?' Petra asked.

'No, though he could have been. He had a wonderful – but untrained – voice. He was a roadie with one of the top bands. We were on the same touring circuit for a while.' Betty dropped her eyes, suddenly shy. 'I'm sure you can guess the rest. When I told him I was pregnant, he said he didn't want anything to do with the child. The following week his show left town. I never heard from him again.'

She shrugged and Petra waited politely for her to continue. 'In those days, our options were limited. It was either a back-street abortion with almost certain infertility as a result, or keep the baby. As I told you, I was young. I thought it would be easy and I never stopped to ask myself what effect my lifestyle might have on Cliff.'

Betty's voice was full of self-recrimination. Petra hastened to reassure her. Like a lot of performers, Betty needed strokes. Her mood could soar and plummet like a soufflé – up one minute, down the next. Petra laughed at her choice of image then pulled herself up short. Betty's tales of the past were fascinating, but it was time to bring the conversation back to the present. She had questions that needed answers.

In the distance, a telephone rang twice. A moment later, there was a tap on the door and Luis entered.

'There's a call for you, Ma'am. It's the police.'

'Thank you, Luis. I'll take it in the bedroom. I won't be long, my dear,' she said to Petra. 'You carry on.'

Petra assumed that the police were calling in connection with the explosion aboard Ken's boat. In the three days that had gone by since then, she had seen them in the distance at the marina but had no contact with them.

While she waited for Betty to return, she flipped through some of the more recent photo albums. There was no doubt that Betty still enjoyed the limelight. Most of the photographs showed her with Joe at various functions, both of them smiling and perfectly groomed. On the surface, at least, they were a golden couple.

Turning the pages quickly, Petra nearly missed a rather different image. Joe was standing in the roof garden in front of the siren fountain, his arm close around the shoulders of a girl dressed in a black and white maid's uniform. The skirt was very short and the neck of the blouse rather low. Petra took a careful look at the girl's face. She had aged and filled out since the picture was taken, but there was no mistaking Bianca Casales.

So Bianca had been working for Joe and Betty. But where was Betty? Was she the one taking the photo? Somehow Petra doubted it.

The sound of the door opening made Petra jump. Hastily, she closed the album and slid it underneath another one. Betty was back. She had disposed of the police in short order, she said, after reminding them forcefully of their shortcomings as investigators.

'You saw how obstreperous Ken was today, and there've been one or two previous occasions on which I had to call the police. They were never any help though. Better to sort it out myself.'

Petra had her suspicions as to what Betty might have done to "sort out" Bianca, but decided not to tackle her on the subject. Instead, she asked the question that had been smouldering in her head for the last few days.

'I'm intrigued to know why you went out on Ken's boat last Friday, given your relationship with him.'

'He's not always so tiresome. He can be charming. At first when he asked me I wasn't keen, but it was one of those mornings when the ocean beckons. It should have been a lovely day.' Betty glanced at the gold Bulgari watch on her left wrist. 'Goodness, how time flies! You'd better be going, my dear.'

Miss Birch was waiting in a grey Prius at the foot of the marble steps when Petra and Martin emerged from the hotel at four o'clock. She looked askance at Martin.

'I didn't know you were bringing anyone else,' she said to Petra.

'Martin's a friend of mine from Toronto. A journalist.'

'Hmm. You're not anything to do with the party that was supposed to visit last week, are you?' she asked, fixing a hawk-like eye on Martin. 'I made special arrangements to give them a tour of the sanctuary then everything was cancelled.'

'I know nothing about that, but I'd be delighted to write a piece about your work as a volunteer here, Miss Birch.'

Petra watched Miss Birch's face change from aggravation to something approaching pleasure.

'Call me Jayne,' she said. 'Come along!'

The sanctuary was built on a promontory overlooking the water on the opposite side of the island from *Neptunis*. It consisted of a series of pens and compounds for the birds plus a small administration block that housed the office, a clinic and a food preparation unit. Jayne Birch showed them round and introduced them to the young female keeper who cared for the birds during the day. She mentioned that a local man acted as security guard at night.

'Do you have a lot of problems with security?' Petra asked.

'Unfortunately, not everyone agrees that the birds should be saved. There have been several instances of cruelty and vandalism.'

Martin pulled out his notebook. 'What are the most common injuries you see?' he asked, his pencil poised.

'Man is responsible for the majority,' Jayne said, glaring

at him. 'Broken wings and damaged feet from contact with man-made objects; physical trauma from oil spills; entanglement with the nets and lines of irresponsible fishermen ...' Jayne reeled off a long list of examples until Petra began to feel as though she were back at school.

'It's the larger birds like the pelicans that suffer the most,' Jayne continued as they entered another compound. She had a name for each one and clucked with concern as she commented on their plight. 'Our objective is to release them back into the wild as soon as possible.'

'Is the success rate good?' Martin asked.

'Very. Our main problem is funding. We could do so much if we had more sponsors like Kendall Graceby. Kendall often brings back wounded birds from the out islands he frequents on his fishing trips. And once a month during the winter, he organizes special bird-watching cruises and donates half his income from them to the sanctuary. I'm not sure he'll be able to continue now that his boat is out of commission. If he doesn't, we'll be faced with an unmanageable deficit.'

'I'll do my best to publicize the sanctuary's good work and attract new donors,' Martin promised. 'I can do a photo spread and I have some experience in fund-raising.' He was full of ideas and soon Jayne was hopping with joy like the birds whose broken legs she managed to mend.

Petra covered her ears. Enough was enough. She wandered back to the pelicans and began giving them new names.

Later, in the quiet of her suite, Petra poured herself a nightcap from the well-stocked bar and flopped down onto the sofa. She had said goodnight to Martin and made her own way back to the Mermaid Suite, taking care to remain alert. She wouldn't easily forget the lesson she'd learned on the night of her arrival. Once again, she heard Tom Gilmore's voice in her head. *Never make assumptions. Never leave yourself vulnerable.* The RCMP Liaison Officer in London was a good teacher and a true friend.

It had been a long day. Betty was delightful to spend time with, but demanding in the way of people used to having staff or servants around them. And then there had been Jayne Birch and her birds. In record time, Martin had had her eating out of his hand. Petra was forced to admit that, despite a mild case of nose-out-of-joint jealousy, she had developed a sneaking regard for Jayne and her sanctuary. Even Ken Graceby deserved a few Brownie points for his altruism, which was no doubt what he was trying to achieve.

Petra walked across the room and opened the balcony doors. The docks were silent and deserted. Perhaps *Gloriana* would glide into port during the night and be there to greet her in the morning.

CHAPTER

9

Sometime during the latter stages of the night, Petra's dream turned into a nightmare. As with all nocturnal adventures, the action was patchy, the locations constantly changing, the faces distorted, and the logic non-existent. The fear, however, was real.

Petra ran screaming away from the harpoon that would puncture her innards if she didn't escape, and dived into the pool. A kaleidoscope of images passed in front of her eyes as she plunged downwards: Ken – or was it Cliff? – taunting her with a gargoyle's leering grin; Bianca dancing in a tutu, apron and tights; Betty in a pink feathered headdress, supported on one bandaged, emaciated leg.

Something fat and slimy brushed Petra's foot. She kicked it away. Her lungs were burning with the effort of holding her breath, collapsing under the pressure of the water. The echo of a motor rang in her ears. They were catching up to her. She fought her way out of a long dark tunnel into a patch of sunlight and hit her head on something soft: a sodden bundle of rags. With Sam's face.

Petra gasped for air and opened her eyes. The noise was real. She jumped up and crossed to the balcony doors. She had left the shutters open so that the light would wake her. Instead, it was the faint buzz of diesel engines borne on the early morning breeze that had penetrated her fitful sleep.

In the middle distance, she saw a boat, heading towards the marina. As it approached, the rising sun bathed the elegant profile and pure lines of the hull in liquid gold. Petra caught her breath. Each sunrise and each boat was different. The fusion of the two, whatever their form, never failed to move her. Hastily, she pulled on a sweatsuit and running shoes, took the waiting elevator to ground level and ran towards the marina. *Gloriana* was coming alongside as she reached the dock.

'I can take the bow line,' she yelled to the crewman who was standing on deck, rope coiled in his hand, ready to leap off. He acknowledged her offer with a nod and threw her the rope. After making fast the bow, Petra moved rapidly to receive the forward spring line. She cleated it with a flourish. As the captain brought the stern in, a second crewmember jumped onto the dock, secured the stern line then the aft spring line. All tied on. Petra took a step back from the edge of the dock to study the motor yacht.

Betty's boat was a classic Hargrave-designed tri-deck Burger, some 40 years old, and at least 30 metres long. Slim and sophisticated like Betty herself, *Gloriana* carried her years as well as her owner did. Some remnants of art deco styling were evident in the rounded corners of the main deckhouse fore and aft. The hull, Petra knew, was made of welded aluminium, which was light, strong, and easy to maintain. She wondered what engines powered the displacement hull and how well the vessel would handle in heavy seas. Although she had caught sight of *Gloriana* on the North Channel of Lake Huron in Canada, she had never had the opportunity or an excuse to go aboard.

Captain James Freedy cut the engines and smiled. *Gloriana* was in. He pushed the hair out of his eyes and straightened his shoulders. The run had been a long one and he was ready for some food and a rest. He had timed their arrival perfectly so that they could slip into the marina while most of *Neptunis* slept.

He slid the port side door open and stepped out into the fresh morning air. His First Mate, Abe, was talking to someone on the dock. 'Good job, Abe, even if you did have a little help!' he shouted.

Petra heard the undertone of laughter in a voice that tugged at her heart. What she saw framed against the yacht's glistening white deckhouse was a California beach version of her first love, Romeo. The palette of colours was different – the blacks and browns of Italy replaced by the bleached tow and copper of America – but the sparkle was the same, the magnetism undeniable. She ran a hand through her uncombed hair and tweaked her sweatsuit top. If only she had made herself more presentable before running down to the marina. Though if she had, she would have missed this moment.

The California beach boy was saying something and staring at her with a bemused look. Petra didn't react. She stood mesmerized by the boat and by the man she knew must be Betty's captain, James Freedy.

'Thanks for your help!' James repeated. 'I try to avoid

the fanfare of a prime-time docking.' He lifted his hands in a gesture of frustrated bewilderment. 'Would you like to come aboard?'

Before he could retract or postpone the invitation, Petra placed her hands on the teak-topped coaming and her left foot on the fibreglass step that was built into the side of the boat. With a strength and agility that surprised James, she pulled herself up onto the deck. She kicked off her running shoes, revealing pale feet with crimson-painted toenails, then turned to face him.

'I know I shouldn't, Captain, but here I am. Minx, Petra Minx. I presume that wasn't a rhetorical question.' Her blue-green eyes danced as she extended a slim but strong hand adorned with similarly varnished fingernails.

James considered her carefully. The sweatsuit and the gymnastics didn't quite jibe with the nail lacquer. He noticed Abe watching them and yelled at him to get on with hooking up the power cable and the water supply to the boat.

'James Freedy. Pleased to meet you. And no, it wasn't rhetorical, just rather rash. Miss Graceby's very particular about who she allows to come aboard *Gloriana*. She'll have my hide if she's watching.'

'From what I know of Miss Graceby, it's too early for her to be up and about, and I won't tell. Anyway, I'm sure she wouldn't mind; she's already asked me to join her for a cruise.'

'In that case, I'll give you the grand tour.' James ushered her through the port side door into a passage that ran across the width of the yacht, roughly amidships. 'We have two helm stations, the upper helm on the flybridge,' he said, pointing to a flight of stairs on Petra's right, 'and the lower helm here.' He gestured to Petra's left, where three steps led forward and up to the lower helm. 'I'm sure you'd rather see the salon and the staterooms, though.'

Without waiting for her reply, he led the way aft through a doorway and into the salon. A light airy mix of apple green, pink and cream took Petra by surprise. She had expected gleaming rich-brown teak with a wealth of damask and brocade. Instead there was velvet and lace and fine silk, French Provincial furniture with an antiqued white finish, and a glass and marble bar in the forward port corner. Through the sliding doors that separated the salon from the aft deck, Petra could see white wicker chairs with candy-striped cushions in green, pink and cream, set around a Perspex table with wrought iron legs. Betty's artistic hand had been at work. The result was clean, attractive and feminine.

James beckoned Petra to follow him. He seemed to use words sparingly, but none were necessary – she would have followed him anyway. He took her back to the midships passage then forward along a short corridor and into the formal dining room. Here, as in the salon, the windows were tall and wide, opening the room to the world beyond. The candy-stripe repeated itself in the upholstered seats of the eight shield-back dining chairs that stood round the satinwood table. The symmetry appealed to Petra's sense of order.

Beyond the dining room, through a doorway, lay the galley – revamped by Betty just a season ago. Stainless steel appliances and a black granite counter, Petra noted.

'The crew quarters and lounge are through that door, in the bow,' James said, pointing to a door on the opposite wall of the galley. 'Off limits to guests, of course!' His slightly lop-sided smile took any sting out of his words. 'Now for the staterooms. They're on the lower deck.'

Petra followed James back to the passage amidships. The companionway leading to the staterooms was just inside the entrance to the salon. The full-width master stateroom was as palatial as she had anticipated, the colour scheme entirely different. A large oval bed shimmered in sand-coloured silk, floating like an island on a sea of blue carpet sprinkled with gold stars. The carpet reminded her at once of the star-studded ceiling of Notre-Dame Cathedral in Old Montreal. A comfortable sitting area, a small book-lined study and two bathrooms linked by a dressing room completed the owner's suite.

James said little as they continued their tour. He showed her the VIP cabin on the port side with its queen bed and a generous bathroom en-suite. Opposite, on the starboard side, were two smaller guest cabins that shared a bathroom. Petra nodded approvingly at the purple and gold bedcovers and the way in which the colours were picked up in a border that ran round the beige carpets. Betty's taste was lavish but flawless, and the housekeeping not to be faulted.

'Is that the engine room?' Petra asked, as they passed a heavy door she had noticed on their way down.

'Yes. As I said, the crew quarters are in the bow – Captain's stateroom, crew lounge, laundry and three crew cabins.'

'Can I take a look at the engine room?'

One of James's eyebrows lifted slightly. 'Sure. I didn't think you'd be interested.'

'Why not?'

He gave a laconic shrug. 'No reason. Most women aren't.'

'I'm not most women.'

'Right. I see that now.'

For some reason, James's reply irritated Petra. She liked him and wanted him to like her. Suddenly though, his attitude was annoying and arrogant. She couldn't imagine why she had thought he was like Romeo.

She opened the engine room door and walked in ahead of him. The twin Caterpillar D-343 TA diesels were spotless. The floor was so clean that she could have picked up a peanut and eaten it without hesitation. There were two generator sets, a water maker for turning salt water into fresh water, an impressive bank of air-conditioning units, a well-organized workbench, a complete set of mechanical gauges, and an array of dials and switches. A humble Marine Unit Sergeant's dream.

'I see you have fuel polishers as well as Racors,' she remarked, noting how James's eyebrow – the same one – lifted slightly as expected. 'Do you have problems with dirty fuel here in the islands?'

'Some places are notorious, so we avoid them. It's the idiots from the mainland that get caught out. *Caveat emptor*, you know.'

Buyer beware indeed, Petra thought. Appearances were deceptive. So far, James's personality was lagging behind his looks.

'Are you hungry?' he asked abruptly.

The simple question diverted her thoughts to her stomach. Borrowing a line from one of her favourite movies, she replied: 'I could eat.'

James grinned. 'Antwone Fisher. So we have more in common than our love of fine boats.'

Petra was forced into a smile. 'I guess so.'

In the crew lounge, Abe had set out a copious breakfast of fresh fruit salad, hot croissants with scrambled eggs, muffins with strawberry jam, and lots of coffee. Petra and James loaded their plates and carried them up to the flybridge. Behind the three helm chairs, there was room for a small crowd on an L-shaped seat with green and white striped cushions. They sat side by side with their backs to the dock, facing the marina. Although it was still early, the sun was beginning to strengthen. Over in the boatyard, a couple of men in coveralls stood looking at a blackened hull. James whistled.

'Somebody ran into a bit of trouble!'

'Somebody you know quite well, I think.'

'Who would that be?'

'Ken Graceby.'

'You're kidding!'

'No, I'm serious. You can just make out the boat's name. *Geyser*. I was there when it happened.'

'What do you mean? Who are you?'

'A friend of the family once removed.' Petra trotted out her cover story and described the events of the previous Friday morning. 'I suppose Cliff didn't think to notify you.'

'He wouldn't. Boating isn't really his thing. Ken might

have tried to contact me, but we've been on the high seas since we left Bermuda three days ago.'

'That's a thousand nautical miles! Why did you go to Bermuda? Wouldn't it have been better to follow the American coast down from Nova Scotia?'

James shrugged. 'I might be captain, but I don't choose the route. I do what I'm told. We avoid making landfall on the east coast of the United States if at all possible. Joe LePinto was adamant about that, and Miss Graceby's the same. Joe told me once that they ran into trouble with the American authorities after taking a boat to Cuba, so he swore he'd never dock a boat of his on the eastern seaboard of the U.S. again.'

Petra had heard many stories of boaters running afoul of the U.S. government after cruising to Cuba, though she thought the restrictions had been relaxed recently.

'How long have you been captaining *Gloriana*?' she asked.

'Just this season. Before that I was First Mate. But I've worked on her for so long it seems like forever.'

Petra guessed that Betty would have replaced Ken as captain shortly after she had complained to the police about him in April. Ken would not have taken kindly to being demoted. 'So you've known the family a long time,' she said.

'Ever since Joe accepted *Gloriana* in part payment of a debt over ten years ago. She'd been used as a party boat, and the interior, especially the teak, was in bad shape. I did a lot of repairs and custom woodwork for him, as well as refinishing the bar and the staterooms.'

'There's hardly any teak inside the boat now.'

'That's Betty's "new look". After the accident that killed Joe, she insisted on a complete makeover of the interior. Said she'd never really liked his choice of furnishings.'

'Which do you prefer?'

'I'm easy. As I said, I just do as I'm told.'

Petra swallowed a mouthful of muffin. 'What about Ken? According to Samson, he used to captain *Gloriana*.'

'Who's Samson?'

'One of the bellboys.'

'You have strange friends!'

'He's not a friend, just a good source of information.'

A slight furrow appeared on James's brow. Immediately, Petra regretted her flippant remark. She would have to watch her reactions. It would be easy to be seduced by James's charm. She didn't really know him and had let her guard down.

'Information about what?' James asked.

'The resort. He knows how everything works and often delivers stuff to the marina, particularly for Mr. Ken as he calls him.'

'Now I know who you're talking about! Ken says he's a nuisance – always there when you don't want him and never around when he's needed.'

'That seems harsh. I'm sure he's just doing his job. Was Ken upset when he lost the position of captain?'

'He didn't lose the position of captain, as you put it. He had other priorities and I took over, that's all. Ken and I work well together. It doesn't make much difference which of us is captain.'

But one of you has to call the shots, Petra thought, and I think I know who it is. She was wondering how to phrase her next question when Ken's voice floated up from the dock.

'Jamie!' Ken vaulted out of the golf cart and knocked on *Gloriana*'s hull. 'Are you there?'

James put his hand on the back of the seat and twisted round to look down at the dock. He was almost touching Petra's shoulder. She could feel the warmth of his body and smell his skin. A faint tang of salt, redolent of the open ocean he had just crossed, a hint of spice and tobacco, not from cigarettes, which she abhorred, but perhaps the lingering remains of an after-shave or his natural aroma. Either way it was pleasant, and she made no attempt to move.

'Hey, man! Come aboard, there's breakfast down below. Get some and join us!' James shifted his wrist, suddenly aware of his companion. 'Your face is so pale,' he said, 'it's hard to believe you've ever been in the sun, yet you know your boats.'

Petra felt the colour rise in her cheeks. A wing of black hair fell across her forehead. She brushed it away and tensed as he leaned towards her. It was almost a relief when he lifted a few strands of her hair with his thumb and finger and watched the light catch it as it fell back onto her scalp.

'Pretty,' he murmured.

Petra drew back. 'It's a mess this morning. I must go.' She jumped up as a squeal of tyres announced the arrival of a second vehicle. On the dock below she saw Cliff and Betty in one of the resort's blue and gold golf carts. Cliff must have arrived by car since she hadn't noticed a helicopter landing. He brought the cart to a standstill and hurried round to help his mother out. Despite the early hour, Betty looked smart and trim in a cream pantsuit with a flowered blouse. Her silver hair was beautifully dressed, each wave flowing unbroken into the next. Once again Petra wished she had devoted a few more minutes to her morning ablutions.

But it was too late to worry about her appearance. James was already on his way down to welcome them. She watched as he emerged from the deckhouse and waited to greet them at the top of the boarding ladder, which Abe had put in place. Betty climbed the six steps of the ladder slowly but steadily, her hand holding the rail for safety. Petra ran down the flybridge stairs to meet her.

'What a lovely surprise, my dear! You're already on board!' Betty kissed Petra on both cheeks and flung open her arms. 'How do you like my baby?'

'She's beautiful. I was on the dock when she came in and I wormed my way aboard. I hope you don't mind.'

'Not at all. You're as good as family – perhaps better. I'm glad you like her, and I see you've met my gallant Captain James.' Betty patted his arm. 'I want to hear all about the repairs that were done in Bermuda.'

At that moment, Ken appeared from the direction of the crew quarters holding a plate laden with food. Cliff, following close on his mother's heels, raised his eyebrows at his son but forbore to comment. Instead he acknowledged him with a foreman's salute. Petra looked from one man to the other. She was pleased that Cliff had come back as promised, but Ken was another matter. She hadn't seen him since the previous morning when he had left Betty's suite in anger.

Petra shied away as Ken took a step forward, a scowl twisting his features. Then she realized he was looking past her to the dock where a third golf cart was whirring along towards them. Samson, with Martin at his side, brought the cart to a shuddering stop at the bottom of the boarding ladder.

'*Power & Motoryacht* magazine asked me to get some pictures,' Martin called out. 'Would you mind if I took a few, Miss Graceby? Your yacht is awesome.'

Ken glowered at Martin. 'Asshole! Get out of here. We don't need you!'

'Ken! Mind your manners. You know how I love having my picture taken. And this is my boat.' To Martin, she said: 'Pay no attention to my grandson, young man. Let's have a group photo.'

'Thank you, Ma'am. Ladies, stand in front of the men, please. Everyone smile.'

'What fun! This is just like the old days,' Betty cried. 'How do I look, Cliff? Come along, Ken, you too! Put that plate down. You're a handsome devil when you don't frown.'

Petra was impressed by Betty's determination to avoid conflict. She seemed to have forgotten the argument she had had with Ken the day before and had succeeded in defusing what could have been a very difficult situation.

'We'll all go for a cruise tomorrow morning,' Betty announced. 'You too, Martin. Ten o'clock sharp, here on the dock. We'll have lunch on one of the out islands and you can take some more pictures.'

'I'm afraid I'm leaving today, Ma'am,' Martin replied. 'Perhaps I can join you another time. Petra, I need to talk to you before I go.'

'I'll come with you now. Thank you so much, Betty …' She stopped short as both Cliff and James spoke her name.

'Petra!'

Betty looked at each of the men, then at Petra. 'My, my! You're popular, my dear, and I'm not surprised. Off you go! Enjoy yourself. We'll see you later.'

Riding back in the golf cart with Martin and Sam, Petra wondered why she was suddenly the centre of attention. Not something she was accustomed to, but she could easily get used to it.

CHAPTER

10

Martin left *Neptunis* at noon, after making Petra promise to spend a few days with him in Toronto. She did so reluctantly, stressing that it depended on A.K. allowing her that freedom. As she stood on the steps waving goodbye, Ken appeared. He cornered her before she could hurry away and offered to take her on a tour of the island. They could stop, he said, at a bird sanctuary in which he was involved.

Petra studied his face. What the hell was he playing at? Was he offering her an olive branch or attempting to get her alone somewhere? Would it be worth accepting the invitation – and the risk – in order to find out more about his attitude towards his grandmother and her money?

'Thanks for the offer,' she said cautiously. 'But I'm really tired.'

'Too busy with your boyfriends, eh?'

That did it. Petra turned on her heel and didn't mention that she'd already been to the sanctuary.

On her way through the lobby, she bumped into Sam whose eyes lit up when he saw her.

'Miss Petra, Miss Petra! I'm just going to lunch. Come with me and I'll show you where I live.'

Still fuming at Ken, she let out an exasperated sigh. 'I can't, Sam. Another time perhaps.' His face crumpled like a child's and she almost changed her mind.

When she got back to her room, there were two phone messages. The first was from Betty, apologizing for not being able to spend time with her that afternoon. The second was from James who wanted to discuss anchorages on Lake Huron's North Channel. It would have been interesting to compare notes but Petra decided not to return his call immediately. Better not to seem too eager.

She was sitting down to rest and to think when the hotel phone rang again. This time it was Cliff, inviting her to go swimming with dolphins. He was insistent and persuasive. In the end, she ran out of excuses and agreed to go. It might give her a chance to find out more about Joe LePinto and the accident that had killed him. According to Martin, Cliff had been driving Joe's Bentley when they ran off the road. Had it been Ken, she might have suspected that it wasn't an accident at all.

Cliff picked her up at two o'clock. He was as well groomed as ever and seemed to be in an expansive mood. Petra threw her bag into the golf cart and jumped in beside him. He leaned over to kiss her cheek. His cologne had a fresh citrus smell, clean and light, quite different from the faint salty tang of James Freedy's skin.

Cliff drove sedately through the gardens towards the aquarium.

'Can we stop for a minute?' Petra asked as they came to an outdoor enclosure. 'It's feeding time for the seals.'

'Sure, if that'll make you happy.'

'I love to watch them catch fish. It's the child in me.'

'You sound just like my mother!'

Once Petra had had enough of the seals, Cliff headed for the far side of the resort where a series of ocean-side pools had been sculpted and enhanced to produce a magnificent combination of artifice and nature. Winding channels led from the main saltwater pools where the dolphins swam to side pools full of rocky islets.

It was a gorgeous afternoon for sunbathing and dipping in and out of the water. Petra slipped off the beach dress she had bought from the shopping arcade and watched covertly as Cliff pulled off his golf shirt and stepped out of his shorts. His body would have been considered good for a man half his age. His perfect tan suggested frequent visits to the spa – in which case it would continue beneath his swimming trunks. She blushed as he turned without warning and caught her assessing him.

'Do you like what you see?' he asked.

'I see bottle-nosed dolphins,' she said, as three of the graceful mammals arced out of the water and began to swim towards them. 'Do you know they never really sleep? They always keep one eye open so that one side of the brain is active.'

'And do you know that they spend over fifty percent of their time having sex?'

'Yes, but I understand that it's the female who chooses when to mate and with which male.'

'You're very well informed.'

'A girl needs to know these things! Let's go and join them.'

The dolphins were slippery, curious and as lovable as Petra remembered from her high-school graduation trip to Mexico. Then she had been in love with Romeo and had gone on the trip only to avoid being left out. Now she had no significant other and was content to focus on her career. Cliff was flirting with her, but she could handle his type.

He proved to be a competent swimmer with an easy style. She accepted his challenge to race and was pleased when he only just beat her to the opposite side of the pool.

'I suspected I might have trouble beating you,' he said, panting. 'You're completely at ease in the water, aren't you?'

'I'm a swimming and aquafit instructor.' As she had been years ago before joining the RCMP.

'That explains it then.'

'Race you back,' Petra called and pushed away from the rocks before he could question her.

Later, as the sun began to slide lower, Cliff climbed out onto a flat rock that still radiated heat. He helped Petra up beside him. She sat dangling her feet in the clear water, watching the brightly patterned fish dart back and forth.

'Can you scuba dive?' he asked her.

'I can. I learned on Lake Huron. There are plenty of wrecks there, but the water is really cold, even in summer. In some ways I'd rather stay on the surface and snorkel, where the colour is and where I can feel the sun on my back.'

'There are some amazing reefs around here. I'd like to take you diving.'

'Aren't you going back to Las Vegas soon?'

'Are you trying to get rid of me?'

'I'm leaving myself in a day or two,' she said.

'Well, come and see me in Vegas then.'

'That's where Joe died, isn't it?'

There was a slight pause before Cliff answered. 'Yes. I suppose my mother told you how it happened.'

'I know it was a car accident. She didn't go into detail. You were driving, I believe.'

Cliff nodded. 'The four of us were on our way to dinner at a favourite place of Mother's outside the city. One minute everything was fine; the next, we skidded off the road into a tree. Joe was in the front passenger seat. He was alive when the ambulance arrived, but died before they could get him to hospital.'

'How awful for Betty – and for you and Ken! The impact must have been huge if Joe's airbag didn't save him.'

'The bag malfunctioned, and he never wore a seat belt – said he hated the things. Mother was sitting behind Joe. Her right hip and leg were badly damaged. Ken suffered cuts and bruises and a mild concussion. I was lucky to get away with a broken arm and a bad headache.'

'So what caused the accident?'

'Well, I hadn't been drinking or taking drugs, and the car had been in for a routine service only three weeks before. Everything should have been good.'

Should have been but wasn't, and something didn't smell right, Petra thought. Cliff spoke too glibly about the whole episode, almost as if he had rehearsed what he wanted to say. 'You don't sound too upset,' she said, watching him wipe the back of his hand across his forehead.

'I've had to put it behind me, we all have. There's no sense in dwelling on it. If you come to Vegas, I'll show you the monument my mother erected to Joe. Now, how about a last dip?'

'Enough is enough. And I need an early night, so if you'd been planning to invite me out to dinner, I'm going to decline.'

'Even if it's the Coco Caverna Club? You wanted to go back there.'

'I did, but three times in five days would be too much.' Petra chuckled as a perplexed look crossed Cliff's face.

'You seem to insinuate yourself everywhere. I don't know how you do it. I swear there's more to you than meets the eye.'

'What you see is what you get!' Petra insisted. 'Jus' a li'l ol' girl from Sudbury, Ontario, havin' a vacation.' Suddenly, she shivered and withdrew her feet as a boldly striped fish began to attack her ankles. 'That's enough for me. Let's go. I don't think this is the place to be after dark.'

All this ran through Petra's mind next morning as she got ready for the cruise on board *Gloriana*. From her limited wardrobe, she chose blue shorts and a simple white V-neck T-shirt. She spent more time than usual applying sunscreen and a little make-up. Betty would be immaculate, and she had to show James that she wasn't always a mess. More important though, Petra reminded herself, was the opportunity the day would give her to observe the three Gracebys together at close quarters. A.K. would be on her case if she didn't report back soon.

When she arrived on the dock, Betty and Cliff were waiting to greet her. Dressed in navy blazers and white slacks, with only pink and green shirts to differentiate them, they could have been fraternal twins. James, Ken, Abe and another man, busy preparing the boat for departure, wore the crew uniform of beige shorts and green T-shirts embroidered with the logo *M.Y. Gloriana* in gold italics.

Petra watched Abe remove the boarding ladder and lay it on the dock. She looked around for Sam, expecting to see his cheery face, but there was no sign of him. He must have delivered provisions to the boat then left to go about his other duties. She felt bad about disappointing him yesterday and wanted to apologize and tell him she would love to visit his lodgings later.

James was driving from the upper helm. Betty took the seat on his right, while Petra sat on his left and studied the instrument panel. Although *Gloriana* was more than four decades old, Betty and Joe had spared no expense to equip her with the latest navigation technology.

As they approached the exit to the sea, Betty tightened her grip on the console in front of her. Immediately, James put a reassuring hand on her arm and murmured: 'No worries this morning, Ma'am. Would you like to take the helm once we're out of the fairway?'

'I think I will, provided you stay here with me.'

'Of course, and I fancy this young lady could handle *Gloriana* without any trouble.'

'I've never driven anything like this, only small boats up at my uncle's cottage in Killarney,' Petra said. 'That's where I saw *Gloriana* this summer.'

'Why didn't you come and tell me then that your father had died?' Betty demanded. 'I could have given my condolences to your mother personally.'

Petra swallowed hard. The worst thing about cover stories was that they didn't cover everything. 'My mother didn't come to Killarney this year. She spent the summer in Rhode Island with a friend, so she didn't know you were in the area,' she finished rather lamely.

'Well, perhaps I can meet her next summer.'

'I believe she's planning a trip to New Zealand.'

James shot Petra a quizzical look. 'Quite a globetrotting mother you have!'

His eyes – blue flecked with gold – were full of laughter. Petra hadn't been conscious of them yesterday, just the whole disconcertingly attractive package. A lick of blonde hair fell across his forehead and he pushed it away. He held her gaze for another few seconds before turning to speak to Betty.

Petra watched him check the radar and blow the horn before they exited the marina. Then he activated the route and the autopilot. 'Where are we heading?' she asked.

'A coral cay about twenty-five nautical miles from here. We should be there by noon. The swimming and snorkelling are fantastic.'

'And we'll catch some fish for lunch,' Betty added.

'I didn't know you liked fishing,' Petra said.

'I used to fish when I was a child, but Joe didn't like it much, so for years I didn't bother. Now I can please myself.'

Betty's comment reminded Petra of the many couples she knew whose interests didn't coincide. Her friend Jim was a hunter and outdoorsman, his wife Mary loved ballet and theatre; Greg played golf, Jeanie played bridge; Uncle Don lived for boats, Aunt Amy hated the water. As Aunt

Amy repeated every summer at the cottage, if you didn't enjoy the same things, the glue had to be so much stronger to make the partnership work. Petra wondered whether Betty and Joe's relationship had been as idyllic as Betty had indicated. It would be a shame if their fairytale were a sham.

Petra filled her lungs with the salt air and focussed on the deep turquoise water. A ten knot southeasterly breeze was creating a light swell. Betty took the helm and after the first few minutes seemed completely relaxed. James stood behind her and continued to keep an eye on the instruments. *Gloriana* rode the waves well, her stabilizers preventing any roll.

When Cliff and Ken joined them on the flybridge, Betty relinquished the helm and the conversation flowed back and forth. Just like any ordinary family on a day out, Petra thought, as they discussed the pros and cons of jet drives for smaller boats. The only discord was when Betty suggested that she might buy a Hinckley picnic boat to keep on the North Channel. James agreed that it would be fun and useful, whereas Cliff and Ken immediately questioned the expense.

By the time they arrived at the entrance to the lagoon, the sense of camaraderie was once again strong. There were a few anxious minutes as James threaded *Gloriana* through the reefs that could hole the boat and send her to the bottom.

'The deeper the blue, the deeper the water,' he sang, searching for the path through the pale banks of coral.

'Just like on Georgian Bay,' Petra said. 'There are plenty of unmarked rocks, but if you slow down and watch the colour variations in the water, you can detect most of them. Have you ever been to the Fox Islands?'

'I don't think so. Where are they?'

'About five nautical miles southeast of Killarney, in uncharted waters. They're the most beautiful group of pink granite islands in the area: windswept, virtually barren, uninhabited except by a few campers in summer – classic Group of Seven painting material. You couldn't go near them in *Gloriana*, but you could use your runabout.' She swivelled her seat to look beyond Cliff and Ken. A Boston Whaler filled the aft section of the upper deck behind the flybridge. There was also what appeared to be a motorbike under a cover.

A couple of hours later, after a lunch of fresh fish caught and prepared by Abe, Petra made her way to the galley to help him tidy up. There was a lot to be admired in the big man with the shiny black skin and tight curly hair who went about his work without complaint.

'Abe, that was fabulous! You're a mean man with a fishing rod. Betty couldn't get a look in with you there! You must be from the islands.'

'Yes, Ma'am. Born and bred right here in the Bahamas.'

'How long have you been crewing aboard *Gloriana*?'

'Rightly speaking, I'm not part of the crew. Mr. Joe favoured his people from Puerto Rico. I jus' fill in whenever there's a vacancy or something special to be done. This time, I went to Bermuda to help Cap'n James with the repairs she needed.' He beamed at Petra.

'What about the other guy? Is he a regular crewmember?' she asked.

'Depends what you mean by regular. Mr. Joe use' to hire new crew each spring to take *Gloriana* to the North Channel. Lots of islanders needed to learn marketable skills, he said, and he wanted to give them a chance.'

'As he did through his Culinary Institute,' Petra added.

'The Institute still sends *Gloriana* a chef every year, sometimes other staff too.'

'What happens to the ones who've finished their tours of duty?'

'They've enough training and experience to move out into the world. Leastways tha's what Mr. Joe said.'

An unusual way of running a motor yacht, Petra thought. Good crew and shipboard staff were hard to find and commanded a premium. Most yacht owners fought tooth and nail to hang on to the best ones. Joe LePinto had had some very fixed ideas about how he wanted things done.

The intercom phone rang in the galley. Abe picked it up.

'Right, Cap'n, be there in three.' He turned to Petra. 'We're hauling anchor and heading home. Miss Betty's having a lie-down. You jus' relax now and enjoy the trip back.'

The phone rang again. Abe listened to the voice giving orders on the other end and rolled his eyes. 'OK, OK, as soon as we're off anchor.'

'What was that about?'

'Mr. Ken wants coffee for two on the aft deck. Not the most convenient time.'

'I'll make it and take it to them, I've nothing else to do.'

'Thanks, lady. You're a good 'un!'

Ten minutes later, Petra carried a tray to the salon. As she entered, she noticed that the drapes were almost closed across the aft deck doors. A shaft of sunlight fell through the gap. The doors were open. Ken's voice was clear as he spoke to his father.

'This could be the answer to all our problems. A few pick-ups and deliveries and we're home free. It's a no-brainer.'

'You're the one with no brains, boy! There's always a catch somewhere.'

'I don't see any difference between this and what's been done in the past, except that they'll pay big time!'

'If they're willing to pay big time, there's a big difference, believe me. Look, let me think about it. If we can negotiate some safeguards, it might be feasible.'

Petra heard the starboard engine engage and resumed her slow walk through the salon towards the aft doors. The boat moved forward then stopped. She was hoping to hear more snatches of conversation, but James was using the engines to position the boat directly over the anchor. Apparently the windlass was stalling as it tried to retrieve it. In an attempt to overturn the anchor, James engaged both engines then alternated from forward to reverse. The seesaw motion of the boat finally caught Cliff's attention.

'Is James having a problem? Go and see what's happening, Ken.'

'The anchor's probably fouled itself on some rock. One of the crew will have to dive down if he can't work it free.'

'Coffee, Gentlemen!' Petra called as she approached the sliding doors to the aft deck. She balanced the tray in the crook of her left arm and used her other hand to pull back the drapes.

Consternation showed in their faces.

'What the hell are you doing?' Ken asked.

Petra put the tray down on the table in front of them and smiled brightly. 'Just helping out.'

'Little Miss Goody Two-Shoes! Still after the gold, are you?' Ken stood up and spat over the side rail.

'Watch your tongue, boy!' Cliff growled. 'Ignore him, Petra. I don't like to say it about my own offspring, but he's a rude sod.'

He's more than that, Petra thought. He's loathsome.

Once the anchor was free, the run home was uneventful. Petra spent the first half-hour alone on the flybridge with James discussing the instrumentation and studying local charts. She was more than conscious of his nearness, but made an effort to sublimate her feelings in the minutiae of boating technicalities. When he offered her the helm, she accepted with a quickening pulse and a determination to surpass his expectations. Betty, followed by Cliff and Ken, arrived in time to witness her metamorphosis from girl next door to skilled pilot. If they noticed the change, they didn't mention it.

Gloriana pulled into the dock a little after five o'clock. The sun was already beginning to set and a cool wind ran through the marina. Petra stayed out of the way during the docking process. James had declined her offer of help with a laughing admonition to act like a guest this time, not a member of the crew. It was Abe who jumped down onto the dock, secured the boat and was now reinstalling the boarding ladder.

Petra looked eagerly for Sam, who normally would be waiting to lend a hand. She had enjoyed the day but was disturbed by what she had overheard. Ken seemed intent on getting himself into trouble and Cliff might not be far behind. Sam's lively chatter would be a welcome distraction.

Instead of Sam's friendly face, Petra was surprised to see the harbourmaster walking rapidly towards them. His expression was dour and his brow laced with sweat despite the wind. He exchanged a few words with Abe and carried on walking towards *Gloriana*. Petra saw one of the resort's golf carts turn the corner of the building and hoped it was bringing Sam. But the man at the wheel was Dick Reed, the manager. Seated next to him was an officer in a khaki uniform. Sam was not with them. Abe had re-boarded *Gloriana* and was calling out for James. Betty appeared on the side deck, accompanied by Cliff.

'Quite a reception committee, Mr. Reed! I hope we've done nothing wrong,' Betty called as the golf cart rolled to a stop. 'Is there a problem?'

'Not as far as you're concerned, Miss Graceby. However, there's been an incident at the resort that you should be aware of.' He gave a nervous cough. 'In fact, the Inspector needs to speak to you.'

'Right now? Can't it wait until I've disembarked and freshened up?'

'No, Ma'am, I'm sorry,' the Inspector said, his foot already on the first step of the ladder. 'I'd like everyone to stay on board until I've had the chance to ask a few questions. May I come aboard?'

'If you must, Inspector.'

A vice clamped around Petra's heart as she listened to the exchange. She had a dreadful feeling that the Inspector was bringing news she wouldn't want to hear.

The Inspector looked at the seven people assembled in *Gloriana*'s salon, eight counting Dick Reed. 'I'm afraid I have some bad news, Ma'am,' he said, addressing Betty. 'One of the resort's bellboys was found this morning in the ocean pool area.'

'You say "bad news", Inspector, so I presume he's dead,' Betty said acerbically.

'That's right, Ma'am.'

Petra's naturally pale complexion turned a pure white. 'I knew it,' she muttered.

'What did you say, Miss?' the Inspector asked.

'Nothing,' she said. 'I had a premonition that something awful was going to happen.'

The Inspector threw her a suspicious glance. 'How could you possibly know … ?'

'Inspector,' Betty interrupted, 'for millennia, women's instincts have proved far more accurate than the most sophisticated diagnostic tools that science has to offer. Petra is my guest and I'd thank you to remember that.'

'No offence intended, Ma'am,' the Inspector replied.

'I still don't understand why you find it necessary to bother me with this tragedy. Surely Mr. Reed is the one to deal with it.'

'Of course, Ma'am. The problem is that we found an envelope addressed to you in the deceased's jacket pocket.'

'He was found on land then?' Cliff said.

'No, Sir; he was in the water. His jacket was lying on a rock nearby.'

'But he hated the water!' Petra burst out.

The Inspector gave Petra a hard look. Her face now was flushed and her manner agitated, unlike Miss Graceby who had taken the news calmly. 'Who are you talking about?' he asked.

'Samson, the bellboy. It's him, isn't it?' Petra answered. 'He couldn't swim and was afraid of drowning.'

'I don't know where you got that idea from,' Ken scoffed. 'He used to help out on my boat when I needed extra crew.'

'Ladies, Gentlemen, please,' said the Inspector. 'The deceased has indeed been identified by Mr. Reed as Samson Taho. I believe you all knew him. I need to ask when you last saw him.'

'Does that mean you suspect foul play?' James asked.

'Not at present. There are indications that he was stung by some kind of fish, which may have incapacitated him. An autopsy will be carried out. We are merely trying to trace his movements and narrow down the time of death.'

Almost in a trance, Petra gave a short statement to the Inspector. She left *Gloriana* in the company of Dick Reed. He was visibly distressed and several shades whiter than when she had met him at the marina on the day of her arrival. The only thing unchanged was his torrent of words that began to swamp Petra as soon as he put the golf cart into gear.

'Terrible, terrible! The dolphin pools and the aquarium are closed. What am I going to say to the guests? Our reputation, you know. What a disaster! What a disaster!'

Fighting her own feelings of despair at the loss of her

friend, Petra ignored him. As they turned the corner of her building, she tapped him on the arm. 'I'll get out here.' She had in mind to fetch a jacket from her suite and walk over to the dolphin pools, to see where Sam had spent his last moments. Only yesterday she had been cavorting in the water there with Cliff and the dolphins. Now that place of fun, laughter and beauty had become the scene of a fatal accident.

Or worse. Petra's brain shot into gear. She began to sift through the events of the past few days, recalling a number of instances where Sam had been referred to in disparaging terms. It might be nothing, but he had irritated at least one person. What if his death hadn't been an accident?

Deep in thought, she heard someone call her name and looked round. Bianca Casales was hurrying down the path towards her.

'Petra, can I talk to you?' she shouted.

Petra hesitated. She wasn't in the mood for conversation, but if Bianca had something to tell her, it might have a bearing on Sam's death. 'Of course, come on up,' she said. She would have plenty of time to go and pay her respects to her friend later. And if she could find out what had happened to him, she promised she would.

CHAPTER

11

Images of Sam cascaded through Petra's mind as the Air Canada plane touched down in Toronto: Sam wrenching open the door of the taxi on her arrival in Nassau; Sam yelling with enthusiasm; Sam hefting suitcases far heavier than himself; Sam hurtling down to the marina in the golf cart; Sam's face – cheeky, creased, brown as the proverbial berry, bright and unfailingly cheerful. He had responded with a smile even when she rejected his invitation to visit his lodgings, although she knew he was deeply hurt.

Above all else, Petra regretted that selfish rejection. True, she had been tired that morning, but the main reason behind it had been to put as much distance as possible between her and Ken Graceby. It was a poor motive, though, for disappointing Sam, who had placed such value on her friendship. Hot tears pricked at the back of her eyes. She blinked them away and looked for her luggage on the carousel.

Martin had come to meet her. As soon as he saw her, he rushed forward. The set of her jaw told him that she was struggling to hold on to her emotions. He squeezed her shoulder and prised her bag from her grip.

'I'll take that. Are you all right?'

Petra nodded, not trusting herself to speak.

'You can tell me all about it when we get back to my place. And if you like, we can go out for a meal this evening.'

Petra shook her head. 'I don't feel like food.'

'Then we'll just drink!' Martin steered her through the crowds of people waiting to meet loved ones, holding her arm firmly but with infinite tenderness. For once, Petra was glad of his presence.

That evening, they sat on the balcony of Martin's apartment overlooking the waterfront in downtown Toronto, a bottle of wine on the table between them. Because it was November and the air was clear and cool, Martin had found a parka belonging to his sister for Petra to wear. He insisted on covering her legs with a blanket. 'This isn't the Caribbean. There's no sense in your catching a cold.'

'Martin, I'm OK now. Don't fuss. Just give me another glass of that Rioja.' His solicitousness was beginning to irritate her.

'You sound much more like your usual self.'

'Thanks to you, I am. Pouring my heart out this afternoon was a cathartic experience. I'm sorry for the waterworks. I don't understand why I reacted so strongly to Sam's death.'

'Don't beat up on yourself, Petra. Sometimes we can't control our feelings the way we'd like to. And you know that whatever happens, I'm here for you.'

'I know, Martin, and I'm truly grateful.'

To change the subject, Petra looked about her. 'You've done well for yourself. This apartment and the view are superb.'

Above and below, lights twinkled. Figures appeared in silhouette against floor-to-ceiling windows, television screens flickered with an eerie green glow. Ferries plied back and forth to the islands, less frequent than in summer but still their sole link to the mainland.

'I've always wanted to be close to the water,' Martin said. 'I made good money in Japan and saved most of it. Now I can afford to live in this rarefied atmosphere. And I can lock up and go whenever I need to. No problem with security.'

'True, but what I don't like about big cities is the anonymity.'

'It has its uses, as you should know after your years in special investigations.'

'Agreed, but at heart I'm a small town girl.'

'For a small town girl, you travel a lot and get involved in some extraordinary situations.'

'I'm just in the right place at the right time – or the wrong place at the wrong time if you're a cynic!'

'I'm a sceptic, not a cynic. I know you never tell me everything.' Martin looked expectantly at Petra, who ignored him and carried on sipping her wine. 'After you phoned to tell me about Sam,' he continued, 'I did some research on lionfish. That's what stung him, isn't it, and precipitated his death?'

'Apparently, but it's very strange. No one's ever seen lionfish in those waters.'

'According to what I read,' Martin said, 'they're native to Indo-Pacific waters. Occasionally they're found in the Caribbean and off the southeastern coast of the U.S. They have red and white stripes like some exotic zebra, and venomous spines.'

'Right! Beautiful but deadly.' Petra gazed at Martin, her expression suddenly sombre under the balcony light. 'You know Sam didn't have any family. *Neptunis* was his whole life. He'd worked there for thirteen years. I spoke to Dick Reed after the preliminary enquiry. He assured me the resort would make arrangements and take care of Sam. That was the only time Reed addressed me directly! He was pretty shaken up.'

'How did the enquiry go?'

'It was all over very quickly. The Gracebys closed ranks and when Betty was confronted with the envelope addressed to her, she said she didn't recognize the handwriting and had no idea who might be writing to her.'

'I wonder who did.'

'I can tell you. It was Bianca Casales.'

'Are you certain?'

'Yes. She came to see me the day Sam's body was discovered. She was really worried because she'd given Sam a note to deliver to Betty.'

'What's the big deal about that? What did it say?'

'She wouldn't tell me. She just said she wanted to apologize to Betty.'

'What for? When we were at the Club, didn't Bianca say that Betty fired her?'

'Yes. She used to work as a housemaid for Betty and Joe. Joe gave her the job to help her find her feet after she arrived in the Bahamas. She was so grateful that she'd do anything for him. I found a photo of them together in one of Betty's albums. They were really close.'

'Were they lovers?'

133

'That was my first thought. Bianca denies it, but after Joe died, Betty fired her. She went to work at the Coco Caverna Club then started dating Ken Graceby.'

'Which Betty wouldn't like at all!'

'There's more to it than that. About a year ago, Bianca and Ken came to see Betty. Betty found Bianca in her bedroom fingering some of her jewellery and called the police.'

'Jeez!'

'Bianca insists it was all a mistake. She's not a bad girl and is very fond of Ken. She's convinced he's heading for trouble.'

'And you didn't say anything about Bianca at the enquiry?'

'I couldn't, Martin. I was only there as an observer, and they'd have given her a really hard time after Betty's allegations. I'm sure she didn't have anything to do with Sam's death.'

'Probably not, but I'd still like to know what the note she wrote Betty contained. Information Ken would rather keep under wraps, perhaps? I wouldn't underestimate him – he's bad news,' Martin said.

'I know, though he can turn on the charm when he wants to.'

Martin looked earnestly at Petra through his glasses. 'I have a theory,' he said. 'Either Bianca was following Ken's instructions and looking for something in Betty's bedroom, or she was staging a diversion so that Ken could carry out a search – in the study, for example.'

Petra nodded. 'Possible. But what for? That's the million dollar question.'

'I guarantee it was something worth at least that much to our Ken!' Martin replied.

CHAPTER

12

Next morning, Petra stood by the window nursing her coffee and watching the first planes of the morning take off from the Toronto Island Airport. The waters of Lake Ontario were a steely grey, and a depressing November drizzle was falling. It reminded her that winter was not far away. Soon, boating patrols, marine search and rescue operations, and unexpected assignments in exotic locations would be nothing but a distant memory.

After the excitement of the last six weeks, she found it hard to contemplate returning to a world of border protection and federal law enforcement in Northern Ontario. By January, the snow would be over a metre deep and the streets icy even when they had been cleared. Criminal activities tended to be more localized as a result. The drug dealers, smugglers and counterfeiters, even the mafia bosses, seemed to fly south with Canada's "snowbirds".

Petra wished she could migrate with them. In the aftermath of her father's death, she had asked A.K. to take her off special investigations so that she could be close to her mother. Now she was developing a taste for them again.

But she had heard nothing from A.K. since he had given her permission to stay in Nassau for the preliminary enquiry into Sam's death. Presumably he wanted her to send him her assessment of the situation then report back to her unit in Sudbury.

As if to answer her unspoken question, the phone in her jacket pocket began to vibrate.

'You're back in Toronto then?'

'Yes, Sir.'

'How was the enquiry?'

'Quick and inconclusive.'

'And the Gracebys?'

'One big happy family when I left.'

'Hmm. Take a day or two to relax and get me your report ASAP. I trust your judgement.'

Thanks, A.K., Petra thought as she slipped the phone back into her pocket. The compliment was welcome, but how was she to combine R & R with writing a concise yet comprehensive report that would adequately convey her impression of the Gracebys? To finish in a couple of days, she would have to start work at once.

Petra fired up her computer and began her research. She discovered that Betty Graceby was born in a small village near Ingotville, Ontario, an only child with a husky voice and a determination to succeed far beyond the boundaries of her local environment. Like her deceased husband, Joe LePinto, Betty had not forgotten her roots and had, over the years, made generous donations to various charities and campaigns.

In the archives of the *Sudbury Star*, Petra found an interesting article. Written in August of the previous year, it described the council's plans for turning the Ingotville area into a destination. Ingotville had once been a centre for silver mining and was one of Ontario's most historic towns. A feasibility study was being carried out to assess various proposals that had been submitted, including the creation of an arts centre and jewellery museum. According to the paper, an as yet unnamed benefactor had expressed interest in the project. This must have been what Martin had been referring to during their lunch at *Neptunis*.

Petra spent an hour searching for more recent information before giving up. There were no further references to the project, no mention of the feasibility study being completed, nothing. She was certain, though, that work must be going on behind the scenes, unless it was just one of the rumours that abounded in political circles. But if the story were true and Betty Graceby the "unnamed benefactor", no effort would be spared to bring the project to fruition – including saving her and her fortune from the competing claims of her family.

Petra spent the rest of the afternoon organizing her notes and thinking about what to include in her report. She decided there was no need to mention the possibility that Betty might be the sponsor of the Ingotville arts centre. All A.K. had asked her to do was determine if there was any substance to Betty's complaints of harassment and violence by her grandson, Ken.

It occurred to Petra that Betty's first complaint against Ken, and Bianca, had been made just a few months after the publication of the article about the arts centre. If Ken had read the article, he might have wanted to search Betty's papers for proof or information. He could have asked Bianca to act as a decoy, as Martin had suggested ...

If, might, could have ... Petra rubbed her forehead. It was a possibility, but a bit far-fetched, and A.K. abhorred speculation. Almost certainly, A.K. knew more than he was telling her. She would leave it at that and not try to second-guess him.

The following day, Petra began drafting her report. Once she started, the words flowed and she completed the first part in record time. The conclusion was not so easy.

She had found nothing to substantiate Betty's allegations against her grandson. Ken was a nasty piece of work and clearly interested in Betty's money, but in her opinion their relationship was volatile, not violent. Although the investigation into the explosion aboard *Geyser* was not yet complete, the Bahamian police seemed fairly sure that he had had no intention of endangering his grandmother's life, nor his own. Petra agreed. As for Cliff, he was forceful with his mother in the way that many people with elderly parents were, yet protective and outwardly solicitous of her welfare. In the end, Petra concluded that the only action she could recommend would be a general watch on Ken Graceby. A dysfunctional family was a matter of concern, but for now at least Betty seemed able to take care of herself.

CHAPTER

13

Petra rejoined her unit with mixed feelings. She was pleased to see her colleagues, particularly her partner, Ed Spinone, but the slow pace was frustrating and she itched for more excitement. Gradually, though, she readjusted. After a few weeks it was as if she had never been away.

At Christmas time, she sent Betty a card, not knowing whether it would reach her, and she received an unexpected gift from Martin – a silver-framed photo of her with Betty, Cliff, Ken and James on board *Gloriana*. She stood it in pride of place on her dressing table. Whenever it caught her eye, she thought about contacting Betty but forgot as soon as she was called out to an incident. Every so often, she would catch herself looking at James in the picture and thinking how like yet unlike Romeo he was.

Petra had no communication from A.K. and could only assume that no news was good news: he must have accepted her assessment that no further action was necessary in the Graceby Affair, as she called it.

The snow fell thick and fast and by the middle of January it was, as Petra had predicted, over a metre deep. She bent low over the handlebars of her Bombardier snowmobile. The biting wind whistled past her ears, and although her standard issue fur cap kept her head warm, the cold stung her cheeks and made her lips sore. Behind her goggles, her eyes watered from the effort of focussing on the white trail ahead.

Despite the discomfort, Petra was in her element. She loved the snow in winter almost as much as she loved the water in summer: skimming over the crisp surface of the trails between the trees, hearing the "plop" as heavy lumps of snow fell from the branches, watching for tree stumps and holes that might cause her to veer off into the icy undergrowth. When one of her colleagues complained about the engine noise, she reminded him that it was like power versus sail: you could listen to the swish of the water against the hull or the swoosh of the snow under your skis, but to get somewhere fast you needed a motor.

She came to a junction and turned left onto a narrow trail that wound through dense stands of fir and pine. The local snowmobile club had used red and white striped stakes like barber's poles to mark the trail. Already the snow was so deep that some of them barely showed above the surface.

Rounding a bend, she came to a sudden stop. One of the markers was lying right across the path. She dismounted and bent to pick it up. Underneath were animal tracks and a trail of blood. Illegal hunters, damn them. As she pushed the red and white stake back into the bank of snow, she remembered Sam.

Petra's throat constricted and a wave of guilt washed over her. It receded, but couldn't absolve her of the fact that she hadn't kept the promise she had made to herself the previous November. She hadn't even bothered to follow up and find out whether the autopsy had been completed.

Thoughts of Sam led to thoughts of Betty. Petra realized it was unlikely she would ever know what had happened to Sam, but she could try and find out if Betty was planning to give a chunk of her fortune to her birth region of Ingotville.

Once she made up her mind, she acted decisively. In February, she put in a request for three days of mid-week leave. Ingotville was over two hundred kilometres from Sudbury. Conditions would be wintry and the drive would be slow, so she would need to stay in Ingotville for two nights.

A Google search for accommodation turned up two motels: The Traveller's Rest and The Northern Lights. When her request for leave was approved, she booked a superior room with fridge and microwave at The Traveller's Rest since the owners of The Northern Lights had apparently gone to Florida until the end of March.

Very sensible, Petra thought, as she drove north on the highway that led to Timmins and Cochrane. She slowed down as she came up behind a truck with orange flashing lights that was spreading salt on the road in anticipation of snow. April, with longer days and warmer temperatures, would have been a more suitable time to make the journey. And she should have known better than to stop at the roadside diner near North Bay. The proprietor had recognized her as RCMP from an incident the previous year and spent half an hour bending her ear.

Already it was mid-afternoon and she had forty kilometres to go. The lack of traffic on the road made it hard to stay awake. Added to that, the light was beginning to fade and the temperature to plummet. For a moment, Petra wished Martin were with her. She had considered asking him to accompany her – with his nose for news, he was good at sniffing things out – but had dismissed the idea as bad policy. He was persistent enough without further encouragement.

A few minutes before four o'clock, she pulled up in front of The Traveller's Rest and went to check in. Her superior room was at the end of the block and consequently icy cold. She tossed her overnight bag onto the bed and fiddled with the thermostat. It didn't seem to make any difference. Perhaps she could downgrade to a smaller, snugger room in the middle. But those had no fridge or microwave, the clerk explained when she went to ask, and the restaurant at The Northern Lights was closed, so the microwave would come in handy. Petra resigned herself to sleeping with her socks on and feasting on a frozen TV dinner from the corner store. That or a takeaway pizza.

Ingotville was bleak when Petra ventured out next morning after a less than restful night. A pre-dawn storm had dumped fresh snow on the ground, making walking difficult. As she trudged down the street, she found it hard to imagine Ingotville reborn as a destination. She had to remind herself that it would look different once the thaw came and everything – including the blackflies – grew with an astonishing energy to make up for months of stagnation.

A few mansions remained from the town's silver-mining days of glory. They were dilapidated now, turned into rooming houses, but still impressive. The town hall, where Petra expected to find the municipal office, was a red stone structure built during those same long-gone days. It was boarded up and surrounded by scaffolding. Could it be that the plans for rebirth were already in motion? There was no one to ask.

As she was assessing her options, an Ontario Provincial Police car pulled up beside her.

'Need any help, Ma'am?'

Petra reached into her jacket for her ID. 'Yes, if you know where the municipal office is.'

'Jump in and we'll take you there. What's the RCMP doing in these godforsaken parts at this time of year?'

Petra's police cousins knew nothing of any plans to revitalize the area and expressed doubt that much could be done. Ingotville was suffering the same fate as Industrial Revolution one-horse towns across the continent. They dropped her outside the municipal office that was being housed temporarily in a disused storage building on the outskirts of town.

She opened the door to the office and stepped into an overheated space. A girl with a silver stud in her nose and a silver ring through her right eyebrow was sitting behind a metal desk, poring over her iPad. She lifted her head and stared at Petra as though she had never seen a human before. Petra shook her head. Was disfigurement with silver a condition of employment in this cradle of abandoned mines? Or a reminder of what once had been and might be again with the help of Betty's gold?

Putting on a smile, Petra set out to charm information out of the metalled girl. She drew only blank looks.

'Huh? There's nothing going on here. This place is dead.'

'I've come a long way. Can I speak to your boss?'

'He should be in on Monday.'

'That's five days from now!'

'Yeah.'

'Do you know Betty Graceby?'

'Betty who?'

'Graceby. The singer and dancer. She was born near here.'

'Never heard of her. I like The Grabsnatchers.' The girl brightened as she wiped a greasy finger several times across her iPad and held it out to Petra. 'No guys in their band. "Snatch it while you can" is their latest hit.'

They'd better get a move on, Petra thought, seeing the bleached hair and enough metal to make a scrap merchant rich. She gave a shrug. 'Never heard of them, so I guess I'd better be going.'

'Come back Monday if you like. Mr. H usually gets in around twelve.'

'And leaves at two?'

'What?'

'Do you have a card? A business card.'

'Oh, right. No. This is just temp'ry.'

'I thought you were a fixture.'

'What?'

'Don't worry, I'm outta here.'

With raw material like that, Petra thought, as she started the long walk back to The Traveller's Rest, Betty would be throwing her and Joe's hard-earned money away. There was no future in Ingotville as far as she could see. Of course, all the inhabitants couldn't be quite so obtuse, unless silver poisoned in the same way as lead.

After a second cold and restless night in which images of Betty in a silver breastplate were muddled up in a dream about Sam fighting lions in a Roman amphitheatre, Petra rose early, checked out of The Traveller's Rest and drove dispiritedly back to Sudbury. The whole expedition had been a waste of time.

CHAPTER

14

Frustrated and tired after the long drive home, Petra let herself into her small apartment, dumped her bag on the floor and opened the hall closet to hang up her ski jacket. A mass of gear for all four seasons greeted her eyes. The rail groaned as she pushed things aside to make space. Something fell off the shelf above and disappeared. Cursing like Ken Graceby, she threw her jacket onto a chair. Time for a clean-out, but not now.

She launched the organizer on her laptop, checked her schedule and made a note to start spring cleaning in a couple of weeks. Then she checked her email. Three unread, including one from Martin. She wasn't feeling sociable so left it until last.

Her electricity bill for the two months ending February 15 was double what she'd been expecting. The special course in dog handling that she'd applied for was full. The next one was in six months' time. Petra banged the lid of her computer shut and went to bed.

In the morning she remembered to read Martin's email.

Three weeks later, Petra met Martin at the Toronto International Airport to fly to Las Vegas. It was the first

Saturday of the March break school holiday – not the best time to travel. Hundreds of families heading for the sun, a red terrorist alert level, and the United States' usual distrust of everyone wanting to visit their country made for irritatingly slow lines at Security and Immigration.

As they ran to the departure gate, their names boomed out over the public address system. With scarlet cheeks, they boarded the plane and made their way down the aisle to the only vacant seats – two with extra legroom in the exit row on the left-hand side. Judging by the looks on their faces, several passengers had been planning to move into them immediately after take-off.

'Remind me never to have children,' Martin grumbled as he flopped into his seat.

'I'll hold you to that. Timbuktu for you if you do!' Petra patted his arm affectionately. 'I don't think I've thanked you properly for arranging this. I've never seen Betty Graceby perform.'

'No one has in recent years. This is the first concert she's given since Joe LePinto died. It's causing quite a sensation.'

'I wonder what changed her mind about performing, and how on earth did you get tickets?'

'Betty sent them as a thank-you for those photos I took of you all on board *Gloriana*. She wants me to take some more – exclusive, she said.'

'You're a smooth one!'

Martin's eyes lit up behind his glasses. 'And now for the rest of my surprise. I've booked us in at The Poseidon.'

'That's Cliff Graceby's hotel!'

147

'Right on! When we were in Nassau last November, he was touting it as an ultra-deluxe boutique hotel, so I thought I'd do a review.'

'Good idea.'

'I booked two rooms,' he added, pretending to concentrate on the view through the window.

Petra's initial reaction was one of relief. He wasn't trying to take advantage of the situation. Then she saw the wry smile on his face and wished, just for an instant, that things could be different. He was such a *nice* guy.

Cliff's hotel was on a side street, close to The Strip, a few blocks away from that most revered of Vegas establishments, the Bellagio. It should have been a good address. The portico was imposing, though the paint on the columns was beginning to peel. On either side of the glass entrance doors stood a marble horse two to three metres high, facing towards the centre. Each of the horses was attended by a lithe naked groom.

'A nice pair of Marlys,' Martin commented as the doors opened. 'You know the originals are in Paris at the entrance to the Champs Élysées.'

'I'm sure Betty donated these.'

'No doubt, and how apt,' Martin said. 'According to my research, Poseidon was the Greek god of earthquakes, the sea and horses – and he's identified with the Roman god Neptune.'

'A few rungs lower down the ladder, I'd say,' Petra remarked as she surveyed the lobby. It was furnished in Empire style with velvet couches and gilded side-tables.

Had it not been for the faded cushions and the rings and scratches on the tabletops, the effect would have been chic and elegant. There was no bellboy, and no clerk standing behind the marble-topped reception desk at the far end of the lobby.

Petra walked across to the desk. A piece of white card propped against a pile of tourist maps said "Ring bell for service". She rang the bell and waited impatiently for the service to materialize. The plane had arrived late and they had less than an hour in which to check in, freshen up, change into evening dress and get to Betty's concert.

Someone had left a copy of that morning's *Vegas Chronicle* on top of the desk. Petra picked it up and stared at the headline. *"Can Graceby still grace? It's double or quits!"* The rather snide female columnist pointed out that at seventy plus years of age, after a hip replacement and several operations to repair damage sustained in the accident that killed Joe LePinto, Betty could hardly be expected to shake the famous Graceby legs in the same way as before, even if her singing voice could still enthrall.

'Look at this,' Petra called to Martin who was examining some framed engravings of Egypt and the Nile. She thrust the paper into his hands. 'It's garbage! My bet's on Betty. She'll show them,' she said, with a confidence she hoped wasn't misplaced. Frustrated, she rang the bell again.

On Petra's third insistent ring, a door in the panelled wall next to the desk opened. A tall woman with frizzy black hair and chocolate skin stepped into the lobby.

'OK, OK, hold your horses. I'm here.' The woman, of indeterminate age, planted her hands on incredibly skinny hips. 'You must be Minx & Johnson. You sound like a pair of lawyers.'

Petra held out her hand. 'I'm Minx, Petra Minx, and this is Martin Johnson. And you are?'

'Ebony. Bony to some, 'cos I'm all skin and bone.'

Martin was running his eye up and down Ebony's athletic figure as if he were assessing her chances of beating the world sprint record. Her black leather hotpants clung like a second skin to her slender frame.

Petra nudged him. 'Martin, you're staring.'

Ebony rattled the copper bangles that adorned both her wrists. 'You'd better come through to the bar. I'm on my own tonight. His lordship and m'lady are high-rolling it over at the Arcadia Palace.' The word "m'lady" was imbued with heavy sarcasm. Ebony turned and strode towards the door in the panelling. As she walked, the high ribbed heels on her copper-coloured sandals flashed orange warning lights.

Martin put his finger to his lips and pointed to the flashing lights. Without comment, they followed Ebony into a dimly lit room that appeared to be a combination bar-restaurant. A row of booths with red plush seats ran along the inside wall. In the centre of the room, wooden tables and chairs were grouped around a raised circular dais. Several tables on the street side were set with stainless steel cutlery on plastic tablemats. The windows were heavily draped in red and gold velvet. In a corner near the bar, a group of obese white men were playing poker; they looked up as Petra and Martin entered.

'Not quite what I was expecting. It looks like a cross

between an English pub and a New Orleans brothel,' Martin whispered.

'How would you know?'

Martin tapped his nose.

Ebony turned and threw him a disdainful look. 'This used to be a top-class French place until his lordship and m'lady had other ideas.'

'By "his lordship", I presume you mean Cliff Graceby,' Petra said. 'I thought he lost his wife to cancer not long ago.'

'Ah, another one who's met the man! Wives aren't difficult to lose – or find for that matter – in Nevada. I'm the original wife. This one's probably number three wannabe: definitely bad news or I'm a Dutchman!'

Petra smiled at Ebony, a smile of genuine delight that lit up her heart-shaped face. 'And that you're not!'

What Ebony was, Petra realized, was Ken Graceby's mother, which would explain the African cast she had noticed in his features on her first day in Nassau. Cliff Graceby's sob story about his late wife was an old trick she should never have fallen for. He was too glib by half and it wouldn't surprise her if he were involved in all kinds of shady dealings. She would plan her revenge in due course. The most important thing was to get to Betty's concert.

The ballroom at the Arcadia Palace Hotel and Casino was bursting at the seams. None of the high rollers wanted to miss Betty Graceby's performance. Now that dinner was over, the tension was building. Black-coated waiters wove through the tables, delivering coffee and *petits fours*, and topping up glasses with wine or champagne. Belle Époque mirrors down the sides of the room reflected the crystal and silver and the rivers of diamonds worn by the female patrons.

In front of the stage, right in the middle, stood one empty table. An ice bucket containing a magnum of champagne had been sitting there since the beginning of the evening. Heads turned as four people made their way towards it.

The babble of voices rose to a crescendo then subsided as the newcomers took their seats. Immediately, the chandeliers dimmed. Above the emerald velvet curtains that concealed the stage, a row of lights began to flash in sequence. A hush descended over the crowd.

Petra and Martin slid through the doors at the rear of the ballroom just in time to see the curtains part. Petra felt the coolness of the wall as she leaned against it in her backless red dress. Martin, wearing a black tuxedo like the rest of the men, had diminished the sartorial effect by choosing a frilly shirtfront.

The gap in the curtains revealed nothing but darkness. A few whispers broke the silence. Then the sound of a gong reverberated through the room. Petra focussed her attention on the stage, her stomach full of butterflies. This was a defining moment for Betty and her fans: the return of a legend to the place that had made her famous.

Slowly, the curtains drew back. As they did so, the lights in the ballroom were extinguished. For a few seconds, there was total blackness. Nobody spoke. Then a chair creaked and a girl gave a nervous titter.

Just as Petra's eyes were adjusting to the darkness, a

spotlight came on. In the centre of the stage stood a circular structure bedecked with shimmering gold hangings. Reminiscent of the tents belonging to desert rulers in Hollywood epics, it was guarded by two turbaned young men wearing nothing but loincloths and scimitars. The oil on their bodies gleamed in the soft light like the patina on a pair of bronze statues.

A melody, in a minor key, played in the background. The two young men seized their scimitars and swept the hangings apart. There was a sharp intake of breath as the audience absorbed the fact that the alcove behind was empty. The hangings dropped back into place. Betty was playing an elusive game.

The plaintive melody continued. The guardians of the golden tent planted their feet and squatted gently, flexing the muscles of their thighs. Then, from between the hangings, the toe of a golden shoe appeared. Slowly a foot emerged, followed by a slim ankle, a neat calf, and a knee.

The silence in the room was absolute. Petra clutched Martin's arm. Her pulse began to race as the Graceby leg dipped and rose in time to the music. She could only begin to imagine the effort required as the thin but shapely leg executed a series of perfect circles before drawing back into the diaphanous folds of the fabric.

The tempo changed, and the crowd began to clap to the rhythm of a Scott Joplin tune. The two young men leapt to attention and slashed the hangings aside. A figure rose from the canopied daybed. Petra held her breath. Betty Graceby stood, poised and elegant, in front of her adoring public once again.

Like the Chiparus bronze dancers of the 1930s, she wore a burnished helmet over her silver hair and a short pleated tunic cinched at the waist. With a coy smile on her face, she turned her head to the right, extended her arms at a forty-five degree angle and flicked her wrists upwards. The skirt of her tunic ballooned out, and she executed a few steps of the Charleston on her spike-heeled shoes. She struck another pose and danced again, held the next pose then danced some more.

The simple moves brought the house down. Betty must have worked non-stop with her physiotherapist to be able to raise and lower her limbs with such style and precision, and no hint of tiredness.

Having proved her agility, Betty bowed her head and waited until silence fell. Then she lifted her face to the audience and began to sing.

Petra listened and watched in fascination as Betty captivated the room with a range of songs from wartime favourites to modern classics. It was a virtuoso performance, cleverly staged to highlight her strengths and mask any weaknesses in delivery. The two male attendants, ballet-trained, supported her, lifted her and passed her between them, perfect foils for her lightness and grace. After nearly two hours on stage, Betty launched into a throaty number that sent ripples up and down Petra's spine.

As the last notes faded away, the room erupted. So much for the columnist in the *Vegas Chronicle*. Martin was stomping his feet and shouting "Bravo!" Petra clapped until her hands were sore as Betty took her bow. Betty acknowledged the contribution of the male dancers and the band that had played throughout the evening then turned to her left. A handsome man emerged from the wings bearing an enormous bouquet of flowers. A head taller than Betty, older than her son Cliff, he was in his mid-sixties Petra estimated.

Resting the bouquet on his left arm, he picked up Betty's right hand and brought it to his lips, looking deep into her eyes as he did so. 'My darling, you were magnificent,' he said for all to hear. Releasing her hand, he placed his unencumbered arm around her shoulders and addressed the crowd.

'You have just witnessed an extraordinary performance by someone whose talent has been missed by us all for far too long. Please join me in thanking Betty for daring to tread the boards again and giving us once more a night to remember.'

'Who's that?' Petra whispered to Martin.

'An impresario by the name of Larry Fishton,' he murmured. 'It looks as though he's on very good terms with Betty.'

Betty accepted the bouquet and seized Larry's hand, lifting it high in the air. 'It's my turn to express my thanks – in fact, my eternal gratitude – to you, Larry, for persuading me to end my self-imposed retirement, and to you all for being such a tremendous audience. However, I must tell you that I don't intend to return to the concert circuit. I'm much too old to do this more than once in a while, but I will continue to perform in selected venues and, from time to time, for you, my dear friends, here at the Arcadia Palace.'

The crowd was already on its feet, whistling and clapping, begging for an encore.

'That's all for tonight, Ladies and Gentlemen,' Betty said. 'Frankly, I'm pooped!' She kissed the tips of her fingers to the audience and turned towards Larry. For a moment, they stood together in an intimate embrace. Then they left the stage and the curtains closed.

Petra whistled under her breath. 'They sure appear to be close friends. That's wonderful: it's given her a new lease on life.'

'Agreed,' Martin said, 'but take a look at Cliff Graceby. He's sitting at that table in the middle.' He pointed to where four people sat, right in front of the stage, on one side of a large circular table.

Cliff Graceby was glaring at Larry Fishton, who had reappeared on stage and was holding the curtain open for Betty to take a final bow. Cliff was clenching his jaw so hard that Petra thought he might stand up and shake his fist at the impresario. On Cliff's right sat a platinum blonde, then a girl with short russet-red hair and, next to her, Ken Graceby. Ken leaned across to his father and touched his arm. Cliff shook him off and snapped his fingers at a passing waiter. Suddenly, the blonde got up, thumped Cliff's shoulder and walked away.

'I think it's time to go and say hello, don't you, Martin?' Petra said with a grin.

CHAPTER

15

Shock registered on Cliff Graceby's face as he took in Petra's porcelain skin and vivid blue-green eyes. 'What the hell … ?'

'I was hoping for a warmer welcome than that.' She noticed immediately that his face was more florid than it had been four months earlier and his forehead etched with fine lines.

'Sorry … you're the last person I was expecting.'

'Who were you expecting?' she asked lightly, pointing to the empty chairs next to him. Ken had succeeded in controlling his astonishment better than his father. In fact, he looked perfectly at ease, sitting with his arm draped round the shoulders of the girl on his left. Petra offered her hand first to him then to the fresh-faced young woman beside him. After a brief exchange of pleasantries, she responded to a tap on her shoulder and turned to include Martin in the group. 'Ken, Cliff, I'm sure you remember my friend, Martin Johnson.'

To her surprise, Ken made no comment about Martin's attire or the camera with its flash attachment that hung amid the ruffles just above his blue cummerbund. Instead, he stood up to shake hands and showed no sign of the aggression that had marked his behaviour in Nassau.

Linda, whom he introduced as his partner, had an easy smile and a warm manner. She patted the vacant chair and invited Petra to sit between her and Cliff. 'Some big shot was supposed to join us tonight but he didn't show, and Cliff's lady friend has just run off – that's why his nose is out of joint.'

'You don't know what you're talking about,' Cliff snapped. 'And you,' he said, addressing Martin in a tone full of venom, 'I know your kind. No doubt you're planning to sell all our secrets to the press.'

'Clifford, that's no way to talk to anyone. I shouldn't have to keep reminding you boys. Martin and Petra are my special guests and I expect you to behave accordingly.' Unnoticed by any of the group, Betty had arrived on the arm of the tanned blonde-haired Larry Fishton. Two waiters hurried to assist them with their chairs.

'I'm so pleased you could share this evening with me, my dears,' Betty continued. 'Pay no attention to that ungrateful son of mine. Now wasn't that a blast?'

Betty radiated happiness. She was euphoric at the success of the show and full of the forty-five day cruise that she and Larry were about to take from Fort Lauderdale to Los Angeles and back, via the Panama Canal. She had undertaken to give two concerts on board the ship, one on the outbound voyage, one on the return. Petra was delighted to see Betty imbued with a new sense of purpose and self-worth. After a trauma such as the death of a loved one, it was an essential part of the healing process.

While Martin discussed the performance with Betty and Larry, Petra took the opportunity to get to know Linda. Ken sat smiling as she told Petra how she had met him in Nassau when she took a wounded dove to the bird sanctuary. She loved the outdoors and seemed an uncomplicated soul. Ken had lost his abrasiveness, whether through Linda's ministrations or not, Petra couldn't tell. In any event, the result was a much more agreeable personality.

Cliff was the only member of the group who refused to join in the conversation. He sat in grumpy silence, wiping his nose frequently and downing champagne. Just before midnight, he appeared to take hold of himself. Leaning towards Petra, he apologized for his moroseness, blaming it on the difficulties the hotel industry was facing due to unreliable staff, the looming economic crisis, et cetera. Petra listened with only half an ear, much more interested to hear Betty lauding Ken for his involvement in the sanctuary. Martin, she noted, had left the table to patrol the room. The magazine that had paid for his trip was expecting some iconic images of the rich and famous.

A waiter bearing a tray of empty glasses paused to whisper something in Cliff's ear. He stood up at once, muttered 'Sorry, Mother, I have to go,' and followed the waiter through the tables.

Many of the guests were leaving the ballroom to continue the evening in the casino, yet there was something odd about Cliff's hurried departure. Petra craned her neck to see which way he had gone. Betty, Linda and Ken were engrossed in a story Larry was telling about a diva whose strapless dress refused to stay up.

Picking up her purse, Petra murmured 'Excuse me' and made her way as quickly as she could to the back of the room. In the crush around the door, Cliff had come face to face with a man in a batik shirt. He was the same height and build as one of the men she had seen at *Neptunis* on the boat Ken had chartered. As Cliff stopped in front of the man, two taller, stouter gentlemen in ill-fitting penguin suits closed in behind him. The man in front of Cliff tapped him on the chest, turned to the door, and the platoon marched out.

It was a classic manoeuvre. Petra followed them through the foyer, skirting animated groups of people discussing Betty's performance. She hurried to catch up until she found her path blocked by another man in evening dress. He towered above her, as impregnable as a castle wall.

'Can I help you?' he asked, planting stubby-fingered hands on her shoulders.

Petra attempted to shake him off with a shimmy and a side step but realized it wasn't going to be that easy. She winced as the giant tightened his grip and brought his face down close to hers, so close that she had to turn away to avoid his sour breath. As she did so, she heard Martin's voice.

'Hold it, Sir, Madam! Thank you! Very nice!' Heads turned to watch, the camera flashed and Martin appeared at the side of the giant. 'The lady's looking for me. She doesn't need your help.'

The giant looked confused. Petra stepped forward and, with great deliberation, trod first on his right foot then on his left. She focussed her energy and brought all her weight to bear before giving him an angelic smile and walking away on Martin's arm.

'Right place, right time. I owe you one, Martin.'

'Actually, you owe me two. I got some excellent shots of Cliff's handlers.'

'He does seem to be digging himself in deep.'

If Cliff had heard Petra's words at that moment, he probably would not have disagreed. The tall man in the batik shirt sitting on the opposite side of the green baize-topped card table was not going to take no for an answer. During the winter months, against Cliff's better judgement, Ken had made several runs without incident. Each time, he had picked up a couple of "refugees" and delivered them to the designated drop-off point. He asked no questions, told as few lies as possible and pocketed the dough. Apparently this was no longer enough.

Cliff wiped his nose. On the table was a pack of cards. The man in the batik shirt picked it up and dealt himself three, laying them face down on the table. He placed the rest of the pack in front of Cliff and said 'Cut!'

Cliff did as he was told. The dots on the back of the cards jumped like fleas on a feral cat as he fought to control his nerves. This was not a game he knew how to play.

The man in the batik shirt turned the middle card over to reveal the Joker. 'That, my friend, is you. A man with a weakness.' Slowly, he turned over the two cards flanking the Joker: the King of Spades and the King of Hearts. 'Take a card.'

Cliff slid the top card off the pile. It was the second Joker, which he placed on the table in front of him.

'That is also you. Take another.'

This time Cliff drew the Jack of Clubs.

'That is your idiot son.'

The man in the batik shirt picked up the remainder of the pack and dealt himself another row of cards, turning each one face up as he did so. Without exception, they were Aces, Kings and Queens. 'The cards are stacked against you.'

Cliff pushed back his chair. 'This is all smoke and mirrors. You're wasting my time.'

The man in the batik shirt nodded to his two goons who moved swiftly from the door to stand behind Cliff. 'I don't think so, Mr. Graceby. And remember this, where there's smoke, there's fire.'

'You'd better tell me what you want.'

'Transport for two into the Northern U.S. This summer. We'll take care of the paperwork.'

'You're crazy!'

'That's for us to decide.'

'What's the matter with Florida, the usual pipeline? Or the Bahamas, the same as before?'

'Too many police, too many informers. We've been watching your movements. We know you can do it.'

'This is a whole new ball game. Too far. Too risky.'

'Come on, Mr. Graceby, what alternative do you have? You do this job to our satisfaction and you'll see how easily the money will flow.'

Cliff closed his eyes. A variety of emotions flitted across his face. 'I'll think about it.'

'Don't think too long, my friend. My customers are not known for their patience.'

Cliff kicked a Coke can dropped by some lout of a tourist viciously out of his way as he left the Arcadia Palace Hotel a few minutes later. Above him, the desert sky was a canopy of dark blue velvet. The stars were tiny pinpricks, eclipsed by the flashing neon and gaudy displays below. Everything was a mess. In this cardboard city where fortunes could be won and lost in an evening, it seemed as though he would never shake off the bad luck that had dogged him his whole life. If Joe LePinto had not stopped him from dating his daughter Elena … if Joe had adopted him as a son and taken him into the business … if Joe had bequeathed him part of his fortune instead of leaving it all to Betty … if Betty were not so tight-fisted … things would have been different. He and Ken would not have been forced to bargain with the old fool. What had started as a fair exchange of money for silence was becoming a millstone around Cliff's neck.

The raucous cries coming from the bar at The Poseidon told Cliff that the Saturday night pole dancing was finding favour with the patrons. He pulled the door open and was met by a fug of cigarette smoke. Provided he kept up his payments, the clean-air police would stay well away. A bunch of French-Canadians, all male, were in town for a quick fling, no holds barred. Vegas was cheap, safe and clean compared to other destinations such as Haiti and Cuba, the dusky beauties on offer less likely to leave a legacy that would be difficult to explain at home.

For the moment, Ebony was the centre of attention, pivoting round the pole in her orange flashing heels. She swung low and bent backwards, arching her back and rubbing herself up and down the pole. Several hostesses in red leather shorts and black Spandex tops stood watching. Cliff grabbed one of them by the arm and pushed her towards a pot-bellied sex tourist whose eyes were popping.

'Go shake your booty for that guy! And double the rate. Twenty for a table dance, fifty for anything more.'

She shot a resentful look at Cliff as he grabbed the next girl in line. 'You come with me,' he said, dragging her after him as he strode out of the room.

Petra had been forced to agree with Martin that it would be sheer folly to try and follow Cliff. They had no idea where he was being taken nor by whom, but it didn't look good. It took them a while to work their way back through the ballroom against the tide of people heading for the casino. When they returned to Betty's table, Ken was staring at his grandmother with his mouth half open. Petra thought immediately of the awful word "gobsmacked" she had learned in England. He looked exactly as though he had been smacked in the face.

'I've asked Betty to marry me,' Larry said by way of explanation. 'And she's agreed to consider it.'

'See what a stunning ring Larry's given me,' Betty said, holding out her hand for Petra to admire the art deco platinum piece set with diamonds. 'I feel like a young girl again, but I've told Larry I need time to think about it. Getting married would change things a lot.'

Not least for her son and grandson, thought Petra.

'For the better, my darling, for the better,' Larry said.

A series of emotions flashed across Ken's face – anger, revulsion and something like desperation.

'I think Ken's having trouble visualizing me as a newly wed,' Betty remarked.

'But it's wonderful news.' Linda beamed at Betty and squeezed Ken's hand.

'Oh, it's great,' he said. 'Just what we've been waiting for! Grandmother getting hitched in the Elvis chapel.'

'Why don't we all get married there?' Larry suggested. 'Make it a threesome. Show Vegas how it's really done!'

Many toasts later, Petra and Martin swayed arm in arm back to The Poseidon. Petra had taken off her Jimmy Choo look-alike shoes and was carrying them in one hand.

'How about it, Petra?' Martin asked. 'Vegas never sleeps. There's bound to be a 24-hour walk-in chapel. We could get married tonight.'

'And rue it in the morning?'

A look of despair passed across his face and he pulled his arm out of hers.

Oh God, she'd done it again: spoken without thinking first. And why did she have to keep pushing him away?

CHAPTER

16

When Petra emerged from her room at The Poseidon next morning, Martin's black shoes were lying outside his door. What the hell were they doing there? He had been wearing them last night. Had he left them for polishing without realizing that one of the girls from the bar could have construed it as a signal that he would welcome a visit? There'd been plenty of scantily clad girls hanging around the lobby when they got back from the casino and no security guard at the desk.

After Betty's champagne, they had both been more than a little unsteady and had gone upstairs straightaway. Martin had wished her goodnight, given her a peck on the cheek and disappeared into his room before she could formulate her apology. 'Look,' she had wanted to say, 'I know your proposal was genuine, Martin. I'm sorry I treated it as a joke, but we'd regret it for sure. Your friendship is what matters to me.' But the words had remained unsaid. Had he been so crushed that he'd needed to seek solace elsewhere?

Petra shook her head to clear it and knocked on Martin's door. There was no point in trying to guess his state of mind. Better to spend time with him and jolly him back to reality. It was ten thirty and she desperately needed a coffee and something sweet. For all Cliff's boasting about The Poseidon, the hotel apparently didn't run to room service of the kind that signified food.

There was no sound from Martin's room. Petra knocked again. Still no answer. That was weird. He was usually up early, even after a night on the town. Perplexed, she caught the elevator down to the lobby and went into the bar-restaurant.

Ebony was there, washing and polishing glasses. Otherwise it was empty. Petra took a seat at the bar. 'You work hard. Don't you ever have any time off?'

'Not much. It's no big deal. What can I get you? Coffee?'

'Yes please, black, and a Danish. Do you live on the premises?'

'Servant's garret, in the basement though, not the attic.'

'What about Cliff Graceby?'

'Opposite end of the spectrum – penthouse fit for a lord.'

Ebony had a surprisingly educated way of describing things as well as a self-deprecating streak. Her life seemed to revolve around her place of work – as Sam's had at *Neptunis*.

'I'd have thought it was awkward, having your ex in the same space.'

'Nah! We divorced years ago, and he couldn't do what he does without me.'

'Meaning?'

'Somebody's got to run this place, the staff, the training and the rest.'

'Is it easy to get staff?'

'It depends what you're willing to accept. Locals cost more, but they're no more reliable.'

'Isn't it difficult to bring people into the U.S.?'

'There are channels.'

Petra swallowed a mouthful of Danish. 'Were you born in the U.S.?'

'No, Haiti.'

'So how did you get here?'

'I came as a student.'

'Let me guess,' Petra said. 'The LePinto Culinary Institute in Florida?'

'Right on.'

'Then you stayed and got a job here?'

'Twenty-five years ago. More coffee?'

'Please, I need it.'

Ebony put down her drying cloth. She refilled Petra's mug and slid the plate of Danish pastries towards her. 'Help yourself. I think I'll join you.'

'Let's move to a booth then. It'll be more comfortable.' Petra carried her coffee and the plate of pastries over to the middle booth and sat down.

Ebony slid onto the banquette opposite. 'What's your connection with the Gracebys?'

'Friend of the family.'

'Then you know Miss Graceby bought this hotel for Cliff. That's how I met him.'

'Did you get married here?'

Ebony snorted. 'Cliff wouldn't have married me at all if I hadn't gotten pregnant with Ken. He wanted me to get an abortion. Then Miss Graceby found out and insisted he do the right thing. She's a doll.'

Petra nodded. That made some sense. Betty knew how hard it was to bring up a child as a single mother, and Joe LePinto came from the old school where family was everything. Yet she couldn't imagine them relishing the idea of a Haitian daughter-in-law, even if Joe's parents were from Puerto Rico.

'They weren't too happy about the African component,' Ebony added with a trace of irony but no bitterness. 'LePinto only accepted it because he wanted Cliff to stay away from his daughter Elena. He couldn't stand the fact that they were in love …'

'Whoa! Rewind! If you and Cliff were together, where does Elena fit in?'

'Cliff took up with me on the rebound.'

'So he went out with Elena?'

'He sure did. She was studying here in Vegas, living with LePinto, when Miss Graceby arrived on the scene with Cliff. He and Elena hit it off straightaway.'

'And Joe was furious?'

'What would you expect? Cliff was into motorbikes and leather and who knows what else. LePinto had better things in mind for his daughter. He sent her back to her mother in Buenos Aires. Cliff never really got over it.'

'Has he seen Elena since?'

'Not to my knowledge.'

'Is she still in Argentina?'

'No idea.' Ebony looked at Petra curiously. 'How come you don't know all this if you're a family friend?'

'Betty and Joe knew my father. Betty's never said anything to me about Elena and Cliff. It's a fascinating story.'

'I guess she wouldn't. It's ancient history now. I don't even know why I'm telling you, except that you're easy to talk to.'

The door to the bar opened. Ebony jumped up and began to clear the table as Cliff walked in. His timing was uncanny.

'Don't you have better things to do than gossip?' he said to her in a tone that reminded Petra of the way Dick Reed, the resort manager at *Neptunis*, had spoken to Sam.

'I invited Ebony to sit with me,' Petra said. 'She needed a break.'

Cliff rubbed a hand across his forehead. 'Sorry. I'm not at my best this morning. And I apologize for my behaviour last night. I'm under a bit of stress at the moment.'

No shit, Petra thought. He didn't have to say anything, it showed in his face. Yet he had maintained his physique and his stylishness. Designer jeans, black shirt and leather jacket, the light, lemony cologne. Not a bad package. What she wanted to do was determine the real cause of the stress that was ageing him rapidly.

The obvious place to start was with the man in the batik shirt. Who was he? Just a messenger, or the one giving the stress? He had support, that much was clear, so which organization did he belong to? Why was he pressuring Cliff? For the time being, Petra had no answers. On the other hand, Betty seemed to be out of the equation now that she had Larry. And as long as she was fine, Petra didn't give a damn about Cliff Graceby and his son. They weren't her responsibility, although Betty would be upset if anything happened to them.

'Why don't we go for a walk?' Petra suggested.

'Walk? Not on my radar. Tennis, swimming, boxing, yes; walking, no. How about we take my Harley up to the dam for lunch?'

So he was still into motorbikes. Petra hesitated. She wasn't good with bikes and it would be impossible to talk while they were on the road. Nevertheless, it would give her a chance to get closer to Cliff and once they arrived at the restaurant, she could try to get some answers.

'Come on. I'll lend you a helmet.'

'Only if you show me Betty's memorial to Joe. You promised you would, remember?'

'Of course,' he said, attempting a smile that didn't quite work.

Ebony waved to Petra from behind the bar where she was sorting cutlery. 'Take it easy.'

Cliff's motorbike was a lime green Harley with high rise handlebars. The pillion seat and footrests were comfortably broad – a bike made for two. Petra sat astride the bike waiting for Cliff to pull out into the street. She calmed her nerves by imagining she was on the back of a jet ski. Speed over water never fazed her; speed over ground had, ever since Romeo's death more than a decade ago. It still did, but she was learning to handle it better.

The streets were quiet on a Sunday morning. Despite the urban sprawl, it wasn't long before they were out of the city. The stark scenery of the desert contrasted sharply with the glitz and glamour of the downtown core. The road was dusty, the air clear and dry.

Petra remembered a piece of trivia she had picked up from Martin. In Vegas there were no storm water drains because it never rained. He'd been there once when the heavens had opened and the streets had turned into raging torrents. Nobody ever went to Vegas with an umbrella or gumboots.

Half an hour out of town, Cliff pulled over to the right and skidded to a stop on the side of the road. He kicked down the stands and dismounted.

Petra lifted her visor. 'Is this it?'

'Yes,' he said, gesturing to where a greenstone cross stood a short distance away from the road.

'Can I take a closer look?'

'Be my guest.'

Cliff folded his arms across his chest and stayed by his Harley as Petra picked her way across an expanse of rough ground towards the cross. When she came close, she was puzzled. The carving on the cross showed an eagle soaring above a desert landscape against a backdrop of mountain peaks. It was beautifully executed, but there was no date or inscription. Petra looked across to the other side of the valley. The jagged skyline was the same as in the carved decoration. The cross could have been a monument to Nature herself.

Cliff seemed to anticipate her question. 'Mother insisted she didn't want to wear her heart on her sleeve so that every Tom, Dick and Harry could make a mockery of her love for Joe. Mother Nature had taken him to her bosom and there he would lie.'

How like Betty! Strength of character with a dash of the theatrical. 'So it was just a terrible accident,' Petra said.

'As I told you, there was no other explanation. Ken picked up the car after it had been in for service. He reported no issues. The police were satisfied it was an accident, Mother too.'

'But it must have been hard for her not to blame you as the driver, even if it wasn't your fault.'

Anger sparked in Cliff's eyes. 'Don't go stirring up trouble where there isn't any. The matter's closed. Let's go. I could use some food.'

Fifteen minutes later, Cliff parked the Harley and unzipped his leather jacket. The St. Christopher medallion shone bright against his tanned chest in the open neck of his black cotton shirt. He took off his helmet and ran a hand through his silver hair. Petra undid her jacket, took off the borrowed helmet and shook out her long black hair. Feeling a little more presentable, she walked with Cliff to the restaurant. He seemed to have forgotten his outburst.

'Is this where you were bringing Betty and Joe?'

'Yes. They used to love this place. Now Mother won't come here.'

The terrace overlooking the lake was already crowded with people enjoying the view and the sunshine. After a few words with the maître d', Cliff led Petra to a small table in the corner.

'You seemed to be getting along well with my ex,' he said when they were seated.

'Exes, currents, wannabes, I'm an easygoing person.'

Cliff cocked an eyebrow. 'Really? As I think I said before, why do I get the impression that there's more to you than meets the eye. Not that what the eye sees is in any way disappointing.' He glanced at the deep V-neck of her blue shirt where the black and silver cross hung tantalizingly low.

'Are you flirting with me again?'

On the way to the lake, sitting tight behind Cliff, Petra had had ample time to reflect on her feelings for him. "Ambivalent" about summed them up. She had also had time to work out her revenge for his misrepresentation of the truth about his wife's death.

'If you are,' she continued, 'it's a waste of effort. Martin asked me to marry him last night, and I'm going to accept his proposal.'

'There must be something in the Vegas air,' Cliff said sourly. 'First my mother, now you. And Ken and Linda are like turtledoves.' He sniffed.

'I'm so pleased, especially for Betty. She was stunning last night. You must have seen her give some fantastic performances over the years.'

'Yeah, I got dragged to most of them and left backstage. At least until I was old enough to look after myself.' Cliff sniffed again and pulled out a handkerchief. 'Allergies,' he said, wiping his nose.

Petra considered him carefully. Maybe, maybe not. Allergies weren't the only thing that inflamed the nasal membranes.

'How was your meeting?' she asked, changing horses.

'What meeting?'

'When you left the table last night at the Arcadia Palace, Linda said you were supposed to see some big shot.'

'Oh that! We had a good talk then the guys wanted to play poker.'

174

'Are you a gambler?'

'I like the occasional game of poker, not the tables.'

'High stakes?'

'Not really. I can't afford to lose too much.'

And that was probably the truth, Petra thought, given the state of The Poseidon and the fact that Cliff had inherited nothing from Joe. She was curious to know more about Cliff's relationship with Joe's daughter, Elena, and wanted to ask Cliff about her, but first she needed to consider what Ebony had told her. Otherwise she might go about it the wrong way.

As Petra ate her steak, she wondered when and why The Poseidon's restaurant had ceased to be a gourmet French bistro and turned into a sleazy joint. Sex tourism, if that was what Cliff was involved in, brought in lots of cash, yet he didn't seem to have any. Who was he beholden to? The Mafia?

'You were complaining about the difficulties in the hotel industry,' she said. 'Is that why you changed the restaurant?'

'People don't want heavy sauces any more; they want pasta and lighter fare – pesto, carpaccio, olive oil with their bread … and French wines are too expensive.'

'But what about the décor and the waitresses' attire?'

'Saturday night is theme night for the tourists.'

'And that kind of thing brings them in?'

'Yes, it does. There's a lot of competition here in Vegas. Anything that differentiates us is good.'

'Not exactly boutique hotel material! You need to spruce up the lobby, update the look.'

'What are you now, an interior decorator?'

'Just trying to help.'

'Well don't. I don't need it.' Cliff scratched his head. 'I'm sorry. It seems as though I'm always apologizing to you. I'm under a lot of pressure right now. I hope you'll bear with me.'

'And if I won't? What then?'

Late in the afternoon, Petra and Cliff arrived back at The Poseidon. Martin was sitting in the lobby with a worried frown on his face. He leapt out of his chair as soon as they walked in.

'I've been looking all over for you, Petra, including the Arcadia Palace. Where the hell were you?'

Petra bridled at his possessive tone. If she had had any intention of considering his proposal, that would have put the kibosh on it. 'I could ask you the same thing. I knocked on your door three times this morning. You'd already gone out.'

'I left you a phone message …'

'Which I didn't get,' she interrupted. 'Nothing works in this place.'

'Larry called and asked me over to The Venetian to take some publicity photos of him and Betty in a gondola. That's where they'll be getting married.'

'But Betty said she wouldn't be seeing anybody today. She wanted to rest.'

'I realize that. She apologized profusely for not saying goodbye. Made me promise to give you her love and tell you she'd see you this summer on Lake Huron.'

'Prima donnas, all of you!'

'There's no need to get so uptight, Petra! They gave me an exclusive. Do you understand what that means?'

'Don't patronize me, Martin!'

'Whatever happened to the wedding bells?' Cliff said, his lips twisting into a smile. 'I'll leave you two lovebirds to sort yourselves out. Let me know when you're ready to go to the airport. Ebony will get you a limousine.'

'What on earth is he talking about?' Martin asked.

Petra shrugged. 'I suggest we leave plenty of time to catch our flight.'

Cliff and Ebony came to the lobby to see them off. Ken and Linda had gone back to the Bahamas where, according to Cliff, Ken's fishing charter business was booming. While they waited for the limousine to arrive, Cliff tipped Petra under the chin and drew her towards him. 'Tit for tat,' he said. 'I'm sorry you're leaving. You should stay longer.'

'But I'm a working girl, remember!' she said with deliberate innuendo. 'And you have a hotel to run.'

'I'll always make time for you. Just say the word.'

Petra was relieved to see the limousine pull up outside. She managed to avoid Cliff's full-on-the-lips kiss although he pressed himself against her and held her for longer than she would have liked. Once she was seated safely in the car, she closed her eyes.

'He has a real hard-on for you,' Martin said. 'You could easily be Number four wannabe.'

'Don't be vulgar, Martin. You're not Ken Graceby, and I have no intention of being seduced by Cliff Graceby. The only reason I accepted his offer of a drive and lunch was to try and find out more about his operations. Those goons last night were serious. I don't suppose you saw them during your wanderings today?'

'Not a chance. Those kinds of guys melt into the walls and only reappear when there's mischief to be made.'

Petra stared out of the window as the limousine rolled along The Strip. Vegas was a shining pool of light in the black sea of the Nevada desert. The traffic was slow but kept moving until they got close to The Mirage where a crowd was gathering. People threaded their way through the stopped cars, ignoring the hooting. Martin looked at his watch.

'The volcano's about to erupt.' He leaned forward to switch on the TV that was set in the console in front of them. 'We'll see it better on screen. Then we can catch the local news.'

At eight o'clock precisely, the volcano spewed its fire to the delight of the masses. It was one of Vegas's most enduring attractions. As soon as it was over, the onlookers began to disperse, many of them to try their luck in The Mirage's casino. The limousine driver cursed as a bearded hippie tapped on the hood of the car and forced him to a complete stop again. 'I'm getting out of this mess,' he grunted, turning onto a boulevard that led to the freeway.

Petra closed her eyes again. Martin turned the TV down until it was just audible. They were about a mile from the airport when the newsreader said: 'We have some breaking news from The Strip. A fire has broken out a few blocks away from The Venetian. It appears to have started in the kitchens of The Poseidon Hotel. Our reporter Johan Glazer is on the scene.'

Petra jerked awake. 'What? Oh my God! Turn it up, Martin!'

'Shit!' Martin said. 'If we'd left a bit later, I could have had a real scoop!'

The face of a young man with pointed ears appeared on a screen behind the newsreader. 'Johan, what can you tell us about the situation at this time? Are there any casualties?'

'The fire service arrived on the scene a few minutes ago. It appears that the fire has not yet spread to the guest rooms, and the hotel has been evacuated. We don't know if anyone is trapped inside the kitchen area, but so far there are no reports of any casualties.'

Petra seized Martin's arm. 'We've got to go back. Betty might be there. She may be in danger. You could get some pictures, and we'll probably still make our flight.'

'You're even crazier than I thought, Petra, but OK. Take us back to The Poseidon,' he shouted to the driver. 'As fast as you can!'

Petra sat with her eyes glued to the TV, her breath coming in small gasps. She hadn't felt right leaving town without seeing Betty again. Now she wanted to make sure Betty wasn't hurt. In the distance, she heard sirens wailing. Suddenly she felt the urge to bite her nails, something she hadn't done since she was thirteen years old.

The street on which The Poseidon stood was blocked off by a couple of police cars with their lights flashing. Petra had her door open almost before the limousine came to a stop. 'Don't go anywhere. Stay here,' she instructed the driver. 'We'll be back.'

Keeping close to the buildings, she skirted the police cars and ran down the street. Martin caught up with her before she reached the hotel.

Petra remembered that The Poseidon's bar-restaurant overlooked a side street. She surmised that the kitchens would be behind it. The firefighters had hooked up their hoses and were pouring water onto the building. She ducked past a burly cop and ran towards the main entrance of the hotel. 'I'm family,' she gasped as he grabbed the back of her jacket. 'My grandmother's inside.'

'Nobody's inside, Ma'am. All the guests and staff have been evacuated.'

At that moment she heard Martin's voice. 'Petra! Over here!'

Across the street from the lobby was a clutch of people. Cliff was standing with his hand on Ebony's slim shoulders, a look of impotence on his face. Hers was a mask of anguish. Next to them, Larry was holding Betty close. Her expression was hard to read.

Petra ran to Betty. 'Thank God you're safe! I was so worried.'

'There's no need to be, my dear, I'm a tough old bird. It would take more than something like this to get rid of me. And naturally, we'll rebuild. It's a wonderful opportunity to revamp the restaurant.'

Cliff's phone began to ring. He moved away from the group to answer it. 'What is it?'

'Just a reminder, Mr. Graceby, that we're waiting to hear from you. I'm sure you'll come to the right decision.'

Petra and Martin boarded the plane just as the gate was closing. Red-faced and panting from the exertion of running through the airport, they collapsed into their extra-legroom seats and grinned at each other.

'Was that worth it, or was that worth it?' Martin asked.

'Incredible!' Petra exclaimed. 'I guess I'll let A.K. know that all things considered Betty Graceby is in fine form.'

CHAPTER

17

It was Canada Day, July the First: a holiday for most people, but not for Petra. At the end of May, she had been posted to Little Current, the largest town on Manitoulin Island and the gateway to the pristine waters of Lake Huron's North Channel. For a few short months, the island and the surrounding cruising grounds would be inundated with visitors, and the RCMP would be run off its feet.

Two flotillas were due in port that afternoon, one from Lake Michigan, the other from Georgian Bay. Each of the sixteen powerboats in the American flotilla had to be searched for guns, drugs, excess alcohol and anything else considered contraband or suspicious by the Canadian authorities. The fourteen sailboats in the Canadian group had to be welcomed and made to feel at home. It would take three teams of Customs and RCMP officers several hours to complete the task.

Petra glanced at her watch as she left the marina at Kincardine after an early breakfast with her friends. Eight o'clock. Conditions were good. The run back in her Seaswirl Striper would take about five hours, putting her in Little Current in plenty of time for her three o'clock shift.

Petra's Striper was her pride and joy: pride because she had saved ten thousand dollars towards it; joy because her father had matched her savings before he died. He had done the same for her sister Mira, although she had opted for a sailboat.

The Striper, which her father had named *Petrushka*, was a fast, compact, hardtop cruiser. It was a good sea boat, great for fishing and easy for one person to handle. Today there was no need to test the boat's capabilities: the surface of the lake was like glass. Petra began to whistle one of her father's favourite songs.

Two hours north, she ran into a bank of fog. She had seen it looming on the horizon well before she reached it. Now it was clinging to everything like wet dog hairs to a blanket. She switched on her foghorn and her running lights, and reduced her speed. Fog was a bummer. It could add hours to her journey time and if she weren't back for the start of her shift, she'd be chewed out by her colleagues.

Travelling as fast as she dared, Petra strained to see through the sea of white. The radar showed no targets, but not every vessel on the water had a good radar profile as she had learned over the years. Her eyes began to ache. This was no Scotch mist; it was as thick as porridge and getting worse.

Petra slowed down even further and resigned herself to a difficult day on the water. The temperature had plummeted and she reached for a jacket. She ran a hand through her dank hair and found herself thinking about Betty Graceby and her yacht, *Gloriana* – both of them so elegant. Most likely they would be making their way to the Great Lakes for the summer, in the capable hands of Captain James Freedy. What would Betty think if she could see Petra now? And what would she say if she found out Petra was RCMP?

In the three months that had gone by since her trip to Las Vegas, Petra had occasionally relived the excitement of Betty's concert, but was otherwise content in the knowledge that her friend was safe and happy. She had come to think of Betty as a friend, although the word didn't adequately describe her feelings. They were a complex mixture of respect, admiration, awe, and – dare she say it – love.

A large target appeared on the radar. Petra stopped trying to analyze her feelings for Betty and focussed on the screen. The target was off to her right and moving fast, travelling in the same direction. It would be the car ferry out of Tobermory, carrying hordes of visitors to Manitoulin Island. She reduced her speed another notch to let the ferry get ahead.

An hour later, Petra burst out of the fog into brilliant sunshine. She waved cheerily to a fishing boat that was heading towards the fog and opened the throttle. With luck, she would be back in Little Current in time to meet the flotillas.

When she rounded the last headland before the run-up the bay, she swore under her breath. Ahead of her lay the channel that led past the lighthouse to the Little Current swing bridge. Her Striper was low enough to pass under the bridge, but she would have to wait her turn. A long procession of boats was making for the bridge, which would open at two o'clock.

Petra counted a dozen or more sailboats and realized it must be the flotilla from Georgian Bay. Traffic at the bridge would be stalled for a long time while they picked their way through against the current. She turned *Petrushka* to port, wondering whether it would be quicker to head for the marina on the near side of the bridge and call her partner, Ed Spinone, to pick her up from there.

As she was debating the question, Petra caught sight of the boat at the front of the procession: a classic white-hulled motor yacht with a teak rail above a dark accent stripe. A tremor ran through her body. It couldn't be *Gloriana*, could it, just as she had been thinking about Betty? The shape and the length were right. Petra's hand shook as she grabbed her binoculars. Yes, there was no mistaking the boat's name. Betty was back!

It was the moment she had been waiting for subconsciously ever since the last remaining particles of blackened snow and ice had melted into the new grass. Despite the disparity in their ages and lifestyles, her attachment to Betty was like an umbilical cord.

With a prickle of excitement, Petra gazed across the water. She raised her binoculars and focussed on the upper helm where a single figure stood at the controls. His tousled blonde hair gleamed in the sun.

A bell began to clang. The bridge was opening. The sailboats formed a proper line behind *Gloriana*, who gathered speed.

Petra scanned the yacht again. Where was Betty? She should have been at James's side for a triumphant return to her summer cruising grounds. Larry too, assuming he was with her. Perhaps they preferred to sit inside.

She watched James pilot *Gloriana* safely through the bridge. He was looking forwards and never once glanced in her direction even though she was willing him to turn his head. As they disappeared from sight, her elation gradually subsided.

The last sailboat dawdled through the bridge. Petra checked her watch. If she docked the Striper at the RCMP's boathouse and changed into uniform there, she would have half an hour to play with. It should be enough. She decided to follow *Gloriana* to see where she was heading.

She overtook the sailboats and increased her speed as much as she could in the narrow channel. A string of power boats flying American flags was coming towards her: the other flotilla. Ahead of her, in the distance, *Gloriana* was turning to starboard. Petra left the buoyed channel and cut across an area that showed depths of one metre or less over a rocky bottom. Local knowledge was everything.

The minutes ticked away. Petra turned north in pursuit of *Gloriana*. If she could follow the yacht for another few miles, she would have a good idea where Betty was going. Judging by the route they were taking, she guessed they were making for the Bay of Islands. She knew she was right when *Gloriana* turned east and continued heading towards the Bay where a number of islands could accommodate a large yacht.

By the time Petra had docked her Striper and changed into uniform, both flotillas had arrived. The main dock wall and the municipality's new finger piers were overflowing with boats. Later, she walked away from the last American power cruiser to be checked and stood talking with Ed at the end of the dock.

'A lot of shit on those boats, but nothing that'll do any damage,' he said.

'You're probably right.'

'I don't suppose you've seen the advisory that was issued this morning.'

'What was that about?'

'The increased use of boats for terrorist-related activities. We're to report anything suspicious to Division H.Q. immediately. I brought you a copy.' He handed her a sheet of paper.

'Thanks. What do they think? That we walk about with our eyes closed?'

'Well even if we don't nab any terrorists tonight, we'll have fun with rival flotillas in port!'

'Don't I know it!' she said.

Next morning's newspaper announced the arrival of the area's most famous summer visitor with appropriate fanfare. The photo had been taken from near the lighthouse as *Gloriana* steamed towards the bridge. Petra downed the last of her coffee and folded the paper in half. As she did so, a small paragraph at the bottom of the front page caught her eye.

"The Mayor of Ingotville has announced revised plans for turning the municipality into a destination. After talks with a major benefactor who wishes to be unnamed, it has been decided to proceed with a contest for the design of an arts centre. The contest will be open to all Ontario firms of architects and the details will be published in the next few weeks."

Well, well! Finally Ingotville seemed to be making progress. During the bleak trip she had made there in February, no one in town appeared to know anything about the project. Now at least they had decided on an arts centre – just the kind of project Betty Graceby would enjoy supporting. But Ken and Cliff would be livid if they knew she was planning to give away such a large sum of money. One thing they both lacked was enough cash to maintain the lifestyle they considered their birthright. Not to mention the fact that Cliff might be developing an expensive drug habit. How far would the Graceby boys go to secure their future?

As soon as the weekend was over, Petra promised herself that she would find *Gloriana* and go and see Betty. She was anxious to renew their friendship and ask her about the arts centre. In the meantime, she would fire off an email to Martin and ask him to do some digging.

CHAPTER

18

For the next few days, Petra was busy from daybreak to nightfall. Vacationers poured across the bridge from the mainland. The car ferry from Tobermory was bursting at the seams on each of its crossings. With so many vessels in the area, the number of distress calls doubled – groundings, mechanical failures, Men Over Board, lost dinghies … The Coast Guard was overwhelmed and the RCMP helped out where it could. When Petra wasn't driving the Marine Unit's boat, she was patrolling the town dock and local marinas on the lookout for terrorists, drugs, and other illegal activities.

Petra worried that *Gloriana* had already moved on. She asked her colleagues in Gore Bay if they had seen the yacht. 'Such a beauty,' she was careful to say, to mask the personal nature of her interest. No sightings were reported and she kept hoping that Betty was still in the area. The Bay of Islands offered several possibilities for a yacht like *Gloriana*, but the most likely place she decided was a recently built private fishing resort. Betty loved fishing.

It was July the Fifth before Petra finished work early enough to visit Betty. She changed out of her uniform and pulled on jeans and a pink short-sleeved T-shirt with a boat neck. Then she went to the marina where she kept *Petrushka*.

In less than ten minutes, she was underway. There was a moderate easterly wind behind her. If it continued, it could kick up a nasty chop that she would be driving into on her way back. For now though, being on the water in her own boat gave her a wonderful sense of freedom. She opened the throttle and let the tension that had built up over the last few days drain away.

Half an hour later, she entered the Bay of Islands and began looking for the private resort where she figured Betty was staying. She was pleased when her instincts proved correct and she caught sight of *Gloriana* on the other side of a narrow spit of land. Turning into the cove, she counted three other vessels tied up at the two parallel docks. One of them was a Hinckley picnic boat. A Talaria T-40, about thirteen metres long. Named *Bettina*.

Petra couldn't see anyone on the docks or on the lawn that sloped gently upwards to a cluster of buildings. The buildings consisted of a two-storey main house flanked by six single-storey chalets, three on each side. They had been designed to blend in with their surroundings through the use of wood and natural stone.

The main entrance to the house appeared to be on the left-hand side where the second storey was topped by a tower with a rose window. Large picture windows and a wooden deck ran along the front of the house. Petra noted that there was a ramp at each end of the deck and a short flight of steps in the middle.

She reduced her speed and idled towards the docks. She desperately wanted to see and speak to Betty. The sun was warm, the cove protected from the prevailing summer winds. It was a perfect afternoon for sitting outside and enjoying the views across the water to adjacent, uninhabited islands. Yet the whole place looked deserted. Ken and James must have taken a boat out. Perhaps Betty and Larry were with them. Even so, there should be a member of staff at the resort, someone who would know what was going on.

Petra decided to risk going ashore uninvited rather than turning round and trying again another day. She docked the Striper on the end of the first dock, climbed out and made her way across the lawn to the front door of the main house. There was a brass knocker in the shape of an anchor, but no bell.

As she raised her hand to knock, the door opened. On the threshold stood a strongly built middle-aged woman with short mousy hair. Petra was not sure whether the woman had seen her approach or had been about to leave the house. She was dressed in what looked like a uniform: dark grey trousers and a pale blue tunic.

'What do you want? Who are you?' the woman said.

'Petra, Petra Minx. I'm a friend of Betty Graceby's. I was wondering if she's in.'

'No. She's not available.' The woman began to close the door.

Petra immediately put her foot against it to stop her from shutting it in her face. 'Not in or not available?' she asked.

'Both.' The woman's clipped speech held the trace of an Irish or Scottish accent.

Petra stood her ground, not prepared to concede so easily. She looked beyond the woman into the entrance hall. On the opposite side of the hall was an elevator and in the alcove next to it, a wheelchair. On the arm of the wheelchair lay a green blanket embroidered with the name *Gloriana* in gold thread.

With mounting anxiety, Petra pushed against the door. Suddenly, she was afraid of what she might find in the house.

'You can't come in,' the woman said.

'Betty asked me to visit.'

'She's not seeing anyone. I have my instructions.'

'I'm sure she'll see me.'

'I'm afraid not.' The woman put her weight behind the door and pushed back.

Petra felt as if she were in a dream where she was beating constantly on a door, trying to force it open. The door wouldn't give way, but she had to succeed. If she didn't, something terrible would happen. She gathered her strength and shoved hard. The woman stepped back. Advantage Petra.

Pressing forward, Petra managed to get both feet over the threshold. She dodged sideways to miss the woman's outstretched arm and raced through the hall, shouting 'Hello, Betty!' over and over. On the right was a door that Petra hoped led to the sitting room. She wrenched it open and entered, the woman on her heels.

'Betty!' she cried then stopped in alarm.

Her friend was lying on a chaise longue near the window, her legs covered by a green blanket. Her face was ashen and her eyes lacked the vitality they had possessed a

192

few months earlier. Nevertheless, Betty made an attempt to sit up when she recognized Petra.

'My dear! I was hoping you'd visit.'

'If I'd known you were unwell, I'd have come sooner. But last time I saw you, you were so full of life: dancing like someone half your age, in love with Larry ...' Petra clasped Betty's hand. 'Where is Larry?'

'We're not together any more.'

'Why not?'

'Miss Graceby needs rest,' the woman interrupted, moving to guard Betty like a police officer outside a celebrity's hospital room.

'Don't fuss, Patricia. I'm all right, and even better now Petra's here. Ask Pepe to bring us some coffee and pastries. And fetch the wheelchair. We'll sit outside.'

Patricia scowled at Petra, but brought the wheelchair without further protestation. She helped Betty into it and prepared to wheel her outside.

'Petra can take me from here. Go and find Pepe.'

Petra was relieved to see that Betty was still very much in the driver's seat. On the other hand, the fact that she had asked for a wheelchair was a surprising and unwelcome development. Betty had aged and lost weight. Petra was determined to discover what was wrong. She manoeuvred the wheelchair through the sitting room doorway, across the hall and out of the front door.

'Where would you like to sit?'

'On the deck, but I'll stay in this chair. It's too much trouble to get in and out of, my dear. I have no energy any more.'

193

'Is that because of what happened between you and Larry?'

Betty laughed and, for a moment, seemed like her old self. 'Not at all. We're still friends. He turned out to be a fool. Some aspiring actress launched a paternity suit against him. I didn't want to be involved with that kind of nonsense and we simply agreed to go our separate ways.'

'So why do you feel like this?'

'I don't know. I had a fall about a month and a half ago in the Bahamas.'

'At *Neptunis*?'

'No. At the bird sanctuary Ken supports.'

Petra looked hard at Betty, noting again the lack of sparkle in her lavender eyes.

'Ken was showing me round. One minute we were walking and talking, then I must have tripped over something. It all happened very quickly. No bones broken, just a badly sprained ankle and a lot of bruising. I suppose that's when I began to lose my strength.'

'You're lucky you didn't damage your hip!'

'I am indeed. But enough about me! Tell me what you've been doing, my dear. Here's Pepe with our coffee.'

A man of medium height with black hair and coppery skin was walking along the deck, carrying a large tray. He set it down on the table in front of Petra, grunting when Betty thanked him. Petra gave him a smile and murmured her thanks. He turned away quickly, not meeting her eyes. His beige slacks and crimson batik shirt reminded her of the goon Cliff had encountered on the night of Betty's concert in Las Vegas. His appearance was so similar that she might have thought it was the same man if he hadn't had a ridge of scar tissue across the bridge of his nose.

'You serve, my dear, and help yourself to the pastries. Pepe is a wizard in the kitchen.'

'He looks like someone I met in Las Vegas,' Petra said as she filled Betty's cup. 'Has he been with you long?'

'Just since we left the Bahamas. He's our summer chef. Joe always supplied a chef for *Gloriana* from the Culinary Institute. He said preparing three meals a day for the whole summer would give them the best experience.'

'The pastries look delicious.'

'They are. I don't know what his secret is, but I should be putting on weight, not losing it.'

Pepe had filled a large rectangular platter with rows of sweet, sticky, bite-sized pastries. Each row contained a different type. The common denominator was a billion calories, Petra thought, thanks to his heavy use of almond paste, honey and nuts.

'I didn't know Puerto Ricans made this type of dessert,' she commented after consuming one from each row and trying to resist helping herself to more.

'They probably don't, but the Institute teaches all kinds of cuisine.'

'Pepe doesn't look as though he eats many of his own delicacies. My father used to say you can never trust a skinny chef.'

Betty sighed. 'Joe did too. I miss him more than ever now that I'm not quite myself. We had such good times together. He knew exactly how to boost my morale. If he were here, I wouldn't need that nurse Cliff insisted on hiring.'

'You mean Patricia?'

Betty nodded. 'She treats me like a child, doesn't want me to see anyone or do anything, and practically force-feeds me with vitamins.'

'Can't you get rid of her?'

'If I did, Cliff would replace her, and I do need some help. Better the devil I know until I get my strength back.'

As if on cue, Patricia came out of the house carrying a small tray. She set it down on the table beside Betty. On the tray stood a large glass of water and a dish containing three tablets of different sizes and colours. 'Miss Graceby needs to take her vitamins. You should go, Miss Minx.'

'What are they?'

'Calcium, glucosamine and a multi-vitamin,' Patricia replied, irritation in her voice. 'Please leave us.'

Patricia's tone awakened Petra's stubborn streak and she sat back on her haunches like a recalcitrant mule. 'I'm not in a hurry. I'd rather stay unless Betty wants me to go.'

'Of course not, my dear, you've only just arrived. Ken and James will be back soon. I know they'll want to see you.'

James might, but Petra wasn't so sure about Ken. His reaction would be interesting. Betty's welcome had been everything she could have hoped for. Patricia was a bitch with a tendency to purse her lips. What once might have been brisk efficiency had morphed into a controlling bossiness. She was standing like a jailer in front of Betty, a tight expression on her lightly freckled face. Cliff had been wrong to think he was doing his mother a favour by hiring her.

'I wish I could do something to help you,' Petra said, taking no notice of Patricia.

'You can! Come with me on a cruise to Fayette – it's a magical place. I go every year. How about next week?'

'That would be fantastic, Betty, but I don't think I can.' She searched rapidly for a suitable excuse that would jibe with what she had told Cliff about being a swimming instructor. 'I'm working at a summer camp.'

'Ask for a few days off, my dear. You've nothing to lose.'

And everything to gain, Petra thought. If she went to Fayette, she would have ample opportunity to talk to Betty.

'You're not well enough to go anywhere,' Patricia said to Betty, a grim expression on her face.

'Please don't forget that you work for me, Patricia. When I want your opinion, I'll ask for it. I'm perfectly capable of making my own decisions.' She waved a hand towards the dock where Ken and James were tying up a boat. 'Here come the boys.'

Ken led the way across the lawn.

'What's she doing here?' he asked, pointing a finger at Petra.

'Don't be rude, Ken. Petra saw us on the water the other day. She's come to see me.'

Ken was as abrasive as he had been in the Bahamas. There was no trace of the bonhomie he had shown in Las Vegas when he had been with the lovely Linda. At a guess, they had parted company too.

James was another matter. It was seven months since Petra had seen him. He was as lanky and athletic as she remembered, and just as attractive. As soon as he saw her, he pushed the hair out of his eyes and gave her a wide grin.

'Hey, Petra!' He stuck out his hand, changed his mind,

and grabbed her shoulders. His touch sent a bolt of electricity through her body as he pulled her to him. She stiffened and drew back from the embrace, afraid of his magnetism and how she might respond. Falling for his charm as she had when she first saw him had no place in her plans.

Betty leaned forward in her wheelchair. 'I've asked Petra to join us on our cruise to Fayette. We'll go next week if she can manage it; if not, the week after. Timing's not important.'

'But …'

'I know what you're going to say, Ken. We've made reservations and arrangements to meet Cliff in a few days' time. All that can be changed. *Gloriana* is mine and I set the schedule.' Betty turned to Petra. 'Will you let me know as soon as possible, my dear?'

'I will.'

'It'll be great to have you on board,' James said.

'How the hell will she get home?' Ken asked. 'We're not coming back straightaway.'

'I can rent a car,' Petra responded.

'Nonsense! Cliff can fly you back,' Betty said.

Anger flashed across Ken's face. James gave a shrug as if to say it was nothing to do with him.

'Do you have a problem with that, boys?' Betty continued. 'If so, I shall do a Mrs. Turner and stay here for the whole summer. You know the story, don't you, my dear?'

Petra smiled. All the locals and many regular visitors knew about Elizabeth and Isaac Turner who had arrived in Little Current by ship in the 1870s. Mrs. Turner had taken one look at the view across the water to the La Cloche Mountains and announced to her husband that she was going no farther. If he didn't want to get off the ship, he could keep heading west without her. They had both stayed in Little Current and founded Turners Department Store, which was still in existence.

'I do,' she said. 'Elizabeth Turner was an amazing woman – just like you. I'll do everything I can to come with you to Fayette, Betty.'

On her way home in *Petrushka*, Petra wondered how she could possibly ask for time off during one of the busiest periods of the year. It would be frowned upon by her superiors and colleagues alike even though she had hours of accumulated overtime.

She gripped the wheel hard, her palms slick with moisture as she remembered Betty being helped into the wheelchair. So much had changed since Las Vegas. The downturn in Betty's health was extremely worrying and there were undercurrents she didn't understand. Going to Fayette would allow her to spend time with Betty in relaxed circumstances. Ken and James would be on board, and the hawk-eyed Patricia, but still …

She slowed down as she approached the Little Current bridge. No, it was impossible. There was no way.

Unless A.K. could do something.

CHAPTER

19

Petra was put through to A.K. at once.

'What's up?' were his opening words.

'I need a few days off to accompany Betty Graceby on a cruise.' It had sounded like a boondoggle even as she said it.

'Why?'

As succinctly as possible she had explained her concern at the deterioration in Betty's health then waited for his decision.

'OK. I'll fix a couple of extra days for you next weekend.'

And that was that: she had Friday and Monday off. Her partner, Ed, had been supportive, but the bantering remarks of some of her colleagues had not been as light-hearted as usual. Since she couldn't explain to them what she was doing, she was forced to maintain silence. She quickly realized that the best thing was to avoid them all as much as possible, which gave her a chance to catch up with her email. She updated Martin on what was going on and sent off a mini round-robin to various friends, including Carlo who worked for Interpol in Europe.

Two days before she was due to join Betty, Petra received an email from Martin with a link to a press release that she hadn't seen:

"The municipality of Ingotville is pleased to announce that Council has given the go-ahead for the building of a Centre for the visual and performing arts. Funding has been secured from a high profile donor who wishes to remain anonymous. The Centre will provide research and teaching facilities and include a theatre, a museum and an art gallery that will be open to the public during the summer months. The closing date for submissions to the contest for the design of the Centre is October 31. It is expected that the winner will be announced by the end of the year. The Centre will play a leading role in the revitalization of the area. For further information, please contact Geoff Hamilton."

Petra studied the press release. There was no doubt that the building of a Centre for the visual and performing arts would bring enormous benefits to the local community. If Betty were the sponsor, as she suspected, it would explain a number of things. On the other hand, Betty was far from being the recluse that her family might have liked her to be. She loved being the centre of attention, so why wasn't she publicizing her involvement in such an ambitious project?

In his email, Martin said he was making an appointment to see Geoff Hamilton. It would be useful to know what he found out.

When Petra arrived at the fishing resort in the Bay of Islands to join Betty on her cruise to Fayette, an empty wheelchair was standing on the dock. Betty must be on board. Petra closed up *Petrushka* and picked up her weekend bag. James and Ken were on *Gloriana*'s flybridge, preparing the instruments. 'Permission to come aboard,' she shouted.

'Granted!' James sang back.

'You've no need to ask for permission, my dear,' Betty said as Petra entered the salon. Betty was sitting in one of the candy-striped armchairs, dressed in cream fine wool trousers, a blue and cream striped top and a heavy blue cardigan. She grimaced as Patricia came in with a glass of water and a number of tablets on a plate. Some of them were the same as the previous week, others Petra didn't recognize. 'I'm sick of having to swallow these things!'

'You'd be sicker without them.' Patricia watched while Betty swallowed the tablets one after another. 'There, that wasn't bad.'

'Hmm. I've put you in the VIP suite,' Betty said to Petra. 'If you need Patricia to show you where it is, she will.'

'No problem, I can find it. Are you coming on deck?'

'No, my dear. I feel the cold nowadays and get tired so quickly.'

Patricia sat down in the armchair next to Betty's. 'I'll stay with Miss Graceby.'

'Go, my dear, go! Don't worry about me.'

Petra needed no more urging. It would be impossible to have a private conversation with Betty while Patricia was there.

Outside, the heat was rising despite the breeze blowing from the southwest. They were almost ready to leave. The power cable and the boarding ladder had been stowed. James had started the engines and a dark-haired crewman

Petra had never seen before was on the dock. He removed the spring lines and waited for James's orders. Then he walked towards the front of the boat and prepared to undo the bow line. A second crewmember was standing in the bow, waiting to receive the line.

Petra watched the scene unfold: the first man, who was wiry and well coordinated, untied the line, coiled it quickly and threw it up to his thickset half-section – who missed it completely and let it fall in the water. Instead of pulling it in as fast as possible, he stood with a helpless look on his face. James and the crewman on the dock were both shouting at him to haul the line in. Not until Ken appeared on the foredeck, yelling, did he seem to understand what he had to do. Even then, he didn't appear to put a great deal of effort into hauling what was, by now, a heavy sodden line aboard. The crewman who was on the dock dealt with the stern line in a much more professional manner before giving James the OK.

'What a jerk,' Petra couldn't help saying to James as she climbed the last of the steps leading to the upper helm.

'I assume you mean Al, the guy on the bow. He's summer crew – another recruit from the islands.'

'If I were you, I'd get rid of him straightaway.'

'I wish I had that luxury.'

'You're the captain.'

'Yes, but not the owner or the owner's family. They have strange ideas sometimes.'

'Is it OK if I join you?' Petra asked, watching James manoeuvre *Gloriana* away from the dock. His hands were tanned and strong.

'Sure. Have you ever been to Fayette?'

'No, but I know people who have. It's a Michigan State Park and museum village on the northeastern shore of Green Bay.'

'That's the official description. Actually it's a ghost town, quite spooky at night. In the nineteenth century it was a thriving community. Men from all over the world worked at the smelter. Snail Shell Harbor was a busy port. Now there's nothing there, just one long dock with no water or electricity.'

'It sounds fascinating. How long will it take us to get there?'

'About twenty hours at twelve knots.'

'Will we stop en route?'

James negotiated a tight turn in the channel between two islands before answering. 'Not this time. We're behind schedule and Cliff's meeting us, so we'll travel overnight. Ken and I will take alternate four-hour shifts. We should be there early tomorrow morning.'

They lapsed into silence as *Gloriana* picked up speed. Petra glanced sideways at James. He was not a great talker unless he had something specific to say, but he was an easy guy to be with and, as she had seen in the Bahamas, a skilled captain. Someone she could have fun with – and respect. The problem was that he reminded her too much of Romeo.

Under the force of her scrutiny, he turned his head and met her gaze. She was embarrassed when he dropped his eyes to her body. Because of the July heat and humidity, she was wearing short shorts and a sleeveless top with a scoop neck. The top perhaps revealed more than it should and the shorts left all of her long legs exposed. She slid off her seat and stood near the starboard rail facing outwards.

The North Channel was busy. The anchorage in the Benjamins, a picturesque group of pink granite islands, was full of boats, both power and sail, despite the tricky entrance. Many of them were rafted together. Petra was assailed by guilt: her colleagues would be kept well occupied throughout the weekend and she doubted whether any of them would have time off. Was she justified in asking A.K. to arrange things for her or was she worrying needlessly about Betty, who was after all in her seventies? She had no evidence of anything sinister, just a strong gut feeling that was intensifying by the day.

To ease her conscience, Petra left James and went to find Betty. She was still in the salon. On the table by her chair was a plate with a half-eaten cookie on it. They chatted for a while about the crowds on the water, then Betty began to reminisce about places they had taken *Gloriana* when Joe was alive. She had always talked a great deal about Joe, but when Petra first met her she had had a zest for living and an independence Petra had found inspiring. Now she seemed to be turning back the clock instead of moving forward.

'I don't know what's the matter with me,' Betty said. 'I feel nauseous. I never used to get seasick. Nor did Joe. Only once after we'd been drinking too many margaritas in the sun. I'll have to go to my cabin.'

Patricia appeared like a genie out of a bottle bringing what looked like a strawberry milkshake. 'Here's your health drink.'

Betty waved it away. 'I don't want it.'

Patricia placed the glass on the table next to the plate containing the remains of the cookie. 'Why are you so awkward? Let's get you to bed. You can have it in a minute.'

Petra was annoyed with Patricia for interrupting her time with Betty. She had had no opportunity to bring up the subject of the new arts centre or to ask Betty whether she knew Geoff Hamilton. Patricia was one of those irritating people who always seemed to know what was going on. 'Eyes in the back of her head,' her father would have said.

Noticing the glass and the plate, Petra realized it must be time for lunch. Being on the water made her ravenous. She picked up the health drink Betty hadn't touched, sniffed it and took a sip. Not bad, just a slight chemical taste. She was so hungry she was tempted to drink it, but memories of Alice in Wonderland stopped her. She didn't want to shrink or grow. She was still holding the glass when Patricia came back to collect it.

As soon as she saw Petra, Patricia's dour expression turned to anger. 'Don't you know you should never touch other people's medications?'

'I'm not. Anyway, it's just a health drink, isn't it?'

'Naturally! But it could have been a liquid prescription formula. You never touch other people's drugs,' Patricia repeated.

For a moment, Petra was reminded of her meeting at the Canadian Consulate in Nassau with Miss Jayne Birch in martinet mode. What did these women get off on? The only answer was power. Power and control over everyone around them.

Returning to the flybridge, Petra found that Ken had taken over from James. He ran his eyes up and down her body as she took the seat to his left. Once again she wished she had worn less revealing clothes.

They were travelling along the north coast of Manitoulin Island towards the strait that would take them onto Lake Huron. The water traffic decreased progressively as they left the popular cruising grounds between Little Current and Gore Bay. Ken gave the chartered boats from Gore Bay a wide berth. They were easy to spot and while most of the helmsmen were competent, some had little experience of boats and even less of the local waters.

Ten minutes later, James appeared carrying a hummus dip with raw vegetables. Pepe, the chef, was behind him with a large plate of sandwiches. As Pepe climbed the stairs, an express cruiser raced by, throwing a heavy wake. Pepe clung to the handrail and let out a shout. It was surely an expletive, in a language that Petra didn't recognize right away. He recovered himself quickly and handed the plate of sandwiches up to James, who tried not to grin.

'Thanks, mate. You should be used to this by now!'

Pepe glowered at him as he backed down the stairs.

'I know you get your chef and some of your summer staff through the LePinto Culinary Institute, but this takes the biscuit,' Petra said in a semi-serious tone.

'Nice one, Petra!' James said. 'Help yourself.'

Encouraged, Petra continued. 'That guy who dropped the line in the water has no idea how to coil a rope properly. Maybe I should give him some lessons.'

'He'd like that, I'm sure.'

'Shut up, you two, I'm trying to concentrate,' Ken snapped. 'Not everybody likes boats.'

Petra shook her head and sighed. Ken had no sense of humour at all. 'Then why have them on board?'

He made no reply.

The afternoon passed quickly on the water. Some people found it tedious to travel for hours at a time with seemingly little to do, but Petra never lost concentration and never got bored. She stayed up on the flybridge, remaining alert, chatting to James whenever Ken was not there and watching the two of them in silence when he was. She learned that James had grown up in Australia and moved to California as a young man. He and Ken made a good team. Ken showed no resentment at having been demoted from the position of captain and, as James had indicated, sometimes the family called the shots. Which must be why they had a dud crewmember aboard.

At five o'clock, Betty sent word to say that she was feeling better. Dinner would be served in the dining room at seven for herself, Petra, James and Ken. Nico, the able seaman, would take over the helm and Patricia would eat in her cabin.

Petra was the only one drinking alcohol during the meal. James and Ken couldn't since they would be driving the boat, and Betty declined even a small glass of wine. Petra also declined until Betty insisted so much that she gave in and allowed Pepe to serve her. As was often the case on smaller crewed yachts, Pepe was doubling as waiter and wine steward. The red California Zinfandel had good colour and spice. It was the perfect complement to his Moroccan lamb *tagine* served with couscous.

'That was excellent, Pepe,' Betty said as she put down her knife and fork. She had eaten a reasonable portion and clearly enjoyed it. 'I'm sorry we're losing you. I seem to get my appetite back when you're cooking.'

Pepe didn't acknowledge the compliment. He simply nodded and disappeared into the galley. A minute later, Petra was surprised to see the idiot who had let the bow line fall in the water come in to clear the plates. He kept his eyes lowered and managed to handle the plates without dropping them.

After he had gone, she turned to Betty. 'Is Pepe leaving? I thought he only just came to work for you.'

'Yes, but I can't stand in the way of his career. He's going to Joe's top restaurant in Chicago. Cliff will pick him up in Escanaba and bring his replacement.'

Once again, Petra wondered at Betty and, above all, Joe's unusual way of doing things. Constantly changing staff seemed par for the course for them. Perhaps it was a means of avoiding over-familiarity and thus provided a certain protection, or maybe they were just eccentric.

Pepe arrived with a plateful of his signature pastries and the offer of coffee to complete the feast.

'We'll have it on the aft deck,' Betty said. 'Give me your arm, Ken.'

James bowed out to return to the helm. They would soon be entering the shipping lanes to the south of Mackinac Island, then passing under Mackinac Bridge that marked the juncture of Lakes Huron and Michigan. The stream of high-speed ferries running between the island and the mainland, plus the freighters transiting from one lake to another, made for a very busy stretch of water.

Petra sank into one of the basket chairs on the aft deck and chose a pastry. She would have to try and ration herself. The dress she had put on for dinner was a clingy purple knit that she liked because it could be rolled up in a bag and simply shaken out. Cottons and linens creased too much. It also went well with the black and silver heirloom cross that hung between her breasts. But it showed every ounce of fat.

Ken fussed over his grandmother then sat down next to Petra. He was a peculiar guy, subject to terrific mood swings – violently angry one minute, caring and kind the next. For the moment, he was in calm territory, as he had been during dinner. He hadn't commented on Petra's appearance nor, for once, undressed her with his eyes. Maybe because he hadn't been drinking alcohol. Whatever the reason, politeness dictated that she stay with him and Betty, although she would have liked to have been on the helm alongside James.

The outside air was cooling down, but it would be another hour or so before darkness fell. The majestic old hotel on Mackinac Island was nevertheless ablaze with lights as they passed.

'I'd like to stay there someday,' Petra remarked. 'It would be a better place to go on honeymoon than Niagara Falls!' She envisioned going there with James then quickly banished the idea.

'Honeymoon?' Betty queried. 'With that nice young man Martin, perhaps.'

Ken snorted, back in sardonic territory.

Petra seized her opportunity. Betty had given her the opening she needed, or perhaps it had been her own stupid comment about honeymoons.

'Martin and I are just friends. He lives in Toronto and is obsessed with his career. I'm really a small town girl; I wouldn't want to abandon Northern Ontario.'

Betty nodded her agreement. 'Your roots are always your roots. Even if you leave as I did, it's important to maintain them. There may come a day when you want or need to return.'

'Or want to give something back to the community,' Petra added. 'Martin sent me an article the other day about a new arts centre that's being built in Ingotville. Isn't that where you were born, Betty? Have you heard about it?'

Betty looked vague. 'I may have done. Perhaps Martin mentioned it when he was in Las Vegas.'

Ken reacted in exactly the way Petra would have expected. 'What good will an arts centre be in the middle of nowhere? It's a complete waste of money!'

'Martin's been trying to contact someone called Geoff Hamilton to get more information. He doesn't return his phone calls. Do you know him?' Petra asked Betty.

Again Betty looked vague. 'I went to school with a Rory Hamilton. That might be his father, but I've no idea where he is. Why is Martin bothering with such local matters?'

'Martin's a dickhead!'

'Don't be coarse, Kendall. Martin is a talented young man; he took some wonderful pictures of me, and of us all.'

'What do you want pictures for? You've got thousands!'

'If it pleases me to have more, I will. And just as a reminder in case you're thinking about money, I'll spend mine as I like. Now shouldn't you be relieving James so that he can get some rest?'

When Patricia came to fetch Betty at ten o'clock, Petra retired to her cabin. It was too early to sleep so she lay on her bed thinking. Betty's reactions when she mentioned the arts centre and again when she had asked about Geoff Hamilton were difficult to assess. Certainly, if she were involved in the project, Petra would have expected her to boast about it. Kudos to performing artists was like oxygen to a fire: they thrived on it and would starve without it. Ken's outburst about wasting money was typical of the way he reacted when large amounts were being spent on anything or anyone other than himself. But it could also indicate that he knew about the project and suspected his grandmother of funding it.

Ken would be on the helm until midnight. On an impulse, Petra decided to pay him a visit. She made her way quietly up to the main deck, not wanting to disturb Betty or Patricia, who had the cabin next door to Betty's stateroom.

The salon was in darkness. Petra turned into the dimly lit passage that ran the full width of the boat. Off the passage, on the starboard side, was the corridor that led forward to the dining room and galley. In the centre of the passage facing forward were three steps leading up to the lower helm. The upper helm was accessed via a set of aft-facing stairs on the port side.

Petra was about to climb the stairs that would take her to the upper helm when she heard someone coming down the corridor from the dining room. Without stopping to wonder why she might not want to be seen, she ducked into the lower helm and waited in the shadows. She saw the figure of a man glide by and heard him climb rather laboriously up to the flybridge. She moved towards the bottom of the stairs. Voices carried on boats.

Ken gave a grunt in his usual fashion. 'What do *you* want? Coffee service, is it?'

'You told us we'd be there by now.' It was Pepe, the chef, his tone aggrieved.

'So? What do a few more days matter?'

'They matter to us.'

Ken laughed, a shrill laugh. 'Because you have to do what I say for a bit longer, eh? Is that it?'

'Another thing, you didn't tell us there would be a guest on board. That wasn't part of the deal.'

'I didn't know my grandmother was going to invite anyone, and I didn't plan for her to be ill.'

'Plan? You plan nothing. We do the planning.'

Silence. Petra could imagine Ken shrugging. She felt like shrugging herself, since she had no idea what was going on. Chefs always had to plan, but Pepe was talking in the plural. Was it a form of royal "we" or was he including his crewmate from the LePinto Institute who didn't like boats and didn't appear to have any culinary skills?

Pepe spoke again, menacingly. 'We won't tolerate any more delays. You'd better hurry it up.'

'No can do, mate. You chose the long way round. You could have made other arrangements. Just stay in the kitchen, out of my hair. We can't dock until morning.'

Petra heard Pepe turn and walk towards the stairs. He was coming down. She moved back into the lower helm and waited for several minutes, giving him ample time to return to the galley. Then she listened. Apart from the purr of the motors, the silence was absolute. It was safe to return to her cabin.

As she ran down to the stateroom level, she felt the hairs on the back of her neck stand on end. She stopped at the foot of the stairs and looked behind her. Nothing. But she couldn't shake off the feeling that someone had been there – and she couldn't stop thinking about Pepe and Ken's conversation as she got ready for bed.

Pepe had spoken to Ken – threatened him even – in a way that would have been unthinkable in a normal owner/crew relationship. Ken had given as good as he got. So what was the real link between them? And why was Pepe so anxious to get wherever it was on time?

Suddenly, Petra had more things to think about than Betty's sponsorship of the Ingotville arts centre. It was over an hour before her mind settled down sufficiently for her to fall asleep.

CHAPTER

20

Something woke Petra shortly after dawn. She listened for wind and wave noise, but couldn't hear anything out of the ordinary. She pulled the bedcovers up under her chin and snuggled down. Although she tried to get back to sleep, the altercation between Pepe and Ken was still uppermost in her mind. Why was Pepe so keen to get to Fayette? Was it just because he was leaving for a better job? Somehow she didn't think so.

She might as well get up and go looking for coffee to really fire up her system. At this hour, Pepe was unlikely to be in the galley. She would make a pot and take it up to the bridge where Ken – and maybe James – would be on the helm. In any case, she didn't want to miss *Gloriana*'s arrival in Fayette.

She pulled on a pair of jeans, a navy sweatshirt and deck shoes, and let herself quietly out of her cabin. She ran up the stairs to the main deck level. The salon was in darkness as it had been the night before, but her eyes adjusted quickly. No one was about and the only sound was that of the engines. She took a quick look in the lower helm. The instruments cast a bluish glow and she glanced at the chartplotter. The moving red ship that was *Gloriana* showed that they were navigating a fairly narrow channel between outcrops of rock.

Petra made her way along the corridor that led to the dining room and the galley. In the dining room, the blinds were up. The faint light coming from outside was enough to see that everything had been tidied away after the previous night's dinner. The chairs had been pushed in under the table and an arrangement of fresh flowers placed in the centre. Betty's newly renovated galley was through the door at the far end of the room.

On the other side of the galley, through another door, was the sitting and dining area for the crew, then the four crew cabins all the way forward. James had told her they were off-limits, yet Petra doubted the door was kept locked. Pepe must have come that way when he went to see Ken. She would have loved to take a look round, but it would be too risky to venture in there now. She would have to content herself with the galley.

Petra opened the door and felt for the light switches, expecting to find a row of them just inside on the left. Nothing. And nothing on the right either. They weren't in the usual place. She cursed *Gloriana*'s designer and fumbled around in the darkness, the only sound her muttered imprecations. In frustration, she swiped her hand across the wall and swept something off the counter. It fell to the marble floor with a crash.

'Shit!' The heavy object was resting against her foot, apparently not broken but probably dented. She bent down to retrieve it. As she did so, she sensed that she was not alone. This time it was more than just a feeling. Before she could react or pick up the object to use as a weapon, she felt the beefy arms of a man encircle her waist. He lifted her up and began to drag her towards the door to the crew quarters.

'What the hell are you doing? Let me go!' Petra jabbed at him with her elbows. He responded by kicking her legs from under her, carrying her as easily as he might have carried a rag doll. She realized he was not going to give up without a fight, unlike Ken in Nassau. She would have to plan her way out of trouble. Once again, she ran through what Tom Gilmore had drilled into her. *Bide your time. Don't waste your energy. Think.*

First question: where had her assailant come from? It was highly unlikely anyone could have boarded the boat while they were underway. In any case, why would they? Which meant that he had to be a member of the crew. It wasn't Ken or James, so that left Nico, Pepe or Al.

Petra decided to call for help. If Ken was on the helm, James might be close by, in the crew quarters – though that didn't seem to square with the fact that she was being dragged in that direction. The guy was crushing her ribcage, squeezing the air out of her. She pumped her legs and tried to scream. He clamped his arms harder round her chest, just below her breasts. Things weren't looking good.

Suddenly, the dining room and the galley were flooded with light.

'What the fuck's going on here?' James ran the last few steps to the galley.

Petra's assailant dropped her as soon as the lights came on. She had already worked out who it must be and recognized him immediately. Al, the useless crewman. He backed towards the door that led to the crew quarters, but James had seen him and came storming in.

'I heard a crash! I thought there was an intruder! I was just doing my job,' Al shouted.

'Oh yeah? I doubt it! You've not done your job properly yet. What happened, Petra?'

'I knocked something off the counter when I was trying to find the lights. This guy grabbed me from behind while I was trying to pick it up. I don't know what the hell he thought he was doing, but he sure didn't want to let go!' Petra gave Al a dirty look.

'Did he hurt you?'

'No.'

'Are you sure?'

'I'm sure.'

James hesitated.

'Look, there's no harm done. Just keep him away from me. And if I were you, I'd get him off the boat as soon as you can.'

James turned to Al. 'You'd better apologize to the lady. And you're relieved of your watch.'

There was a moment's silence during which Petra wondered whether Al would challenge James's authority. Tough guys didn't do apologies. Then he muttered 'Sorry. It was a mistake.'

'It sure was! Go to your cabin and stay there until we're ready to dock.'

Petra went to sit in the dining room while James made a large pot of coffee. She wanted a few minutes to think before he grilled her. She had deliberately made light of the incident, though privately she suspected that Al had been waiting for an opportunity to harm her. It was the only conclusion that made sense if she looked back at what had happened since she had come aboard *Gloriana* less than twenty-four hours ago.

From the beginning, Al had been out of place. She hadn't had any contact with him on a one-to-one basis – hadn't even known his name at first – but she'd made plenty of scathing remarks about his ability as a seaman, which he could have heard. And laughing with James at his ineptitude, which was a stupid thing to do in retrospect, would probably have been enough to make an enemy of him. Then he must have seen her leave the lower helm a few hours ago and realized she could have overheard Pepe and Ken talking. If there was a connection between Al and Pepe, Al would have continued to watch her and seized his opportunity to do one of three things: take revenge on her for ridiculing him, find out what she had overheard, or assuage his lust. Whatever the case, she would have to take extra care from now on.

Petra was sitting with her eyes closed when James came in from the galley.

'Wakey, wakey! I want to show you where the light switches are.'

'I don't believe it,' she said as he pointed to an out-of-the-way corner below the counter. 'That's something Betty didn't get right.'

'I agree, but there's also the switch I used as you come into the dining room. A good job I was on my way to get coffee. Tell me again what happened when Al attacked you.'

Petra repeated the story and dismissed the incident as a confluence of circumstances. 'It probably never would have occurred if I hadn't drawn attention to myself by knocking the paper towel holder to the floor.'

'God knows why Ken hired that guy, Álvaro or whatever his name is,' James said with a frown.

When they went up to the flybridge, Ken, instead of scoffing as Petra expected, appeared genuinely concerned and angry with Al. Again, she made light of the incident and suggested that they put it out of their minds to concentrate on the water.

Standing at the helm with Ken and James a couple of hours later, Petra felt a mounting excitement as they approached Fayette. James had described it in such glowing terms that she couldn't wait to see what it was really like.

Ken began to slow down as they passed a wooded hill that merged into higher ground beyond. In the distance, Petra could see grey limestone bluffs. She kept her eyes on the land and water ahead, knowing they would only be able to detect the entrance to the harbour when they were much closer. Without warning, two sailboats appeared. She picked up her binoculars and focussed on the spot where they had materialized. There was no break in the shoreline that she could see.

James chuckled at her serious expression. 'Don't worry, kiddo! You'll see it soon enough.'

Ken picked up the intercom and rang down to the crew quarters to alert Nico and Al that they were needed on deck.

Gradually, the hill fell away and sheer grey cliffs rose up behind it. Petra continued to scrutinize the foreshore for the first sign of a break. Then she saw it. A smile spread across her face. Within seconds, the inlet became apparent and it was hard to believe it had remained hidden for so long. On her right, a low curly tail of sand, stones and scrub replaced the hill. On her left, the cliffs plunged straight down into the water. Usually, she preferred symmetry. Here there was none.

But as Ken steered *Gloriana* into the entrance channel, Petra gasped in amazement. Directly ahead of them, not far from the water's edge, was an enormous stone structure with the missing symmetry. In the centre stood two monumental towers, five or six storeys high, flanked by long stone buildings with grey roofs. The towers were twice the height of the side arms – blast furnaces built in the 1860s to smelt iron, James explained. More buildings dotted the flat isthmus of land that had been cleared of trees long ago. Some had been restored, others left with gaping holes where the windows had been.

'Most of the buildings have had new roofs put on to preserve them,' James said. 'When production was at its peak, over five hundred people lived here.'

Unexpectedly Ken joined in the conversation. 'And vessels from all over the Great Lakes used this harbour,' he said, turning to starboard. 'It's a natural deepwater port.'

Beyond the sand spit, the harbour opened out and the wooden dock came into view. Apart from one small powerboat at the far end, it was empty. Ken headed for the middle where yellow tape had been tied between the wooden piles that fronted the dock, blocking off a section long enough to accommodate *Gloriana*.

'Our friends got the message then,' he said.

Seeing Petra's doubtful look, James added: 'We've been coming here for so many years, the Rangers always make sure there's space for us. They'll be along later.'

'OK guys, no more chatter. Time for docking.' Ken switched on the loud hailer so that he could communicate with Nico, who had already prepared the bow line and was waiting for instructions. 'I'll bring the bow alongside the second pile, Nico. Once you've got a line on, tell Al to jump off and get the stern line. Then we'll worry about the rest.'

'All the lines are rigged, but I don't know where Al is. I can jump off.'

Ken called Al on the stern loud hailer twice with no reply. 'Where the fuck is he?'

'I'll go down if you like,' Petra said without thinking. For a moment, she worried that she might have given something away. Then she remembered she had helped them dock in Nassau and also driven *Gloriana*, so they knew she was a seasoned sailor even if they didn't realize she was a Marine Unit Sergeant.

'No way, you're a guest. I'll go,' James said. 'Stay here and supervise young Ken.'

'It's Al that needs the supervision,' Petra countered, noting the flush on Ken's face.

She went to stand amidships to observe James and his crew. Al was a sleazeball of the worst kind and needed to get his shit together – to use her police colleagues' vernacular – if *Gloriana* was to be run properly. Yet she knew that wasn't going to happen. There was some other reason he was on board. She just had to figure out what.

James was on the bow, exchanging a few words with Nico. The sun lit up the curls in the nape of his neck and turned them to spun gold. Cute, the way they lifted in the morning breeze and fanned out over his collar.

As if he could feel Petra's eyes on him, James turned and looked up. A *frisson* of something she didn't want to acknowledge as desire ran through her. To cover her confusion, she gave him a thumbs-up, for which he blew her a kiss – merely a thank-you kiss from a flirtatious pirate, she told herself.

James walked towards the stern, checking the lines as he went. Just before he reached the aft deck, Al emerged.

James's voice floated up to Petra above the noise of the engines. 'You put one more foot wrong, buster, and you won't go any farther.'

He gave Al a hefty push between the shoulder blades to help him on his way as Ken brought the boat alongside. It was only a short jump and Al managed to keep his balance. He glowered at James before moving to the stern to catch the line James threw him. He caught it but let go as *Gloriana* moved in a sudden gust of wind, retrieving it just as it began to fall into the water. Petra shook her head in frustration. He certainly wasn't a seaman.

Petra fell in love with Fayette at first sight. As soon as they docked, she leapt off the boat and spent an hour exploring. It was only hunger and the thirst for more coffee that drove her back to *Gloriana*.

When she went to see if breakfast was being served, she found Patricia in the galley making toast for Betty who was still in bed and would not get up until later.

'But Betty loves Fayette!' Petra exclaimed. 'And I understand why.'

'She needs rest,' Patricia said firmly.

'I'd like to take her out.'

'I'll see how she is after lunch.'

'We can use the wheelchair.'

'As I said, I'll see.'

Not 'I'll ask Betty' or 'How nice of you to offer, that would be good for Betty,' Petra thought as Patricia left the galley. She couldn't imagine a worse type to look after an enthusiastic, independent person like Betty who rarely complained. If Betty had been involved in the interview process, she wouldn't have chosen Patricia. It was Cliff who had been the driving force in hiring her after Betty's fall in Nassau. That seemed to be when the decline in Betty's health had begun. Strange that accidents happened when one of the Graceby boys was around.

With a worried look on her face, Petra took stock of the galley. The vitamins Betty was taking didn't seem to be helping her regain her strength at all. Perhaps she was taking too many. Yet Patricia must know what the right dosage and combinations were … And then there were the health drinks. Where were they kept? It would be interesting to see what they contained.

Petra opened a pair of cupboards that were full of cups and glasses then glanced in the remaining over-the-counter cupboards: china in one; tea, coffee, sugar and spices in another. She moved across to a tall narrow cupboard that proved to be a pullout pantry. Starting at the top, she worked through the shelves one by one, examining anything that had potential and putting it back.

'What are you doing?'

Petra flinched at the hostile tone in Pepe's voice. He took a step towards her. The scar on his nose reminded her that chefs were territorial and prone to wielding kitchen knives.

'Looking for chocolate cookies – for Miss Graceby,' she said hurriedly.

Pepe stared at her with hard eyes. 'There are none on board. I was told not to use chocolate.'

'What about macadamia?'

Pepe was looking at her very oddly. Petra decided to cut her losses. It had been a spur of the moment decision anyway to try and find Betty's "medication". She didn't know why she had bothered. Patricia was a trained nurse.

'How about those almond pastries you make?'

'I'll be happy to take some to Miss Graceby.'

Who would be very surprised to receive them.

'Would you like some with your breakfast – Miss?' he added as an afterthought.

Petra sighed. 'Yes, thank you. I'll be in the dining room.'

Another billion calories.

21

Petra took the handles of Betty's wheelchair firmly from Patricia. 'I can manage from here.'

Patricia opened her mouth to say something, but Betty shooed her away. 'It'll do me good to be out in the fresh air. I want to see what's changed since last year.'

'Well, don't get cold and don't stay out too long.'

'She loves to have the last word,' Betty grumbled. 'It's hot this afternoon. Everyone's in shorts like you, my dear, except me,' she said, pointing to a group of tourists then at the blanket covering her legs.

One of the Park Rangers was leading the group to the smelter building where the replica of Fayette at its peak in the 1880s was housed. Petra had studied the model that morning and picked up a guide at the Visitors' Center. Already she could visualize the hustle and bustle that would have characterized the town during the days when it was producing day and night to meet the demand for pig iron.

'We'll go to the other side where the labourers' cottages are,' Betty said decisively. 'It'll be less crowded. We can talk there.' She began to point out to Petra some of her favourite buildings on the site. 'Every time I come here, I see differences. You must visit the museum in the Company Manager's house, my dear. There's a nice collection of furniture, artifacts and coins.'

Petra turned to look back at the dock and the restored two-storey house that stood halfway up the hill above it: perfectly positioned so that the boss could keep an eye on the comings and goings in the harbour. She glimpsed a man leaving the dock: a man in a green shirt and beige shorts, stocky like Al … He began to climb the hill towards the house. Petra shrugged. Perhaps he was a history buff.

The wheelchair rolled easily along the hard-packed sand and gravel paths. When they reached the cottages, Betty directed Petra to the right. 'There's a very secluded spot along here where we can sit and enjoy the view.'

'Isn't there a campsite nearby?'

'Yes, but they won't bother us.' Betty gestured to the left. 'It's over there.'

Once they left the cottages behind, the path turned inland and began to narrow.

'Watch that branch, Betty,' Petra said as she struggled to push the wheelchair over the rough ground.

'No worries, my dear, as Captain James would say. This is all part of the fun.'

Just when Petra thought they would have to turn back, they came to a clearing on the water's edge. She set the brake on the wheelchair and stood gazing across the bay. Although the sky above them was clear, a heat haze prevented her from seeing to the other side. The water lapped on the rocks below where she stood, and a cormorant surfaced suddenly a little way offshore.

'Three years ago, Joe and I saw a white pelican here,' Betty remarked. 'I couldn't believe it. I had no idea they came this far north. The Rangers said we were incredibly lucky. But Joe never made it back to Fayette after that, so I wonder.'

'You don't believe in omens and Fate and things like that, do you? I thought you were more practical.'

'All performers are superstitious, my dear, but I don't believe in Fate. I believe we control our destiny to a large extent.' Betty paused to stare at the sunlit water. 'The only problem is that right now, I feel as though I'm not controlling mine. And it's a feeling I don't like.'

Petra put a hand on her shoulder and squeezed it gently. 'If there's anything I can do, I will.'

'Then get me out of this stupid chair. Help me up and we'll sit on the GraPinto rock. That's what we used to call it,' she said, pointing to a flat-topped rock big enough for two to sit on.

If Patricia had been there, she would have forced Betty to stay in the wheelchair. Petra didn't give a damn. As long as Betty was warm and comfortable, it couldn't do her any harm. She laid the blanket on the rock and helped Betty to stand. Once Betty was on her feet, she seemed quite stable and was able to walk the few steps to the rock without Petra's aid.

'That's better,' Betty said, taking off her sunglasses. 'Now I can tell you what I wanted to. I've been talking to my lawyers and making arrangements in case something happens to me. Don't look so horrified, my dear. I'm worried about my health. I'm not a spring chicken any more. I want everything to be in place.'

'Surely this is just a bad patch.'

'I'd like to think so, but lately I've been depressed. And with Joe gone …'

'You still have Cliff and Ken.'

'Yes, but it's not the same. I've never lived through my child and grandchild, as some people do. My whole life revolved around performing, and Joe of course. Now both are finished.'

'You can still perform, as you did in Las Vegas in March. You were brilliant! The audience couldn't get enough of you! If you wanted to do more, I'm sure you could. You'll get through this bad time, I know you will.'

Betty gave a tiny smile. 'You're right, my dear. Perhaps I'm being too self-indulgent. Let me explain what I've been doing.' She began to swing one of her bird-like legs. 'There's plenty of money for everything. I'll provide for my family – not for a life of Riley, though. If Cliff and Ken think that, they'll have to think again. Anyway, I'm very angry with Cliff. He's trying to sell The Poseidon.'

'I thought you were going to create a new restaurant.'

'That was my plan – to launch another of Joe's "White Nights". Cliff said it would take too much money and too much effort to make it work. I don't agree. We could have renovated the whole hotel, made it a destination of choice for the very wealthy. Nowadays they want privacy and exclusivity, not big hotels where everyone ogles them …' Betty's face lit up as she warmed to her theme.

Petra wondered how Cliff would survive without the

cash flow from The Poseidon, assuming there were any. Betty had bought the hotel for him in the beginning, so the proceeds of the sale should revert to her. Perhaps Cliff had other irons in the fire.

'What was Cliff's real objection?' she asked.

'I don't know. We have a ready source of trained staff. It would have been something for him to be proud of.'

'Like Joe with his Culinary Institute and Hotel School. Joe left an incredible legacy,' Petra said, trying to steer the conversation in the direction she wanted it to go.

Betty nodded. 'I always admired the way he gave so generously of his time and money to help those he called his "kith and kin". His foundation is an inspiration to us all.' She paused and Petra waited impatiently for her to continue.

Somewhere in the trees, a bird called, loud and rasping.

Betty lifted a finger and tilted her head to listen. 'That sounds like a jackdaw. They love nesting in chimneys and old buildings. The Rangers have a terrible time keeping them out.'

Petra cursed inwardly. Why did older people have such a hard job concentrating? The slightest thing seemed to throw Betty off track.

'You were talking about Joe's foundation and what he's done for his kith and kin,' she prompted. 'He's left his mark and will be remembered for as long as it exists. If ever I were rich enough, that's the kind of thing I'd do for my hometown.'

Betty remained silent. Then she turned her lavender eyes on Petra and asked: 'Can you keep a secret?'

'Of course.' Petra crossed her fingers. This was it! Betty must be the unknown sponsor of the Ingotville project. She could see her name in lights on the marquee above the entrance: The Betty Graceby Centre for the Performing Arts. A legacy to inspire generations of youngsters.

'I'm going to use some of Joe's money to set up a Marine Staff Training Academy, specifically to train shipboard crew. It'll be an extension of his foundation and allow selected graduates from the Institute to specialize in onboard service. There's a dearth of proper staff nowadays.' Betty fluttered her eyelashes. 'What do you think of that?'

Petra was flabbergasted. She had been so certain Betty was going to reveal her intention of funding the new arts centre in Northern Ontario that it took her several seconds to recover. 'But you recruit staff every year from the Institute for *Gloriana.*'

'That's true, and some are better than others. The Academy will build on what Joe put in place. We'll teach nautical skills as well, so that shipboard staff can double as crew and dock staff. There are far more motor yachts in the eighty to a hundred and twenty-foot range today than there were even a few years ago. They need crew, but don't have the space or the budget for a lot of people. *Gloriana* is a perfect example.'

What Betty said made eminent sense, yet Petra was hugely disappointed. The concept was a clever one and certain to make money, so that wasn't the issue. Perhaps it was the fact that Betty was pursuing Joe's initiatives rather than her own. Sure, it was Joe's money that would be financing the project and he had been a constant background presence throughout the conversations she had had with Betty, but now, as Betty's health deteriorated, he was taking over. LePinto pervaded everything they did and everywhere they went. Petra was beginning to resent him. Soon, if she weren't careful, she might hate him as much as Ken did.

How could she persuade Betty, without burning any bridges, that there were better projects to promote? Betty had her own fortune, her own ideas, her own legacy to leave, and survival in the collective memory to ensure. In spite of her love for Joe, she had never taken his name; she had different tastes – fishing and boat décor, for example. She was perfectly competent and independent-minded. What was stopping her from realizing some of her own dreams? She certainly had the means.

'So what do you think, my dear?' Betty asked, breaking what had become a long silence.

'I'm amazed!'

'And so will the boys be, when I tell them tonight.'

Petra settled Betty into the wheelchair and pushed her carefully back along the path the way they had come. They did not say much. Petra was immersed in her thoughts and Betty had less energy than at the beginning of the afternoon. But their silence was companionable: anyone looking at them could easily have assumed they were grandmother and granddaughter or great-aunt and great-niece out for a stroll.

Patricia was standing on the dock. As soon as she saw them, she made a rapid beckoning motion. 'I was speaking to Clifford. He wants to talk to you. He wasn't at all pleased when I told him you were out. And you've been gone a long time,' she scolded, turning her cold grey eyes on Petra. The freckles on her face seemed to darken and grow more prominent when she was angry.

'Stop fussing, Patricia. If anyone is to blame, I am, not Petra. I'll see you this evening, my dear. Pepe's preparing a celebratory dinner.'

The dock had filled up while Petra had been out with Betty. Fayette was popular with boaters, especially at weekends. Petra boarded quickly to avoid a couple of teenagers who wanted to ask questions about the yacht. She felt guilty, but it was up to James and Ken to handle the public. She wondered how they would react to Betty's news. She was still trying to come to terms with it herself.

She decided to go for a walk. Exercise would do her good. Pushing the wheelchair didn't count. There was plenty of time before dinner and the tour bus crowds had gone. From the bluffs, the view of the whole site and the dock filled with boats of different sizes would be terrific.

As she disembarked, she heard a noise on the upper deck. She looked up, thinking it might be James or Ken. Instead it was Al. He had taken the cover off the motorbike and was bending over the fuel tank.

Petra strained to see what he was doing and was about to step back a few paces when something prevented her. She moved closer to the side of the yacht where she could stay out of sight. She heard footsteps and Pepe's voice.

'Ken told me what happened. You're a fool.'

'I tell you she was spying on us.'

'So keep an eye on her, but don't jeopardize the project. Is that machine in good shape?'

'Yes.'

'Then everything's ready for tonight.'

Petra walked rapidly down the dock, hoping she hadn't been seen. She was right, Al had been watching her. She would have to be careful. And something was scheduled to go down that night, something to do with the motorbike. She had no idea what. Maybe Al was a better mechanic than ship's crew. With a small sigh at her inability to figure out what he and Pepe were up to, she set off towards the bluffs.

Halfway round the foreshore, she stopped to stare up at the smelter buildings that dwarfed everything around them. She felt as insignificant as an ant faced with an elephant. White seagulls with grey wings and bright yellow beaks stood sentinel along the edge of the roofs, one on each crenellation, the distance between them exactly equal. It was an extraordinary sight.

So too was what she saw as she turned the corner of the building. A dark-haired youth in jeans and a black shirt was standing in the shadow of the wall, his back to Petra. Facing her was a girl with light brown dreadlocks, wearing an ankle-length tie-dye skirt straight out of the hippie era of the 1960s. Her ample bosom was unsupported, her nipples hard beneath the Indian gauze blouse that was tied in a large knot just above her navel.

"Dreadlocks" opened her embroidered shoulder bag and pulled out a packet of cigarette papers. She extracted one, dropped the packet into her bag and took out a small rectangular tin. With one practised hand she flipped it open.

Holding the paper in her left hand, she shook some of the contents of the tin carefully into the centre crease. She closed the tin, put it back in her bag, used both hands to roll the cigarette and pulled out a lighter. As soon as she lit it and took a drag, Petra smelled the cloying sweetness of marihuana.

The young man reached out a hand and snatched the joint.

'No you don't, Ken Graceby. That's mine, all mine.' Dreadlocks inhaled deeply, blew the smoke out into his face and flung her arms round his neck. She pulled his head down and kissed him on the lips.

Petra was nauseated – not by the smell, but by the company Ken was keeping. Betty would be outraged if she knew, and Petra's job was to protect Betty. She took a pace forward, sorely tempted to remove the joint from the girl's waving hand and grind it into the ground.

At that moment, James walked round the opposite corner of the building. 'Hey, man! What's going on?' he shouted. Then he caught sight of Petra and called her name.

Ken whirled round. 'Jesus Christ! You're like a leech. I can't get away from you!'

Dreadlocks put a proprietary hand on Ken's shoulder, drawing him closer. She lifted her chin and took another drag on the joint. 'Who's the chick?'

'Guest of my grandmother's.'

She pinched the end of the joint and sucked at it, looking Petra up and down. 'She can join us. Jamie too.'

Petra shook her head. 'Thanks but no thanks. I don't smoke.'

'What a surprise! Little Miss Goody Two-Shoes doesn't smoke. And she doesn't like …'

'Knock it off, Ken,' James interrupted. 'You can be a jerk sometimes.'

'I bet you like parties,' Dreadlocks said, reaching out to touch Petra. 'We're having one tonight at the bar just past the campsite. After dark, on the shore. A pig roast. Lots of booze, lots of guys – no pigs though – and Jamie'll be there, won't you, Jamie?' She didn't wait for him to answer, but rubbed up against him, the pot keeping her on the boil. 'He likes a drag now and then, not to mention a few other things. Am I right, Jamie?'

James pulled out of range and threw Petra a half-embarrassed glance. 'You guys do what you want. We'll decide about the party later.'

'Suit yourself,' Ken muttered.

'Don't tell me they're an item,' Dreadlocks said as they moved away.

Petra and James climbed to the top of the bluffs, saving their breath until they stood looking out over the harbour. Across the other side, the boats at the dock looked like toys, except for *Gloriana*.

'So who's the girlfriend?' Petra asked.

'Nadine? She's one of the regular campers, spends most of the summer hanging out here. Ken doesn't have great taste in women.' He paused. 'Unlike me!'

'Aha! You fancy you can pick them better, do you?'

'I try. How about being my date for the party?'

'But Betty's organized a special dinner.'

'We'll go afterwards. It's Saturday night. She'll expect us boys, as she calls us, to go off and do something.'

'She wouldn't like the company Ken's keeping.'

'She knows he won't stay in. So whaddaya say?'

Petra stifled the voice in her head that was telling her to watch what she was doing.

'OK.'

Pepe might be an introvert but his taste was spot on. Petra marvelled at his ability to produce a three-course gourmet meal on a yacht that hadn't been near a decent shopping centre for several weeks. Of course the motorbike would enable someone to go shopping for fresh produce if there was a reasonable store not too far from the marina. In Fayette, though, he had had to make do with what was on board. Tricolour salad of fresh buffalo mozzarella, sliced tomatoes and avocado, salmon steaks with anchovy sauce accompanied by ratatouille and croquette potatoes, fruit pavlova with vanilla ice-cream: a feast to delight the eyes and the palate.

Petra leaned back in her chair. She was seated on Betty's left, opposite James. It was impossible to avoid looking at him. Their eyes met once or twice and he smiled at her as if they were sharing a secret. Petra was very conscious of Ken on her left but glad that she didn't have to face him across the table. Patricia had that pleasure.

Petra tried not to let her tension show as she waited for Betty to make the big announcement. It was difficult, though, and once or twice she lost track of the conversation.

'Pepe, you've excelled yourself again,' Betty said as the

chef brought coffee and miniature Baklava to the table. 'We shall miss you.'

Pepe muttered something that could have been a thank-you and glanced sideways at Petra as she added her praise to Betty's.

'Bring more champagne so that we can drink a toast,' Betty continued. 'There's something I want to tell you all.'

Petra inclined her head and tried to look curious.

Ken raised his eyebrows. 'You're not going to buy another boat, are you?'

'No,' Betty laughed.

'Is it to do with Fayette?' James asked.

'No, no. Nothing like that.'

Betty scanned their faces. 'I'm setting up a Marine Staff Training Academy in Florida, to complement the work of Joe's Culinary Institute and Hotel School. The training will cover all aspects of shipboard service, both the household and the crew side.'

James whistled. 'That's a fantastic idea, Ma'am.'

'Yeah, absolutely fantastic!' Ken said, thumping the table with his fist. 'It'll sure eat up the millions. Does Dad know about this?'

Betty nodded. 'He does. I told him this afternoon. It's a shame he isn't here, but I wanted you all – including Petra – to know. There'll be no time tomorrow. When Cliff joins us in Escanaba, he'll fly Petra back to Canada before taking Pepe to Chicago. This seemed like the best opportunity to let you know what I've been planning for a while.'

Petra still thought Betty was – to use one of her father's favourite expressions – barking up the wrong tree. Ken, of course, was appalled at the idea of Betty spending her money on anything other than him and his father. James, in his laconic, all-accepting way, was pleased. Patricia didn't comment.

'How far into the planning have you got?' James asked. 'I'd be happy to help in any way I can.'

'I'm using one of Joe's waterfront plots in Palm County and one of his companies to do the construction work. My lawyers are drawing up the agreements as we speak.'

'You must be out of your fucking mind, Grandma! That land should be used for high-rise condos and a marina,' Ken said. 'That would be much more lucrative.'

'Go and wash your mouth out, young man, and don't tell me what to do! When you've made your fortune, you can spend it how you like. Meanwhile, I'll spend mine as I please.'

There was a stunned silence. Betty had spoken to Ken as if he were a five-year-old. Roughly, he pushed back his chair and stood up. A mixture of disgust and loathing distorted his features. With slow-motion deliberation, he drained his glass and slammed it down on the table. Then he threw Betty a look that made Petra shudder and stumbled out of the room.

For what seemed like an eternity, no one spoke. Petra couldn't think what to say to her friend whose big performance had ended in a shambles. Then James said: 'He didn't mean to be rude, Ma'am.'

'Oh yes he did. And I meant what I said too. Patricia, give me a hand. I'm going to bed.'

CHAPTER

22

Petra pedalled furiously along the road behind James. He was on a mission and the road was narrow and unlit. Fortunately there were few cars and the light from the almost-full moon enabled her to keep up. She was still wearing the outfit she had chosen for Betty's celebratory dinner: a black and white tunic top with elbow-length sleeves over thin black leggings, and silver Roman sandals. By sheer coincidence, not bad gear for cycling.

Petra didn't feel in the least like partying, but she had agreed with James that they could not accomplish anything by staying on board the boat and should follow Ken. Who knew what he might do given the mood he was in and the amount of alcohol he had consumed?

From inside the yacht, they had heard Ken wheeling the motorbike he had unloaded earlier along the wooden dock. As soon as he reached the compacted sand path, he went roaring off, scarring the walkways between the ancient buildings, caring nothing for the prohibition against motorized vehicles on the site.

James had produced two folding bicycles from a storage closet near the engine room, bicycles that Betty and Joe used to use. How ironic, Petra thought, that they were being used now to go after someone who hated both of them.

The bar Nadine had mentioned was a twenty-minute ride from Fayette, about eight kilometres away Petra estimated. The parking lot was little more than a flattened expanse of ground littered with stones. It was full of SUVs and pickup trucks with outsize wheels. There was even a customized Hummer, yellow with a black skull-and-crossbones motif.

The motorbike contingent had taken over the far end of the parking lot. James pointed out Ken's black and orange Honda, which was, for the time being, still standing. He and Petra left their pushbikes with a handful of others that were propped against the side of the first building they came to.

Nadine had called it a bar, but at first sight it was more like a sprawling collection of old outhouses or sheds. Some of them had open fronts, revealing worn tables and chairs scattered beneath a few naked low-wattage bulbs. Not the most prepossessing place Petra had ever seen, though that didn't seem to detract from its popularity. The average age was probably under twenty-one.

Petra wrinkled her nose. Pot mixed in with the cigarette smoke. No surprises there.

'The bar is in that building in the middle,' James said, indicating a larger, sturdily built chalet with picture windows and a deck full of teak tables and chairs.

Petra picked up a beer mat advertising Bell's Oberon Ale. 'At least they have half-decent beer.'

James raised one lazy eyebrow. 'I had you figured for a wine girl.'

'You didn't have me figured then. Beer's cool, in the summer.'

'Bottle or glass?'

'Bottle.'

'I'll get you one. Wait here. Then we can look for Ken.'

James disappeared into the seething mass of people that filled the chalet. Petra chose a seat on the deck and settled down to wait. Music with a pounding bass boomed through speakers that hung precariously from poles. A group of kids laughed raucously, the girls shrieking in their high-pitched voices until Petra's ears began to ache.

Beyond the deck, pale sand sloped down to meet dark water. The moon – high, like most of the people there – cast an oily sheen over the surface. Every minute or so, a thin black cloud scudded across its luminous white face, heralding change.

After a while, Petra began to feel antsy. More people were arriving, the noise was intensifying; there was no sign of James or her beer. A girl at the next table screamed at the top of her voice as one of her drunken mates pushed ice cubes down her cleavage. The scream was followed by the ripest swear words Petra had heard for a long time. The next thing, no doubt, would be two "young ladies" trying to tear each other apart with their fake fingernails or puncture each other's calves with their heels.

Wrong. The next thing was a stoned biker in leathers who collapsed like a house of cards onto the seat next to Petra. He ogled her with animal instinct and unfocussed eyes.

'Hey, baby. You're hot. I could use a fuck. How 'bout it?'

Petra rolled her eyes even though he was in no condition to notice. She cursed James's tardiness and made for the entrance to the bar. In the time she had been waiting, which was now the best part of half an hour, the crush had extended and thickened like an unstoppable canker. She pushed her way through a loud group standing in the doorway, weaving to avoid the roving hands of the alpha male. In the process, she bumped into an already unsteady pre-Raphaelite whose thick copper tresses shouted volumes at her bright pink tunic. The girl's glass tilted and deposited its red wine contents on the white portion of Petra's top.

'Sorree.'

Petra swore. It was at least as much her fault as the girl's, though that didn't make the result any easier to accept. What a zoo. If she'd been on duty back home, half of the revellers would have been in the paddy wagon by now, the other half not far behind.

She continued to worm her way through the crowd, keeping her eyes peeled for James. A small space opened up in the forest of thirsty carousers around the bar. Petra pushed into it, to the disgust of a guy and his girlfriend who tried to claw her back. James was nowhere to be seen.

As Petra elbowed her way out, a commotion on the far side of the room caught her attention. A bunch of half-naked, over-excited teens were jumping up and down, yelling the words to the dance music that poured out of the speakers. Petra caught a glimpse of someone in the middle. A guy with his back to her. A guy whose floppy fair hair curled over the collar of his shirt into the nape of his neck: James, holding two bottles of Oberon Ale high in the air, prancing and twisting like a manic jester while a ringletted blonde tried to unbutton his clothes.

Fucking idiot. Petra's usual restraint in the use of swear words went out the window. She felt like bellowing, putting her head down and charging out of the bar. He was as far from cute as it was possible to imagine. And whether he was any fitter than Ken to captain Betty's classic yacht, she doubted. Betty would be so disappointed.

Petra stomped out to the deck. Someone had left half a bottle of Carlsberg Lager on the table next to where she had been sitting. She picked it up and sniffed it. It smelled OK. In fact it smelled damn good. She was about to take a swig when her training reasserted itself, resurfacing at the same time as Patricia's admonitions against taking other people's medicine.

To distance herself from the antics she had just witnessed, Petra walked rapidly away from the crowds towards the shore. In the pit where the pig had been roasted, smouldering embers were all that was left of the fire. A faint aroma of pork crackling lingered in the night air. Or perhaps it was her imagination working overtime.

The sound of clapping, coarse laughter, and a male voice crying 'Way to go, man! Way to go!' drew her away from the pit. She followed the direction of the noise to a path that led between thick bushes. Heavy rap from a boom box suddenly drowned out the voice. Her eyes widened as she stopped on the edge of the bushes and took in the scene.

A short distance away, a mixed group in various stages of undress sat in a circle around a fornicating couple. Ken Graceby was on top of Nadine, straddling her on his knees.

His bare arse lifted pale in the moonlight as he bent his mouth to her nipples. Nadine's skirt was bunched up round her waist, her hips rising to meet him. Roughly, she pulled Ken's head up and he thrust into her. Another girl came from behind to join them. She pressed herself against Ken's writhing buttocks and rode with him until he withdrew from Nadine and turned his attention to her.

The shouts and catcalls grew louder. Already Ken's place inside Nadine had been taken. Petra wanted to rush in and tear the couples apart. Apparently none of them had ever heard of AIDS.

Filled with revulsion, she turned away. She had seen too much, transfixed by the sight of such blatant sexuality. First James, now Ken … Men were imbeciles.

Petra stumbled through the bushes, trying to find the path that would take her back to the beach. She tripped over a rock and felt herself falling … felt strong hands catch her under the armpits and haul her back to her feet.

'Careful, kiddo,' James said with a grin. 'You're gonna damage that beautiful face of yours.'

'Take your hands off me! I could smash your face in!'

'What's got into you? I couldn't find you.'

Petra heard her tunic rip on a branch as she tried to push past James. He grabbed her shoulders and gave her a light shake. 'Calm down, you're going crazy.'

'What the fuck were you doing with those little tarts? Half an hour I was waiting for you.'

'Whoa! Those kids are harmless. I've seen them grow up.'

'Grow up? You need to grow up yourself!'

'What about you? Do I detect jealousy?'

'No way, mate. I suppose you're going to join Ken.'

'Ken?'

'Banging his way through a bunch of hippies, closely followed by the rest of the county.'

James laughed.

'How can you laugh at something like that? They're animals.'

'Look, Petra, it's almost a ritual here, once a summer. They're all willing participants.'

'Is that where you were going? To join them?' she repeated.

'That stuff doesn't turn me on.'

'Cheerleaders obviously do.'

'High spirits, a few beers, there's nothing else the matter with them.'

'High is right!'

'Come for a walk with me, Petra. I'm sorry. Let's start the evening over. I'll show you the end of the beach.'

She resisted strongly as he pulled her towards him and tried to get an arm round her shoulders. Men were such jerks. They thought an apology was all it took to restore the situation.

Someone had turned up the music behind the bushes. The loud rap banged off Petra's ears and her mind refused to let go of the scene that could so easily turn into rape.

'OK,' she said reluctantly. It wasn't OK, but it would take her mind off Ken.

She walked stiffly alongside James who led her towards the shore that lay quiet and silvery in the moonlight. They stood at the edge of the water, gazing across the gentle waves that lapped at the stones. Thank God he didn't attempt to make conversation. She wanted to wrap herself in a cocoon of silence, focus on repair and regeneration until she was ready to emerge. The strident world could wait.

'Jamie! Jamie!'

'Where's our Jamie?'

'You can't hide from us!'

'We know what you like!'

Chanting voices carried on the breeze. A posse of four hunting down their man.

Petra turned. Leading the pack was the ringletted blonde she had noticed before, the one who had been trying to unbutton James's clothes. Somewhere along the line she had shed her tank top, leaving her high breasts bare. As soon as she identified James, she raced forward twirling her top like a lasso.

'Your fan club,' Petra muttered. 'Have fun.'

She didn't stop running until she reached the place where they had left Betty and Joe's bicycles. Panting, she looked around. It was definitely the right place. She recognized the building, but the bikes had gone. They were quite distinctive: dark green and white like *Gloriana* with a gold B & J intertwined on the rear mudguard. She spent ten minutes searching the vicinity in case someone had moved them. Nothing. Shit. And more shit. Betty would be none too pleased.

Petra weighed up her options. She could walk back to Fayette, take someone else's bicycle, or find Ken's motorbike and ride it home. She didn't fancy walking eight kilometres and running the risk of being hassled or run down by drunkards or druggies once they started to leave the party. The idea of appropriating someone else's bicycle on the eye for an eye principle was tempting, but the perp was unknown so it wasn't fair to go that route. The third option held the most appeal, despite the fact that she knew she would be nervous. Still, she could keep the speed down and would be returning the motorbike to the relative safety of the dock. Ken and James would be left without transport. Serve them right.

There was one major problem, though. Keys. Years ago, she had seen Romeo and his friends, Ben and Carlo, hotwire a bike after Ben's keys had fallen in the water while they were jostling each other on a bridge. If she could find a piece of wire, she might remember how to do it. Or someone might help her if she played the damsel in distress card.

Petra crossed the parking lot to the motorbike corner and searched for Ken's Honda. Amazingly, it was still there, and his helmet was hanging from the pillion. Not only that, he had left his keys in the ignition. Either he had been too drunk and angry to notice, or he wasn't concerned about theft of an item paid for by his grandmother, especially after her announcement regarding the Marine Staff Training Academy. Whatever the case, there was more honesty among bikers than cyclists, and somewhere in the starlit heavens Orion must have been watching over her.

The ride back to Fayette took only a few minutes. When Petra reached the entrance to the park, the Rangers' cottages were in darkness. At the Visitors' Center she stopped and switched off the engine. Despite some dim lights inside, it was silent and empty. She freewheeled down the long hill that led to the smelter buildings, enjoying the feeling of being alone. Once or twice scurrying in the undergrowth reminded her of the presence of nocturnal animals and as she turned a corner, the sickly-sweet smell of skunk drifted across the road. At the bottom of the last slope, she skidded to a halt, dismounted and began to wheel the motorbike. She parked it beside the path at the north end of the dock, not wanting to wake everyone by pushing it along the boards. She pocketed the keys but left Ken's helmet as she had found it.

Petra stood for a moment looking at the ripples on the moonlit water. She wasn't yet ready to return to *Gloriana*. A glance at her watch showed that it was 1.30 a.m. Late for small town America, but there was no way she would be able to sleep. The whole scene with James and Ken was too fresh in her mind. She wondered what time they'd get home and how – or if they'd make it back at all. No doubt many of the partygoers would sleep it off where they fell, up to their eyeballs in drugs and alcohol. Had James and Ken been taking drugs? If so, should she tell Betty? Was it any of her business? She needed to sit and think.

Fayette was an eerie place to be at this hour. The Rangers had closed the buildings at dusk, leaving a handful of lights to shine through glassless windows and empty doorways like ghostly beacons in a sea of darkness. A deep stillness pervaded the site, as if it was a graveyard for the hundreds of souls that had toiled in the quarries and sweated in the heat of the furnaces. Yet Petra could feel no evil in the stone relics of the past.

Suddenly, she felt a surge of energy as if someone had given her a shot of adrenaline. She wanted to see Fayette from above in the moonlight, to look down on the sleeping boats and contemplate the juxtaposition of past and future. It would be a balm to her spirit. Then perhaps she could rest.

It was too far to walk to the bluffs as she had before dinner, but the Company Manager's house was on the hill above the docks. There would be an unspoiled view of the harbour from its verandah. She recalled seeing Al walking up there earlier that day when she was taking Betty out in the wheelchair. With a slight shiver, she set off up the slope to the house. A few steps led up to the verandah. The front door was closed and no light shone through the fanlight above it. Out of habit, Petra checked the door. Locked. The windows on either side were covered by heavy shutters.

The wooden floor of the verandah was still warm. Petra sat down, clasped her hands round her bent knees, and stared out over the harbour. She couldn't get the sordid scenes from the pig-roast venue out of her head: James making a fool of himself with over-sexed, under-age airheads who didn't know better, and Ken in stud mode, having it off with the local trailer trash. She didn't think James had been under the influence of drugs – his eyes had been clear and laughing bright. Ken was a different matter. His behaviour had come as a shock but no real surprise. Ever since her first night in Nassau, she had been half expecting it. She had no idea if he'd been stoned, or worse, or whether it was simply the result of an inferiority complex mixed with too much alcohol and testosterone. So what if anything should she do?

As she sat pondering, she heard a faint scraping sound. She moved her feet and the deck creaked. Then she heard another creak. Petra drew herself upright to listen. A minute or two passed and she tried to relax, but once her mind started playing tricks, it was time to go.

She stood up quietly. As she did so, something squeaked at the back of the house. Like a hinge. There might be a back door that the Rangers had failed to secure properly. At night the cooling air created downdraughts that could cause old doors to bang and break off their hinges.

Petra saw the door as soon as she turned the corner. It was hanging open and a little askew. The lock had been jimmied. The question was when. She debated whether to go in and investigate but without backup or a weapon it would be foolhardy. Whoever had broken into the house could still be inside.

She sensed movement and turned to look behind her. In the same instant she felt the cool blade of a knife pressing against her throat. A strong gloved hand twisted her right arm and forced it behind her back. She let herself go limp. No point in ending up with a dislocated shoulder.

Her aggressor was not much taller than she was. His arm was thick and hairy. Although she hadn't seen his face, she had an idea who it might be. She made a noise in her throat.

'Shut up,' he growled, confirming her suspicion.

Al was crushing her arm, and the cold steel against her larynx was making her gag. He bundled her over the threshold into the house, threw her on the floor and pulled the door shut.

'If you make one sound, I'll cut your throat,' he said, brandishing the knife close to her face.

She didn't doubt for a minute that he might. The best policy would be to do as he said and bide her time. As her eyes adjusted to the darkness, she saw him bend over and open what appeared to be a fairly heavy bag. Although he was still holding the knife, he was concentrating on the bag, for the moment not paying her any attention.

With her left hand, Petra felt for the black-studded silver cross she always wore. The hidden stiletto that had protected the faith of her ancestors had been useful before, but right now she knew it wouldn't be enough. It would only enrage Al if she attempted to use it. There was a chance, though, that she could make it through the door before he found what he was looking for. All she had to do was stand up, open the door and run. It was worth a try. He didn't seem to want to cut her throat just yet.

CHAPTER

23

Al's reflexes were faster than a snake's. He grabbed the back of Petra's tunic before she had a chance to open the door, spun her round and smashed his fist into her face. She was smart enough to move her head to the left, so that it caught her jaw on the right-hand side. Nevertheless, it was a heavy blow.

Petra hunched over and dropped to her knees to protect her body in case he decided to attack her with the knife. Instead he dragged her farther into the room, holding her right arm in an iron grip. This time he didn't let go. Her jaw was already throbbing furiously. She tried to ignore the pain and work out what his next move would be. If she could figure out what he wanted, she would be in a much stronger position, but the lack of light prevented her from seeing the expression in his eyes.

He was squeezing her arm so hard that his fingers began to burn through her flesh. She felt him reach for something and waited for the searing pain of his blade. It would be pointless to embark on another futile attempt at escape. Tom Gilmore would be so disappointed in her for not thinking her way out of the situation.

Al's fingers dug even deeper into her muscles. Then she heard a click. The beam from the flashlight blinded her as he shone it into her face.

'Don't try anything,' he growled, waving it up and down her body.

His eyes were black, impassive, creepy. The opaque eyes of someone without emotion. She let her own blue-green gaze bore into him like a laser, but remained silent. He wasn't giving anything away; neither would she.

He flashed the beam of light through a doorway into another room. 'We're going in there. I don't want any trouble. I'll be right behind you with the knife. Get up!'

Al pushed her through the doorway into what she saw was the kitchen. A pine table stood against the whitewashed wall opposite. He shone the light under the table and forced her to her knees. Her thin leggings caught on the rough stone floor.

'See that trapdoor? You're going to undo those bolts and lift it up.' He dragged the table partially out of the way.

Petra nodded, grateful for small mercies. It didn't take a nuclear physicist to figure out that he was going to lock her in the cellar. She felt the tip of Al's knife in her back as she struggled with the bolts. The blasted things were stuck. Without warning, the first one slid back before she could move her finger. She shook it hard. Shit! That hurt.

'Come on, come on! I haven't got all night.'

She continued to work on the second bolt until she was able to force it open. She sat back on her heels and felt a hole develop in her leggings. Al was breathing down her neck, brandishing the knife.

'OK, now the door.'

Petra dug her fingernails under the edge of the heavy piece of wood and lifted it up. Al shone the beam round the cellar, lighting up a stout but rusted iron pole that stood in the centre, supporting the ceiling above.

'Right. Move it!' He bundled her down a short flight of wooden steps. 'I want you over there. Put your arms round the pole. No, don't hold it.' He placed the flashlight on the floor.

Petra wondered what the odds were of being able to kick the flashlight out of the way, dodge Al's knife, run up the stairs, slam the trapdoor shut and sit on it while she bolted him in. A zillion to one. Better to live to tell the tale and set the police on him in the morning.

Al grabbed her hands and forced her wrists together, squeezing them tight. From the right-hand pocket of his leather jacket he took a length of rope and tied her wrists securely. Then he patted her down. Not in the lascivious way Ken would have done if she had been at his mercy, but in a totally asexual way. He paused as soon as he felt the keys in her tunic pocket and gave a grunt of satisfaction when he pulled them out. Immediately he picked up the flashlight and turned to leave.

'Aren't you going to gag me? Aren't you afraid I'll raise the alarm?'

'No one will hear you. By morning I'll be miles away. Even if they look for me, they won't find me.'

He ran up the steps and closed the trapdoor. Petra heard him bolt it and pull the table back into place. After that, silence. No doubt he would leave the house through the back door, latching it as he went out. He was thorough and violent, but had not used as much force on her as he could have done. Something had held him back. He wasn't a rapist or even a guy trying to get his rocks off. What was he then? A petty thief hoping to get away with the loot and no consequences, providing he didn't really hurt anyone?

That didn't compute. He hadn't taken her jewellery or her watch or the cash in her pocket. Only the motorbike keys. It was as though he had been expecting to find them on her. Had he been watching from the Manager's house, waiting for Ken to return with the bike? Was that what had been set up for that night? Petra began to add up everything she knew about him and Pepe.

Cold was seeping through the walls and floor of the cellar. The whole side of her face was aching. She guessed it must be between two thirty and three in the morning. The Fayette town site opened to visitors at eight. The Rangers would do their rounds and open the museum some time before that. *Gloriana* was due to leave for Escanaba at nine. If she could shout loudly enough to make herself heard, she might be rescued and back on board before Betty missed her. If not, she would have to rely on someone noticing her absence. Perhaps when they found out Al was missing, James or Ken would start asking questions.

Petra realized she was still standing in the same position as when Al had left. She could slide her arms up and down the pole, but he had tied her wrists tightly, making it impossible to abrade the rope on the rough surface. Experimentally, she bent her head towards her wrists. It was not that difficult to reach them. And her cross was still round her neck.

If she could free her wrists, she would have a better chance of attracting attention by banging on the trapdoor. She manoeuvred herself into a position where the pole rested in the crook of her left arm. Then she bent her right arm and tucked it tightly into her chest. This brought her fingers close enough to reach her cross. On the third attempt, she managed to press the base of the crosspiece with enough force to release the spring mechanism. The five-centimetre stiletto fell to the floor with a clink.

Petra felt for the stiletto with her foot then moved herself round the pole so that when she knelt down, she was able to pick it up with her fingers. She clamped it between her teeth, ignoring the slight grittiness.

Now came the most difficult part. The object was to cut the rope without cutting her wrists. Patience was the key. Like Houdini, she had practised using the stiletto at home in private, feeling slightly stupid and never revealing to anyone the secret of the cross.

She worked on the rope, trying not to get frustrated at her slow progress. Suddenly, the blade slipped as one of the strands parted. She jerked her head backwards before it could do more than prick her skin. Now the job should be much easier.

When the next strand parted, Petra knew she was nearly free. She pulled her wrists apart and the last piece of rope gave way. She dropped back onto her heels.

After a break, she picked up the stiletto and replaced it in her necklace. She searched for the pieces of rope and put them in her pocket. Her wrists were sore but not badly damaged. She stood up and began stretching to loosen her limbs. She estimated it had taken about an hour to free herself, which meant at least another three hours of waiting before she could expect any help. The best thing would be to get some sleep if she could.

James woke up with a mild hangover and a feeling that he had ruined his chances with Petra. While he didn't want any long-term female involvement, he couldn't deny the spark of attraction between them. Unfortunately, because of their personalities, it had been like rubbing two sticks together to start a fire. The flames had spread rapidly then started to burn out of control. He didn't think it was all his fault.

He rubbed his temples and pulled on beige slacks and his *Gloriana* Captain's shirt. The crew area was quiet, except for a light snoring coming from Ken's cabin. James had persuaded him to leave the party, sated and drunk, in the early hours of the morning. Luckily, after discovering that the motorbike had disappeared, they had been able to hitch a ride back to Fayette.

James went into the galley in search of coffee. Pepe was there, beginning preparations for breakfast. 'Have you seen Al and Nico?' James asked.

'Not yet.'

'I'm going to need them on deck.'

'Not my department.'

James helped himself to a mug of coffee and went out on deck. Snail Shell Harbor was shrouded in mist. Not that unusual in July. Normally it would burn itself off quickly. Breakfast was at eight, departure scheduled for nine. Betty would probably not put in an appearance until mid-morning when they reached Escanaba. He and Petra might be the only ones around for breakfast. He didn't know what to do to appease her. His behaviour had been stupid, but if he apologized again, he'd come across as a wimp. Shit. There was no easy way out.

Petra would have agreed. She had been shouting as loudly as she could and banging on the trapdoor for twenty minutes at least. Nobody seemed to be out walking or jogging in the vicinity and old stone houses were built sturdily to withstand the elements. It was unlikely her cries would be heard until someone actually entered the house. She started shouting again. The Rangers weren't in any hurry to open up on a Sunday morning.

Suddenly she heard footsteps above her head. The table was dragged away and the bolts pulled back. The face of one of the Rangers she had met the day before appeared at the top of the steps.

'Oh my God! How did you get down there?' He grasped Petra's hands and pulled her up the steps.

She stood blinking in the daylight. 'Thanks, Mike. It's a long story. I thought you'd never come.'

From then on, things moved quickly. Mike radioed his colleagues, who brought coffee and cookies and a warm jacket for Petra. She asked him not to radio *Gloriana* or fetch anything from the boat. Two State Police Troopers arrived within half an hour. They examined the back door of the house and one of the display cases upstairs which had been broken open. According to Mike, a dozen Civil War Silver Dollars and a Venezuelan 20 Bolivar gold coin from 1889 were missing. The troopers took statements from them both. Petra gave a description of Al, but – unwilling to reveal the secret of her cross – omitted to mention that he had tied her wrists round the pole in the cellar.

During the night, before falling asleep, she had decided that the best way to play it was to say that she had surprised him leaving the building with a bag; he had hit her on the jaw, bundled her down the stairs into the cellar and locked her in. Betty would be horrified if she heard the full story and Petra was keen to spare her anxiety, especially in her delicate state of health.

When the troopers had finished their examination of the house, Petra walked with them towards the dock. The early morning mist had turned into a full-blown fog that didn't look as though it would lift anytime soon. It wreathed the site in a bright white dampness that lent a surreal touch to Petra's memories of her night in the cellar.

'We need to talk to the captain and Miss Graceby, since this Al was a member of the crew,' said the senior trooper.

'Could you talk to her grandson Ken instead? Miss Graceby isn't well.'

Seeing how serious Petra was, the trooper nodded. 'We'll start with the captain and take it from there.'

James saw them coming. The look of concern on his face as he recognized Petra wiped out some of her frustration with him. Quickly she told him the short version of what had happened.

'May we come aboard?' asked the senior trooper. 'We'd like a few words with you and Miss Graceby or her grandson.'

'Miss Graceby had a very bad night. She's in bed, being cared for by her nurse. Her grandson is on board. I'll call him.'

Petra was seized with worry. On the other hand, she was glad Betty was not around to see her before she had time to treat her face and change her clothes.

James led them to the dining room where they seated themselves round the table. Ken joined them a few minutes later, looking angry but none the worse for wear.

'Found my motorbike, have you?' he said as soon as he saw the troopers. 'Some bastard took it. I had to hitchhike home.'

Before they could respond, Petra raised her hand. 'I borrowed it to get back here and parked it at the end of the dock. You left your keys in the ignition,' she said to Ken. 'Now Al has them. He took them off me before he locked me in the cellar. Said he'd be miles away by now.'

A shadow passed across Ken's face.

'Have you any idea where Al might be heading?' the trooper asked.

'None at all,' Petra said.

James shook his head.

'He's probably just gone for a joyride,' Ken said. 'There's no need to make a fuss. Even if he's gone for good, it's only a motorbike, and he was a lousy crewman.'

James looked as astonished as Petra at Ken's sudden change in attitude towards Al and his disappearance.

'What about him stealing from the museum? And attacking me when I tried to stop him?' she protested.

'Yeah, but he didn't take much, did he? And you're not hurt.'

261

'Do you wish to press charges, Ma'am?' asked the senior trooper.

'No,' Petra said, with an emphatic shake of her head. The most important thing at this stage was to protect Betty and disturb her as little as possible. Once she was back in Little Current, she would figure out what to do. If necessary, A.K. would back her up and explain to the Michigan police that she was working under his aegis. But for the time being, she would keep a few secrets.

24

'I want to see Petra!' Betty insisted when Patricia came to remove her breakfast tray. 'You're treating me as if I were senile.'

'There's no need to get into a state. Why haven't you taken your vitamins? You must take them.'

'I mustn't do anything. Go and find Petra.'

Patricia pressed her lips into a tight line, as she did when she didn't get her own way.

A few minutes later, Petra tapped on the door of Betty's stateroom. She had showered and dressed, taken ibuprofen for her aching jaw and covered it in concealer. Her hair was hanging loose about her face and she hoped Betty wouldn't notice the bruising.

Betty smiled as Petra entered the room. She was propped up on pillows and wearing a bright yellow bed jacket, but her lavender eyes that had been so much a part of her magnetism seemed to have shrunk into her head. The dark circles that underscored them were deeper and more noticeable than ever before. Aghast, Petra sat down on the chair next to the bed, on Betty's right, keeping her face turned away.

'How was your night out?' Betty asked with unintentional accuracy. She studied Petra's face. 'You look tired.'

'Noisy. Late. I didn't get much sleep.'

'Neither did I, my dear. Too much rich food, I'm afraid. It's all Pepe's fault for producing such a fabulous meal.'

Not exactly, Petra thought, but Betty made no mention of Ken.

'I can't believe you're losing Pepe.'

'I think he finds the boat claustrophobic. He's fretting to get off, and now we're delayed because of the fog.'

'It should clear by noon. The sun's trying to break through.'

'I hope it does. I need to see Cliff and ask his advice. Escanaba has critical mass and a half-decent hospital.'

'Hospital? You don't feel that bad, do you?'

'I had a terrible night, my dear. I woke up dripping with sweat, feeling as though a huge weight had been pressing down on my face, suffocating me. Patricia told me I shouted for help at the top of my voice. I'm glad you weren't disturbed. By the time Patricia got to me, I was hyperventilating. That's why I feel so drained this morning.'

'It was probably just a nightmare. As you say, Pepe's food was very rich.'

Although her words were designed to reassure Betty, Petra felt a jolt of fear. Too many odd things were happening. She recalled her own nightmare the night before Sam's death in the Bahamas. Her right hand shook as she raised it to push back an errant lock of hair. Just in time she remembered that she wanted to keep her damaged face hidden.

264

Betty had begun talking, her tone urgent. 'I want you to do something for me, Petra, something very important. No one else must know about it, you understand?'

'Of course. I'll do whatever I can, Betty. What is it?'

'I want you to find Elena. Joe's daughter.'

'Elena? Isn't she in Buenos Aires?'

'I don't know where she is. Joe's only contact with her was through her mother, Sofía, who died years ago.'

'What about when Joe died?'

'Elena didn't come to his funeral and there was nothing about her in his will.'

'And you want to find her?'

'Yes. I've been doing a lot of thinking recently. It's only right that she should have a portion of Joe's fortune.'

'Are you sure, Betty?'

'Absolutely. Joe provided for Sofía during her lifetime. Then he left everything to me after endowing his Institute and Foundation.'

'What about your lawyers? Can't they find Elena?'

'I had some communication with them about her, but I don't want Cliff or Ken to know about this. They stick their noses into everything. I'm sure they read my correspondence at every opportunity. You're a resourceful girl; you can use the Internet or whatever you young people do nowadays. And I'll pay for anything you need: advertisements for example, private investigators if necessary.'

Petra felt winded by the enormity of Betty's request and its implications. Although she had no vested interest in the security of the Graceby boys' future, Betty was already planning to spend millions on the Marine Staff Training

Academy. How would they feel about sharing what remained with Elena? She suspected they would be livid if they found out what Betty had asked her to do. With her, and with Betty.

'Why me, Betty? Am I the best person to do this?'

'You're the only one I can trust. I realize what I'm asking of you, my dear. I need your help.' Betty quickly brushed away the tears that filled her eyes.

'You'll have to give me as much information as you can – Elena's full name, date and place of birth, mother's name, last known address, etc. And I won't be able to do anything until I get back to Little Current.'

'I know, my dear. I've written down everything I can think of.' She handed Petra a sealed envelope.

Petra leaned closer and took Betty's right hand in hers. 'I can see how much it means to you. I hope I'm successful. How can I contact you? If you're on the boat, it won't be easy.'

'It's all in the envelope,' Betty said. 'Now, tell me what happened to your face.'

The fog lifted gradually and by noon it was clear enough for them to leave Fayette. Although *Gloriana* was well equipped with radar and perfectly able to travel in fog, Betty had instructed James that she preferred not to do so unless it was absolutely necessary. The danger came not from her boat, but from the numerous small boats that had no radar or radar profile and travelled too fast for the prevailing weather conditions.

Petra was sorry to say goodbye to Fayette. The town had grown up in the pollution-laden days of nineteenth-century industrial production and Man's craft was everywhere, yet there was a touch of mysticism in the way nature had reclaimed the site. Petra was left with a deep sense of history and an abiding feeling of peace.

She sat on the aft deck with Betty and watched the smelter buildings recede as they exited the channel. Betty had recovered enough to get up and dress. Pepe brought them an early lunch. He seemed even more morose than usual, although it didn't diminish his efficiency and the food was up to his normal high standard. He must know Al had gone and the circumstances of his disappearance.

As they approached Escanaba, Betty became more animated. Cliff was waiting on the dock to meet them. Standing tall in khaki slacks and a cream shirt, his silver hair glistening in the sun, he looked as debonair as the day Petra had met him in Nassau. In the four months that had passed since Las Vegas, she had forgotten how much charisma he had. Only as they came alongside could she see the deepening lines across his forehead and around his eyes. He stepped straight off the dock onto *Gloriana*'s deck.

'Cliff! There you are!' Betty said, reaching out a hand.

'How have you been, Mother? Has Patricia been taking proper care of you since you left the Bahamas?'

Betty grimaced. 'Officious and overprotective, that's what she is. I'm not taking any more vitamins or drinking any of her concoctions. My body's reacting against them.'

'Don't be too hasty, Mother. Patricia knows her stuff.'

Ken came down from the flybridge to greet his father. He threw a nervous glance at his grandmother. 'Yeah,' he added. 'She's specially trained in geriatric care.'

'What do you mean, geriatric? Don't write me off yet, young man.'

Petra had to suppress a laugh at the outrage on Betty's face. There was plenty of charge in Betty's battery now that Cliff had arrived, and she appeared to have forgotten her clash with Ken the night before. Up and down like a rollercoaster, that's how their relationship worked.

Petra waited for Cliff to speak to her. He had glanced in her direction but so far not addressed her directly. Naturally, family came first. That was normal, but at the end of her visit to Vegas he'd promised always to make time for her.

When he did speak, he was all business. 'As soon as you're ready, Petra, I'll fly you home. We don't have much time. I have to get Pepe to Chicago today. I'll fly back tomorrow with the new chef and stay for a day or two, Mother.'

'My bag's packed,' Petra said. 'I only need a few minutes.'

'No rush, my dear. Surely, Cliff, it isn't a crisis if you don't leave with Pepe until the morning? You can fly to Chicago and back in one day.'

'It's all arranged, Mother.'

Ken nodded. 'Leave things as they are, Grandma. Dad knows what he's doing. Dad, I have to talk to you.'

'And I want to touch base with Pepe. Make sure he knows what's happening.'

Cliff and Ken departed together, leaving Petra alone with Betty.

'Thank you for sharing Fayette with me, Betty. It's a very special place. I can imagine the clatter of the ships being unloaded in the harbour, the babble of voices, the roar of the fires.'

'You're very special, my dear. And thank you for agreeing to help me.'

At that moment Patricia walked onto the aft deck with a small tray. Betty waved it away. 'You needn't bother, Patricia. I'm not taking any more supplements. You can say what you like.'

'Nonsense!' Patricia sat down next to Betty and began talking earnestly to her. Petra took the opportunity to excuse herself.

Ken opened the door of his cabin for Cliff and shut it carefully once they were inside.

'We have a problem, Dad.'

'We? Or you?'

'We.'

'Is it serious?'

'Yes.'

'Come on then, tell me.'

'As you know, the plan was for me to leave the motorbike on the dock at Fayette. Al was to take it and disappear. I would have ranted about the motorbike being stolen, but done nothing about it. Vehicle thefts happen all the time.'

'Right, so come to the point.'

'Before Al left last night, Petra surprised him up at the Manager's house, stealing stuff from the museum. He roughed her up and locked her in the cellar. The Rangers found her this morning and called the cops. Now they're looking for him.'

'Shit! Just what we need! Why would he do that? Does Pepe know?'

'Pepe saw the cops come aboard and asked me what they wanted as soon as they left. I had to tell him. The cops checked out Al's cabin and asked for information on all of us, even though we already called it in to Customs.'

'Did they find anything in Al's cabin?'

'Nada. It was as clean as a whistle.'

'How come Petra was involved? Weren't you there to see Al off?'

Ken looked sheepish. 'Things got a little out of hand.'

'Let me guess. It was Saturday night, party time. Were you getting something on with Petra?'

'I've got better things to do than lay frigid broads!'

'You shouldn't have been laying anything. You had a job to do, and you blew it! You're a fucking fool!'

Cliff looked at his son in exasperation. It was Ken who had talked him into transporting Pepe and Al, against his better judgement. The fee – half up front, half on completion – would have given them ready money for quite a while. Then he wouldn't have had to worry about being leaned on by dealers or protection men; he could have forgotten about The Poseidon and Ebony, and taken off on his bike …

'So what are we going to do?' Ken asked.

'How the fuck do I know? One thing's for sure: we won't see any more of the dough. In fact, we'll be lucky to keep the first lot and our skins. These guys play hardball. Go and get Pepe. We'll have to negotiate.'

Cliff ran a hand through his silver hair and sat down on the edge of the lower bunk. There was no room to pace in

Ken's compact cabin. Once again, it seemed that the things he touched were turning to lead not gold. He didn't believe Ken's half-story for an instant. The boy was rude and unstable, yet he had his own kind of charm and the ladies lapped it up. Perhaps Petra had given him the come on, then the cold shoulder when the situation got out of hand. She might have agreed to meet him at the Manager's house or gone up there to avoid him … Cliff could only speculate.

Al's behaviour was a complete aberration. He seemed to have added his own agenda to what had been a perfectly simple plan. Cliff kicked the edge of Ken's bunk. Fuck and more fuck! Why couldn't anyone do what they were supposed to do? Now he'd have to deal with Pepe and the cops.

Ken returned with Pepe. Cliff took one look at the chef's closed expressionless face and knew it was going to be even more difficult than he had anticipated.

'What the hell were you and Al thinking of?' he shouted, startling even Ken. 'Robbery with violence? Forcible confinement? You must be mad!'

'I had nothing to do with that. If you'd kept your end of the bargain, we'd have been out of here weeks ago.'

'Not weeks, one week.'

'You've broken our agreement.'

'Like hell I have! This cock-up is Al's fault. If we get investigated by the cops because of it …'

'Cool it, Dad!' Ken interjected. 'James and Nico are around. Voices carry.'

'Al won't get far. He's as good as dead.' Pepe's face was grim. 'I need a phone.'

'Haven't you got your own?'

271

'Give me yours.'

Cliff gave it to him.

Pepe dialled an eleven-digit number that rang twice before it was answered. He spoke rapidly in heavily accented Spanish. The conversation moved back and forth. Pepe seemed to be issuing instructions then answering questions. He began to raise his voice. Suddenly he broke off and turned to Ken. 'What about the girl, Petra?'

'She told the cops she's not pressing charges.'

'That's good, but you never know.' He talked for another few minutes then closed the phone. 'OK. As I said, you've broken our agreement. So there's no more money.'

'Then there's no transportation to Chicago,' Ken snarled. 'You dagos are the ones who fucked this up, not us.'

Cliff saw a dangerous glint come into Pepe's eyes. 'Look, there've been mistakes on both sides. We don't want any more police involvement. I'll get you out of here this afternoon; you can go wherever you want after that and do what you like about Al. If anyone asks questions, I'll say I took you to the hotel restaurant as planned. It's not my problem if you don't hang around to start your new job – and it's not a crime. But I want the rest of the money transferred to my account before we take off for Chicago.'

Ken had left the monetary side of things to his father to arrange. Cliff had set up a separate account to receive the money for this job. The first half had been paid in just before they set off from Nassau. Cliff had moved it immediately to a different account. If they got the second installment of a hundred thousand dollars, they'd be laughing.

Pepe was talking on the phone again. A minute later, he snapped it shut and put it in the pocket of his grey chef's trousers. 'OK. We're making a transfer of fifty thousand. You can check it before we leave.'

Cliff saw Ken about to protest and shook his head in warning. It could have been worse. 'Can I have my phone back?'

'No! I'll keep it for now.'

Petra left Patricia and Betty together in the salon. Apart from one or two last-minute items, her bag was ready. She calculated that unless she were very unlucky, she had about five minutes before Patricia gave up trying to talk Betty into taking her vitamins. Then in all likelihood Patricia would go to the galley or come down to her cabin. It was a risk Petra was prepared to take in order to find the health drinks and supplements. She was becoming more and more convinced that there was something wrong with them.

Patricia's cabin was adjacent to Betty's stateroom, opposite Petra's suite. It shared a bathroom with another cabin that was currently not in use. Both cabins were probably locked. Patricia was that type of cagey person. Petra tried the door anyway and was surprised when the handle gave under her light pressure. Cautiously, she opened the door and looked inside.

It was as neat as she would have hoped a trained nurse's cabin to be, and consequently easy to search. The hanging closet contained several changes of uniform and a few other clothes. The dressing table and night table surfaces were bare, except for a hairbrush and comb and a water glass.

Petra took a quick look in the drawers and cupboards. Nothing of interest. She crossed to the bathroom.

Above the washbasin and toilet was a cupboard with a mirrored sliding door. Petra slid the left-hand section of the door to the right and found a toothbrush, toothpaste and a basic moisturizer. When she leaned over and slid the other half of the door to the left, it caught on something. She put her hand in and found a large packet blocking the runner. Petra pulled it out. It contained exactly what she had been looking for: small sachets of powder to be mixed with water. She extracted two, put them in her jeans pocket, replaced the packet and continued searching.

Time was disappearing fast. Patricia could appear at any moment and there was nowhere to hide. She could try slipping out through the cabin next door, but if Patricia did catch her, she would just have to tough it out.

Petra paused, not sure whether she had heard footsteps on the stairs. After a few anxious seconds, she ran her hand back along one of the shelves and took out three plastic bottles of vitamins, one after the other. They weren't very full. Quickly, she unscrewed the caps and poured out two tablets from each bottle. Any more than that and the eagle-eyed Patricia might notice. Petra wrapped them in a tissue and put them in her pocket with the sachets. She replaced everything in the cupboard and moved the sliding door back into the position in which she had found it. Then she left the cabin. With luck, Patricia would never know she had been there.

Five minutes later, Petra carried her luggage up the stairs. As she set it down in the midships passage, she saw movement through the window on the port side. Pepe was standing on the side deck with a phone to his ear.

'Sí, cincuenta mil,' Petra heard him say in Spanish. 'Yes, fifty thousand.' Then: 'Vale, vale.' OK. As she watched, he ended the call, closed the phone and dropped it over the side of the boat into the water.

What the hell was going on? First Al, now Pepe. Petra had a feeling she was going to be very busy when she got back to Little Current.

CHAPTER

25

'There's been a change of plan,' Cliff announced when Petra returned to the salon. 'Pepe's needed urgently at the restaurant in Chicago. I'll take you as far as Sault Ste. Marie on the American side. You'll have to make your own way from there. That'll save flying time and having to go through Customs and Immigration in Canada.'

Betty remonstrated with him to no avail. Secretly, Petra was relieved. It was no problem to find transportation from The Soo to Little Current and she had been wondering how to handle the situation if one of her colleagues came to check Cliff in at the Manitoulin Island Airport. Banter could easily blow her cover.

Petra's eyes were damp with unshed tears as she said goodbye to Betty. They hugged each other tight. 'You'll be back on the North Channel soon, won't you, Betty?'

'Yes, my dear. We'll spend a few days here then go to Sister Bay to see the goats on the grass roof of the restaurant there. It's twee, but I always enjoy watching them. I wish you could stay with us.'

'I do too. Unfortunately, I have to get back to work.'

Patricia shook Petra's hand without cracking a smile.

James had gone to check in with the harbourmaster. He came aboard just as Petra was leaving with Cliff. Petra wondered if he had deliberately stayed out of the way until the last minute. No doubt it was for the better. She wouldn't feel comfortable starting a relationship with Betty's captain and trying to maintain it. It wasn't just a question of distance dating, which never worked well; there would be something quasi-incestuous about it, because of the strength of her feelings for Betty. But he was attractive, and if the situation had been different, and if he hadn't acted like such a jerk in Fayette …

The twin-engine Cessna was ready and waiting when Cliff and Petra arrived at the Delta County Airport. In the taxi, there had been none of the flirtatious sweet talk of Nassau or even Las Vegas. Cliff kept quiet, engrossed in his own thoughts. Now, strapped in the plane, Petra looked sideways at him. He was working through his pre-flight checklist and talking to the control tower. Then they were cleared for take-off and airborne within a few minutes. Petra didn't mind flying, though she still preferred water rather than air around her. Water was a much better medium in an emergency.

She was determined to make the most of the short flight to The Soo and had made a mental list of topics to discuss with Cliff. First up, Al and Pepe.

'I bet you never thought you had a thief on board *Gloriana*,' she said, watching Cliff's reaction.

'The boat's my mother's domain,' he replied, as slippery as any politician.

277

'Weird, though, that Al and Pepe came so far on the boat, and now going, going, gone! It's almost as if they were stowaways.'

'That's a ridiculous thing to say.'

Maybe, but Cliff's hands tightened on the controls and the red began to spread up the back of his neck.

'My friends are always telling me I have an overactive imagination,' she said.

Cliff grunted.

Petra ticked Al and Pepe off her mental list. Time to find out as much as possible about Elena. Cliff might have maintained contact with her without letting on to Betty or Joe. There was only one way to broach the subject quickly – by taking the bull by the horns.

'Betty was telling me you used to date Joe's daughter, Elena,' she said, keeping the same naïve tone and modifying the truth slightly to protect Ebony. 'Have you stayed in touch with her?'

'Haven't given her a thought for years!'

'Not even after you and Ebony got divorced? People often take up with former partners.'

'Not my style.'

'But Elena was your style when you were young. What was she like? Tell me about her.'

'Why do you want to know?'

'I'm curious.'

'What do you want to know?'

'What do you think I should know?'

Cliff threw her a sidelong glance. 'Haven't we been through something like this before?'

Petra nodded. 'Come on, the ball's in your court. You have to tell. I asked first!'

'OK. You win. Elena was a raven-haired beauty. Lively, quick-witted, naughty when Joe wasn't looking. A bit of a minx – like you, if I'm not mistaken.'

Petra put on her most demure expression. 'Me?'

'Yes, you.'

'If you loved her so much, why on earth didn't you find her again?'

'Listen to Miss Romantic! She was only flirting with me. Six months after she went back to Buenos Aires, she eloped with a polo player. It was all over *Hello Magazine*: "Elena LePinto and Fran Arturo". She didn't care for me.'

'You really believe that? She probably ran away because she was upset. You could still track her down.'

'What? And have her ask for a share of Joe's fortune? Anyway, why are you so interested in Elena all of a sudden?'

Time to change the subject.

'Talking about fortunes, what about the worthy Patricia? A real gem. She must be spending a fortune on vitamins for your mother,' Petra said.

'No one's spending a fortune on anything. I buy them in bulk from a friend.'

'You do? Can you get me some?'

Instead of dismissing her flippant question immediately, Cliff appeared to give it serious consideration.

'Cross-border. It might be difficult. But not impossible. It depends on the quantity. And the delivery method.' There was a faraway look in his eyes as if he were talking about something entirely different.

'I was joking! I don't need vitamins, and I think your mother would be better off without them.'

'Are you some sort of health expert as well as an aquafit instructor, interior decorator and matchmaker?'

'I've done some courses in Nutrition.'

'What haven't you done?'

'Flown a Cessna.'

'I suppose you'd like to try.'

'Definitely.'

Petra was dying to read the information Betty had given her about Elena. It took all her willpower not to rip open the envelope as soon as she had waved goodbye to Cliff. She had kept it sealed and well hidden from him during the flight. He would have recognized his mother's script instantly, as he had in Nassau, and wondered why she was writing.

During the taxi ride from the airport, Petra forced herself not to touch the envelope, knowing she would be interrupted by passport control at the Canadian end of the international bridge. At the bus station, the queue for tickets moved with glacial slowness. Finally, she boarded the late afternoon bus to Sudbury and chose a seat at the back, as far away as possible from a group of teenage backpackers.

She took the envelope out of her shoulder bag and opened it. It contained two folded sheets of paper. The first was a letter. As she read it, Petra could hear Betty speaking to her.

"Petra my dear,

You will have had time to reconsider your offer of help, and I hope you haven't concluded that I'm an eccentric old lady whose delusions deserve to be ignored. In my heart, I know

that will not be the case. You and I are soul mates. We
understand each other in the deepest possible way. I could
not care more for you if you were my own daughter. Be
careful, my dear. Joe's legacy is a weighty one.
With love,
Betty"

Petra's eyes misted over as she finished reading. She shook
her head. It was stupid to be so sensitive. Betty was used to
having lots of people at her beck and call. On the boat, there
was no one else to do her bidding. Petra was a convenient
stooge.

No, that wasn't true. It was exhaustion talking. Less
than twelve hours ago, she had been banging on a trapdoor,
locked in a cellar ... Since then, she hadn't had time to sleep
or think or rationalize her experience. No wonder her head
was a mess.

'Get a grip on yourself, girl.' This time it was her father
talking. Petra folded Betty's letter and looked eagerly at the
second sheet.

"Elena Maria LePinto Sanchez, born Palm Beach,
Florida, USA, September 1, 1958
Father: José Maria LePinto Inara, born San Juan, Puerto
Rico, May 14, 1925, died Las Vegas, USA, May 14,
2006
Mother: Sofía Maria Sanchez Guzman, born Buenos
Aires, Argentina, June 18, 1933, died Buenos Aires,
January 24, 1988
Mother's last known address: Pastelería Guzman, calle
Santiago, Buenos Aires, Argentina"

The second half of the page was a summary by Betty of

what had happened in 1979 and subsequent years. It corroborated what Cliff had told Petra on the plane.

"When Joe found out Cliff had been dating Elena, he sent Elena back to her mother in Buenos Aires. This was in September 1979. Six months later, in April 1980, she ran away with a prominent Argentinian polo player, Fran Arturo, creating a huge scandal. He divorced his wife and according to the tabloid press married Elena in 1982. Elena had no communication with her father after she ran away, and her mother Sofía died in 1988. As far as Joe was concerned, Elena no longer existed. I know this grieved him throughout his life, which is why I wish to find her and make amends."

Once again, Petra blinked away tears. Families could be such diabolical things. Blood ties, like blood stains, were virtually impossible to erase, although in many instances it would be the best thing to do.

Petra wondered whether she should tell A.K. that Betty was looking for Elena. He had contacts at the highest levels that could expedite the search. On the other hand, it was a personal request from Betty to Petra in her capacity as a friend, and Betty had asked her to be discreet. As far as Petra could see, it was not an emergency situation. Betty's health was of concern, but she was not terminally ill or losing her mind to Alzheimer's, despite what Cliff and Ken might like to think.

The easiest place to start was with the Internet. Simply typing in "Elena Maria LePinto Sanchez" might produce results. If that failed, she would email Martin and get him involved. She would also contact Carlo, her Italian friend who was employed by Interpol. It was less than a year since she had found him working undercover on the same megayacht as herself. Without her help, he would never have obtained the evidence he needed to bag several individuals for making and dealing drugs. He owed her one. The only problem might be getting him to reply. As his nickname Mercutio implied, he was mercurial and hard to pin down.

If those initiatives produced nothing, she would have to consider using the methods Betty had suggested and was prepared to pay for: advertising, or hiring a private investigator. That would be a much more serious step and difficult to orchestrate. At that point she would have to ask herself how far she would be prepared to go to help Betty. Elena's reappearance would reduce Cliff and Ken's inheritance significantly, but might it not be good for Cliff to be reunited with his former sweetheart?

Stop being such a sentimental fool, Petra told herself. She realized she was crushing the letter from Betty in her hands.

At the bottom of the second sheet, Betty had set out *Gloriana*'s itinerary for the next few weeks. The yacht was continuing her cruise round Green Bay then spending time in Harbor Springs, Michigan, before returning to the North Channel. With relief, Petra saw that Little Current was not on the list of intended stops. It would be extremely difficult to keep the fact that she was a Marine Unit Sergeant in the RCMP a secret from Ken and James if *Gloriana* docked in town.

Betty had underlined the dates when she planned to be in Killarney and suggested that Petra join her there for a few days. If she could manage it, she would. By then, she hoped to have some information on Elena's whereabouts.

Petra folded the sheets of paper, put them back into the envelope and placed the envelope safely in her bag. She stood up and made her way forward to speak to the bus driver. He confirmed that they would be at the turn-off to Little Current in half an hour. She lurched back to her seat and pulled out her phone. Her partner, Ed Spinone, was expecting her call. He agreed to meet her at the junction.

His white Ford was there when the bus pulled up.

'Hi, Petra!' he said as she thanked the driver and jumped to the ground. He grabbed her bag and threw it into the back seat of the car. 'How was life in the fast lane?'

'Not that fast. An eye-opener, though, in terms of nineteenth-century history.' She told him about Fayette and the way it had insinuated itself into her psyche.

'So that's it? Nothing special to report?'

'Negative.'

Ed studied her hard in the fading light. Petra gritted her teeth. He had the same natural instincts as the Italian breed of gun dog after which his family was named. If a Spinone couldn't sniff out the scent that would lead to the game, no one could.

'It can't have been that uneventful,' he said. 'You look all in. You know we're on at six tomorrow morning?'

'Don't worry. I'll be bright-eyed.'

A couple of hours later, Petra was sitting in her pajamas poring over the computer when her phone rang. She had already done a rapid search of the Internet and turned up plenty of Elenas, Marias and Sanchez's in different combinations, but nothing with LePinto. She had also scanned the information from Betty into her computer and emailed Martin, attaching the pertinent sections.

Writing to Carlo was not so easy. A short interruption would give her brain time to work out what to say. She picked up the phone.

'I thought you'd be back. How did it go?'

Wordy for A.K.

'Betty's fine. Planning to open a Marine Staff Training Academy in Florida.'

A loud silence.

'In Florida?'

'Right. Not Northern Ontario. And there's something else.'

'Oh?'

'Two highly unlikely crewmembers. Hispanic/Latino troublemakers at a guess. Both left the yacht in Michigan. Ostensibly one's a chef, the other, a thug and a thief.'

'Send me a report. Are you OK?'

'Fine.'

A.K.'s curtness was catching. The line went dead before she had time to elaborate.

Instead of writing to Carlo, Petra rushed off a report to A.K. Hearing his gruff yet compassionate voice on the phone had reminded her how solid an ally he was. Although she was exhausted, she marshalled her thoughts and divided the report into two sections: One – Introduction of foreign elements into the United States; Two – Betty Graceby: Health and ambitions.

In the first section, she set out her reasons for suspecting that Pepe and Al were not what they purported to be. She kept it brief. From the start, they had been totally out of place on Betty's yacht. Pepe had been too good, Al too incompetent. It was the Graceby boys who had hired them, not James or Betty. She described Al's attacks on her person, his theft of the silver dollars and gold coin, Pepe's strange behaviour, and Cliff's reaction to her probing. Quickly she read through what she had written. A.K. was a strong believer in a cop's "gut feel", but there was more to it than that.

This thing went way back. She remembered snippets of conversation she had overheard between Ken and Cliff in Nassau and on board Betty's yacht, and the photos that Martin had taken – tussling with Ken over them at *Neptunis*, and confusing the goon who had stopped her from following Cliff in Las Vegas. She added another paragraph and left it at that. A.K. would decide what was significant and whether to alert the U.S. Department of Homeland Security. And Martin would send her the photos if they were needed.

In the second section, Petra explained her concerns over Betty's health and her suspicions that the supplements sourced by Cliff were contributing to Betty's deterioration. Then she discussed Betty's charitable ambitions and her description of Joe LePinto's legacy as weighty. Petra still did not want to mention Betty's search for Elena to A.K. That was a private matter between her and Betty. Satisfied with the report, she emailed it to A.K. and turned her attention back to Carlo.

After staring at her computer screen for ten minutes, Petra could think of no suitably jokey or folksy way of enlisting his help. The only thing to do was to go straight for the jugular. It was too late and she was too tired for anything else.

'Carlo, it's payback time. I need a favour,' she wrote. She attached the information she had sent Martin, put a reminder on her calendar to send the supplements away for analysis, and fell into bed.

26

Martin emailed Petra to say he was in Thailand on a working holiday and wouldn't be back in Toronto for at least a week. As soon as he returned, he would find out what he could. Petra took out her anger and disappointment on a newly arrived American cruiser by confiscating two bottles of California wine and four of beer. It was only when Ed remarked after the fact on her aggressiveness that she realized she was becoming like A.K. Instant results, that's what she wanted.

There was no word from Carlo.

Over the next week, Petra went about her work methodically, but with less than her usual enthusiasm. Ed was not the only one to notice. Twice he asked her out for a drink – something she usually enjoyed. She fobbed him off with feeble excuses. Once she took the Striper out and returned to the marina after only forty minutes.

She spent most of her off-duty hours trawling the Internet for information. In vain. Although she attempted to disguise it from those around her, her level of frustration was reaching crisis proportions. At the end of the week, she emailed Martin again.

'Where are you? I need help!'

After some hesitation, she sent another message to Carlo. 'Your debt is incurring interest. Please get off your sexy ass.'

Despite the fact that she had told herself there was no urgency in locating Elena, Petra felt a growing sense of panic as the days went by and she continued to receive no news from either Martin or Carlo. Betty would be fretting. Men simply couldn't be relied on.

The laboratory in Ottawa to which she had sent one sachet of powdered drink and a sample of each of the supplements was also slow to respond. Surely the results should be ready by now. The testing wasn't cheap and she had couriered the package to the lab instead of using the mail. She had asked them to email the results and archive the samples in case they were needed later. The remaining sachet and samples were tucked away in her lodgings. She was wondering whether to ask Ed to log them in as evidence.

'What's eating you, Petra?' he asked on the tenth day after her return from The Soo.

'Nothing.'

'Don't give me that crap. You've been wound more tightly than an old-fashioned watch spring ever since you got back. No one can say anything to you without having their heads bitten off, least of all the poor Americans you've been checking in. If you're not careful, there'll be complaints to the brass.'

'Are you complaining about me?'

'No, just giving you a friendly warning.'

'Well I don't need it.'

Petra knew she was being a bitch, but couldn't help herself even when she noted a change in Ed's attitude. He stopped trying to use verbal persuasion and attempted to steer her into calmer waters by being silently supportive while reining her in as unobtrusively as possible so that she didn't overstep the mark. They both recognized that there might come a point when he could no longer pull her back from the edge.

On the Friday at the end of Week 2, Petra received a text message from Martin. 'Driving up tmoro. Will call from ferry. What r ur hours? Mx.'

Petra's brain went into overdrive. Why was he coming? Why hadn't he emailed? What was wrong?

She texted back. 'Off duty 6p Sat till 6a Sun.' She couldn't bring herself to sign off with anything like a happy face.

Still worrying, Petra declined Ed's invitation to join him and his wife for dinner and sat down at her computer that evening to check her email again. Three stupid jokes and an invoice from the marina for a minor job that had taken twice as long and cost twice as much as it should have done. She nixed the jokes and sent the marina a demand for more information. Hell! Was nothing right in the world?

She was about to close her computer and go out for a Chinese takeaway when she noticed a new email in her inbox. The lab results were in! Eagerly, she opened it. Ignoring the standard covering letter with its caveats and thanks for the business, she scrolled to the nitty-gritty. The sachet contained glucose, fructose, sodium, potassium, natural and artificial strawberry flavour in a powder base to be mixed with water and consumed as a drink. Nothing unusual. Nothing untoward.

She scrolled down the page. There must be something in the supplements.

Calcium, 600 mg, with 200 mg of Vitamin D to facilitate absorption.

Glucosamine HCl 1500 mg, with Chondroitin Sulfate 1200 mg. A high dose but safe.

Multi-vitamin with minerals: Vitamins A, B6, B12, C, D, E and K; sodium, potassium, magnesium, zinc, etc., etc. The list was endless. All within normal limits.

All quite safe.

Petra read the data again. In her haste, she must have missed something. No, everything was kosher. Then there must be a mistake. She fired off a strongly-worded query to the lab and burst into tears.

The water coursed down her cheeks and onto the keyboard. She didn't care. What she did care about was Betty and her health. It had all seemed so plausible: Betty's decline had started with a minor fall, Cliff had hired a bitch of a nurse and supplied her with stuff to force on Betty… Petra really thought she'd discovered what the problem was. Now she didn't know. It looked as though her overactive imagination had taken the facts and fashioned a fantasy.

Yahoo was telling her that Betty Graceby was trending now – Top of the Pops in fact, as news of the Marine Staff Training Academy caught the imagination of Web surfers everywhere. Betty's plans appeared to be becoming more ambitious by the day. Cliff and Ken would really like that!

Petra was reminded of Betty's Training Academy the following afternoon as she walked along the docks. A three-masted schooner lay port alongside, her sails neatly furled. It was a training ship manned by teenage crew. Every summer it arrived in Little Current for a few days' break from the wind and the waves. The crowds on the boardwalk were dense, and the queue for the ice-cream stand snaked halfway round the building. Nobody was jumping the line or otherwise disturbing the peace, so Petra carried on walking, her mind elsewhere.

She had gone over the lab results one more time the night before while she ate her Cantonese chicken and fried rice. The lab had responded that morning with a detailed explanation of the margin for error. Infinitesimal. So the deterioration in Betty's health couldn't be attributed to scheming by Cliff and Patricia, period.

An hour before the end of Petra's shift, six American boats arrived and had to be inspected. To Ed's astonishment, she made up for her previous over-zealousness by letting them sail through the examination. He hoped the pendulum would settle down in the middle now that it had swung both ways.

By the time Petra reached her lodgings, Martin was sitting outside in his green convertible, waiting as patiently as a hound for its master.

'I knew you'd be along soon!'

'Sorry, late arrivals. Six in an hour and a half. Not bad.'

'So they weren't loaded with contraband!'

'If they were, I didn't see it. Nothing wrong with turning a blind eye now and then.'

Martin looked at her with amusement. 'That's a departure from your usual "all power to the uniform" way of doing things.'

Suddenly Petra felt drained. She leaned towards Martin and gave him a peck on the cheek. 'Why are you here?'

'I've booked us into a cottage at the Wikwemikong Lodge. Drinks at 7.30, dinner at 8, and I'll have you in your uniform again and back here by 6 a.m. Promise!'

A lump rose in Petra's throat and for a few seconds, she couldn't speak. 'OK, but I'll do the in and out of uniform thing myself. Give me ten minutes to change and grab an overnight bag.'

Martin refused to enter into any discussions while he was driving to the Lodge. 'Just relax. I'll tell you all about my holiday massage experiences in due course. You need candlelight and a good bottle of Bordeaux to really appreciate them.'

He parked the convertible by the side of Cottage No. 8 and opened the trunk. Petra had simply put her bag on the back seat, not realizing he had brought all the ingredients for a feast. Smoked oysters, Black Angus steaks, three different salads, freshly baked baguette, a plastic container full of French cheeses, and a box of after-dinner dark chocolates. From a second cooler, Martin took out two bottles of Saint-Émilion, a half bottle of port and two litres of water.

'If we run out of anything, we can get more from the Lodge,' he said, placing citronella candles around the wooden deck that overlooked the water.

One thing about the Canadian North in summer was the size of the mosquitoes. The shortness of the season required them to direct all their energy towards growth and reproduction. Judging by the amount of food and drink Martin had brought, his thoughts might be tending in the same direction.

Petra watched him with a warm, fuzzy feeling. It was the first time she had seen him since Vegas, but he was the same old Martin. Solicitous. Kind. Thoughtful. Like the best kind of older brother. She was glad they weren't going into the restaurant to eat. There was so much she wanted to share with him – though not her bed – and she knew he must have news of Elena. For now, though, she was content to follow his advice and relax.

'So you went to Thailand to do a piece on the state of the country four and a half years after the tsunami that killed hundreds of tourists on Boxing Day 2004. How do you manage to incorporate massage parlours into that?' she asked, sitting back in her Muskoka pine chair, sipping her first glass of wine.

'You can tailor anything to fit,' he replied. 'Slant, spin, call it what you will. The tsunami is just something to hang my hat on at the beginning of the piece.'

'Like the one you wrote on Vegas in April?'

'You didn't like it?'

'I think you were paid to say some of the things you said.'

'It'd take more than a few meals and drinks to seduce me. How about you? Are you ready for a second glass?'

'You know I can't be seduced, Martin.'

'I can still try.'

Petra fell silent. Some issues could never be worked out between them. She wished he would accept that.

'OK, so here's the latest on the greatest thing to hit Ingotville, Ontario, since the meteorite that wiped out its dinosaur population fifty million years ago,' he said, punching the air in a gesture that reminded her of Sam.

'Make that sixty million,' she said, forced into a laugh.

'OK, sixty. Now for the hot poop. I spoke to Geoff Hamilton. Turns out he was on sick leave but is now back in the saddle. The arts centre is a definite go. Green all the way. And that's one of the major criteria in the design contest. The centre must be environmentally sensitive, eco-friendly, and independently sustainable, as well as meeting a few other doublespeak requirements. I suggested a New-Age Taj Mahal with four wind turbines to replace the minarets at the corners, a vast central dome covered in solar panels, and hydroelectric-powered fountains – or wave-powered if they want to move it to the Bay of Fundy.'

Petra choked with laughter and Martin had to beat her between the shoulder blades to bring her back to life.

'Seriously,' he continued when she had recovered, 'the project is well on its way to fruition. I developed an excellent rapport with Geoff, although I couldn't persuade him to tell me who the secret sponsor is.'

'Did you push him?'

'As hard as I could. All in good time, he said, and promised to keep me informed. In fact, he's asked me to act as their Press Liaison Officer when the time comes.'

'What's your opinion, Martin? Do you think Betty is the sponsor? I did until she told me about her Marine Staff Training Academy.'

'There's a lot of hype on the Internet about that,' Martin answered. 'In fact, I plan to ask her for an interview so that I can do an exclusive.'

'Ever the journalist! But what do you think? One doesn't preclude the other.' Petra drained her wine and helped herself to another smoked oyster.

'No, but both would require big, big bucks.'

'And since she's giving a share of her fortune to Elena …'

Petra broke off as Martin stood up and waved the neck of the bottle he was holding at her wine glass. He filled it nearly to the top then filled his own. He placed the empty bottle on the table and sat down heavily in his chair, the expression on his face sombre. The suspicion Petra had harboured since receiving Martin's message the day before condensed into a certainty. Everything he did had a motive.

'Petra …'

'I know something's wrong, Martin. Otherwise you wouldn't be here.'

'I hate to be the bearer of bad news, but I couldn't just send you an email or phone. I'm so sorry. Elena's dead.'

Petra stared at the water. 'I guessed as much. When did it happen?'

'Ten years ago.'

'That long? She must have been only about forty.' A minute went by before she spoke again. 'How did she die?'

'Suicide.'

Petra closed her eyes. 'How did you find out?'

'It wasn't easy. In the end, polo was the key.' Martin's voice was gentle. 'Even though her marriage to Arturo didn't last more than five years, she stayed on the circuit like some sort of groupie.'

'In Argentina?'

'She moved to Spain where she met and married a player named Ian McInley. Canadian, according to one of the specialist magazines. That didn't last long, either.'

'Any children?'

'None that I can find.'

'How did she kill herself?'

'Alcohol combined with barbiturates. Not the most heroic death.'

'What a waste.'

When Petra opened her eyes after a long trance-like silence, the citronella candles were flickering in the breeze. Martin was preparing to light the barbecue. He had left her to think her own thoughts and to mourn what now could never be.

'How am I going to break the news to Betty?' she whispered.

'There's only one way.'

'I know. It was a rhetorical question. She'll be devastated. She was bent on making amends for Joe's rejection of Elena. Now there can be no closure. I'll have to go and see her in Killarney as soon as she gets back.'

'Do you want me to come with you?'

'No, Martin, thank you. This is something I have to do myself.'

CHAPTER

27

A ten-day hiatus gave Petra time to put Martin's revelation about Elena into perspective and to plan how she would present the news to Betty. Suicide was not an easy form of death to deal with. Family members often blamed themselves for not being able to prevent it, and there was always a shadow of suspicion that it might occur again somewhere down the line.

When she checked the itinerary Betty had given her, Petra saw that *Gloriana* was due to be in Killarney over the coming weekend. Perfect. Killarney was only an hour or so away by water, and she was scheduled to be off duty Saturday and Sunday. She had been stationed in Killarney the previous summer and knew it well.

On Friday afternoon, Petra called The Fisherman's Lodge and Marina in Killarney. A girl named Liz answered the phone. She confirmed that Betty Graceby's yacht had arrived at lunchtime and checked in for at least a four-night stay.

'Can I take a message for Miss Graceby?'

'No, thanks. I'll get in touch with her myself.'

Saturday morning, the skies were clear, the wind light, and the forecast benign for the whole weekend. Petra set off from Little Current in *Petrushka* just before noon. After a lifetime as a performer, Betty was not at her best early in the morning and given her recent weakened state of health, Petra judged it would be better to arrive once lunch was over. She still found it hard to believe the laboratory's assertions that the test results on the health drink and vitamins were valid. She was toying with the idea of sending the other set of samples to a different lab for a second opinion.

During the sixty-minute trip to Killarney, Petra rehearsed what she would say to Betty. The difficult thing would be to soften the blow before it hit. Betty was hoping to redress what she had come to feel was a great injustice. She was investing a great deal of herself in the search for Elena, as she was in the Marine Staff Training Academy. Bad news might damage her health even further.

The closer Petra came to Killarney, the more she worried. She passed Cash Flow Rock without noticing and slowed down automatically as she entered the channel from the west. *Gloriana* was docked on the town side, about halfway along the narrow cut that separated Killarney from George Island. As she drove by the yacht, she averted her gaze and hoped no one would be on deck. She wasn't yet ready to be recognized or confronted by James, Ken, Patricia or the remaining crew. Her plan was to check in to the marina at the Lodge, tidy herself up and collect her thoughts before walking over to visit Betty.

Petra pulled into a vacant slip directly in front of the Lodge and secured *Petrushka*. There were surprisingly few boats in the marina. No doubt the calm weather forecast for the weekend had tempted boaters to anchor out. She walked over to the dock office and found a note pinned to the door: "For assistance, please go to the bar".

Petra headed back to the front of the building. During the day, The Fisherman's Lodge was quiet. In the evenings it was a magnet for locals and visitors. The restaurant had a reputation for fine dining at reasonable prices, with live piano music Wednesday through Sunday. The bar had a vibe all its own. Frequented mainly by a young, late-night crowd, it drew the hikers, canoeists, kayakers and fishermen, as well as some of the boaters and their crew. The place could be raucous until the early hours, and the cops, as Petra knew from last summer, sometimes had to be called to settle things down.

The screen door that gave access to the bar from the patio squeaked atrociously as Petra pulled it open. Inside, the heavy wooden chairs and tables were clean but bare. The bar was unmanned. She went into the hall and across to the restaurant. The room was empty although the tables were set for dinner; the piano was closed and covered. The whole place had a deserted feel that disturbed her.

Somewhere deep inside the building, a phone rang three times then stopped. Footsteps echoed down the wooden stairs and through the hall. Petra returned to the bar. A girl was standing behind the counter, trying to fit an unopened bottle of Scotch into one of the dispensers.

'Are you in charge of the marina?' Petra asked.

'Just a mo'. This bloody bottle's jammed.'

The girl pushed a mass of curly blonde hair out of her

way and examined the tap on the dispenser. The roots of her hair were dark. Petra rested her elbows on the counter. She noticed a butterfly tattoo on the girl's right shoulder blade, outside the scope of her faded tank top. Her arms were muscled and a deep brown. Her legs too, beneath the rolled-up short shorts. No excess fat there. An outdoor girl – one that looked the part.

Petra was an outdoor girl too but kept it well hidden under her pale, almost translucent skin. 'Can I help?' she asked.

'No, I've got it. What can I do for you?'

'I've tied my Striper up out front. I'd like to stay overnight.'

'At the dock?'

'Yes.'

'No problem. Just fill out this form.'

Petra paid the $30 fee in cash. Although she could easily have found dockage through her RCMP connections, she preferred to retain her anonymity.

'Aren't you the person who phoned yesterday asking about Betty Graceby?'

'You must be Liz. You have a good memory for voices.'

'A good memory, period. It's useful in this job. Are you a friend of the Gracebys?'

Petra nodded. 'A friend of the family.'

'I've met Ken Graceby. He comes in for a few beers.'

'I can imagine. Have you been working here long?'

'Last year I worked part-time, this year I'm full-time.'

'You look after the marina as well as the bar?'

'Only for a couple of hours while the guys are at lunch.'

Petra caught sight of the clock above the bar. The afternoon was slipping away. 'Thanks for checking me in. I have to go. See you later.'

Liz was already reaching up to tidy the less used bottles of aperitifs and liqueurs.

Petra approached Betty's yacht with a familiar sinking feeling in her stomach. It was never easy to be the bearer of bad news. She noticed that the Boston Whaler was not in its cradle on the top deck, and she couldn't see it anywhere in the water nearby. It would certainly make life easier if the boys weren't on board, although she would still have to get rid of Patricia in order to have a private conversation with Betty. Another outing in the wheelchair might be on the cards.

Petra knocked hard on the side of the boat. All the blinds were down on the windows facing the dock. 'Hello! Betty? Permission to come aboard,' she shouted. When there was no answer, she repeated her call.

Petra walked the length of the yacht. There was no sign of movement. Where was everyone? Patricia at least should be on board. Then the blind covering the aft deck window was pulled up. Betty peered out.

'Petra! I thought I heard your voice in my daydreams. Come aboard!'

A few minutes later, Petra was seated in one of the candy-striped chairs on the aft deck, next to Betty.

'What a pleasant surprise, my dear! I was going to ask Cliff to phone you to let you know we were here.'

Betty's voice had a lilt that hadn't been there a few weeks ago. She had colour in her cheeks and was moving about without assistance. Her lavender eyes danced, the dark circles beneath them much diminished. Something had changed.

'You look wonderful, Betty. Patricia's tonics must be working at last.'

'Patricia? She resigned before I had her fired. I gave Cliff an ultimatum: her or me.'

'So who's looking after you?'

'Cliff, and Fernando, the new chef. His food's not as exquisite as Pepe's, but it's still excellent and he's a very caring person. He'll help me if I need help after Cliff leaves. I persuaded Cliff to join us for a week.'

'Cliff's here now?'

'Yes, not on board though. They all went fishing this afternoon. Your timing couldn't be better.' Betty studied Petra's face. 'I'm sure you have news for me.'

Petra bit her lip. Trust Betty to strip away the protective outer layers and go straight to the heart of the matter. Petra crossed her legs and uncrossed them, unsure now how to begin.

'Whatever it is, my dear, you came here to tell me something, so go ahead. What have you found out?'

'There's no easy way of doing this.' Petra spread her hands and looked into Betty's eyes, seeing her own sadness reflected in them. 'Betty, I'm afraid Elena is dead.'

Betty bowed her head. After a minute's silence, she looked up. 'I had a horrible feeling that might be the case as soon as I saw you today. You don't reach my age without realizing that death is very much a part of life. Tell me the details.'

Betty sat without moving, her hands clasped in her lap, while Petra recounted what Martin had found out. As Petra fell silent, Betty sighed heavily. 'You know it doesn't surprise me, my dear. Elena threatened suicide more than once during the years she was living with Joe when he was trying to control her. She had an unstable streak and was a tearaway like Cliff. They were well suited. Had we let them stay together, they might have sorted each other out. I regret now that we didn't. But one can't live on regrets, they're even more unhealthy than Patricia's vitamins!'

Petra had to smile at Betty's joke. After the briefest of intermissions, the show must go on.

'That's better, my dear. We must forget about Elena, and not mention anything about it to Cliff or Ken. Since I can't undo the past, I'm going to concentrate on the future. My Marine Staff Training Academy is generating enormous interest. Do you think I should call it The GraPinto Academy?'

'Why not? It unites you and Joe in an endeavour that would have meant as much to him as it does to you.'

'You're such a comfort and support, my dear. I knew I could count on you.'

'All I've done is bring you bad news about Elena.'

'Sad news, but not bad.'

'What's not bad, Mother?' Cliff said, appearing in the doorway to the salon.

'Your hearing, Clifford, and my health now that Patricia has gone. I was just telling Petra how much better I was feeling. What I may not have told you is that I threw the remaining health drinks and vitamins over the side in Harbor Springs.'

Cliff nodded in Petra's direction. 'If you did, you threw away a lot of money, Mother.'

'Well, what were you going to do with them? Take them yourself?'

Betty was in a feisty mood, hitting back at Cliff instead of letting him manipulate her. Was it a reaction to the news about Elena or her new modus operandi since Patricia's departure? Cliff looked weary and grey-faced. Not like a man who had just been out fishing in one of Ontario's most beautiful areas. Petra kept her tone light.

'Did you catch anything, Cliff?'

'I'm not into fishing. I've been sleeping.'

'I'm afraid Cliff has the VIP cabin, my dear,' Betty said. 'If I'd known you were coming ...'

'That's not a problem. I can stay on board *Petrushka* or drive home tonight.'

'I won't hear of it. You can have Patricia's old cabin, and Cliff will book dinner at the Lodge for all of us. I gave Fernando the evening off. You can sample his Eggs Benedict tomorrow.'

'But ...'

'No buts, Cliff. Everything's arranged.' Betty winked at Petra.

Petra arrived at the restaurant with a certain amount of trepidation, not knowing how the evening would unfold. She was wearing her purple knit dress and black strap sandals. The outfit suited her mood and the underlying solemnity of the occasion.

Betty had put on a simple black linen dress with a wide red leather belt. She embraced Petra warmly and gave no sign that anything was amiss. Cliff appeared cool and unruffled in a black silk shirt and a cream tropical suit like the one he had been wearing in Nassau. He opted for formality and shook Petra's hand.

Petra studied his face, trying to decide whether he had overheard her final words to Betty before making his presence known that afternoon. There was a better than even chance that he had. But if so, did it matter? It would only have mattered if Elena had been alive to receive a share of Joe's fortune.

Ken and James followed Cliff's lead and shook hands with Petra. In the circumstances, it was probably best. She had decided to play it cool as far as they both were concerned. The way they had behaved in Fayette still bugged her, but this wasn't the right time or place to tackle them about it.

As they took their seats, the piano player looked up and smiled in recognition at the Gracebys. He was playing a medley of classical favourites that he followed with some jazz. Then he moved on to popular songs. Before long, everyone in the room was chatting easily.

Perhaps the evening wasn't going to be as much of an ordeal as she had anticipated, Petra thought. She showed her amusement when Ken and James struck up a conversation with four well-oiled fishermen at the next table.

'What are you laughing at?' James asked her. 'They're going to take us to the Fox Islands tomorrow morning. You know those islands. Come with us!'

'I was looking forward to Fernando's brunch. And I came to see Betty…'

'Go while I'm still sleeping, my dear,' Betty said. 'Cliff will be up in time to keep me company until you get back – if he doesn't drink too much, that is.' She looked pointedly at her son.

Petra had never before heard Betty comment on Cliff's drinking. Betty herself had been abstemious, a habit she had acquired as a performer and one that was hard to break she had told Petra. But Cliff had been refilling his glass with wine at double the rate of anyone else's. Betty was no fool. She would suspect that he had heard more of their conversation than he had let on.

With a sardonic smile that made him look like Ken, Cliff raised his glass to Betty. The pianist began asking for requests. An Irish girl stood up and ran through her repertoire of nostalgic ballads. The noise level rose as people joined in the choruses. When one of the diners called for "Amazing Grace", Petra saw tears glisten in Betty's eyes. She leaned across the table.

'Will you sing for us, Betty?'

There was a moment's silence. Then Betty lifted her chin and gave a determined nod.

'No!' Cliff shouted.

'When you were little, Cliff, you used to beg me to sing,' Betty said.

'That was then.'

'And this is now.' She laid a hand on his arm. 'I think I should, Cliff. It's only right.'

CHAPTER

28

By the time Petra repaired to the bar with James, Ken and Cliff, her emotions were in tatters. Betty's rendering of "Amazing Grace" had brought her so close to losing control that she had had to leave the table and go into the hall to avoid making a fool of herself. It had also provided a measure of closure she had not thought possible.

As they walked in, the smell hit Petra like the stench of seaweed at low tide. Stifling heat, beer, sweaty bodies, unwashed camping and hiking gear with a whiff of mosquito repellent. The density of the scrum at and between the tables was way above the allowable limit and the decibels high enough to meet her father's definition of a rumpus.

Ken elbowed his way through the crowd to the bar. Between the end of the L-shaped counter and the wall was a small area with sufficient room for the four of them to stand. He waved them over. Petra felt like a diminutive kingpin in the middle of the three men. James began asking her about the Fox Islands. She described them with enthusiasm, emphasizing their rugged appeal.

Liz was behind the bar, working alongside a young man with tattooed sleeves. She was dressed for the evening in a red cut-off tank top with a drooping neckline and a black tube miniskirt that barely covered her backside. Ken called across to her and shouted out their order.

'Hey!' she said when she delivered the two red wines and two beers. 'Where were you guys last night?'

'Grandma insisted we eat on board then Jamie wanted to hit The Anchor, didn't you, mate?' Ken said.

James lifted his left eyebrow and grinned. 'If you say so.'

'I thought you were the captain,' Petra interjected before she could stop herself.

'Ah! *Petrushka*. The little family friend.'

'Minx, Petra Minx.'

'No need for introductions, you know who I am. And who's this? Another friend?' Liz asked, pointing to Cliff.

'My father,' Ken answered without apparent embarrassment.

Liz cocked her head and appraised Cliff. 'No way! Not old enough and too smooth.' She pushed one of the glasses of wine towards him.

'My ex and I were very young when we had this cub,' Cliff responded, letting his eyes descend slowly from the barmaid's face to her crotch.

Petra and James exchanged glances. The sexual charge in the air was palpable. Liz had the wired hungry attitude of someone out to find something better in life. If it came in the form of a man old enough to be her father, so be it. She tossed her oiled curls and rested her forearms on the bar so that her tank top revealed more of her compact conical breasts.

'Mature is good,' she announced.

The tension decreased a notch as Liz moved away to serve other customers who were clamouring for her attention. Petra's forehead was damp with perspiration. Some of the patrons were taking their drinks onto the verandah to take advantage of the nighttime breeze. Inside the bar, the air was becoming heavier and heavier with smoke from those too lazy or contrary to go outside for a cigarette. Petra noticed a window high up behind James and reached for the handle.

James pushed her gently out of the way. 'Good move, Petra. Bugger the mosquitoes!'

'They won't survive in this atmosphere,' she shot back.

Seeing how easily James opened the window, how fluid and economical his movements were, Petra realized how nice he was to have around. Suddenly she was not sure that she wanted to reopen the issue of Fayette. Bar-hopping and girls in every port seemed to be part of his and Ken's lifestyle, as they were for sailors the world over. She understood that they provided a release from the stress of being on the water, of facing the elements and maintaining, for hours or days at a time, the concentration and discipline required to navigate safely whatever the conditions. Only when she lost that rational focus did the thought of their puerile behaviour begin to bother her.

James's proximity in the small space was disturbing, though. Petra was conscious of his odour: tangy and warm, not unpleasant like many of the bodies in the room. She eased away from him, but found a few minutes later that she was back in the same position as before. Had he moved or she, or both of them?

Cliff was swaying on his feet and interrogating Ken.

'The barmaid, Liz, what's she like? Have you had her?' Cliff steadied himself against the bar.

'Dad! I think you've had enough.'

'You can never get enough, you should know that, boy.' He punctuated his words with a wag of his finger: 'I .. think .. you .. do .. know .. that. "Never enough", that's my motto.'

'Dad, you're pissed. Go back to the boat.'

Sweat was dripping down Cliff's face, even though he had taken off his jacket. He was holding it by the back of the collar and teetering on his feet.

'Come on, Dad, give me your jacket, I'll take you back.' Ken grabbed Cliff's arm. He wrestled with him for a minute and began to escort him out of the bar.

'I've never seen Cliff Graceby like that,' James said to Petra as Ken and Cliff departed. 'He's always so controlled and immaculate.'

'We all have a hidden side.'

'Look, if you're referring to Fayette …'

'I wasn't. There's no point in going over old ground. *Carpe diem*. Let's just live for today.'

'OK. Whatever you say.' With a puzzled look on his face, James went off to fetch two vacant bar stools he had spotted.

Petra and James were deep in conversation when Ken returned a quarter of an hour later minus his father.

'He's out of things for the time being. God knows what's got into him,' Ken said. He clicked his fingers to attract Liz's attention and ordered another round of drinks.

This time when Liz brought them over, she stayed to

chat with Ken. Hedging her bets, Petra noted with a twitch of disapproval. Then she realized Liz was talking about Betty.

'I was reading about Betty Graceby on the Internet. You're a relative of hers, aren't you?'

'Yeah, she's my grandmother.'

'Cool. You must have fun on that boat. Need any crew?'

'Not right now. Anyway, what do you know about boats?'

'Nothing,' Liz said, 'but I could learn. Anything would be better than this. Isn't your gran opening a Marine Staff Training Academy?'

'Yeah, in Florida.'

'I could apply to go there at the end of the season, instead of going to Spain. I can speak Spanish, you know.'

'Oh yeah?'

'Sí. I was born in Spain. You or your dad could put in a good word for me, couldn't you?'

'I guess so.'

'Is your dad coming back?'

'Dunno. He might. He's pretty resilient.'

'Shouldn't you go and see how he is?' Liz suggested, putting her hand on his arm. 'I'll come with you.'

Ken shook his head. 'Can't do it. My grandmother would kill me if I took you aboard, not to mention the captain.' He threw a glance at James and removed Liz's hand from his arm. 'But we could go back to your place when you finish here.'

'What, you and Jamie? There's an idea. I can call Susie, my mate,' Liz said, casting a sideways look at James and ignoring Petra.

Watching the way Liz was operating, Petra felt disgusted and, at the same time, sorry for Ken. Didn't he realize he was being played for a fool? Liz seemed to have no morals when it came to getting something – anything – she wanted. She would eat him for breakfast and spit out the gristle. And now she was trying to draw James into her web.

James grabbed Ken's shoulder. 'Don't involve me in anything, mate. Drink up, Petra. Let's go for a walk.' He slapped his beer bottle on the counter and got down from the stool on which he had been sitting.

'I'll take that,' said an unexpected voice from behind him. It was Cliff, minus his jacket. His hair was damp and slicked back as if he had just taken a shower. He appeared to be at least half sober. He nudged James aside and took his place. Immediately, Liz came to take Cliff's order.

'Back for more?' she said, looking at him with wide fiery eyes. 'I like a man with stamina.'

The sexual innuendos and Liz's unabashed interest in Cliff were beginning to seriously annoy Petra. Her protective instincts rose to the fore.

'He's spoken for, Liz. And if he isn't, you are,' she said, pointing to Ken who was glaring at Liz and at his father. 'Don't you have an arrangement with Ken?'

'Petra, come on, it's none of your business. Leave these three to work things out.'

James seized her arm as she slid off the stool and led her out of the bar.

'Ménages à trois never work!' she said.

'If you like them, they do.'

'Father and son? That's gross.'

'Who says it's going to happen?'

Cliff altered his position on the bar stool and studied the barmaid's figure as she served a new group of loud hikers. Her athletic build reminded him of Ebony, though she was much shorter and had wider shoulders. More of a javelin thrower than a marathon runner. And she didn't have the African colouring. The hair roots plus the olive tone of her skin marked her as a brunette masquerading as a blonde. In this light, her eyes were a rich brown. Spanish eyes reminiscent of Elena's, with the same kind of naughty gleam.

He closed his eyes to blot out the image of Elena as she had been when they met thirty years ago – shaking her dark curls at him, throwing him glances full of promise. To discover so abruptly that she was dead had shaken him to the core. Not that he had wanted ever to see or speak to her again.

Elena had betrayed him and he had closed his mind to any prospect of reconciliation. It was only Petra's questions about her during the plane ride to The Soo that had reawakened a faint interest in what she had become. An interest that lately had begun to grow. But now there was no possibility of changing his mind. A cornerstone had been removed from the foundation of his existence.

Cliff stared off into the distance. A bead of perspiration formed at his hairline and threatened to run down his forehead. He wiped it away. In the mirror behind the bottles along the wall, he caught sight of a girl. A girl with long black hair, like Petra.

Suddenly, through the mirror, he saw with awful clarity: she was the problem! Petra ... Petra Minx ... These issues surfaced when Petra was around. Why had she brought news of Elena to his mother? Betty must have asked her to. They were as thick as thieves.

Fuck Petra. That was what he had wanted to do from the beginning. He should have acted on his impulse. Underneath she was like Elena, he was sure; if he could just break through the barriers she kept putting up …

Teases and minxes, all of them. Fuck 'em all! Cliff slammed his fist on the bar.

'Hey, Dad. Are you OK? What's up?' Ken looked anxiously at Cliff who had been sitting slumped on his stool like a sack of garbage left by the side of the road. He hadn't touched the wine Liz had delivered with a come-on smile that she extended at the last minute to include Ken.

Now Cliff was drumming his fingers on the counter.

'Keep out of it.'

'But Dad …'

'Fuck off, boy. You're bugging the hell out of me. I've got to think things through.'

'Suit yourself. I know when I'm not wanted.'

29

The cocaine kicked in immediately. It magnified every sensation and sent a blast of energy coursing through Cliff's body like molten lava down the side of a volcano. Cliff ground his teeth as he felt the hard hot throb in his groin. He looked wildly round his cabin. His nerve endings were singing under the influence of the drug. He could feel the surrounding space as if it were water. Where was Petra? It was time to make good on the laughing invitation that had been in her blue-green eyes from the beginning. He wanted to see her close those eyes and lift her slim hips to meet his pulsing erection. There was so much they could do …

Where the fuck was she? They had been together. Then he remembered. Petra had left the bar to go for a walk with James, Betty's prick of a captain. It was Liz he was meeting as soon as the bar closed. Liz, whose brown eyes flashed with the savage light of the predator, promising to devour him.

Cliff strode towards the door, paused with his hand on the handle. Betty was asleep in the master stateroom only a few metres away. She might wake up and come looking for him. Best to put the stuff away.

He snorted another half line and rubbed a little into his gums. He put the pouch containing what was left into his wash kit in the bathroom and swept the rest of the paraphernalia into the top drawer of the dressing table. After scanning the room, he opened the cabin door, checked the hallway before walking out and closed the door behind him as quietly as he could.

Petra was using the cabin Patricia used to have, directly opposite Cliff's. Her door was closed. Was she back from her walk and sleeping now, or still out with James? The drug had heightened his animal instincts but contaminated his sense of time.

He eased the door to Petra's cabin open. It was dark and absolutely quiet. No breathing, no human presence. A feeling of acute disappointment seized him. Petra would have to wait until he had finished with Liz.

Cliff left the boat and made his way to the Lodge. Liz had told him to use the side door of the bar, the one with the blue light above it. The thought of her hot lips mouthing the words brought another surge of blood to his loins. Already his penis was on fire. How much longer could it be before it burst out of his shorts like a cork out of a bottle of champagne?

He found the door and let himself into the darkened bar. The air was fetid with sweat and stale cigarette smoke. Where the hell was Liz? Liz or Petra.

In the back corner of the room, near where he had been sitting not so long ago, Cliff heard low grunting noises. There was just enough light from the hall to see two figures: a man and a woman. The man's trousers were halfway to his ankles. Facing him, pressed up against the wall, was the barmaid. The man was pumping her furiously, the muscles in his buttocks driving the action to a violent crescendo.

With a white-hot flare of anger, Cliff propelled himself across the room. He caught his foot on the leg of a chair and cursed loudly. Ken spun round as Liz pushed him away. She stood staring at Cliff, naked from the waist down, her thong discarded on the floor. She licked a finger and put it to her crotch.

'You're late, but not too late,' she said.

Ken gave a sneering laugh. 'Hey, Dad! You asked me how she was. Well, she's hot, real hot. Be my guest,' he said with a nod in Liz's direction. 'You'll only be one of many,' he added as he zipped himself up. He crossed the room and disappeared into the hallway.

Cliff could see the tips of Liz's nipples under her thin cotton top. Below the waist, she was all muscle and legs. His eyes settled on the patch of shiny dark hair at her crotch. She was stroking herself and crooning. The cocaine drove him forwards.

She lifted her finger and held it out to him. 'Unfinished business,' she murmured.

Cliff ran his tongue over his gums, feeling the buzz. He took another step towards her and accepted her invitation. Liz's finger smelled and tasted of sex: raw, uninhibited, animal sex. At that moment, there was nothing else in the world.

Several hours later, Cliff stumbled back to the dock and boarded *Gloriana*. He was fucked. Boy was he fucked. And there would be more to come over the next few days. He paused outside the door to Petra's cabin, the recollection of what he had wanted to do earlier that night causing his penis to stir ever so slightly.

On the other side of the door, Petra tensed as she lay in bed. Something had woken her. Someone was out there. Was it Cliff, on his way back from a rendezvous with Liz? She had caught sight of him leaving the dock just as she had been wondering how to say goodnight to James after their walk along the foreshore. Seeing Cliff hurrying towards the Lodge had reminded her of Liz's flagrant behaviour and convinced her not to replicate it. As a result, she had placed the chastest of chaste goodnight kisses on James's cheek, even though they had sat close together on a bench talking intently for over half an hour.

Petra slowed her breathing and listened. If it wasn't Cliff outside her door, who was it? Ken? An intruder? James? She hadn't thought to lock her door as she would have done in a hotel. Now it was better to stay quiet and still. She remained on her guard, alert to the slightest sound of movement. The seconds became a minute and the minute two minutes, then three, before she heard Cliff's cabin door open and someone close it with what could have been a sigh.

CHAPTER

30

After a night of fitful sleep, Petra dragged herself out of bed at 8 a.m. to get ready to meet James, Ken and the four fishermen who had undertaken to show them the Fox Islands. By 10 however, it was clear that Ken and the other four were no-shows.

'Maybe I should just go home,' Petra suggested.

'Betty will be disappointed if you do, and I want to see those islands,' James insisted. 'You love them and we won't feel the heat and humidity out on the water. We can take the Whaler. Whaddaya say?'

Petra hid a smile. He was as persuasive as Cliff had been in Nassau over the dolphins. 'All right. I've got my GPS.'

When they reached the islands, she directed James through the uncharted waters to her favourite one of the group. It was shaped like a pyramid with a domed instead of a pointed top. Bare orange-tinted rocks sloped down to meet the shallow turquoise water. Later in the day, the setting sun would bring out the pink rather than the orange in the rocks and turn the surrounding water a deeper shade of blue.

James brought the Whaler carefully into a crevice that was just wide enough to accommodate the boat without damaging her sides. Petra jumped out and tied a line round a large boulder.

'Now for my little ritual,' she said. 'The first thing I do whenever I come here is go to the top. See that tree?' She pointed to a stunted pine that was leaning at an angle of 60 degrees. 'That's where I sit, cross-legged like a Buddha. I listen to the birds then I scan the horizon. The air is so clear, you can see for miles … ' The words came tumbling out and Petra stopped in embarrassment. 'You probably think I'm crazy,' she finished as she stepped over a tenacious pocket of grass that was clinging to the barren rock.

'No I don't,' James said. 'I can see how much it means to you. Off you go, kiddo. I'll follow in a minute.'

He let Petra run on ahead to the summit, as if he sensed that he was present as a special invitee, tolerated but not really included.

'I'm glad the others didn't come,' Petra said after completing her ritual. 'Ken and those guys wouldn't have appreciated the beauty of this place.'

'Don't underestimate Ken,' James warned, reminding Petra that Martin had once said the same thing. 'He can be a lout, but basically he's a good guy. He does a lot of the right things for the wrong reasons.'

'And, I suppose, a lot of the wrong things for the right reasons?'

'From his point of view, undoubtedly!'

Petra lay back on the warm rock and placed her hands behind her head. James lay down beside her. She was aware of his closeness, as she had been the night before in the bar at the Lodge. She wondered what he was thinking about and whether he was remembering the walk they had taken together and sitting on the bench afterwards, talking quietly.

Suddenly James rolled onto his side and propped himself up on his elbow. He leaned towards Petra and looked into her eyes. They were as deep and intense as the ocean.

'I'm sorry for what happened in Fayette,' he said. 'You were my date for the evening and I screwed it up.'

'I thought it was Ken who was doing the screwing,' Petra said with forced lightness. 'You don't have to apologize. I probably overreacted after what happened with Betty at dinner.'

James moved closer and Petra felt herself stiffen.

'Relax, kiddo,' he whispered. 'I should have apologized before but I didn't know how. Your island is magic,' he continued, reaching out to stroke her cheek.

His caress was as delicate as a cat's whisker. It sent a shiver through Petra's body from the top of her head to the tip of her toes. Her heart began to race. She knew he was going to kiss her. If she let it happen, it would change the game forever. Was that what she wanted? She wasn't sure. Then his lips brushed hers. She gave up trying to reason and surrendered to the moment.

After what seemed like an eternity, she broke the kiss. 'I have to breathe,' she gasped, gulping in air and clinging to James as though she was drowning.

He looked at her with laughter and a new tenderness in his eyes. 'Better now?'

She gave a small nod and raised her face to his.

In the far distance a loon called. Petra ignored its plaintive warning. James's tongue was awakening sensations that she hadn't felt for a long time.

The loon called again. This time she couldn't block it out. Other noises began to intrude into her consciousness. Noises on the rocks below. Abruptly, she pushed James away.

'What's wrong?'

'We have company. Kayakers,' she said, sitting up to look. 'They camp here sometimes.'

'Shit!'

'I couldn't agree more!' Her pulse was slowly returning to normal. 'We'd better go and see what they're doing.'

'I guess.'

Petra scrambled to her feet and started down the slope.

James caught her hand as he came up beside her, forcing her to slow down. 'Petra, wait! That was … special.'

'I thought Aussies used words like "bonzer" and "swell".'

'They do, but I was trying to be serious. How about we try it again someday?'

Petra shook off his hand and began to run. 'Maybe. But not now.'

The kayakers were unloading bushels of gear, clearly planning to stay the night. Petra spoke briefly to the group leader and headed for the Whaler.

'Why don't you drive?' James said, seeing the taut look on her face. 'You know the way out of here.'

Petra nodded but felt like shaking her head instead. Waters she could navigate, but the maelstrom of feelings

James had stirred up left her rudderless. She needed time to reorient herself.

She startled James as she was about to turn the key by saying: 'No, I'm not going to put the motor on. We'll just drift and see where the current takes us. A few more minutes won't matter.' Maybe that's what she and James needed to do – coast for a while and see what happened.

James looked doubtful. The shallow water was full of rocky hazards. 'I assume you've done this before.'

'I have. Trust me.'

'I do.'

They sat drifting in the Whaler, the motion of the water lulling them into a kind of stupor. Unseen currents carried them safely round the larger rocks and over the top of small ones that wouldn't damage the keel. Petra pretended to concentrate on her GPS. What would she do if James tried to kiss her again? She didn't know.

After a while, James broke the silence. 'I forgot to tell you that the Rangers in Fayette found the bicycles and are keeping them for us.'

'Incredible! Where were they?' Petra asked, relieved to be on safe ground.

'At the campsite.'

'That figures. What about the motorbike and Al?'

James shrugged. 'I haven't heard anything. God knows what Al was doing, breaking into the museum then taking off like a fugitive.' He spoke with such sincerity that Petra knew she hadn't misjudged him.

She glanced at the GPS in her hand, then at the rocks and islets around them. When they reached a cluster of rocks shaped like seals, she sat up and began to watch the screen intently.

'There!' she cried, holding it out for James to see. 'We're about to go over my entrance waypoint!'

James's face was a mixture of incredulity and admiration. 'Now I understand. You own these islands, don't you? You know them so well, you've made them yours and you can't share them with anyone.'

'I wish I could own them, but they're not for sale. And you're right, it's difficult for me to allow anyone in. Every time I come here, I feel ... restored,' she said, blushing.

'Is that what you call it?'

To cover her confusion, Petra switched on the motor and opened the throttle. She didn't know what to say. James had been a considerate companion, sympathetic to her mood, and mindful of her needs. His apology and the kiss had taken her by surprise and swept away her defences, but she liked him and had felt more at ease than at any time since the day Betty had asked her to find Elena. Damn the kayakers!

When Petra and James arrived back at the yacht, they found the three Gracebys sitting in the air-conditioned salon stiff and tight-lipped, avoiding each other's eyes. It was as if a set of invisible walls prevented them from communicating. Betty looked grim, Cliff haggard and red-eyed, Ken irritated. They were all dressed partially in black, which struck a sombre note on such a hot summer's day.

'There you are,' Betty said, pouncing on Petra as if she were a recalcitrant schoolgirl. 'The Foxes, is that where you've been?'

Petra threw a glance at Ken's sullen face. Could he have complained that she and James had gone off without him? He might be so petty, but it was unlike Betty to worry about such a small thing.

'Yes, it was a lovely morning,' she said, aware of the irony.

Betty simply grunted. 'Brunch is waiting.'

Throughout the meal the atmosphere remained oppressive even though Petra tried to describe the stark beauty of the islands and James made an effort to support her. It was as though Betty sensed that something had happened between them.

As soon as they had finished eating, Petra stood up. 'I'd better be going.'

'Very well.'

'Is there a problem, Betty?' Petra asked anxiously. 'Have I done something wrong?'

'Not at all. Perhaps it's the weather. Please don't worry.'

Betty's polite reassurance did nothing to assuage Petra's doubts. Something had tainted their relationship. Petra cast a helpless look at James. What a mess.

CHAPTER

31

It was Sunday night, just before midnight. The drug coursed through Cliff's veins. He was pumped and ready to play. Liz was waiting for him by the side door to the Lodge. He put his hands on her shoulders and pulled her roughly towards him. The top of her head smelled of beer and smoke and musk. He buried his face in the blonded hair and breathed her in. Then he pushed her away, dragging down her top to expose her breasts. They were shaped like lemons, but boy were they sweet to suck!

Memories of their couplings the night before – first in the bar, afterwards in Liz's airless room – flashed through Cliff's brain as he tongued one nipple then the other. He raised his head, frantic to crush his lips against hers and push his tongue deep into her mouth. Her dark eyes held a curious glint: lust mixed with desire, inviting yet holding something back, something that for a split second reminded him so strongly of Elena that he almost shoved her aside. More than once he had fucked Elena hard against a wall before riding off with her on his motorbike to go elsewhere and fuck some more.

Liz twisted away from him. 'Change of plan: my roommate's back.'

Cliff groaned.

'It's OK. I've got my car, and I know a place where only the satellites can see us. They won't give a shit what we do.'

Liz grabbed Cliff's hand and they staggered to her car, a big old maroon clunker. She drove through the deserted streets of Killarney like a hurricane searching for something on which to vent its fury. With a squeal of tyres, she turned onto a road that led to the water. The last half-kilometre was unpaved and uneven. She kept her eyes on the road on the lookout for moose and one hand down the front of Cliff's trousers, squeezing and stroking until he could barely stave off the eruption.

At the end of the road where the gravel terminated in a semi-circle of boulders, Liz brought the car to a stop. She twisted in her seat and bent her head to Cliff's groin. Cliff ground his teeth and forced her skull down and down until she had him deep in her throat. The sensitivity was almost unbearable. He came quickly with an agonized moan of ecstasy tinged with pain.

Liz began to kiss him, thrusting her tongue into his mouth so that he could taste his own semen. Cliff pushed back his seat and lifted her onto his lap. He felt himself responding as she clamped her knees around him and began to move up and down in a furious rhythm punctuated by strangled half-cries. It was like being attacked by some demonic clawed creature that dug into his shoulders and refused to let go. When the moment of release came and the mist cleared from his vision, Cliff was overcome by lethargy and a profound melancholy. Not since he had been with Elena had he experienced such frenzied sex.

Liz clung to him in silence until her heartbeat slowed and she was able to extricate herself. With a return to something like normality, she opened the door of the car and stumbled out. Her skirt was bunched up round her waist, revealing hard sun-tanned buttocks. She wriggled it back into place and leaned into the car to help Cliff. Then she went to the trunk of the car and took out a tartan rug and a striped canvas tote bag. She locked the car and picked up Cliff's hand, as if he were a young child she was taking to school.

'Come,' she said, leading the way through the boulders. 'I'll show you my secret spot.'

'I've found it already.'

'Not this one, you haven't.'

Cliff had no idea where Liz was taking him. At first, he thought it might be to the lighthouse, but she veered off to the left. She was as primed as he was, on what he didn't know or care. After a while, the narrow trail disappeared into a tangle of thornbush, forcing them to scramble through scrub, over rocks and tree roots. Cliff no longer had any sense of time or direction. It seemed as though every few minutes they would stop to fondle and kiss, then Liz would set off again, picking her way across the rough terrain. He was completely in her hands, moving when she told him to move, doing whatever else she told him at her command or instigation.

They emerged onto a plateau overlooking the lake. Cliff's senses were aroused almost to screaming point. Liz placed her bag on the ground next to the ruins of a man-made structure and spread out the rug. There was no need of it for warmth, only to act as a thin cushion between their bodies and the rock. It was one of those hot clammy nights when the temperature refused to drop.

Liz pulled Cliff down onto the rug and took a still cool bottle of vodka from her bag. She opened it and took a long swig before giving him the bottle. She shed her skirt and top and knelt naked in front of him, offering him a breast while she unbuttoned his black shirt. They passed the bottle back and forth, and she continued to undress him until they were both naked.

Like a tomcat driven wild by the sight of a snake, Liz pounced on Cliff's penis and took him into her mouth. He felt for the opening between her legs, caressing and stroking until her clitoris stood erect like a third nipple.

Some time later, Liz took a packet from her bag and added white powder to the rest of the vodka. She shook it violently as if it were a snow globe and passed it to Cliff.

After that, intervals of semi-lucidity alternated with periods of frenetic sex. At the end of one such period of crazed activity, Cliff rolled onto his side, panting with exertion.

'God almighty! What are you doing to me? You'll kill me, Elena!' The name was squeezed out of him as he collapsed onto his back with a final groan. He stared unseeing at the night sky above.

Liz attacked him with her fists and a laugh like a hyena.

Elena had sometimes had a laugh like that.

'Fuck you! Don't keep calling me that! My name's Eliza, same beginning, different end.'

'Eliza, I like that ... Come here, Eliza ... Eliza Doolittle ... Doolittle except fuck me!'

330

'No,' Liz shrieked. 'I'm flying, flying to Spain, where the rain falls on the plain!' She avoided his searching hands, picked up the bottle and drained what was left of the vodka cocktail. Then she began to roll on her side, over and over, away from him, towards the edge of the cliff.

'What's in Spain?' Cliff shouted.

'My mother is!'

Liz stopped, changed direction and came rolling like a barrel towards him.

'Fuck your mother!'

He shoved her away, but she came rolling back, screaming.

'I fucked your son!'

'Fuck off then!'

'I will. He's a good fuck, a very good fuck. Did I mention that?'

Cliff picked up a loose stone and lobbed it at Liz as she rolled away again.

'A fucking good fuck!'

He picked up another stone and tossed it towards her taunting voice.

'Eeny, meeny, miny, moe …'

'Incestuous bitch!'

Cliff dragged himself up onto all fours and scrabbled around searching for missiles. He found a cairn of stones and began flinging them towards the edge of the cliff, one after the other. He could hear them clattering down onto the rocks and gulls crying in the night. When there were no more stones, he fell back on the rug and passed out.

Cliff woke with the dawn. His head was pounding like a pile driver. Shivering, he sat up and saw that he was naked. The rug underneath him was damp, but he pulled a corner of it over his penis, which felt chafed and raw. He looked around for his clothes. A short distance away, he found his black shirt, his underwear and his slacks, lying in a soiled heap against the wall of some kind of ruin. He couldn't find his belt.

At first, he had no idea where he was. Then he began to remember. The barmaid, Liz, had brought him there. Snatches of their antics during the night returned to him in exaggerated colour as if he were watching clips from a lurid skin flick. He closed his eyes to block them out and rubbed his hand over the lower part of his face where rough stubble was growing. Where was she? Her discarded black skirt and lime green top, along with one black ballerina-style shoe, lay close to where he had found his own clothing.

An empty vodka bottle was lying next to a red and grey striped tote bag. The bottle top with part of the seal clinging to it was in the bag, along with a plastic sachet that had contained some type of powder. He had no recollection, but they must have drunk the litre of vodka between them and used the powder too. That would account for how he was feeling. But where was Liz? When he called her name, there was no answer.

The wind was picking up as the sky grew lighter. Cliff could hear waves splashing against the rocks below. He had to get out of there, back to *Gloriana* before Ken and James and his mother woke up. Where the fuck was Liz? She knew the way home, he didn't. If she had gone and left him there …

Fury gripped him then a sobering thought: she would never have left without her clothes. In the pit of his stomach, a knot of panic began to form. Perhaps she had had a change of clothes in her bag. Something warm. Which meant that she had left him to make his own way back. Fucking bitch! They were all bitches. Elena had run out on him, Petra too, now Liz.

Cliff picked up the empty vodka bottle, walked towards the edge of the cliff and flung it onto the rocks. The glass shattered as it landed. He gathered up the rug and stuffed it into the tote bag with Liz's clothes and all the plastic rubbish. He threw the bag as far as he could out over the cliff into the water. Then he began the long lonely walk back to civilization.

The sun was up by the time he found Liz's car. She wasn't there and the doors were locked. A chill settled over him. Taunting him was one thing, playing tricks was another. It was an even longer lonelier walk back to the yacht.

CHAPTER

32

Petra had long since learned to sublimate her personal feelings in her work. On Sunday evening, shortly after her return from Killarney, she volunteered to fill in for a sick colleague. This enabled her to shelve the question of her feelings for James and to avoid thinking about what might have happened to alter her relationship with Betty. She also avoided a phone call from Martin who wanted to know how her trip had gone. Instead of calling him back, she sent him an upbeat email telling him that he needn't have worried. Betty had taken the news with equanimity.

It was only when she was getting dressed for work on Monday morning that Petra realized she had completely misread the situation with Betty. Betty had reacted to the awful news of Elena's death in the only way she knew: by putting on a good show. She had rationalized and made light of it, then concealed her grief in an emotional rendition of "Amazing Grace". As Betty's monument to Joe had demonstrated, Betty was too consummate a performer to wear her heart on her sleeve. Underneath her cool, calm exterior, she would have been hurting terribly and mourning Elena … mourning too the lost opportunity to right a wrong that she felt Joe had committed. That would explain Betty's aloofness on Sunday, and Petra, as the unlucky bearer of the bad tidings, had been duly shot.

Once Petra recognized that fact, she was able to function normally. Her partner, Ed, was quick to spot the change in her.

'These weekends away visiting your wealthy chum on her yacht don't seem to do you much good,' he said, giving her a quizzical look. 'You come back as prickly as a porcupine, with a deep frown on your forehead and a chip on your shoulder. Now suddenly, you're OK again. Want to tell me about it over lunch?'

'I can't, Ed. It's too complicated.'

'Are you suggesting that my brain isn't up to it?'

'That's not what I meant. It's a personal matter, and confidential.'

Ed scrutinized her face. 'Well, any time you change your mind, let me know. We don't want the personal to spill over into the professional again.'

After a sandwich lunch during which Ed chatted about his wife's plans to remodel the kitchen, they received an urgent call to launch the Marine Unit's boat. A floatplane had turned turtle on Campbell's Bay after a bad landing. There had been no passengers and the pilot had managed to scramble out, so no one was hurt. But the plane and debris from the crash constituted a navigational hazard. Lighted marker buoys had to be put in place and the incident investigated before the salvage operation could begin. Petra was pleased to have something to do that would occupy her fully, both physically and mentally, and keep Ed off her back.

Just before 10 p.m. she returned to her lodgings and downloaded her email. She saw immediately that the second laboratory to which she had sent samples of Patricia's vitamins and health drinks had replied. Not much use now, Petra thought; Betty's health was vastly improved and the chances of the first lab having overlooked something were minimal. Nevertheless, she opened the email and scanned the results: first, the usual caveats, then the breakdown of the ingredients in the health drink with their quantities, the same thing for each of the supplements. A waste of money. The analysis was no different from the first one she had paid for.

Then she noticed a paragraph at the end of the report that highlighted the amount of potassium that was in the drink and the supplements if they were considered together. The lab pointed out that in a susceptible person such a high level could cause severe problems if the body did not eliminate it properly.

If someone had asked Petra to make a list of suspected poisons, potassium would not have been on it. Bananas helped to ward off cramp, didn't they? Potassium was an essential mineral, wasn't it?

With a fair degree of scepticism, she Googled her way through a number of apparently trustworthy medical sites and found that too much potassium in the blood could indeed pose problems. *Hyperkalemia* it was called. Older people were more likely to develop the condition because the kidneys became less able to excrete any excess. The most dangerous effects included abnormal heart rhythms, impaired muscle function and digestive issues such as nausea, vomiting and cramping. In severe cases, fatal arrhythmias or paralysis could occur.

Petra flexed her fingers. So she hadn't been completely off her head! The vitamins and health drinks might not have been the cause of Betty's malaise but they could have been a factor, and Patricia should have known and been more careful.

Petra caught sight of the time in the bottom right-hand corner of her computer screen. It was midnight: way too late to call The Fisherman's Lodge in Killarney and ask to talk to Betty to alert her to the dangers of too much potassium. She would have to do that in the morning. But it wasn't too late to fire off an email to Martin. He would be intrigued and probably produce a well-researched article for one of his magazines.

On Tuesday morning, Petra waited impatiently until eleven o'clock before phoning The Fisherman's Lodge. If Betty wasn't up and about, she would ask Liz to give her a message and hope that Betty would call back. The phone at the Lodge rang for a long time. Petra was about to give up when it was answered by a harassed-sounding female.

'Fisherman's Lodge, Liz speaking.'

'That doesn't sound like the Liz I know,' Petra said.

'You want Liz A. I'm Liz B. She's not here. Monday and Tuesday are her days off. She usually goes home to Sudbury. Can you call tomorrow?'

'Actually I wanted to talk to Betty Graceby. Her boat's on your megayacht dock. Can you find her for me or take her a message?'

'I would if I could, but they've gone.'

'Are you sure?'

'Yes. They left right after lunch yesterday.'

'Do you know where they were going?'

'No idea, sorry.'

'Oh well, thanks for your time.'

'If you call tomorrow, Liz A might know. Rumour has it she's very friendly with Betty Graceby's son.'

Pally with her grandson, too, Petra thought. But why had Betty left early, and where had she gone? According to Liz A, *Gloriana* had been booked in at the Lodge for at least four nights. Had Betty cut short her visit in order to distance herself from the place where she had received the news about Elena?

Later that evening, Petra looked for the itinerary Betty had given her. It was still in the envelope with the information about Joe, his ex-wife Sofía and their daughter, Elena. Petra was overcome by a feeling of failure as she ran her eye down the list of dates and ports. She had succeeded merely in driving Betty away, not helping her.

At the bottom of the page below "Killarney", the itinerary simply said "Cruising the North Channel until the beginning of September". Once again Petra would have to ask her colleagues to look out for Betty's yacht and let her know if they saw it.

Despondently, she checked her email. As expected, Martin had replied without delay. 'Great stuff,' he said. 'I'll let you know what I find out.'

What Petra wasn't expecting, though, was a message from Carlo in Italy. It was over three weeks since she had emailed him to ask for his assistance in finding Elena. So much had happened in the interim that she had written him off like a bad debt.

After reading the subject line of his email, she opened it with a degree of apprehension.

"Subject: Elena Maria LePinto Sanchez: antecedents, death and photographs
Bella, Bellissima!
I can make no plausible excuses for my tardiness so I hereby plead guilty. No doubt you will dream up a suitable punishment to be dispensed in due course. The attached report is for your beautiful eyes only. Sorry the result is not more positive. Let me know if you need more.
Yours in leather,
Mercutio"

Petra suppressed a shiver as she read the subject line again. "Antecedents" was such a cold unemotional European word, and death left no room for hope. The idea of photographs perturbed her even more, not because she hadn't come face to face with death before – she had seen plenty of corpses in her years with the RCMP – but because this was personal. Photos brought people to life, even those that featured the dead.

Carlo had sent two attachments: a five-page report followed by a page of photographs. Petra opened the report and began reading. She didn't want to examine the photographs until she had read the entire document.

The first part was a compilation of data from official sources: birth certificate, driver's licences, municipal and tax records, to name but a few. There were numerous identification, file and reference numbers. In spite of her own experience with the RCMP, Petra was awed by the extent of the mined data. Big Brother was alive and well, even if Elena wasn't. With access to the right databases, an identity thief would have no problems at all.

The data repeated the personal information that Betty had provided, gave Elena's known home and work addresses in Argentina and, lower down the listings, in Spain, the dates of Elena's marriage to and divorce from Fran Arturo, the Argentinian polo player, and of her second marriage to the Canadian, Ian McInley. It was a catalogue of Elena's life as the authorities knew it: totally passionless and lacking any human element.

The second part of Carlo's report concerned Elena's death. It confirmed in bald terms what Martin had found out through some clever journalistic research: that Elena had been accompanying McInley on a polo tour; that she had been found dead in their hotel room in Sotogrande; that she had killed herself with a combination of alcohol and barbiturates.

Then the report became more interesting. An enquiry into the circumstances surrounding the death had been launched and the initial finding of suicide upheld – not only on the basis of the empty bottles lying by Elena's side, but also because she had left a suicide note.

Petra's heart fluttered. In the newspaper article Martin had given her, there had been nothing about a suicide note. The press had speculated about the reasons why the forty-year-old wife of a well respected polo player would want to take her life, depression being cited as the most likely underlying cause. Which it probably was. But people who left a note often explained in more precise terms why they had committed suicide. And they always apologized.

The vein in Petra's temple began to twitch as she concentrated all her attention on the next few lines of text. The unsigned note had been filed with the judge conducting the enquiry. It had been found in the pocket of the blouse worn by Elena. Her husband attested that it was in her handwriting. It said:

"I'm sorry, Ian. I can't live a lie any longer. Take care of my daughter."

The judge concluded that there was nothing to indicate foul play or support any verdict other than suicide and declared the enquiry closed.

Petra stopped reading and leaned back in her chair, letting her eyes rest while her mind tried to come to grips with the new information. Betty had asked her to find Elena and Elena was dead, but if she had offspring, Betty might want to pay Elena's share of Joe's legacy to the next generation. That would make the Graceby boys happy!

Eager to read more about Elena's daughter, Petra scrolled to the next page. There was one more terse entry stating the date and cause of Elena's death and the place of her interment. Nothing else. What the hell had Carlo been thinking about? Then Petra realized she had asked only for his assistance in locating Elena. That he had done. Bloody men! If only they could look beyond the obvious and read a little between the lines.

Reluctantly Petra moved on to the photographs. There were just two. The first was a picture of a woman with long, dark, curling hair, wearing sunglasses and a designer dress that ended above the knee. She was sitting watching a polo game, one slim leg crossed over the other. The overall impression was of an attractive, well-off woman, with just a hint of spread around her middle. Only the set expression to her mouth suggested a measure of discontent.

The second picture showed a woman lying on a large bed. It had been taken by the police photographer to record the position of the deceased and the items that had been found near the body. These included a litre bottle with a red and white label, a couple of pill bottles, a glossy magazine, and a broken telephone surrounded by shards of glass. Although it was not a close-up, the picture clearly showed the same woman. It looked as though she had hurled the phone at the mirror in a paroxysm of anger and frustration.

Petra glanced at the photos again but did not dwell on them. Better to concentrate on learning more about Elena as she had been in life, in order to put that life into perspective. Perhaps, when the time was right and she had mended her relationship with Betty, she would be able to talk to her about Elena and tell her everything she had found out.

Petra moved the report and the photographs Carlo had sent into the file she had begun to compile on Elena. It already contained copies of the magazine and newspaper articles from which Martin had derived his information. Martin would be livid that he had failed to discover the fact that Elena had a daughter. There was an unvoiced rivalry between him and Carlo, even though they knew each other only through Petra and she was in love with neither of them. It was a matter of professional pride. But both had used the tools of their trade to the best of their ability and provided her with valuable information.

She wrote first to Carlo.

"Thanks for the dope. Excellent stuff except it didn't go quite far enough. To ensure all debts cancelled including late charges, please send maximum info on Elena's daughter: name, dob, whereabouts, etc.

Yours in blue,

Petra"

Next she wrote to Martin, which was usually easier. This time it proved more difficult. After three aborted attempts, she managed to compile a short note:

"You won't like this, but according to info received from Carlo, Elena left a suicide note indicating she had a daughter, name unknown. Have asked for details.

Petra"

By the time Petra finished sending her emails, it was after 1 a.m. She hoped her two ferrets would get to work quickly so that she could go back to Betty with better news – once she knew where Betty had gone. She put a note on her computer to call the Lodge again in the morning to talk to Liz A and went to bed.

CHAPTER

33

Petra spent the whole of Wednesday working with a mixed force at the Gore Bay-Manitoulin Island Airport. Acting on a tip-off, they were searching all incoming planes for a major shipment of drugs.

As she inspected a Cessna, Petra couldn't help thinking about Cliff Graceby. He had plenty of opportunity to make shipments and deliveries and had even mentioned as much during the flight from Escanaba to The Soo when she had asked about the vitamins Patricia had been giving Betty. Before that, she had tried to shake him up with her questions about Al and Pepe, then Elena, and felt she had succeeded. He was far from being the smooth playboy of the Bahamas. Sartorially he might appear the same, but since Las Vegas he had been on a downward spiral that had culminated in the appalling display of drunkenness on Saturday evening in Killarney. Once upon a time, she had thought him better behaved than his son and more able to control his emotions; now it was clear she had been mistaken. Ken had shown remarkable restraint in dealing with his father.

Petra continued to wonder about Betty's earlier than planned departure from Killarney. Where would *Gloriana* most likely have gone? She had seen no sign of the yacht on Monday or Tuesday when she'd been out and about dealing with the downed seaplane. But the North Channel had plenty of out-of-the-way anchorages, even for boats as large as Betty's – as she had discussed with James during their cruise to Fayette. It had been one of the things that had brought them together.

Petra squared up her shoulders as another light plane came taxiing down the runway. No worries, no regrets.

It wasn't until late Wednesday afternoon that she was able to call The Fisherman's Lodge to ask Liz A about *Gloriana*. The phone rang and rang, as it had on Tuesday. Finally, it was answered by Liz B.

'Sorry for the wait,' she said. 'This place is a zoo.'

'Can I speak to Liz A?'

'She's not back yet. She hasn't called in, and the boss is pissed off. No doubt she'll show up at some point. In the meantime, it's more work for all of us. The hotel's fully booked and the marina's overloaded. Give me your number and I'll tell her you want to speak to her when she does come in.'

Early Friday morning, after a second day of fruitless searching at the airport, Petra returned to the waterfront. A few sailboats were waiting for the bridge to open. There was a crispness in the air that hinted at Fall and the days were getting noticeably shorter. The summer season would come to a sudden end as soon as the kids went back to school in September. Some boats, like *Gloriana*, would begin the long trek to Florida or the Caribbean for the winter.

Suddenly Petra had a horrible thought. What if Liz A had gone off on Betty's yacht with Cliff and Ken – and James? Liz wanted to crew, and they had lost Al. They could be heading south already. Petra hoped to God not; she really wanted to rebuild her relationship with Betty before she left, and the idea of Liz on board *Gloriana* in a confined space with James was too distressing to contemplate.

At that moment, the phone in Petra's pocket began to vibrate. She grabbed it and answered it before it rang.

'Where's Betty Graceby?'

A.K. at his most terse.

'I wish I knew.'

'When did you see her last?'

'Sunday lunchtime in Killarney.'

'With her family?'

'Yes. Cliff and Ken. And her captain, James.'

'What's their next port of call?'

'I don't know. What's the matter?'

'U.S. Homeland Security and the O.P.P. want to speak to them.'

Wow! A double whammy! Homeland Security was not such a surprise with Al and Pepe on the loose, but what could the Ontario Provincial Police want? Unless it were Cliff Graceby for drugs.

A.K. preempted more questions by becoming quite verbose. 'Get ready to go to Killarney to assist the O.P.P. I'll deal with Homeland Security.'

Petra slipped her phone back into her pocket with a feeling of foreboding. Why did A.K. want her to assist the O.P.P.? What had happened in Killarney? Was it something involving Betty? Petra struggled to remember the first telephone conversation she had had with Liz B.

On Tuesday Liz B had said: 'They left right after lunch yesterday', meaning Monday. Did "they" include all of them? Petra had assumed so. What if she had been wrong and it didn't include Cliff … or Ken Graceby? *Never make assumptions* her mentor Tom Gilmore had repeated over and over like a mantra. And could it have included Liz A? Petra's mind started to fly off in a million directions. She took a deep breath to slow herself down. She had to think rationally.

Petra was heading back to the station house when Ed radioed to say that they were needed to help with a search and rescue in Killarney. She met him at the boathouse where their boat was ready to go. As soon as she saw him, she asked him the question that had been making her head spin.

'Is it Betty Graceby?'

'No.'

'Thank God.'

'I knew you'd be worried.'

'I was. I still am,' she said edgily. 'You drive, I'll do the lines.'

Ed took the wheel and started the engines while Petra cast off the lines.

'So what is it?' she asked as they left the bridge astern and Ed brought the boat up to speed. At full throttle, they would be in Killarney within the hour. 'A boater?'

'No. A member of staff from The Fisherman's Lodge.'

'Not the barmaid?'

'Yes. Do you know her?'

'A little. Her name's Liz. A right piece of work.'

'It doesn't sound as though you have much time for her,' Ed said.

'If you'd seen her in action, you wouldn't either.'

'If we don't find her, her action days could well be over.'

'That's ominous,' Petra said. 'What have you heard?'

'She was last seen on Sunday evening. The O.P.P. found her car out near the lighthouse, locked and undamaged. It's been there since Monday – an officer noticed it but didn't report it until yesterday.'

'Any contact with friends or relatives?'

'None. Her father in Sudbury didn't hear from her this week. Normally she spends her days off with him and lets him know if she isn't going to make it.'

Petra nodded. 'Monday and Tuesday are her days off and she didn't return to work on Wednesday. I know because I spoke to her colleague at the Lodge. What do the O.P.P. think?'

'According to her friends, she was supposed to meet someone after work on Sunday night, which would have made it a late-night rendezvous. Either they drove out to the lighthouse for a bit of fun and games, or she went hiking on Monday morning and came to grief on the trails. It's a fairly remote area, as you know. Which scenario would you choose?'

'I don't have to choose,' Petra answered, 'if the way she behaved on Sunday was anything like her performance on Saturday.'

Petra and Ed docked their boat on the Killarney side of the cut just past the liquor store. An O.P.P. car was waiting to greet them.

'We have people out scouring all the trails,' the officer said. 'But if she didn't stick to a trail, it's going to be difficult to find her.'

'Shouldn't we be looking for more than one person?' Petra said.

'Oh?'

'The barmaid, Liz, was supposed to meet someone on Sunday night. I suspect that someone was Cliff Graceby, or his son, Ken Graceby – or both. No one knows where they are now.'

The officer raised both eyebrows. 'OK, I'll check with the boss. We can look out for two people or more; it won't make much difference. My instructions are to ask you to search the coastline from this side of the lighthouse to the old tar vats. We'll have helicopter assistance shortly. Report anything at all that might be significant.'

Petra and Ed began their search as instructed on the Killarney side of the lighthouse. Until mid-morning the water remained relatively calm. Then the wind strengthened and by noon had reached a steady ten to fifteen knots. The waves breaking on the shore made it much more difficult. They drove the boat into every crevice and cranny, nosing between the rocks, stopping to investigate the slightest thing that seemed unusual or out of place.

They checked out a wrecked skiff that Petra remembered from the year before, picked up a couple of old planks, various lengths of fishing line, one empty cardboard box and several plastic bags, as well as a balloon from a child's birthday party. Petra leaned over the side of the boat to retrieve a stout piece of rope that was floating just below the surface of the water. Hauling it in, she found that it was attached to an old boot.

'That's ten points,' Ed said, chortling at the expression on her face. 'There aren't many of those down there nowadays.'

Petra grinned back, the laughter dispelling the tension.

Out beyond the lighthouse, the water was rougher. Petra and Ed bobbed along the shore, straining their eyes to detect any anomaly. The waves made it hard to control the boat at idle speed and to identify alien objects.

In the end, it was a frustrating day. The conditions hampered their efforts to such an extent that they were able to cover only half the territory they had hoped. As dusk fell, they returned to the dock near the liquor store and tied up for the night. Ed radioed the control centre to report their non-progress. There was nothing to report from the air or land crews either.

'You look all in,' Ed said as he walked with Petra to the guesthouse where they had managed to find accommodation for the night.

'I am. These missions are always draining, but it's worse if you know the people involved.'

'Even if you don't like them and the way they behave?'

'Yes, I feel bad about that too.'

'You'll feel better after dinner and a drink.'

'And an early night and dreamless sleep!'

A couple of hours later, Petra was preparing to turn out her bedside light when her phone rang. Her first thought was that A.K. had found Betty. Instead, it was Martin.

Immediately she was wary. If she told him where she was and what she was involved in, he would be up there like a shot and perhaps expect special treatment. There were already enough journalists poking around.

'Petra, I need to talk to you.'

'This isn't a good time, Martin. Can't it wait until after the weekend?'

'After the weekend? No way. I have some information about the arts centre project. The sponsor is actually a consortium, and the guy leading it …'

'Martin, send me an email or call me on Monday. I told you, I'm in bed.'

'Is someone with you?' he asked suspiciously.

'Yes,' she said, taking the only route she could think of to shut him up.

At first light on Saturday, Petra and Ed resumed their search. The wind was not as strong and the waves gradually settled down, making their task easier. They began where they had left off on Friday evening. As they moved farther away from the lighthouse, the coastline became even more fragmented. It was a frustratingly slow process to circumnavigate every island and islet and to explore each indentation. Some led to channels that fed into further bodies of water; others dead-ended after winding their way between outcroppings of rock.

Mid-way through the morning, Ed spoke to one of the officers whose job was to keep curious members of the public from interfering with the hunt, which could only succeed if it was conducted as quickly and as methodically as possible. Police cars controlled all major junctions in town, barricades had been set up on the lighthouse road and all hiking trails in the vicinity cordoned off. Since nothing of significance had been discovered along or adjacent to the main trails, the ground patrols were extending their search. Each block of terrain to be covered was marked off on a topographic map. It had been impossible to stop the spread of the news and the officer reported that the volume of vehicles coming into the area was three times the norm for an August Saturday.

Disheartened by the lack of progress, her eyes tired from the effort of focussing on the ever-moving water and the sun and shadows on the rocks, Petra nevertheless redoubled her efforts. Time was of the essence, as the lawyers liked to say. The more time that elapsed since Liz's disappearance, the less likely they were to find her unharmed. Above them, the helicopter was working a grid pattern, flying up and down then across and back before moving on to the next sector. From time to time, the timbre of its engine changed as it hovered to investigate some anomaly that might prove important.

Petra ceded the helm to Ed at the end of her two-hour stint. It was his turn to drive while she reverted to being the prime spotter. She rubbed her eyes and picked up the binoculars. Adjusting them slightly, she began to scan the shore. Even with the image stabilizer it was exhausting work.

Just after eleven, they rounded a promontory and entered a bay full of rocks and islands. A reasonably clear channel presented itself on the left-hand side. Ed followed it, concentrating on keeping the boat off the cliffs while staying close enough in for Petra to systematically scan the rocks at their base. Nothing.

The channel made a turn to the left and continued, leading them to a sheltered inlet.

'Aren't we somewhere near the old tar vats?' Ed asked. 'We used to come here as kids.'

Petra consulted her chart. 'They're farther east, over that way,' she said, pointing to yet another break in the shoreline. 'Let's finish this inlet, then maybe we can put in somewhere for a few minutes and have our lunch.'

'You want to stop for lunch?' Ed said with a smirk. 'That can't be my partner talking!'

'I can't see straight any longer. A ten-minute break won't hurt.' A small voice inside Petra's head reminded her that it might make all the difference. 'OK, you're right. Keep going.' She pointed out a ribbon of water that filled the space between steep-sided rocks. 'Let's have a look in there.'

'It's not wide enough for the boat. You'll have to get out on that ledge.'

Ed brought the boat neatly alongside a level section of rock that could have been made for the purpose. Petra stepped off as easily as if she had been on a train pulling into Union Station in downtown Toronto. She made directly for a jumble of boulders that blocked her view of the narrow waterway. Finding a path through was not so easy. She managed to climb to the top of the pile without losing her footing or her hat, then realized that the only solution on the other side was to slide down on her butt.

As Petra disappeared from view, Ed manoeuvred away from the ledge; he would hold the boat off until she reappeared. The radio was silent. All he could do was wait.

Petra scrambled over the orange rocks. The midday sun

was gradually bringing her temperature to boiling point. The seat of her uniform pants was already scraped and she cursed as she caught her knee on a particularly vicious corner. Ahead of her, the blue ribbon of water tapered to nothing.

It was the colours that caught Petra's attention: blue .. orange .. red .. and grey .. and a splash of lime …

A striped canvas bag was lodged between two boulders, half in half out of the water. Petra climbed down to take a look. It was a good-size bag with a stout zipper that was partially open, revealing soft goods of some kind. She leaned closer, not wanting to touch the fabric but to see … T-shirt material, lime green … a shade worn by women.

She grabbed her radio and called Ed.

CHAPTER

34

When Petra and Ed returned to Killarney a couple of hours later, there were enough people on the dock to fill a small cruise ship. News had travelled fast via the Internet, the social media, the local TV and radio stations. The fish and chip shop had run out of fish, and the police were running out of both resources and patience.

Petra brought the boat into the dock and killed the engines as soon as Ed had secured the lines. They climbed out amid a barrage of flash bulbs.

'Hold it, Madam, Sir – Officers – thank you, very nice!' A voice Petra would recognize anywhere rang out above the din.

'Martin!'

'Petra!' he said in a reproachful tone. 'You could at least have let me know what was going down! Then I'd have been ahead of the pack.'

'Martin, that's been the last thing on my mind. In any case, you know I couldn't. This isn't me on vacation in the Bahamas.'

'Well, can you give me a few juicy details about what you found – to give me an edge?'

Petra shook her head. 'Your persistence does you credit, but it won't wash with me. I'm on duty. There'll be a press release at some point. You'll have to wait for that.'

'Even if I have information to exchange?'

'If you have pertinent information, Martin, you should be talking to the uniforms in charge.'

The canvas bag had been photographed in situ and delivered to the control centre. Photographs of the contents had been taken and each item logged in and bagged. The key now was to determine whether any of them belonged to the missing girl. Petra and Ed waited while the O.P.P. went to bring in Frankie, the barman from The Fisherman's Lodge, Liz B, and Liz A's friend, Susie, to help identify the items.

According to Frankie, Liz A had been wearing the same black tube miniskirt on Sunday night as she wore whenever she was on evening shift. It showed off her rump and was the type of skirt that encouraged interest in the bar, with a consequent effect on its sales and her tips. To complement the skirt, he was sure she had worn a low-necked top – red, he thought, or maybe yellow. Something bright, anyway. He had paid more attention to the bottom end.

Liz B and Susie confirmed that the lime green cotton and Spandex T with the scoop neck belonged to Liz A. As did the black ballerina shoe, the canvas bag, and the rug. They didn't recognize the leather belt that Petra had found on the rocks half in the water not far from the bag. Liz A's tube skirt didn't need a belt, and it would have been much too long for her. It looked to be a fairly standard high-end man's belt: Italian black leather with a silver buckle. Petra thought Cliff Graceby had been wearing one like it on Saturday night, but couldn't be sure. The O.P.P. would check for prints just in case.

As soon as it had been confirmed that the bag contained items belonging to the missing girl, the police ordered all available hands to join the search. Petra and Ed took to the water again, the helicopter resumed its droning criss-cross, the land crews scoured the area near where the bag had been found. No one knew whether it had been dumped or thrown or left there by mistake; whether it had come from the land or the water side; whether waves and currents had carried it from where it had been dumped, thrown or left by mistake … There were so many variables, and the terrain was inhospitable and difficult to access. It was almost impossible to search completely. They needed a bit of luck.

Petra and Ed continued to comb the rocks and waterways in their designated zone with grim determination. As the afternoon wore on, they stopped trying to bolster one another's morale. They said less and less to each other, simple gestures replacing words that might take them into the gallows-humour territory they didn't yet want to explore. The worst thing was rounding a corner and hoping to see something – although "hope" was the wrong word when the "thing" might be a body.

At sundown Petra and Ed received the order to call it a day. Lady Luck had remained elusive. They drove the boat slowly back to Killarney. There was nothing to look forward to there except the long wait until dawn when they could start again.

The crowds that had greeted them earlier had dissipated. The police presence, the helicopter, the search-and-rescue boat had become the status quo, and public interest waned as the hours went by without further discoveries. A sandy-haired reporter detached himself from the few people remaining on the dock and blocked Petra's path.

'Another photo, Officer! For the record!'

'Not now, Martin. Leave me alone. This isn't the right time or place.'

'It is,' he said. 'I must talk to you. Please.'

'Martin, persistence is one thing, harassment is another.'

Ed intervened. 'I'll have to ask you to move on, Sir. We have a meeting to attend.'

Petra opened the door of the patrol car that had come to fetch them.

'It won't take a minute,' Martin insisted, holding on to the door. 'And I promise you it's really important.'

Petra noted the urgency in his tone and how flushed his cheeks were. 'I can't believe you're doing this, Martin. All right, meet us at the Lighthouse Inn after dinner, between 9.30 and 10.'

The bar at the Inn was packed but Ed managed to secure two beers. He brought them out to the garden where Petra had found a table. She took her bottle and chinked it against Ed's.

'Here's to tomorrow. Let's hope we find Liz.'

Above them, the three-quarter moon shone with a brilliant whiteness against the inky sky. Farther away, to the east and the west, stars peppered the darkness.

'I don't see any clouds coming in. It might be a good day,' Ed said.

They sipped their beers and lapsed into silence, waiting for Martin. When he arrived, he was not alone.

'Petra, I'd like you to meet someone,' he said.

Petra looked at his companion: a man with greying hair, a high, open forehead and a craggy face that would have won him female attention in some circles. He appeared to be about the same height as Cliff Graceby, a few years older perhaps, but without Cliff's slickness or arrogant bearing.

Suddenly, Martin seemed nervous. His words came out in a rush. 'This is the man I was telling you about, Petra. The one who's putting together the consortium to finance the arts centre in Ingotville.'

Petra frowned slightly. 'I wish this could have waited, Martin. I'm in the middle of a search and rescue.' Martin's priorities were all wrong. But his companion looked kind and didn't deserve to be treated rudely. She got to her feet and extended her hand. 'How do you do? Minx, Petra Minx.'

'McInley, Ian McInley. Thank you for agreeing to meet me, and for what you're doing.' His handshake was firm.

Petra paused as she assimilated his response to her greeting.

McInley. Ian McInley. A name she had heard before.

She turned to Martin.

He nodded his head like a woodpecker, his glasses glinting in the moonlight. 'Yes, Petra. This is what I wanted you to know, even if it's of no interest to the police. Mr. McInley was Elena Arturo's husband. When I met him yesterday in Sudbury to discuss the arts centre project, I worked it out immediately.' Martin saw the spark of hope in Petra's eyes and gently pushed her back onto the chair on which she had been sitting. 'He has something to tell you.'

Petra studied McInley's face, noting the distress in his

eyes and the bags beneath them. 'Is it about your daughter?' she asked, with sudden insight.

Ian McInley's years on the polo field had given him a hardiness that had stood him in good stead throughout that period of his life and the tragedy of his wife's death. For a few seconds, it deserted him; then he began to speak, softly and earnestly.

'Yes, although she's only my daughter by adoption. Liz – Eliza as she was baptized – never came to terms with her mother's death. She was tormented by anger and guilt, as I was, but she was too young to deal with those feelings. I tried every way I could think of to help her, especially during her turbulent teenage years. Lately, she had seemed better.' For the first time, Ian's voice faltered. He turned away and looked off into the distance.

Martin laid a restraining hand on Petra's arm as she opened her mouth to speak. 'Let Ian finish. There'll be plenty of time to discuss the whys and the what-ifs.'

'Now I know it was futile,' Ian said, turning back to face Petra and Ed. 'The girl you're looking for is Elena's daughter – my daughter.'

'Liz Arthurs?' Ed asked.

'Arturo. She called herself Arthurs.'

'Not McInley?' Petra said.

'No, because she blamed me even more than she blamed herself.' His eyes misted over. 'I've told the police her real name, but what am I going to tell her little girl?' he whispered.

Petra sat for a long time in the garden with Ed after Martin had led Ian McInley away.

'I agree, Ed, that Elena's story is of no relevance to the police in the current investigation,' she said. 'But what about Liz? She's a single mother. It's imperative that we find her.'

'Petra, we can't do any more than we're doing already. It's six days since Liz was seen and five since she abandoned her car. You know how unlikely it is that we'll find her alive.'

'I know, but there's still a chance. It's not over yet.'

It occurred to Petra as she lay on top of her bed in the darkness that the tragedy that had begun with Joe LePinto's decision to separate Elena and Cliff might never be over. Sleep eluded her, even though it was two in the morning and she knew she would be back on the water at first light to continue the search. How was she going to explain everything to Betty? How would Betty take it? Where was Betty? When would A.K. have news? What about Carlo? Should she text him, to tell him not to bother, that she had discovered what she needed to know?

Any action was better than no action. Petra sat up, switched on the bedside light and fired up her phone. One message received. From Carlo.

"Elena Arturo gave birth to a daughter in Santiago de Compostela, Spain, April 12, 1988. Name of child: Eliza Arturo. Father unknown."

Petra's last thoughts before she finally drifted off to sleep were for Betty.

The body of Eliza Arturo McInley was washed up on the shore near the lighthouse on Sunday.

EPILOGUE

Three months later, in November, a year after their first visit, Petra and Martin flew to Nassau to visit Betty Graceby. They arrived at the Toronto International Airport with ample time to spare; their business class flight, courtesy of Betty, was peaceful; the ride to *Neptunis*, in a car sent by Betty, cool and comfortable.

As the driver cruised to a halt at the foot of the marble steps, the door on Petra's side was pulled open. A wave of humid fragrant air poured into the car.

'Welcome to *Neptunis*, Ma'am. This way if you please.' The major-domo stood erect in his blue and gold uniform, holding the door as Petra slid out of the car. 'Follow me, Ma'am; Sir,' he added as Martin came round from the other side. 'Your luggage will be delivered to your suite.' Double Sam's height, twice as serious, correct and professional – but half as lively and endearing. Petra couldn't prevent a lump from forming in her throat.

Sam's ghost was everywhere as Petra followed the major-domo up the steps, past the immense statue of Neptune with his trident and his bevy of mermaids. Martin caught up with them in the reception hall. The tropical fish were still there in the enormous tanks.

'Wait till you see our aquarium and the shark cages, and the mermaid caves down by the pool,' Petra murmured. She waved to the receptionist with the owlish black glasses who gave not a flicker of recognition.

'Petra? Are you all right?'

'I will be.'

Betty's houseboy, Luis, was standing next to the elevator that served the Siren Suite. He welcomed Petra with a broad smile that included Martin. 'Welcome, Miss, and you too, Sir. Miss Graceby's in the roof garden. She said to bring you right on up.'

Petra stepped into the garden, expecting to see Betty sitting under the striped canopy near the siren fountain. Instead, she was standing talking to a man with greying hair who no longer had bags under his eyes. A short distance away, under the watchful eye of Bianca Casales, a little girl with curly blonde hair and skin the colour of amber was sitting, naked, in the middle of a green plastic paddling pool shaped like a frog.

Betty hurried towards Petra and Martin. 'My dears,' she said. 'I'm so glad you could come. I hope you're comfortable in the Mermaid Suite together.'

Petra blushed. 'There's more than enough room for us to spread ourselves out, isn't there, Martin?' He hadn't quite forgiven her for telling him she had been in bed with someone in Killarney.

Betty tilted her head to one side like a bird. 'Well, my dear, you must play it as you wish, but in my opinion he's charming. Now what do you think of my little tadpole?

363

Come along both of you and say hello to Sophie – and her nanny, Bianca.'

Betty took Petra's hand and drew her towards the paddling pool. 'One thing Joe never considered when he designed this garden was grandchildren, certainly not great-grandchildren. And I don't care for swimming, as you know, so he didn't include a pool. I was just suggesting to Ian that I have one built for Sophie. We can leave the fountain in the centre. What do you think?'

Petra thought that Betty looked ten years younger than she had during the summer. Her lavender eyes glowed every time she mentioned Sophie or turned to look at the little girl. She appeared to have no trouble being on her feet, in fact she was moving with complete ease. Perhaps Patricia's vitamins had been causing a problem after all.

'I think that's a terrific idea, Betty, and you look wonderful! Sophie has given you a new interest in life.'

'As if I didn't have enough to do with the GraPinto Marine Staff Training Academy! We're making great progress. And Ian has finally persuaded me to join the consortium to sponsor the arts centre in Ingotville. He's been trying for ages. Until you told me who he was, I had no idea he had any connection with Elena.'

Petra exchanged a few words with Ian McInley and left him talking to Martin and Betty about the arts centre. She went to greet Bianca who was crouched down next to the paddling pool, quietly staying on the fringe; she was helping Sophie fill a variety of shapes with water. Petra suspected it would be a while before Bianca felt completely at ease in the new Graceby household.

Martin strode towards them with his cameras. 'Let's have a group photograph. Betty and Ian, stand behind the frog pool, if you please. You too, Petra. Bianca, move closer to Sophie. That's it! Everyone smile! Fantastic! Now how about one by the siren fountain?'

Six days later, Petra and Martin were sitting amicably on the balcony of the Mermaid Suite overlooking the marina. It was the first opportunity they had had to relax after a whirlwind week of outings and visits, lunches and dinners – the bird sanctuary, the out-islands, the Coco Caverna Club, Luis's fabulous food. The calories had piled on, and there had been so much to absorb.

A light breeze ruffled the fronds of the palm trees as they gazed out over the marina. The line-up of boats was as impressive as the previous year.

'*Gloriana* isn't here yet,' Martin observed.

'No. Old habits die hard. I heard from James that they're still in Bermuda,' Petra replied, blushing slightly.

'I'm surprised Betty's boat wasn't impounded.'

'I'm sure the powers that be had a hand in that. *Gloriana* was well on her way south when they caught up with her. As usual, she didn't touch the U.S. and Cliff was long gone.'

'Do you know where he is?'

'A little bird told me he's in rehab farther south.'

'Aha!' Martin tapped the side of his nose. 'What about Ken?'

'He's playing dumb and blaming his father for everything. Says he's just a charter fisherman.'

Martin peered at Petra through his glasses. 'There are

more and more terrorist groups on this side of the Atlantic, establishing themselves in places like Venezuela and using Cuba as a conduit, but it'll be difficult to prove Cliff and Ken knew who they were smuggling into the States.'

'Particularly if they maintain they were just continuing Joe LePinto's tradition of helping people from the islands.'

'No doubt Betty has the best lawyers working to straighten out the mess,' Martin said. 'The bottom line is: money talks, and they want hers up in Northern Ontario. She doesn't seem overly concerned about "the boys" as you call them.'

'She's hiding her feelings, as she always does. Underneath, I know she's hurting. She was livid with Cliff when she found out about his habit, and with both of them for misusing her beloved boat and besmirching Joe's reputation.'

'It's incredible to think that she knew nothing about their schemes or Joe's. I was right about his Cuban connections.'

'You don't need to sound so smug, Martin! Betty admits that she knew Joe was born in Cuba, not Puerto Rico, but insists that's all.'

'And you believe her?'

'I do. But I would have expected you to be pressing her for more information,' Petra said.

'Like you, I feel an almost filial obligation towards Betty. So until we know what's going to happen to the Graceby boys, I'll concentrate on the singing great-granny image. My readers will love that.'

Petra took a sip from her glass of Veuve Clicquot pink champagne. 'There's one more thing I need to do, Martin, before we leave.'

'Besides packing?'

'Yes. I want to say farewell to Sam. Dick Reed told me they sprinkled his ashes in the dolphin pools. Come with me, please.'

Petra sat on the rocks in quiet meditation, keeping her feet well out of the water. After a time, she turned to Martin. 'Thank you, Martin. This is a pilgrimage I had to make. Sam's monument is here, at *Neptunis*. In future when I visit, I'll be able to celebrate his memory and remember him as he was when I first met him.'

On the way back, they stopped at the aquarium. Petra showed Martin the zebra-striped lionfish. 'There's the culprit,' she said.

That night, during the last supper in the Siren Suite, Betty made a surprise announcement.

'I'm organizing a trip to Spain with Ian and Sophie, to visit Santiago de Compostela where Liz was born and to pay our respects to Elena. It would be wonderful if you and Martin could join us, my dear,' she said to Petra. 'Next April, on Liz's birthday.'

Petra's face fell. 'I'm so sorry, Betty. I can't. I've promised Carlo I'll go to South Africa with him, for his cousin's wedding. But you go, Martin, it'll make a great story,' she said, ignoring the daggers in his eyes.

ACKNOWLEDGEMENTS

First of all, my sincere thanks to everyone who supported me during the writing of this novel, particularly my family and the readers of the early versions who helped me to find the "red thread" that holds the story together. Without your feedback and encouragement, this book would not have made it into print.

Several people mentioned that they thought they had seen a mixture of British and American spelling. I have elected to follow Canadian usage which falls somewhere between the two because my heroine, Petra Minx, is Canadian, and I spent half my life in Canada. However, since I was born and educated in the U.K., you may notice a few lapses, for which I apologize.

Marion Leigh

The Politician's Daughter

by Marion Leigh

When Emily Mortlake, daughter of a high-flying Toronto politician, disappears after taking a summer vacation job aboard a megayacht, RCMP Marine Unit Sergeant Petra Minx is sent undercover to investigate.

Please enjoy this excerpt from Petra's first adventure, set in the Mediterranean.

Thunder woke Petra briefly at 4 a.m. on Tuesday morning. With a groan, she rolled over and fell back into a profound, almost drugged, slumber. When the sound of waves slapping on the hull brought her to her senses again, the room was bright. For a moment, she was disoriented. Then her eyes fell on the seascape on the opposite wall: white surf smashing onto barnacle-covered rocks, a pair of gulls soaring into an azure sky sprinkled with clouds. She was in Monte Carlo, aboard motor yacht *Titania*.

Memories of the night before came in waves, each one more insistent: her first, unnerving encounter with Don

León that had been nothing like she'd expected; the acute embarrassment of being stripped half-naked in front of a group of unknown men; then the shock of seeing Mercutio. Could it really be him? Or had being on the Côte d'Azur resurrected images from the past and superimposed them on the present? No, it was a one in a million chance, yet she was sure.

The name Mercutio had fallen from her lips as soon as the dark curly-haired man had turned to face her at Don León's command. When he responded to his boss's question with an expansive 'Bellissima!', she had needed no further convincing. His voice was the same as it had been a decade ago. She had often thought of him and Ben during those years, but always found another excuse for not making contact.

Even before he had managed to whisper a few words in her ear later, as he was pouring her a glass of wine, she knew that she must not reveal their relationship. Whatever he was doing on board *Titania* required discretion, just as her mission did.

Published by Rudling House, June 2011
ISBN 978 0956276 032